George Augustus Henry Sala, Hablot Knight Browne

The strange adventures of Captain Dangerous

who was a soldier, a pirate, a merchant, a spy, a slave among the Moors

George Augustus Henry Sala, Hablot Knight Browne

The strange adventures of Captain Dangerous
who was a soldier, a pirate, a merchant, a spy, a slave among the Moors

ISBN/EAN: 9783744738835

Printed in Europe, USA, Canada, Australia, Japan

Cover: Foto ©Andreas Hilbeck / pixelio.de

More available books at **www.hansebooks.com**

THE

STRANGE ADVENTURES

OF

CAPTAIN DANGEROUS,

WHO WAS

A SOLDIER, A PIRATE, A MERCHANT, A SPY, A SLAVE AMONG
THE MOORS, A BASHAW IN THE SERVICE OF THE GREAT
TURK, AND DIED AT LAST IN HIS OWN HOUSE
IN HANOVER SQUARE.

A Narrative in plain English

ATTEMPTED BY

GEORGE AUGUSTUS SALA.

LONDON:

C. H. CLARKE, 13 PATERNOSTER ROW.

SOLD BY ALL BOOKSELLERS AND AT ALL RAILWAY STATIONS.

NOTE.

I HAVE to state, once for all, that for the "plain English" in which I have attempted to write this story, the English of Swift, of Pope, of Addison, and of Steele, has not been adopted as a model. Such a feat of elegant pedantry has been already admirably accomplished in Mr. Thackeray's noble story of *Esmond;* and I have no wish to follow up a successful imitation by a sorry caricature. I have simply endeavoured to make my hero write as a man would write who was born and bred in the early part of the eighteenth century, whose reading had been confined to the ordinary newspapers and story-books of his time, and who, in his old age, had preserved the diction of his youth. The Captain's orthography has been modernised; for to continue through nearly four hundred pages spelling "pic" "pye," "public" "publick," and "tiger" "tyger," would be but a tiresome trick, keeping up no illusion, and of which the reader would soon sicken.

G. A. S.

CONTENTS.

———◆———

viii   *Contents.*

THE STRANGE ADVENTURES

OF

CAPTAIN DANGEROUS.

———◆———

CHAPTER THE FIRST.

MINE OWN HOUSE.

I, JOHN DANGEROUS, a faithful subject of his Majesty King George, whose bread, God bless him! I have eaten, and whose battles I have fought, in my poor way, am now in my sixty-eighth year, and live in my own house in Hanover Square. By virtue of several commissions, both English and foreign, I have a right to call myself Captain; and if any man say that I have no such right, he lies and deserves the stab. It may be that this narrative, now composed only for my own pleasure, will, long after my death, see the light in print, and that some sham Captain, or sham critic, or pitiful creature of that kind, will question my rank, or otherwise despitefully use my memory. Let such gutter-bloods venture it at their peril. I have, alas, no heirs male; but to my daughter's husband, and to his descendants, or, failing them, to their executors, administrators, and assigns, I solemnly commit the task of seeking out such envious rogues, and of kicking and cudgelling them on the basest part of their base bodies. The stab I forego; I wish not to cheat the hangman of his due. But let the knaves discover, to the aching of their sorry sides, that even the ghost of John Dangerous is not to be trifled with.

There is a knot of these same pestilent persons who meet at a coffee-house in Great Swallow Street, which I am some-

B

times minded to frequent, and who imagine that they show
their wit and parts by reviling their Church and their King, and
even by maligning the Honourable East India Company,—a
corporation to which I am beholden for many favours. "Fellow," I said, only last Saturday, to a whippersnapper from
an Inn of Court,—a Thing I would not trust to defend my
tom-cat were he in peril at the Old Bailey for birdslaughter,
and who picks up a wretched livelihood, I am told, by
writing lampoons against his betters in a weekly Review,—
"Fellow," I said, "were I twenty years younger, and you
twenty years older, John Dangerous would vouchsafe to pink
an eyelet-hole in your waistcoat. Did I care to dabble in
your polite conversation or your *belles lettres* (of which I
knew much more than ever you will know years before the
parish was at pains to fix your begetting on some one), I
would answer your scurrilities in print; but this I disdain,
sirrah. Good stout ash and good strong Cordovan leather
are the things fittest to meet your impertinencies with;" and
so I held out my foot, and shook my staff at the coxcomb;
and he was so civil to me during the rest of the evening as
to allow me to pay his reckoning for him.

The chief delight I derive from ending my days in Hanover Square is the knowledge that the house is mine own.
I bought it with the fruit of mine own earnings, mine own
moneys—not gotten from grinding the faces and squeezing
the vitals of the poor, but acquired by painful and skilful
industry, and increased by the lawful spoil of war. For
booty, as I have heard a great commander say in Russia, is a
holy thing. I have not disdained to gather moderate riches
by the buying and selling of lawful merchandise; albeit I
always looked on merc commerce and barter as having something of the peddling and huckstering savour in them. My
notion of a Merchant is that of a Bold Spirit who embarks
on his own venture in his own ship, and is his own supercargo, and has good store of guns and Bold Spirits like himself on board, and sails to and fro on the High Seas whither-
soever he pleases. As to the colour of the flag he is under,
what matters it if it be no colour at all, as old Robin Rough-
head used to say to me,—even Black, which is the negation
of all colour? So I have traded in my way, and am the
better by some thousands of pounds for my trading, now.
That much of my wealth has its origin in lawful plunder I

scorn to deny. If you slay a Spanish Don in fair fight, and the Don wears jewelled rings on all his fingers, and carries a great bag of moidores in his pocket, are you to leave him on the field, prithee, or gently ease him of his valuables? Can the crows eat his finery as well as his carcass? If I find a ship full of golden doubloons and silver candlesticks destined for the chapel of St. Jago de Compostella, am I to scuttle the ship and let her go down with all these good things on board; or am I to convey them to mine own lockers, giving to each of my valiant comrades his just and proper share? The governor of Carthagena will never get the doubloons, St. Jago of Compostella will never see his candlesticks; why should not I and my Brave Hearts enjoy them instead of the fishes and the mermaids? They have coral enough down there, I trow; what do they want with candlesticks? If they lack further ornament, there are pearls enow to be had out of the oysters—unless there be lawyers down below—ay, and pearls too in dead men's skulls, and emerald and diamond rings on skeleton hands, among the sea-weed, sand, and the many-coloured pebbles of the great Deep.

There are those who call me an old Pirate. Let them. I was never in trouble with the Admiralty Court. I can pass Execution Dock without turning pale. And no one can gainsay me when I aver that I have faithfully served his Majesty King George, and was always a true friend to the Protestant succession?

There has been a mighty talk, too, about my turning Turk. Why should not I, if I could not help it? I never turned my coat, as some fine gentlemen who have never been to Constantinople have done. I never changed my principles, although I was a Bashaw with three tails. Better to have three tails than to be a rat with only one. And, let me tell you, it is a mighty fine thing to be a Bashaw, and to have as many purses full of sequins as there are days in the year.

I should have been hanged long ago, should I—hanged for a Pirate, a Spy, and a Renegade? Well, I have escaped the bow-string in a country where hundreds die of sore throat every day, and I can afford to laugh at any prospect of the halter in mine old age. Sword of Damocles forsooth! why my life has been hanging on a cobweb any time these fifty years; and here I am at sixty-eight safe and sound,

with a whole liver and a stout heart, and a bottle of wine to
give a friend, and a house of mine own in Hanover Square.

I write this in the great front parlour, which I have converted into a library, study, and counting-room. The year of
our Lord is seventeen hundred and eighty. His Majesty's
subjects have lost eleven days—through some roguery in
high places, you may be sure—since I was a young man ;
and were I a curmudgeon, I might grudge that snipping off
of the best part of a fortnight from an old man's life. It
may be, indeed, that Providence, who has always been
good to me, will add eleven days—yea, and twice eleven
—to the span of poor old John Dangerous. I have many
mercies to be thankful for : of sins likewise, and grievous
ones, there may be a long list that I shall have to account
for ; but I can say that I never killed a man in cold blood,
that I never wilfully wronged a woman, so long as she
was not obstinate, that I never spake an unkind word to
a child, that I always gave freely from that which I got
freely, and never took from him who had little, and that I
was always civil to the clergy. Yet Doctor Dubiety of St.
George's tells me that I have been a great sinner, and bids
me, now, to repent of my evil ways. Dr. Dubiety is in the
right no doubt ;—how could a Doctor of Divinity be ever in
the wrong?—but I can't see that I am so much worse than
other folks. I should be in better case, perhaps, if these
eyes stood wider open. I confess that I have killed many
men with powder and lead, and the sharp sword ; but then,
had I not shot or stabbed them, they would surely have shot
or stabbed me. And are not his Majesty's fellow-subjects
shooting and stabbing one another at this instant moment*
in the American plantations? No ; I always fought fair,
and never refused quarter when mine enemy threw up his
point ; nor, unless a foeman's death were required for lawful
reprisals, did I ever refuse moderate ransom.

There may be some things belonging to my worldly store
that trouble me a little in the night season. Should I have
given St. Jago de Compostella's candlesticks to Westminster
Abbey? Why, surely, the Dean and Chapter are rich
enough. But I declare that I had neither act nor part in
applying the thumbscrews to the Spanish captain, and subjecting the boatswain and his mate to the ordeal of flogging

* 1780.

and pickling. 'Twas not I, but Matcham, who is dead, that caused the carpenter to be carbonadoed, and the Scotch purser to walk the plank. Those were, I grant, deeds worthy of Blackbeard; but I had naught to do with them. John Dangerous has suffered too many tortures in the dungeons of the Portuguese Inquisition to think of torturing his fellow-creatures. Then, as to what became of Doña Estella. I declare that I did my best to save that unhappy lady. I entreated, I protested; but in vain. None of that guilt lies at my door; and in the crime of him who roasted the Bishop, and cut off the Franciscan Monk's great toes, I have no share. Let every man answer for his own deeds. When I went the Middle Passage, I tried to keep the slaves alive as long as I could. When they died, what was there to do but to fling them overboard? Should I not have done the same by white men? I was not one of those cruel Guinea captains who kept the living and the dead chained together. I defy any one to prove it.

And all this bald chat about sacking towns and gutting convents? War is war all the world over; and if you take a town by assault, why of course you must sack it. As to gutting convents, 'tis a mercy to let some pure air into the close, stifling places; and, of a surety, an act of charity to let the poor captive nuns out for a holiday. Reverend Superiors, holy Sisters, I never did ye any harm. You cannot torment me in the night. Your pale faces and shadowy forms have no need to gather round the bed of John Dangerous. Take, for Pity's sake, those Eyes away. But no more. These thoughts drive me mad.

I am not alone in my house. My daughter, my beloved Lilias, my only and most cherished child, the child of my old age, the legacy of the departed Saint her mother, lives with me. Bless her! she believes not a word of the lies that are whispered of her old father. If she were to be told a tithe of them, she would grieve sorely; but she holds no converse with slanderers and those who wag their tongues and say so-and-so of such-a-one. She knows that my life has been wild, and stormy, and dangerous as my name; but she knows that it has also been one of valour, and honesty and honour. St. Jago de Compostella's candlesticks never went towards her schooling, pretty creature! My share from the gold in the scuttled ship never helped to furnish forth

her dowry. Lilias is my joy, my comfort, my stay, my merciful consolation for the loss of that good and perfect Woman
her mother. Dear heart! she has never been crossed in love,
never known Love's sorrows, angers, disappointments, and
despair. She was married at twenty years of age to the man
of her choice; and I am delighted to know that I never in-
terfered, by word or by deed, with the progress of her wooing; that he to whom she is wedded is one of the worthiest
of youths; and that Heaven has blest me with the means to
enable him to maintain the state and figure of a gentleman.

Thus, although comfort and quiet are the things I chiefly
desire after the bustle and turmoil of a tempest-tossed life,
and the pleasure I take in the gaieties of the town is but
small, it cheers me to see my Son and Daughter enjoying
themselves, as those who have youth and health and an un-
clouded conscience are warranted in doing, and, indeed, called
upon to do. I like them on Sundays and holidays to come
to church at St. George's, and sit under Doctor Dubiety,
where I, as a little lad, sat many and many a time, more
than fifty years ago; but my house is no conventicle, and on
all weekdays and lawful occasions my family is privileged to
partake to their heart's content of innocent and permitted
amusements. I never set my face against a visit to the playhouse or to the concert-room; although to me, who can remember the most famous players and singers of Europe, the
King's Theatre and the Rotunda, and even Drury-Lane, are
very tame places, filled with very foolish folk. But they
please the young people, and that is enough for me. Nor to
an occasional junketing at Vauxhall do I ever object. 'Tis
true I have seen Ranelagh and Marylebone and Belsize, to
say nothing of the chief Continental Tivolis, Spas, Lust-
gardens, and other places of resort of the Great; but fiddlers
are fiddlers, and coloured lamps are coloured lamps, all the
world over, I suppose; and my children have as much delight
in gazing on these brilliant follies now as I had when I and
the eighteenth century were young. Only against masquerades and faro-tables, as likewise against the pernicious game
of E. O., do I sternly set my face, deeming them as wholly
wicked, carnal, and unprofitable, and leading directly to per-
dition.

It rejoices me much that my son, or rather son-in-law,—
but I love to call him by the more affectionate name,—is in

no wise addicted to dicing, or horse-racing, or cock-fighting, or any of those sinful and riotous courses to which so many of our genteel youth—even to those of the first quality—devote themselves. He is no Puritan; but he has a proper sense of what is due to the honour and decency of his family, and refrains from soiling them among the profligate crew to be met with, not alone at Newmarket, or at the "Dog and Duck," but in Pall Mall, and in the very antechambers of St. James's. He rides his hackney, as a gentleman should, nor have I prohibited him from occasionally taking my Lilias an airing in a neat curricle; but he is no bettor on the turf, no comrade of jockeys and stablemen, no patron of bruisers and those that handle the backsword. I would disinherit him were I to suspect him of such practices, or of an over-fondness for the bottle, or of a passion for cards. He hunts sometimes, and fishes and shoots, and he has a pretty fancy for the making of salmon-flies, in the which pursuit, I conclude, there is much ingenuity, and no manner of harm, fish being given to us for food, and the devising how best to snare the creatures entirely lawful.

Lilias Dangerous has been wedded to Edward Marriner these two years. It was at first my design to buy the youth a pair of colours, and to let him see the world and the usages of lawful warfare for a year or two; but my Lilias could not bear the thought of her young Ensign's coming home without an arm or a leg, or perchance being slain in some desperate conflict with savage Indians, or scarcely less savage Americans; and I did not press my plan of giving Edward for a time to the service of the King. He, I am bound to say, was eager to take up a commission; but the tears and entreaties of my Daughter, who thinks War the wickedest of crimes, and the shedding of human blood a wholly unpardonable thing, prevailed. So they were married, and are happy; and I am sure, now, that were I to lose either of them, it would break the old man's heart.

My Lilias is tall and slender, her skin is very white, her hair a rich brown, her eyes very large and clear and blue. But that I am too old to be vain, I might be twitted with conceit when I state that she holds these advantages of person less from her Mother than from myself, her loving father. Not that I was so comely in my young days; but my Grandmother before me was of the same fair Image that I so delight to look upon in Lilias. She was tall, and white, and brown-haired, and blue-eyed. She had Lilias's small and exquisitely-fashioned hands and feet, or rather Lilias has hers. To me these features were only transmitted in a meaner degree. I was a big-boned lusty lad, with flowing brown locks, an unfreckled skin, and an open eye; but my Grandmother's face and form have renewed themselves in my child. At twenty she is as beautiful as her Great-grandmother must have been at twenty, as I am told and know that Lady was, albeit when I remember her she was nearly ninety years of age.

Yes; Lilias's eyes are very blue; but they are always soft and tender and pitiful in their glance. Her Great-grandmother's had, when she was moved, a strange wild look that awed and terrified the beholders. Only once in the life of my Lilias, when she was very young, and on the question of some toy or sweetmeat which my departed Saint had denied her, did I notice that terrible look in her blue eyes. My wife, who, albeit the most merciful soul alive, ever maintained strict discipline in her family, would have corrected the child for what she set down as flat mutiny and rebellion; but I stayed her chastening hand, and bade the young girl walk awhile in the garden until her heat was abated; and as she went away, her little breast heaving, her little hands clenched, and the terrible look darting out on me through the silken tangles of her dear hair, I shuddered, and said, " Wife of mine, our Lilias's look is one she cannot help. It comes from Me, you may have seen it, fiercer and fiercer in mine own eyes; and she, whom of all women I loved and venerated, looked thus when anger overcame her. And though I never knew my own dear Mother, she, or I greatly mistake, must have had that look in hers likewise."

I thank Heaven that those pure blue waters, limpid and bright, in my Lilias's eyes were nevermore ruffled by that storm. As she grew up, their expression became even softer and kinder, and she never ceased from being in the likeness of an Angel. She looks like one now, and will be one, I trust, some day, Above, where she can pray for her dangerworn old sire.

My own wife (whose name was Lilias too) was a merry, plump, ruddy-skinned little woman—a very baby in these strong arms of mine. She had laughing black eyes, and coal-black tresses, and lips which were always at vintage-time. Although her only child takes after me, not her, in face and carriage, in all things else she resembles my Saint. She is as merry, as light-hearted, as pure and good, as she was. She has the same humble, pious Faith; the same strong, stern will of abiding by Right; the same hearty, outspoken hatred of Wrong, abhorrence of Wrong. She has the same patience, cheerfulness, and obedience in her behaviour to those who are set in authority over her; and if I am by times angered, or peevish, or moody, she bears with my infirmities in the same meek, loving, and forgiving spirit. She has her Mother's grace, her Mother's voice, her Mother's ringing voice. She has her Mother's infinite care of and benevolence to the poor and needy. She has her Mother's love for merry sports and innocent romps. Like my departed Saint, she has an exquisitely neat and quick hand for making pastries and marchpanes, possets and sugared tankards; and like her she plays excellently on the harpsichords.

Thus, in a quiet comfort and competence, in the love of my children, and in the King's peace, these my latter days are gliding away. I am somewhat troubled with gout and twitching pains, and fulness of humours, with other old men's ailments; and I do not sleep well o' nights owing to vexatious dreams and visions, to abate which I am sometimes let blood; but beyond these cares—and who hath not his cares?—Captain John Dangerous, of number One hundred Hanover Square, is a happy man.

CHAPTER THE SECOND.

IN the winter of the year 1720, died in her house in
Hanover Square—the very one in which I am now finishing
my life—an Unknown Lady nearly ninety years of age. The
mansion was presumed to be her own, and it was as much
hers as it is mine now; but the reputed landlord was one
Doctor Vigors, a physician of the College in Warwick Lane,
in whose name the lease ran, who was duly rated to the poor
as tenant, and whose patient the Unknown Lady was given
out to be. But when Dr. Vigors came to Hanover Square it
was not as a Master, but as the humblest of servants; and no
tradesman, constable, maid, or lacquey about the house or
neighbourhood would have ventured for his or her life to
question that, from cellar to roof, every inch of the house
belonged to the Unknown Lady. The vulgar held her in
a kind of awe, and spoke of her as the Lady in Diamonds;
for she always wore a number of those precious gems, in
rings, bracelets, stomachers, and the like. The gentlefolks,
of whom many waited upon her, from her first coming hither
unto her death, asked for "my Lady," and nothing more. It
was in the year 1714 that she first arrived in London, coming
late at night from Dover, in a coach-and-six, and bringing
with her one Mr. Cadwallader, a person of a spare habit and
great gravity of countenance, as her steward; one Mistress
Nancy Talmash, as her waiting-woman; and a foreign person
of a dark and forbidding mien, who was said to be her chaplain. In the following year, and during the unhappy troubles in Scotland arising out of the treasons of the Earl of
Mar, and other Scots Lords, one of his Majesty's messengers
came for the foreign person, and conveyed him in a coach to
the Cockpit at Whitehall: while another messenger took up
his abode in the house at Hanover Square, lying in the second
best bed-chamber, and having his table apart for a whole
week. From these circumstances it was rumoured that the
Unknown Lady was a Papist and Jacobite; that the priest,
her confederate, was bound for Newgate, and would doubtless

make an end of it at Tyburn; and that the Lady herself would be before many days clapt up in the Tower. But Signor Casagiotti, the Venetian envoy, claimed the foreign person and obtained his release; and it was said that one of the great lords of the council came himself to Hanover Square to take the examination of the Unknown Lady, and was so well satisfied with the speech he had with her as to discharge her then and there from custody,—if, indeed, she had ever been under any kind of durance,—and promise her the King and Minister's protection for the future. The foreign person was suffered to return, and thenceforward was addressed as Father Ruddlestone, as though he had some license bearing him harmless from the penalties which then weighed upon recusant persons. And I am given to understand that, on the evening of his enlargement, the same great Lord, being addressed in a jocular manner at the coffee-house by a person of honour, and asked if he had not caught the Pope, the Devil, and the Pretender in petticoats and diamonds, somewhere in St. George's parish, very gravely made answer, that some degrees of loyalty were like gold, which were all the better for being tried in the furnace, and that, although there had once been a King James, and there was now a King George, the lady, of whom perhaps that gentleman was minded to speak, had done a notable Thing before he was born, which entitled her to the eternal gratitude of Kings.

Although so old on her first coming to Hanover Square, and dwelling in it until her waiting-woman avowed that she was close on her ninetieth year, the Unknown Lady preserved her faculties in a surprising manner, and till within a few days of her passing away went about her house, took the air from time to time in her coach, or in a chair, and received company. The very highest persons of Quality sought her, and appeared to take pleasure in her company. To Court, indeed, she never went; but she was visited more than once by an illustrious Prince; and many great nobles likewise waited upon her in their Birthday suits. On Birthnights there was Play in the great drawing room, where nothing but gold was permitted to be staked.

Credible persons have described her to me as being,— in the extremest sunset of her life, when the very fray and fringe of her garment were come to, and no more stuff remained wherewith to piece it,—a person of signal beauty.

She was of commanding stature, stooped very little, albeit she made use of a crutch-stick in walking, and had a carriage full of graciousness, yet of somewhat austere Dignity. No portion of her hair was visible under the thick folds of muslin and point of Alençon which covered her head, and were themselves half hidden by a hood of black Paduasoy ; but in a glass-case in her cabinet, among other relics of which I may have presently to speak, she kept a quantity of the most beauteous chestnut tresses ever beheld. "These were my love-locks, child," I remember her saying to me once. I am ashamed to confess that, during my brief commerce with her, the dress she wore, which was commonly of black velvet, and the diamonds which glittered on her hands and arms and bosom impressed themselves far more forcibly on my memory than her face, which I have since been told was Beautiful. My informant bears witness that her eyes were Blue, and of an exceeding brightness, sometimes quite terrible to look upon, although tempered at most times by a sweet mildness ; yet there were seasons when this brightness, as that of the Sun in a wholly cloudless sky, became fierce, and burnt up him who beheld it. Time had been so long a husbandman of her fair demesne, had reaped so many crops of smiles and tears from that comely visage, that it were a baseness to infer that no traces of his husbandry appeared on her once smooth and silken flesh, for the adornment of which she had ever disdained the use of essences and unguents. Yet I am told that her wrinkles and creases, although manifold, were not harsh or rugged ; and that her face might be likened rather to a billet of love written on fair white vellum, that had been somewhat crumpled by the hand of him who hates Youth and Love, than to some musty old conveyance or mortgage-deed scrabbled on yellow, damp-stained, rat-gnawed parchment. Her hands and neck were to the last of an amazing whiteness. The former, as were also her feet, very small and delicate. Her speech when moved was quick, and she spoke as one accustomed to be obeyed ; but at most seasons her bearing towards her domestics was infinitely kind and tender. Towards the foreign person, her chaplain, she always bore herself with edifying meekness. She was cheerful in company, full of ready wit, of great shrewdness, discretion, and observation ; could discourse to admiration of foreign cities and persons of renown, even to Kings and Princes, whom she had seen and known; and was well qualified to speak on public affairs, although she seldom deigned to concern herself with the furious madness of Party. Mere idle prattle of operas, and play-books, and auctions, and the like, were extremely distasteful to her; and although at that time a shameful looseness of manners and conversation obtained even among the Greatest persons in the land, she would never suffer any evil or immodest talk to be held in her presence; and those who wished to learn aught of the wickedness of the town and the scandals of High Life were fain to go elsewhere for their gossip.

I have said that her dress was to me the chief point of notice, and is that of which I retain the keenest remembrance. Her diamonds, indeed, had over me that strange fascination which serpents are said to have over birds; and I would sit with my little mouth all agape, and my eyes fixed and staring, until they grew dazed, and I was frightened at the solemn twinkling of those many gems. In my absurd child-way, it was to my fancy as though the Lady were some great altar or herse of state in a church, and her Jewels so many Lamps kindled about her, and to be kept alive for ever. She robed habitually, as I have said, in Black Velvet; but on Birthnights, when more company than usual came, and there was play in the great drawing-room, she would wear a sack of sad-coloured satin; while, which was stranger still, on the thirtieth day of January in every year, at least so long as I can keep it in mind, she wore her sable dress; not her ordinary one, but a fuller garment, which had bows of Crimson Ribbon down the front and at the sleeves, and a great Crimson Scarf over the right shoulder, so as to come crosswise over her Heart. And on the day she made this change she wore no diamonds, but Rubies in great number, and of great size. On that day, also, we kept an almost entire fast, and from morning to night I had nothing but a little cake and a glass of Red wine. From sunrise to sunset the Lady sat in her cabinet among her relics; and I was bidden to sit over against her on a little stool. She would talk much, and, as it seemed to me wildly, in a language which I could not understand, going towards her relics and touching them in a strange manner. Then she would say to me, with a sternness that chilled the marrow in my bones, "Child, Remember the Day; Remember the Thirtieth of January." And she would often repeat that word, "Remember," rocking herself to and fro. And more than once she would say, "Blood for blood." Then Mistress Talmash would enter and assay to soothe her, telling her that what was past was past, and could not be undone. Then she would take out a great Prayer-Book bound in red leather, and which had this strange device embossed in gold, on either cover, and in a solemn voice read out long

passages, which I afterwards learned were from that service holden on the anniversary of the martyrdom of King Charles the First. She would go on to read the Ritual for the King's Touching for the Evil, now expunged from our Book of Common Prayer; and then Mistress Talmash would pray her to read the joyful prayers for the twenty-ninth of May, the date of the happy restoration of King Charles the Second. But that she would seldom do, murmuring, "I dare not, I dare not. Tell not Father Ruddlestone." All these things were very strange to me; but I grew accustomed to them in time. And there seems to be an immensity of time passing to a solitary child between his first beginning to remember and his coming to eight years of age.

There is one thing that I must mention before this Lady ceases to be Unknown to the reader. She was afflicted with a continual trembling of the entire frame. She was no paralytic, for to the very end she could take her food and medicine without assistance; but she shook always like a very aspen. It had to do with her nerves, I suppose; and it was perhaps for that cause she was attended for so many years by Doctor Vigors; but he never did her any good in that wise; and the whole College of Warwick Lane would, I doubt not, have failed signally had they attempted her cure. Often I asked Mistress Talmash why the Lady—for until her death I knew of no other name whereby to call her—shook so ; but the waiting-woman would chide me, and say that if I asked questions she would Shake me. So that I forbore.

Ours was a strange and solemn household. All was stately and well ordered, and—when company came—splendid ; but the house always seemed to be much gloomier than the great parish-church, whither I was taken every Sunday morning on the shoulder of a tall footman, and shut up alone in a great Pew lined with scarlet baize, and where I felt very much like a little child that was lost in the midst of the Red Sea. Far over my head hung a gallery full of the children of Lady Viellcastel's charity-school; and these, both boys and girls, would make grimaces at me while the Psalms were being sung, until I felt more frightened than when I was on my little stool in the cabinet of relics, on the thirtieth of January. Just over the ledge of my pew I could see the clergyman, in his large white wig, leaning over the reading-desk, and talking at me, as I thought, in a mighty angry manner; and when he, or another divine, afterwards ascended the pulpit above, I used to fancy that it was only the same clergyman grown taller, and with a bigger wig, and that he seemed to lean forward, and be angrier with me than ever. The time of kneeling was always one of sore trouble to me, for I had to feel with my foot for the hassock, which seemed to lie as far beneath me as though it were sunk at the bottom of the Red Sea. Getting up again was quite as difficult; and I don't think we ever attained the end of the Litany without my dropping my great red Prayer-Book—not the thirtieth-of-January one—with a clang. On such occasions the pew-door would open, and the beadle enter. He always picked up the book, and gave it me with a low bow; but he never omitted to tell me, in a deadly whisper, that if I had been one of Lady Viellcastel's boys, he'd skin me alive, he would.

The Unknown Lady did not attend the parish-church. She, and Mistress Talmash, and the foreign person, held a service apart. I was called "Little Master," and went with the footman. The fellow's name, I remember, was Jeremy. He used to talk to me, going and coming, as I sat, in my fine laced clothes, and my hat with a plume in it, and my little rapier with the silver hilt, perched on his broad shoulder. He used to tell me that he had been a soldier, and had fought

under the Duke of Marlborough; and that he had a wife who
washed bands and ruffles for the gentlemen of the Life Guard,
and drank strong waters till she found herself in the round-
house. Always on a Sunday morning, as the church-bells
began to ring, the Unknown Lady would give me a guinea
to put into the plate after service. I remember that the year
before she died, when I was big enough to walk with my
hand in Jeremy's, instead of being carried, that he told me
on Easter-Sunday morning that his wife was dead, and that
he had two children in a cellar who had no bread to eat. He
cried a good deal; and before we reached the church, took me
into a strange room in a back street, where there were a
number of men and women shouting and quarrelling, and
another, without his wig and with a great gash in his forehead, sprawling on the ground, and crying out, " Lillibulero!"
and two more playing cards on a pair of bellows. And they
were all drinking from mugs and smoking tobacco. Here
Jeremy had something to drink, too, from a mug. He put
the vessel to my lips, and I tasted something Hot, which
made me feel very faint and giddy. When we were in the
open air again, he cried worse than ever. What could I
do but give him my guinea? On our return to Hanover
Square, the Lady asked me, according to her custom, what was
the text, and whether I had put my money into the plate.
She was not strict about the first; for I was generally, from
my tenderness of years, unable to tell her more than that the
gentleman in the wig seemed very angry with me, and the
Pope, and the Prince of Darkness; but she always taxed me
smartly about the guinea. This was before the time that I
had learned to Lie; and so I told her how I had given the
piece of gold to Jeremy, for that his wife was no more,
and his children were in a cellar with nothing to eat. She
stayed a while looking at me with those blue eyes, which
had first their bright fierceness in them and then their kind
and sweet tenderness. It was the first time that I marked
her eyes more than her dress and her diamonds. She took
me in her lap, and printed her lips—which were very soft,
but cold—upon my forehead.

"Child," she said, "did I use thee as is the custom, thou
shouldst be whipped, not kissed, for thy folly and disobedi-
ence. But you knew not what you did. Here are two guineas
to put into the plate next Sunday; and let no rogues cozen

you out of it. As for Jeremy," she continued, turning to Mistress Talmash, " see that the knave be stripped of his livery, and turned out of the house this moment, for robbing my Grandson, and taking him on a Sabbath morning to taverns, among grooms, and porters, and sharpers, and bullies."

Yes; the Unknown Lady was my Grandmother. I purpose now to relate to you her History, revealed to me many years after her death, in a manner to be mentioned at the proper time.

CHAPTER THE THIRD.

THE HISTORY OF MY GRANDMOTHER, WHO WAS A LADY OF CONSEQUENCE
IN THE WEST COUNTRY.

My Grandmother was born at Bristol, about the year 1630, and in the reign of King Charles the First. She came of a family noted for their long lives, and of whom there was, in good sooth, a proverb in the West setting forth that "Bar gallows, glaive, and the gout, every Greenville would live to a hundred." Her maiden name was Greenville : she was baptised Arabella; and she was the only daughter of Richard Greenville, an Esquire of a fair estate between Bath and Bristol, where his ancestors had held their land for three hundred years, on a jocular tenure of presenting the king, whenever he came that way, with a goose-pie, the legs sticking through the crust. It was Esquire Greenville's misfortune to come to his estate just as those unhappy troubles were fomenting which a few years after embroiled these kingdoms in one great and dismal Quarrel. It was hard for a gentleman of consequence in his own country, and one whose forefathers had served the most considerable offices therein,—having been of the Quorum ever since the reign of King Edward the Third,—to avoid mingling in some kind or another in the dissensions wherewith our beloved country was then torn. Mr. Greenville was indeed a person of a tranquil and placable humour, to whom party janglings were thoroughly detestable ; and although he leant naturally, as beseemed his degree, towards the upholding of his Majesty's Crown and Dignity, and the maintenance in proper Honour and Splendour of the Church, he was too good a Christian and citizen not to shrink from seeing his native land laid waste by the blind savageness of a Civil War. And although he paid cess and ship-money without murmuring, and, on being chosen a Knight of the Shire, did zealously speak up in the Commons' House of Parliament on the King's side (refusing nevertheless to make one of the lip-serving crowd of courtiers of Whitehall), and although, when churchwarden in his parish, he ever preserved the laudable custom of Whitsun and Martinmas ales for the good of the poor, and persisted in having the Book of Sports read from the pulpit,—he was averse from all high-handed measures of musketooning and pike-stabbing those of the meaner sort, or those of better degree (as Mr. Hampden, Mr. Pym, and Another whom I shudder to mention), who, for conscience' sake, opposed themselves to the King's Government. He was in this wise at issue with some of his hotter Cavalier neighbours, as, for instance, Sir Basil Fauconberge, who, whenever public matters were under question, began with "Neighbour, you must first show me Pym, Hampden, Haslerigge, and the rest, swinging upon a gallows, and then I will begin to chop logic with you." For a long time Mr. Greenville, my Great-grandfather (and my enemies may see from this that I am of no rascal stock), cherished hopes that affairs might be brought to a shape without any shedding of blood; but his hope proved a vain and deceiving one; ungovernable passions on either side caused not alone the drawing of the sword, but the flinging away of the scabbard; and my Grandmother was yet but a schoolmaid at Madam Ribotte's academy for gentlewomen at Bristol when that dreadful, sinful war broke out which ended in the barbarous murder of the Prince, and the undoing of these kingdoms.

Mr. Greenville had two children : a son, whose name, like his own, was Richard, and who was born some five years before his sister Arabella. Even as a child she was exceedingly beautiful, very gracious, fair, grave, and dignified of deportment, with abundant brown hair, and large and lustrous blue eyes, which, when the transient tempests of childhood passed over her, were ever remarked as having a strange, wild, fierce look, shared in sometimes by the males of her family. Her mother, to her sorrow, died when she was quite a babe. The Esquire was passionately fond of this his only daughter; but although it was torture for him to part with her, and he retained her until she was thirteen years of age in his mansion-house, where she was instructed in reading and devotion, pickling and preserving (and the distilling of strong waters), sampler work, and such maidenly parts of education, by the housekeeper, and by a governante brought from London,—he had wisdom enough to discern and to admit that his daughter's genius was of a nature that required and demanded much higher culture than could be given to her in an old country seat, and in the midst of talk about dogs and horses and cattle and gunning and ploughing, and the continual disputes of hot-

headed Cavaliers or bitter Parliamentarians, who were trying
who should best persuade my Great-grandfather to cast in his
lot with one or the other of the contending parties.   His son
Richard had already made his election, and, it is feared, by
having recourse to usurious money-scriveners in Bristol and
London, had raised a troop of horse for the service of the King.
Moreover, Arabella Greenville was of a very proud stomach
and unbending humour.   She might be led, but would not be
driven.   She adored her father, but laughed at the commands
of the governante, and the counsels of the housekeeper, who
knew not how either to lead or to rule her.   It was thus determined to send her to Madam Ribotte's academy at Bristol,
—for even so early as King Charles's time had outlandish and
new-fangled names been found for Schools ; and thither she
was accordingly sent, with instructions that she was to learn
all the polite arts and accomplishments proper to her station,
that she was to be kept under a strict regimen, and corrected
of her faults ; but that she was not to be thwarted in her
reasonable desires ; was to have her pony, with John coachman on the skewball sent to fetch her every Saturday and
holiday ; was not to be overweighted with tedious and dragging studies ; and was by no means to be subject to those
shameful chastisements of the ferula and the rod, which, even
within my own time, I blush to say had not been banished
from schools for young gentlewomen.   To sum up, Miss Arabella Greenville went to school with a pocketful of guineas,
and a play-chest full of sweet-cakes and preserved fruits, and
with a virtual charter for learning as little as she chose, and
doing pretty well as much as she liked.

Of course my Grandmother ran a fair chance of being
wholly spoiled, and growing up to one of those termagant
romps we used to laugh at in Mr. Colley Cibber's plays.   The
schoolmistress fawned upon her, for, although untitled, Esquire
Greenville (from whom my descent is plain) was one of the
most considerable of the County Gentry ; the teachers were
glad when she would treat them from her abundant store of
guineas ; and she was a kind of divinity among the school-
maids her companions, to whom she gave so many cakes and
sweetmeats that the apothecary had to be called in about once
a week.   But this fair young flower-bed was saved from blight
and choking weeds, first, by the innate rectitude and nobility
of her disposition, which (save only when that dangerous look

was in her eyes) taught her to keep a rein over her caprices, and subdue a too warm and vigorous imagination; next, by the entire absence of vanity and self-conceit in her mind,—a happy state, which made her equally alive to her own faults and to the excellencies of others; and, last, by her truly prodigious aptitude for polite learning. I have often been told that but for adverse circumstances Mrs. Greenville must have proved one of the most learned, as she was one of the wittiest and best-bred, women of her age and country. In the languages, in all manner of fine needlework, in singing and fingering instruments of music, in medicinal botany and the knowledge of diseases, in the making of the most cunning electuaries and syllabubs, and even in arithmetic,—a science of which young gentlewomen were then almost wholly deficient,—she became, before she was sixteen years of age, a truly wonderful proficient. A Bristol bookseller spoke of printing her book of recipes (containing some excellent hints on cookery, physic, the casting of nativities, and farriery); and some excellent short hymns she wrote are, I believe, sung to this day in one of the Bristol free-schools. But the talent for which she was most shiningly remarkable was in that difficult and laborious art of Painting in Oils. Her early drawings, both in crayons and Chinese ink, were very noble; and there are in this House now some miniatures of her father, brother, and school-companions, limned by her in a most delicate and lovely fashion; but 'twas in oils and in portraiture of the size of life that she most surpassed. She speedily out-went all that the best masters of this craft in Bristol could teach her; and her pictures —especially one of her father, in his buff coat and breastplate, as a Colonel of the Militia—were the wonder, not only of Bristol, but of all Somerset and the counties adjacent.

About this time those troubles in the West, with which the name of Prince Rupert is so sadly allied, grew to be of such force and fury as to decide Mr. Greenville on going to London, taking his daughter Arabella with him, to make interest with the Parliament, so that peril might be averted from his estate. For although his son was in arms for King Charles, and he himself was a gentleman of approved loyalty, he had done nothing of an overt kind to favour King or Parliament. He thus hoped, having ever been a peaceable and law-worthy gentleman, to preserve his lands from peril, and himself and family from prosecution; and it is a great error to suppose that many honest gentlemen did not so succeed in the very fiercest frenzy of the civil wars in keeping their houses over their heads, and their heads upon their shoulders. Witness worthy Mr. John Evelyn of Wotton and Sayes' Court, and many other persons of repute.

While the Esquire was intent on his business at Westminster, and settling the terms of a Fine, without which it seemed even his peaceable behaviour could not be compounded, he lay at the house of a friend, Sir Fortunatus Geddings, a Turkey merchant, who had a fair house in the street leading directly to St. Paul's Church, just without Ludgate. The gate has been pulled down this many a day, and the place where he dwelt is now called Ludgate Hill. As he had much going to and fro, and was afraid that his daughter might come to hurt, both in the stoppage to her schooling, and in the unquietness of the times, he placed her for a while at a famous school at Hackney, under that famous governante Mrs. Desaguiliers. And here she had not been for many weeks ere the strangest adventure in the world—as strange as any one of my own—befell her. The terrible battle of Naseby had by this time been fought, and the King's cause was wholly ruined. Among other Cavaliers fortunate enough to escape from that deadly fray, and who were in hiding from the vengeance of the usurping government, was the Lord Francis V—rs, younger son to that hapless Duke of B—m who was slain at Portsmouth by Captain F—n. It seems almost like a scene in a comedy to tell; and, indeed, I am told that Tom D'Urfey did turn the only merry portion of it into a play; but it appears that, among other shifts to keep his disguise, the Lord Francis, who was highly skilled in all the accomplishments of the age, was fain to enter Mrs. Desaguiliers' school at Hackney in the habit of a dancing-master, and that as such he taught corantoes and rounds to the young gentlewomen. Whether the governante, who was herself a stanch Royalist, winked at the deception, I know not; but her having done so is not improbable. Stranger to tell, the Lord Francis brought with him a companion who was, forsooth, to teach French and the lute, and who was no other than Captain Richard, son to the Esquire of the West country, and who was likewise inveterately pursued by the Usurper. The brother recognised his sister, to what joy and contentment on both their parts I need not say; but ere the false dancing-master had played his part many days, he fell madly in love with Arabella Greenville. To her sorrow and wretchedness, my poor Grandmother returned his flame. Not that the Lord Francis stands convicted of any base designs upon her. I am afraid that he had been as wild and as reckless as most of the young nobles of his day; but for this young woman at least his love was pure and honourable. He made no secret of it to his fast friend, Captain Richard (my Grand-uncle), who would soon have crossed swords with the spark had any villany been afloat; and he made no more ado, as was the duty of a Brother jealous of his sister's fair fame, but to write his father word of what had chanced. The Esquire was half terrified and half flattered by the honour done to his family by the Lord Francis. The poor young man was under the very sternest of proscriptions, and it was openly known that if the Parliament laid hold on him his death was certain. But, on the other hand, the Esquire loved his daughter above all things; and one short half-hour, passed with her alone at Hackney, persuaded him that he must either let Arabella's love-passion have its vent, or break her heart for ever. And, take my word for it, you foolish parents who would thwart your children in this the most sacred moment of their lives,—thwart them for no reasonable cause, but only to gratify your own pride of purse, avarice, evil tempers, or love of meddling,—you are but gathering up bunches of nettles wherewith to scourge your own shoulders, and strewing your own beds with shards and pebbles. Take the advice of old John Dangerous, who suffered his daughter to marry the man of her choice, and is happy in the thought that she enjoys happiness; and I should much wish to know if there be any Hatred in the world so dreadful as that curdled love, as that reverence decayed, as that obedience in ruins, you see in a proud haughty daughter married against her will to one she holds in loathing, and who points her finger, and says within herself, "My father and mother made me marry that man, and I am Miserable."

It was agreed amongst those who had most right to come to an agreement in the matter, that as a first step the Lord Francis V—s should betake himself to some other place of hiding, as more in keeping with Mrs. Greenville's honour; but that, with the consent of her father and brother, he

should be solemnly betrothed to her; and that, so soon as
the troubles were over, or that the price which was upon his
head were taken off, he should become her husband. And
there was even a saving clause added, that if the national
disturbances unhappily continued, Mrs. Greenville should be
privately conveyed abroad, and that the Lord Francis should
marry her so soon after a certain lapse of time as he could
conveniently get beyond sea. My Lord Duke of B—m had
nothing to say against the match, loving his brother, as he
did, very dearly; and so, in the very roughest of times, this
truest of true loves seemed to bid fair to have a smooth
course.

But alas the day! My Grandmother's passion for the
young Lord was a very madness. On his part, he idolised
her, calling her by names and writing her letters that. are
nonsensical enough in common life, but which are not held
to be foolish pleas in Love's Chancery. When the boy and
girl—for they were scarcely more—parted, she gave him one
of her rich brown tresses; he gave her one of his own dainty
love-locks. They broke a broad piece in halves between
them; each hung the fragment by a ribbon next the heart.
They swore eternal fidelity, devotion. Naught but death
should part them, they said. Foolish things to say and do,
no doubt; but I look at my grizzled old head in the glass,
and remember that I have said and done things quite as foolish forty—fifty years ago.

Nothing but Death was to part them; and nothing but
Death so parted them. The Esquire Greenville, his business
being brought to a pleasant termination, having paid his Fine
and gotten his Safe-Conduct and his Redemption from Sequestration, betook himself once more to the West. His daughter went with him, nourishing her love and fondling it, and
dwelling, syllable by syllable, on the letters which the Lord
Francis sent her from time to time. He was in hopes, he
said, to get away to Holland.

Then came that wicked business of the King's murder.
Mr. Greenville, as became a loyal gentleman, was utterly dis-
mayed at that horrid crime; but to Arabella the news was
as of the intelligence of the death of some loved and revered
friend. She wept, she sobbed, she called on Heaven to
shower down vengeance on the Murderers of her gracious
Prince. She had not heard from her betrothed for many

days, and those who loved and watched her had marked a strange wild way with her.

It was on the third of February that the dreadful news of the Whitehall tragedy came to her father's house. She was walking on the next day very moodily in the garden, when the figure of one booted and spurred, and with the stains of many days' travel on his dress, stood across her path. He was but a clown, a mere boor; he had been a ploughboy on her father's lands, and had run away to join Captain Richard, who had made him a trumpeter in his troop. What he had to say was told in clumsy speech, in hasty broken accents, with sighs and stammerings and blubberings; but he told his tale too well.

The Lord Francis V—s and Captain Richard Greenville —Arabella's lover, Arabella's brother—were both Dead. On the eve of the fatal thirtieth of January they had been taken captives in a tilt-boat on the Thames, in which they were endeavouring to escape down the river. They had at once been tried by a court-martial of rebel officers; and on the thirtieth day of that black month, by express order sent from the Lord General Cromwell in London, these two gallant and unfortunate gentlemen had been shot to death by a file of musketry in the courtyard of Hampton Court Palace. The trumpeter had by a marvel escaped, and lurked about Hampton till the dreadful deed was over. He had sought out the sergeant of the firing party, and questioned him as to the last moments of the condemned. The sergeant said that they died as Malignants, and without showing any sign of penitence; but he could not gainsay that their bearing was soldier-like.

Arabella heard this tale without moving.

"Did the Captain—did my brother—say aught before they slew him?" she asked.

"Nowt but this, my lady: 'God forgive us all!'"

"And the Lord Francis, said he aught?"

"Ay; but I dunno loike to tell."

"Say on."

"Twas t' Sergeant tould un. A' blessed the King, and woud hev' t' souldiers drink 's health, but they wouldno'. And a' wouldno' let un bandage his eyes; an' jest befoar t' red cwoats fired, a' touk a long lock o' leddy's hair from 's pocket and kissed un, and cried out 'Bloud for Bloud!' and then a' died all straight along."

Mrs. Arabella Greenville drew from her bosom a long wavy lock of silken hair,—his hair, poor boy!—and kissed it, and crying out "Blood for Blood!" fell down in the garden-path in a dead faint.

She did not Die, however, being spared for many Purposes, some of them Terrible, until she was nearly ninety years of age. But her first state was worse than death ; she lying for many days in a kind of trance or lethargy, and then waking up to raving madness. For the best part of that year, she was a perfect maniac, from whom nothing could be got but gibberings and plungings, and ceaseless cries of "Blood for Blood!" The heir-at-law to the estate, now that the Esquire's son was dead, watched her madness with a keen avaricious desire. He was a sour Parliament man, who had pinned his faith to the Commonwealth, and done many Awakening things against the Cavaliers, and he thought now that he should have his reward, and Inherit.

It was so destined, however, that my Grandmother should recover from that malady. On her beauty it left surprisingly few traces. You could only tell the change that had taken place in her by the deathly paleness of her visage, by her never smiling, and by that fierce expression in her eyes being now an abiding instead of a passing one. Beyond these, she was herself again ; and after a little while went to her domestic concerns, and chiefly to the cultivation of that pleasing art of painting in oils in which she had of old time given such fair promise of excellence. Her father would have had several most ingenious examples of History and Scripture pieces by the Italian and Flemish masters bought for her to study by,—such copies being then very plentiful, by reason of the dispersing of the collections of many noblemen and gentlemen on the King's side ; but this she would not suffer, saying that it were waste of time and money, and, with astonishing zeal, applied herself to the branch of portraiture. From a little miniature portrait of her dead Lord, drawn by Mr. Cooper, she painted in large many fair and noble presentments, varying them according to her humour,—now showing the Lord Francis in his panoply as a man of war, now in a court habit, now in an embroidered night-gown and Turkish cap, now leaning on the shoulder of her brother, the Captain, deceased. And anon she would make a ghastly image of him lying all along in the courtyard at Hampton Court, with the purple bullet-marks on his white forehead, and a great crimson stain on his bosom, just below his bands. This was the one she most loved to look upon, although her father sorely pressed her to put it by, and not dwell on so uncivil a theme, the more so as, in crimson characters, on the background she had painted the words "Blood for Blood." But whatever she did was now taken little account of, for all thought her to be distraught.

By and by she fell to quite a new order in her painting. She seemed to take infinite pleasure in making portraitures of OLIVER CROMWELL, who had by this time become Lord Protector of the Commonwealth. She had never seen that bold bad man (the splendour of whose mighty achievements must for ever remain tarnished by his blood-guiltiness in the matter of the King's death); but from descriptions of his person, for which she eagerly sought, and from bustos, pictures, and prints cut in brass, which she obtained from Bristol and elsewhere, she produced some surprising resemblances of him who was now the Greatest Man in England. She painted him at full and at half length—in full-face, profile, and three-quarter; but although she would show her work to her intimates, and ask eagerly "Is it like—is it like him?" she would never part with one copy (and there were good store of time-servers ready to buy the Protector's picture at that time), nor could any tell how she disposed of them.

This went on until the summer of the year 1657, when her father gently put it to her that she had worn the willow long enough, and would have had her ally herself with some gentleman of worth and parts in that part of the country. For the poor Esquire desired that she should be his heiress, and that a man-child should be born to the Greenville estate, and thus the heir-at-law, who was a wretched attorney at Bristol, and more bitter against kings than ever, should not inherit. She was not to be moved, however, towards marriage ; saying softly that she was already wedded to her Frank in Heaven,—for so she spoke of the Lord Francis V—s,—and that her union had been blessed by her brother Dick, who was in Heaven too, with King Charles and all the Blessed Army of Martyrs. And I have heard, indeed, that the unhappy business of the King's death was the means of so crazing, or casting into a sad celibacy and de-

vouring melancholy, multitudes of comely young women who
were born for love and delights, and to be the happy mothers
of many children.

So, seeing that he could do nothing with her, and loth
to use any unhandsome pressure towards one whom he loved
as the apple of his eye, the Esquire began to think it might
divert her mind to more cheerful thoughts if she quitted for
a season that part of the country (for it was at Home that
she had received the dreadful news of her misfortune) ; and,
Sir Fortunatus Geddings and his family being extremely
willing to receive her, and do her honour, he despatched
Arabella to London, under protection of Mr. Landrail, his
steward, a neighbour of his, Sir Hardress Eustis, lending his
Coach for the journey.

Being now come to London, every means which art could
devise, or kindness could imagine, were made use of by Sir
Fortunatus, his wife, and daughter, to make Arabella's life
happier. But I should tell you a strange thing that came
about at her father's house the day after she left it for the
town. Mr. Greenville chancing to go in a certain long building by the side of his pleasure-pond that was used as a boat-
house, when, to his amazement, he sees, piled up against the
wall, a number of pictures, some completed, some but half
finished, but all representing the Lord Protector Cromwell.
But the strangest thing about them was, that in every picture the canvas about the head was pricked through and
through in scores of places with very fine sharp holes, and,
looking around in his marvel, he found an arbalest or crossbow, with some very sharp bolts, and was so led to conjecture that some one had been setting these heads of the
Protector up as a target, and shooting bolts at them. He
was at first minded to send an express after his daughter
to London to question her if she knew aught of the matter ;
but on second thoughts he desisted, remembering that in
the Message, almost, (as the times stood) there was Treason,
and concluding that, after all, it might be but some idle
fancy of Arabella, and part of the demi-craze under which
she laboured. For there could be no manner of doubt that
the pictures, if not the holes in them, were of her handi-
work.

Meanwhile Arabella was being entertained in the state-
liest manner by Sir Fortunatus Geddings, who stood in great

favour with the government, and had, during the troubles, assisted the Houses with large sums of money. There were then not many sports or amusements wherewith a sorrowing maiden could be diverted; for the temper of England's Rulers was against vain pastimes and junketings. The Maypoles had been pulled down; the players whipped and banished; the bear and bull baitings, and even the mere harmless minstrelsy and ballad-singing of the streets, all rigorously pulled down. But whatever the worthy Turkey merchant and his household could do in the way of carrying Arabella about to suppers, christenings, country gatherings, and so forth, was cheerfully and courteously done. Sir Fortunatus maintained a coach (for he was one of the richest merchants in the City of London), and in this conveyance Arabella was ofttimes taken to drive in Hyde Park, or towards the Uxbridge Road. 'Twas on one of these occasions that she first saw the Protector, who likewise was in his coach, drawn by eight Holstein mares, and attended by a troop of Horse, very gallantly appointed, with scarlet livery coats, bright gorgets and back-pieces, and red plumes in their hats.

"He is very like, very like," she murmured, looking long and earnestly at the grand cavalcade.

"Like unto Whom, my dear?" asked Mrs. Nancy Geddings, the youngest daughter of Sir Fortunatus, who was her companion in the coach that day.

"Very like unto him who is at Home in the West yonder," she made answer. "Now take me back to Ludgate, Nancy sweet, for I am sick."

She was to be humoured in every thing, and she was taken home as she desired. It chanced, a few days after this, that word came that his Highness the Lord Protector of the Commonwealth of England (for to such State had Oliver grown) designed to visit the City, to dine with the citizens at Guildhall. There was to be a great pageant. He was to be met at Temple Bar by the Mayor and Aldermen, and to be escorted towards Cheapside by those city Trainbands which had done such execution on the Parliament side during the wars, and by the Companies with their Livery banners. Foreign ambassadors were to bear him company; for Oliver was then at the height of his power, and had made the name of England dreaded, and even his own prowess respected, by all nations that were beyond sea. He was to hear a sermon at Bow Church at noon, and at two o'clock —for the preacher was to be Mr. Hugh Peters, who always gave his congregation a double turn of the hour-glass—he was to dine at the Guildhall, where I know not how many geese, bustards, capons, pheasants, ruffs and reeves, sirloins, shoulders of veal, pasties, sweet puddings, jellies, and custards, with good store of Rhenish and Canary, and Bordelais and Burgundian wines, were provided to furnish a banquet worthy of the day. For although the Protectorate was a stern sad period, and Oliver was (or had schooled himself to be) a temperate man, the citizens had not quite forgotten their love of good cheer; and the Protector himself was not averse from the keeping up some state and splendour, Whitehall being now well-nigh as splendid as in the late King's time, and his Highness sitting with his make-believe lords around him (Lisle, Whitelocke, and the rest), and eating his meat to the sound of Trumpets, and being otherwise puffed up with Vanity.

The good folks with whom Arabella was sojourning thought it might help to cure her of her sad moping ways if she saw the grand pageant go by, and mingled in the merriment and feasting which the ladies of Sir Fortunatus's family—the Knight himself being bidden to the Guildhall—proposed to give their neighbours on the day when Oliver came into the City. To this intent, the windows of their house without Ludgate were all taken out of their frames, and the casements themselves hung with rich cloths and tapestries, and decked with banners. And an open house was kept, literally, meats and wines and sweets being set out in every room, even to the bed-chambers, and all of the Turkey merchant's acquaintance being bidden to come in and help themselves, and take a squeeze at the windows to see his Highness go by. Only one window on the first floor was set apart, and here sat the ladies of the family, with Mistress Deborah Clay, the Remembrancer's lady, and one that was sister to a Judge of Commonwealth's Bench, and Arabella Greenville, who was for a wonder quite cheerful and sprightly that morning, and who had for her neighbour one Lady Lisle, the wife of John Lisle, one of Cromwell's Chief Councillors and Commissioners of the Great Seal.*

* This Lady Lisle was a very virulent partisan woman, and, according to my Grandmother's showing, was so bitter against the

The time that passed between their taking seats and the coming of the pageant was passed pleasantly enough; not in drinking of healths, which practice was then considered as closely akin to an unlawful thing, but in laughing and quaffing, and whispering of many jests. For I have usually found that, be the Rule of Church and State ever so sour and stern, folks *will* laugh and quaff and jest on the sly, and be merry in the green tree, if they are forced to be sad in the dry.

There was a gentleman standing behind Arabella, a counsellor of Lincoln's Inn I think, who was telling a droll story of Mr. President Bradshaw to his friend from the Temple. Not greatly a person of whom to relate merry tales, I should think, that terrible Bencher, who sat at the head of the High Commission, clothed in his scarlet robe, and passed judgment upon his lord the King. But still these gentlemen laughed loud and long, as one told the other how the President lay very sick, sick almost to death, at his country house; and how, he being one that was in the Commission of the Chancellorship, had taken them away with him, and would by no means surrender them, keeping them under his pillow, night and day; wherefore one of his brother commissioners was fain to seek him out, and press him hard to give up the seals, saying that the business of the nation was at a standstill, for they could neither seal patents nor pardons. But all in vain, Bradshaw crying out in a voice that, though weak, was still terrible, that he would never give them up, but would carry them with him into the next world; whereat quoth the other commissioner, "*By* —, *Mr President, they will certainly melt if you do.*" And at this tale the gentleman from Lincoln's Inn and he from the Temple both laughed so, that Arabella, who had been listening without eavesdropping, burst into a fit of laughter too; only my Lady Lisle (who had likewise heard the story) regarded her with a very grim and dissatisfied countenance, and murmured that she thought a little trailing up before the Council, and

Crown that, being taken when a young woman to see the execution of King Charles, and seeing one who pressed to the scaffold after the blow to dip her kerchief in the Martyr's blood, she cried out "that she needed no such relic; but that she would willingly drink the Tyrant's blood." This is the same Alice Lisle who afterwards, in King James's time, suffered at Winchester for harbouring two of the Western Rebels.

committing to the Gate-house, would do some popinjays some good, and cure them of telling tales as treasonable as they were scurrilous.

But now came a great noise of trumpets and hautboys and drums, and the great pageant came streaming up towards Ludgate, a troop of Oliver's own Body-Guard on iron-gray chargers clearing the way, which they did with scant respect for the lives and limbs of the crowd, and with very little scruple either in bruising the Trainbands with their horses' hoofs and the flat of their broadswords. As Arabella leant forward to see the show approach, something hard, and it would seem of metal, that she carried beneath her mantle, struck against the arm of my Lady Lisle, who, being a woman of somewhat quick temper, cried out,

"Methinks that you carry a pocket-flask with you, Mistress Greenville, instead of a vial of essences. That which you have must hold a pint at least."

"I do carry such a flask," answered Arabella, "and, please God, there are those here to-day who shall drink of it even to the Dregs."

This speech was afterwards remembered against her as a proof of her Intent.

All, however, were speedily too busy with watching the show go by to take much heed of any word passage between the two women. Now it was Mistress Deborah Clay pointing out the Remembrancer to her gossip ; now the flaunting banners of the Companies, now the velvet robes of the Lord of the Council were looked upon ; now a great cry arose that his Highness was coming.

He came in his coach drawn by eight Holstein mares, one of his lords by his side, and his two chaplains, with a gentleman of the bed-chamber sitting over against. He wore a rich suit of brown velvet puffed with white satin, a bright gorget of silver,—men said that he wore mail beneath his clothes,— boots and gauntlets of yellow Spanish, a great baldric of cloth-of-gold, and in his hat a buckle of diamonds and a red feather. Yet, bravely as he was attired, those who knew him declared that they had never seen Oliver look so careworn and so miserable as he did that day.

By a kind of fate, he turned his glance upwards as he passed the house of the Turkey merchant, and those cruel eyes met the fierce gaze of Arabella Greenville.

"Blood for Blood!" she cried out in a loud clear voice; and she drew a Pistol from the folds of her mantle, and fired downwards, and with unerring aim, at the Protector's head.

My Lady Lisle saw the deed done. "Jezebel!" she shrieked, striking the weapon from Arabella's hand.

Oliver escaped unharmed, but by an almost miracle. The bullet had struck him, as it was aimed, directly in the centre of his forehead, he wearing his hat much slouched over his brow; but it had struck—not his skull, but the diamond buckle, and glancing off from that hard mass, sped out of the coach window again, on what errand none could tell, for it was heard of no more. I have often wondered what became of all the bullets I have let fly.

The stoppage of the coach; the Protector half stunned; the chaplain paralysed with fear; the Trainbands in a frenzy —half of terror, half of strong drink—firing off their pieces hap-hazard at the windows, and shouting out that this was a plot of the Papists or the Malignants; the crowd surging, the Body-Guard galloping to and fro; the poor standard-bearers tripping themselves up with their own poles,—all this made a mad turmoil in the street without Ludgate. But the Protector had speedily found all his senses, and had whispered a word or two to a certain Sergeant in whom he placed great trust, and pointed his finger to a certain window. Then the Sergeant being gone away, orders were given for the pageant to move on; and through Ludgate, and by Paul's, and up Cheape, and to Bow Church, it moved accordingly. Mr. Hugh Peters preached for two hours as though nothing had happened. Being doubtless under instructions, he made not the slightest allusion to the late tragic Attempt; and at the banquet afterwards at the Guildhall there were only a few trifling rumours that his Highness had been shot at by a mad woman from a window in Fleet Street; denial, however, being speedily given to this by persons in Authority, who declared that the disturbance without Ludgate had arisen simply from a drunken soldier of the Trainbands firing his musketoon into the air for Joy.

But the Sergeant, with some soldiers of the Protector's own, walked tranquilly into the house of Sir Fortunatus Geddings, and into the upper chamber, where the would-be Avenger of Blood was surrounded by a throng of men and women gazing upon her, half in horror, and half in admiration. The Sergeant beckoned to her, and she arose without a murmur, and went with him and the soldiers, two only being left as sentinels, to see that no one stirred from the house till orders came. By this time, from Ludgate to Black-friars all was soldiers, the crowd being thrust away east and west; and between a lane of pikemen, Arabella was brought into the street, hurried through the narrow lanes behind Apothecaries' Hall, and so through the alleys to Blackfriars Stairs, where a barge was in waiting, which bore her swiftly away to Whitehall.

"You have flown at high game, mistress," was the only remark made to her by the Sergeant.

She was locked up for many hours in an inner chamber, the windows being closed, and a lamp set on the table. They bound her, but, mindful of her sex and youth, not in fetters, or even with ropes, contenting themselves with fastening her arms tightly behind her with the Sergeant's silken sash. For the Sergeant was of Cromwell's own guard, and was of great authority.

At about nine at night the Sergeant and two soldiers came for her, and so brought her, through many corridors, to Cromwell's own chamber, where she found him still with his hat and baldric on, sitting at a table covered with green velvet.

"What prompted thee to seek my Life?" he asked, without anger, but in a slow, cold, searching voice.

"Blood for Blood!" she answered, with undaunted mien.

"What evil have I done thee that thou shouldst seek my blood?"

"What evil—what evil, Moloch?—all! Thou hast slain the King my Lord and master. Thou hast slain the dear brother who was my playmate, and my father's hope and pride. Thou hast slain the sweet and gallant youth who was to have been my husband."

"Thou art that Arabella Greenville, then, the daughter of the wavering half-hearted Esquire of the West."

"I am the daughter of a gentleman of long descent. I am Arabella Greenville; and I cry for vengeance for the blood of Charles Stuart, for the blood of Richard Greenville, for the blood of Francis Villiers. Blood for Blood!"

That terrible gleam of Madness leapt out of her blue eyes, and, all bound as she was, she rushed towards the Protector

as though in her fury she would have spurned him with her
foot, or torn him with her teeth. The Sergeant for his part
made as though he would have drawn his sword upon her;
but Oliver laid his hand on the arm of his officer, and bade
him forbear.

"Leave the maiden alone with me," he said calmly;
"wait within call. She can do no harm." Then, when
the soldiers had withdrawn, he walked to and fro in the room
for many minutes, ever and anon turning his head and gazing
fixedly on the prisoner, who stood erect, her head high, her
hands, for all their bonds, clenched in defiance.

"Thou knowest," he said, "that thy Life is forfeit."

"I care not. The sooner the better. I ask but one
Mercy : that you send me not to Tyburn, but to Hampton
Court ; there to be shot to death in the courtyard by a file of
musketeers."

"Wherefore to Hampton?"

"Because it was there you murdered my Lover and my
Brother."

"I remember," the Protector said, bowing his head.
"They were rare Malignants, both. I remember ; it was
on the same thirtieth of January that Charles Stuart died
the death. But shouldst thou not, too, bear in mind that
Vengeance is not thine, but the Lord's?"

"Blood for Blood !"

"Thou art a maiden of a stern Resolve and a strong
Will," said the Protector musingly. "If thou art pardoned,
wilt thou promise repentance and amendment?"

"Blood for Blood !"

"Poor distraught creature," this once cruel man made
answer, "I will have no blood of thine. I have had enough,"
he continued, with a dark look and a deep sigh; "I am weary;
and Blood will have Blood. But that my life was in Mercy
saved for the weal of these kingdoms, thou mightst have
done with me, Arabella Greenville, according to thy desires."

He paused as though for some expression of sorrow; but
she was silent.

"Thou art hardened," he resumed ; "it may be that there
are things that *cannot* be forgiven."

"There are," she said firmly.

"I spare thy life," the Lord Protector continued; "but,
Arabella Greenville, thou must go into Captivity. Until I

am Dead, we two cannot be at large together. But I will
not doom thee to a solitary prison. Thou shalt have a companion in durance. Yes," he ended, speaking between his
teeth, and more to himself than to her, "she shall join Him
yonder in his lifelong prison. Blood for Blood ; the Slayer
and the Avenger shall be together."

She was taken back to her place of confinement, where
meat and drink were placed before her, and a tiring-woman
attended her with a change of garments. And at day-break
the next morning she was taken away in a litter towards
Colchester in Essex.*

* Those desirous of learning fuller particulars of my Grandmother's
History, or anxious to satisfy themselves that I have not Lied, should
consult a book called *The Travels of Edward Brown, Esquire*, that is
now in the Great Library at Montague House. Mr. Brown is in most
things curiously exact ; but he errs in stating that Mrs. Greenville's
name was Letitia,—it was Arabella.

CHAPTER THE FOURTH.

MY GRANDMOTHER DIES, AND I AM LEFT ALONE, WITHOUT SO MUCH
AS A NAME.

I HAVE sat over against Death unnumbered times in the course
of a long and perilous life, and he has appeared to me in almost
every shape; but I shall never forget that Thirtieth of January
in the year '20, when my Grandmother died. I have seen
men all gashed and cloven about—a very mire of blood and
wounds,—and heads lying about on the floor like ninepins,
among the Turks, where a man's life is as cheap as the Halfpenny Hatch. I was with that famous Commander Baron
Trenck* when his Pandours—of whom I was one—broke
into Mutiny. He drew a pistol from his belt, and said, "I
shall decimate you." And he began to count Ten, "one, two,
three, four," and so on, till he came to the tenth man, whom
he shot Dead. And then he took to counting again, until he
was arrived at the second Tenth. That man's brains he also
blew out. I was the tenth of the third batch, but I never
blenched. Trenck happily held his hand before he came to
Me. The Pandours cried out that they would submit, although I never spoke a word; he forgave us; and I had a
flask of Tokay with him in his tent that very after-dinner.
I have seen a man keel-hauled at sea, and brought up on the
other side, his face all larded with barnacles like a Shrovetide capon. Thrice I have stood beneath the yardarm with
the rope round my neck (owing to a king's ship mistaking
the character of my vessel).† I have seen men scourged till
the muscles of their backs were laid bare as in a Theatre of
Anatomy; I have watched women's limbs crackle and frizzle
in the flames at an Act of Faith, with the King and Court—
ay, and the court-ladies too—looking on. I stood by when
that poor mad wretch Damiens was pulled to pieces by horses
in the Grève. I have seen what the plague could do in the
galleys at Marseilles. Death and I have been boon companions and bedfellows. He has danced a jig with me on a

---

* The Austrian, not the Prussian Trenck.—ED.
† This does not precisely tally with the Captain's disclaimer of
feeling any apprehension when passing Execution Dock.—ED.

plank, and ridden bodkin, and gone snacks with me for a lump of horseflesh in a beleaguered town; but no man can say that John Dangerous had aught but a bold face to show that Phantom who frights nursemaids and rich idle people so.

And yet, now, I can recall the cold shudder that passed through my young veins when my Grandmother died. Of all days, too, that the Thirtieth of January should have been ordered for her passing away! It was mid-winter, and the streets were white with Innocent Snow when she was taken ill. She had not been one of those trifling and trivanting gentlewomen that pull diseases on to their pates with drums and routs, and late hours, and hot rooms, and carding, and distilled waters. She had ever been of a most sober conversation and temperate habit; so that the prodigious age she reached became less of a wonder, and the tranquillity with which her spirit left this darksome house of clay seemed mercifully natural. They had noticed, so early as the autumn of '19, that she was decaying; yet had the roots of life stricken so strongly into earth as to defy that Woodman who pins his faith to shaking blasts at first, but when he finds that windfalls will not serve his turn, and that although leaves decay, and branches are swept away, and the very bark is stripped off, the tree dies not, takes heart of grace, and lays about him with his Axe. Then one blow with the sharp suffices. So for many months Death seemed to let her be, as though he sat down quietly by her side, nursing his bony chin, and saying, "She is very old and weak; yet a little, and she must surely be mine." Mistress Talmash appeared to me, in the fantastic imagination of a solitary childhood, to take such a part, and play it to the Very Death; and there were sidelong glances from her eyes, and pressures of her lips, and a thrusting forth of her hands when the cordial or the potion was to be given, that seemed to murmur, "Still does she Tarry, and still do I Wait." This gentlewoman was never hard or impatient with my Grandmother; but towards the closing scene, for all the outward deference she observed towards her, 'twas she who commanded, and the Unknown Lady who obeyed. Nor did I fail to mark that her bearing was towards me fuller of a kind of stern authority than she had of aforetime presumed to show, and that she seemed to be waiting for me too, that she might work her will upon me.

The ecclesiastic Father Ruddlestone was daily, and for many hours, closeted with my kinswoman and benefactress; and I often, when admitted to her presence after one of these parleys, found her much dejected, and in Tears. He had always maintained a ghostly sway over her, and was in these latter days stern with her almost to harshness. And although I have ever disdained eavesdropping and couching in covert places to hear the foregatherings of my betters (which some honourable persons in the world's reckoning scorn not to do), it was by Chance, and not by Design, that, playing one wintry day in the Withdrawing-room adjoining the closet where my Grandmother still sat among her relics, I heard high words— high, at least, as they affected one person, for the lady's rose not above a mild complaint; and Father Ruddlestone coming out, said in an angry tone:

" My uncle saved the King's life when he was in the Oak, and his soul when he was at Whitehall; and I will do his bidding by you now."

" The Lord's will be done, not mine," my Grandmother said meekly.

Then Father Ruddlestone passed into the Withdrawing-room, and seeing me on a footstool, playing it is true at the Battle of Hochstedt with some leaden soldiers, and two wooden puppets for the Duke and Prince Eugene, but still all agape at the strange words that had hit my sense, he catches me a buffet on the ear, bidding me mind my play, and not listen, else I should hear no good of myself, or of what an osier wand might haply do to me. And that a change was coming was manifest even in this rude speech; for my Grandmother, albeit of the wise King's mind on the proper ordering of children, and showing that she did not hate me when I needed chastening, would never suffer her Domestics, even to the highest, to lay a finger upon me.

It was after these things, and while I was crying out, more in anger than with the smart of the blow, that she called me into her closet and soothed me, giving me to eat of that much-prized sweetmeat she said was once such a favourite solace with Queen Mary of Modena, consort of the late King James, and which she only produced on rare occasions. And then she bewailed my hurt, but bade me not vex her Director, who was a man of much holiness, full, when we were contrite, of healing and quieting words; but then, of a sudden, nipping me pretty sharply by the arm, she said :

"Child, I charge thee that thou abandon that fair false race, and trust no man whose name is Stuart, and abide not by their fatal creed." In remembrance of which, although I am by descent a Cavalier, and bound by many bonds to the old Noble House,—and surely there was never a Prince that carried about him more of the far-bearing blaze of Majesty than the Chevalier de St. G—, and bears it still, all broken as he is, in his Italian retreat,—I have ever upheld the illustrious House of Brunswick and the Protestant Succession as by Law Established. And as the barking of a dog do I contemn those scurril flouts and obloquies which have of old times tossed me upon tongues, and said of me that I should play fast and loose with Jacobites and Hanoverians, drinking the King over the Water on my knees at night, and going down to the Cockpit to pour news of Jacobites and recusants and other suspected persons into the ears of Mr. Secretary in the morning. Treason is Death by the Law, and legal testimony is not to be gainsaid ; but I abhor those Iscariot-minded wretches, with faces like those who Torture the Saints in old Hangings, who cry, aha ! against the sanctuaries, and trot about to bear false witness.*

There were no more quarrels between my Grandmother and her Director. Thenceforth Father Ruddlestone ruled over her ; and one proof of his supremacy was, that she forewent the use of that Common Prayer-Book of our Anglican Church which had been her constant companion. From which I conjecture that, after long wavering and temporising, even to the length of having the Father in her household, she had at length returned to or adopted the ancient faith. But although the Substance of our Ritual was now denied her, she was permitted to retain its Shadow ; and for hours would sit gazing upon the torn-off cover of the book, with its device of the crown and crossed axes, in sad memory of K. C. I^{st}.

* I do not find it in the memoirs of his adventures, but in an old volume of the *Annual Register* I find that, in the year 1778, one Captain Dangerous gave important evidence for the crown against poor Mr. Tremenheere, who suffered at Tyburn for fetching and carrying between the French King and some malecontents in this country, notably for giving information as to the condition of our dockyards.—ED.

A most mournful Christmas found her still growing whiter and weaker, and nearer her End. At this ordinarily joyful season of the year, it was her commendable custom to give great alms away to the poor,—among whom at all times she was a very Dorcas,—bestowing not only gifts of money to the clergy for division among the needy, but sending also a dole of a hundred shillings to the poor prisoners in the Marshalsea, as many to Ludgate, and the Gatehouse, and the Fleet,—surely prisons for debt were as plentiful as blackberries when I was young!—and giving away besides large store of bread, meat, and blankets at her own door in Hanover Square : a custom then pleasantly common among people of quality, but now—when your parish Overseer, forsooth, eats up the very marrow of the poor—fallen sadly into disuse. They are for ever striking Poor's Rates against householders, and will not take clipped money ; whereas in my day Private Charity, and a King's Letter in aid from the pulpit now and then, were enough ; and, for my part, I would sooner see a poor rogue soundly firked at the post, and then comforted with a bellyful of bread and cheese and beer by the constable, and so passed on to his belongings, than that he should be clapped up in a workhouse, to pick oakum and suck his paws like a bear, while Master Overseer gets tunstomached over shoulder of veal and burnt brandy at vestry-dinners. For it is well known, to the shame of Authority, that these things all come out of the Poor Rate.

Ere my Grandmother was brought so low, she would sit in state on almsgiving morning, which was the day after Christmas ; and the more decent of her bedesmen and bedeswomen would be admitted to her presence to pay their duty, and drink her health in a cup of warm ale on the staircase. Also the little children from Lady Vielleastel's charity-school would be brought to her by their governante to have cakes and new groats given to them, and to sing one of those sweet tender Christmas hymns which surely fall upon a man's heart like sweet-scented balsam on a wound. And the beadle of St. George's would bring a great bowpot of such hues as Christmas would lend itself to, and have a bottle of wine and a bright broad guinea for his fee : while his Reverence the rector would attend with a suitable present,—such as a satin work-bag or a Good Book, the cover 'broidered by his daughters,—and, when he sat at meat, find a bank-bill under

his platter, which was always of silver. And I warrant you
his Reverence's eyes twinkled as much at the bill as at the
plum-porridge, and that he feigned not to see Father Ruddlestone, if perchance he met that foreign person on the staircase, or in the store-office where Mistress Nancy Talmash
kept many a toothsome cordial and heart-warming strong
water.

This dismal Christmas none of these pleasant things were
done. My Lady gave one Sum to her steward, Mr. Cadwallader, and bade him dispose of it according to his best judgment among the afflicted, bearing not their creed or politics
or parish in mind, but their necessities. And I was bereft
of a joyful day; for in ordinary she would be pleased that I
should be her little almoner, and hand the purses with the
groats in them to the poor almsfolk. What has become, I
wonder, of those good old customs of giving away things at
Christmas-tides? Where is the Lord Mayor's dole of beef-
pies to the vagrant people that lurk in St. Martin's-le-Grand,
that new Alsatia? Where is the Queen's gift of an hundred pounds to the distressed people who took up quarters
in Somerset House? Where are the thousand guineas
which the Majesty of England was used to send every New-
Year's morning to the High Bailiff of Westminster to be
parted among the poor of the Liberty? Nothing seems to
be given nowadays. 'Tis more caning than cakes that is
gotten by the charity children; and master Collector, the
Jackanapes, is for ever knocking at my door for Poor's
Rates.

In the middle of January my Grandmother was yet
weaker. Straw was laid before her door, and daily prayers
—for of course the Rector knew nothing about Father Ruddlestone—were put up for her at St. George's. And I think
also she was not forgotten in the orisons of those who attended the chapel of the Venetian Envoy, and in that permitted to the use of the French Ambassador. Doctor Vigors
was now daily in attendance, with many other learned physicians, who almost fought in the antechambers on the
treatment to be observed towards this sick person. One
was for cataplasms of bran and Venice turpentine, another
for putting live pigeons to her feet, another for a potion of
hot wine strained through gold-leaf and mingled with helle-
bore and chips of mandrake. Warwick Lane suggested

mint-tea, and Pall Mall was all for bleeding. This Pall-Mall physician was about the most passionate little man, with the biggest ruffles and the tallest gold-headed cane I ever saw. His name was Toobey.

"Blood, sir! there's nothing like blood!" he would cry to Doctor Vigors; and he cried out for "blood, sir," till you might fancy that he was a butcher or a herald-at-arms, or a housewife making black puddings.

Says Doctor Vigors in a Rage, "You are nothing but a barber-surgeon, brother, and learnt shaving on a sheep's head, and phlebotomy on a cow that had the falling fever."

"Mountebank and quacksalver!" answers my passionate gentleman, "you bought your diploma from one that forges seamen's certificates in Sopar Lane!"

"Go to, metamorphosed and two-legged ass! Where is your worship's stage in the Stocks Market, with pills to purge the vapours, and powders to make my lady in love with her footman, and a lying proclamation on every post, and a black boy behind you to beat on the cymbals when you draw out teeth with the kitchen pliers."

"Rogue!" screams Doctor Toobey, "but for the worshipful house we are in, I would batoon you to a mummy."

"Mummy forsooth!" the other retorts; "Mummy with a murrain! Why, you dug up your grandmother, and pounded her up with conserve of myrrh, and called the stuff King Pharaoh, that was sovereign to cure the strangury."

"Better to do that," quoth Toobey, calming down into mere give and take—for he had, in truth, done some droll things in mummy medicaments,—"than to have been a Fleet parson, that was forced to sell ale and couple beggars for a living, and turned doctor when he had cured a bad leg for one that had lain too long in the bilboes."

This was too much for Doctor Vigors, who had once been in orders, and was still a Nonjuror, winked at, for his skill's sake, by Authority. He was for rushing on the Pall-Mall mummy-doctor and tousling of his wig, when Mistress Tallmash came out of her lady's closet, and told them that she was fainting. This was the way that doctors disagreed when I was young, and I fancy that they don't agree much better now.

She lingered on, however, still resolutely refusing to take to her bed, and seeing me, if only for a moment, every day,

for yet another fortnight. On the Twentieth of January, it
was her humour to receive the visit of a certain great nobleman. Very many of the quality had daily waited upon her,
or had sent their gentlemen to inquire after her ; but for
many weeks she had seen none but her own household. The
nobleman I speak of had lately come down from the Bath,
where he had been taking the waters ; for he was full of
years, and of Glory, and of infirmities. A message went to
his grand house in Pall Mall, and he presently waited on
my Grandmother. He was closeted with her for an hour,
when the tap of my Grandmother's cane against the wainscot
summoned Mistress Talmash, and she, doing her errand,
brought me into the presence.

"My Lord," whispered my Grandmother, as she drew me
towards her, and gave me a kiss that was almost of a whisper too, so feebly gentle was it,—"My Lord Duke, will you
be pleased to lay your hand on the boy's head and give him
your blessing, and it will make him Brave."

He smiled sadly at her fancy, but did as she entreated.
He laid a hand that was all covered with jewelled rings,
and that shook almost as much as my Grandmother's, on
my locks, and prattled out to me something about being a
good boy and not playing cards. He, too, was almost gone.
He had a mighty wig, and velvet clothes all covered with
gold-lace, a diamond star, and broad blue ribbon ; but his
poor swollen legs were swathed in flannel, and he was so
feeble that he had to be helped down-stairs by two lacqueys.
I too ran down-stairs unchecked, and saw him helped, totter-
ing, into his chair, a company of the Foot-guards surrounding
it ; for he was much misliked by the mobile at that time,
and few cried, God bless him ! Indeed, as the company
moved away, I heard a ragged fellow (who should have been
laid by the heels for it) cry, "There goes Starvation Jack,
that fed his soldiers on boiled bricks and baked mortar."

"He is a Whig now," said my Grandmother to me, when
I rejoined her ; "but he was of the bravest among men, and
in the old days loved the true King dearly."

When this man was young and poor, the mobile used to
call him " Handsome Jack." When he was rich and old
and famous, he was "Starvation Jack" to them. And of
such are the caprices of a vain, precipitate age. But I am
glad I saw him, Whig and pinchpenny as he was. I am

proud of having seen this Great Captain and Prince of the Holy Roman Empire. The King of Prussia, the Duke of Cumberland, my Lord George Sackville, Marshal Biron, Duke Richelieu, and many of the chiefest among the Turkish bashaws, have I known and conversed with ; but I still feel that Man's trembling hand on my head ; my blood is still fired, as at the sound of a trumpet, by the remembrance of his voice ; I still rejoice at my fortune in having set eyes, if only for a moment, on John Churchill, Duke of Marlborough.

It was on the Twenty-ninth of January (o.s.) that our servants who had declared to having heard the death-watch ticking for days, asserted that those ominous sounds grew faster and faster, resolving themselves at length into those five distinct taps, with a break between, which are foolishly held by the vulgar to spell out the word DEATH. And although the noise came probably from some harmless insect, or from a rat nibbling at the wainscot, that sound never meets my ear—and I have heard it on board ship many a time, and in gaol, and in my tent in the desert—without a lump of ice sliding down my back. As for Ghosts, John Dangerous has seen too many of them to be frightened.*

That night I slept none. It was always my lot in that huge house to be put, little fellow as I was, in the hugest of places. My bed was as spacious as a Turkish divan. Its yellow silken quilt, lined with eider-down, and embroidered with crimson flowers, was like a great waving field of ripe corn with poppies in it. When I lay down, great weltering waves of Bed came and rolled over me ; and my bolster alone was as big as the cook's hammock at sea, who has always double bedding, being swollen with other men's rations. This bed had posts tall and thick enough to have been Gerard the Giant's lancing-pole, that used to stand in the midst of the bakehouse in Basing Lane ; and its curtains of yellow taffety hung in folds so thick that I always used to think birds nestled among them. That night I dreamt that the bed was changed into our great red pew at St. George's, only that it was hung with dark velvet instead of scarlet baize, and that the clergyman in the pulpit overhead, with a voice angrier than ever, was reading that service

* Captain Dangerous was, unconsciously, of the same mind with Samuel Taylor Coleridge.—ED.

for the martyrdom of K. C. Ist, which I had heard so often.
And then methought my dream changed, and two Great
Giants with heading-axes came striding over the bed, so
that I could feel their heavy feet on my breast; but their
heads were lost in the black sky of the bed's canopy. Horror!
they stooped down, and lo, they were headless, and from their
sheared shoulders and their great hatchets dripped, dripped,
for ever dripped, great gouts of something hot that came into
my mouth and tasted Salt ! And I woke up with my hair
all in a dabble with the night dews, with my Grandmother's
voice ringing in my ears, "Remember the Thirtieth of January !" Mercy on me ! I had that dream again last night ;
and the Giants with their axes came striding over these old
bones—then they changed to a headless Spaniard and a
bleeding Nun ; but the voice that cried, "Remember !"
spake not in the English tongue, and was not my Grandmother's. And the hair of my flesh stood up, as Job's did.

In the morning, when the clouds of night broke up from
the pale winter's sky, and went trooping away like so many
funeral coach-horses to their stable, they told me that my
Grandmother was Dead ; that she had passed away when
the first cock crew, softly sighing, "Remember." It was a
dreadful thing for me that I could not, for many hours,
weep ; and that for this lack of tears I was reproached for a
hardened ingrate by those who were now to be my most
cruel governers. But I could not cry. The grief within
me baked my tears, and I could only stare all round at the
great desert of woe and solitude that seemed to have suddenly
grown up around me. That morning, for the first time, I
was left to dress myself; and when I crept down to the
parlour, I found no breakfast laid out for me—no silver
tankard of new milk with a clove in it, no manchet of sweet
diet bread, no egg on a trencher in a little heap of salt. I
asked for my breakfast, and was told, for a young cub,
that I might get it in the kitchen. It would have gone
hard with me if, in my Grandmother's time, I had entered
that place to her knowledge ; but all things were changed to
me now, and when I entered the kitchen, the cook, nay, the
very scullion-wench, never moved for me. John Footman
sat on the dresser drinking a mug of purl that one of the
maids had made for him. The cook leered at me, while
another saucy slut handed me a great lump of dry bread,

and a black-jack with some dregs of the smallest beer at the bottom. What had I done to merit such uncivil treatment?

By and by comes Mr. Cadwallader with a sour face, and orders me to my chamber, and get a chapter out of Deuteronomy by heart by dinner-time, "Or you keep double fast for Martyrdom-day, my young master," he says, looking most evilly at me.

"Young master, indeed," Mrs. Nancy repeated; "young master and be saved to us. A parish brat rather. No man's child but his that to hit you must throw a stone over Bridewell Wall. Up to your chamber, little varlet, and learn thy chapter. There are to be no more counting of beads or mumblings over hallowed beans in this house. Up with you; times are changed."

Why should this woman have been my foe? She had been a cockering, fawning nurse to me not so many months ago. Months!—yesterday. Why should the steward, who was used to flatter and caress me, now frown and threaten like some harsh taskmaster of a Clink, where wantons are sent to be whipped and beat hemp? I slunk away scared and cowed, and tried to learn a chapter out of Deuteronomy; but the letters all danced up and down before my eyes, and the one word "Remember," in great scarlet characters, seemed stamped on every page.

It should have been told that between my seventh and my eighth year I had been sent, not only to church, but to school; but my grandmother deeming me too tender for the besom discipline of a schoolmaster,—from which even the Quality were not at that time spared,—I was put under the government of a discreet matron, who taught not only reading and writing, but also brocaded waistcoats for gentlemen, and was great caudle-maker at christenings. It was the merriest and gentlest school in the town. We were some twenty little boys and girls together, and all we did was to eat sweetmeats, and listen to our dame while she told us stories about Cock Robin, Jack the Giant-Killer, and the Golden Gardener. Now and then, to be sure, some roguish boy would put pepper in her snuff-box, or some saucy girl hide her spectacles; but she never laid hands on us, and called us her lambs, her sweethearts, and the like endearing expressions. She was the widow of an Irish Colonel who suffered in the year '96, for his share in Sir John Fenwick's conspiracy; and I think she had been at one time a tiring-woman to my Grandmother, whom she held in the utmost awe and reverence. I often pass Mrs. Triplet's old school-house in what is now called Major Foubert's Passage, and recall the merry old days when I went to a schoolmistress who could teach her scholars nothing but to love her dearly. It was to my Grandmother, a kind but strict woman, to whom I owed what scant reading and writing ken I had at eight years of age.

Rudely and disdainfully treated as I now was, my governors thought it fit, for the world's sake, that I should be put into decent mourning; for my Grandmother's death could not be kept from the Quality, and there was to be a grand funeral. She lay in State in her great bedchamber; tapers in silver sconces all around her, an Achievement of arms in a lozenge at her head, the walls all hung with fine black cloth edged with orris, and pieced with her escocheon, properly blazoned; and she herself, white and sharp as waxwork in her face and hands, arrayed in her black dress, with crimson ribbons and crimson scarf, and a locket of gold on her breast. They would not bury her with her rubies, but these, too, were laid upon her bier, which was of black velvet, and with a fair Holland sheet over all.

Not alone the chamber itself, but the anterooms and staircase were hung from cornice to skirting with black. The undertaker's men were ever in the house: they ate and drank whole mountains of beef and bread, whole seas of ale and punch (thus to qualify their voracity) in the servants' hall. They say my Grandmother's funeral cost a thousand pounds, which Cadwallader and Mrs. Talmash would really have grudged, but that it was the will of the executors, who were persons of condition, and more powerful than a steward and a waiting-woman. In her own testament my Grandmother said nothing about the ordering of her obsequies; but her executors took upon them to provide her with such rites as beseemed her degree. In those days the Quality were very rich in their deaths; and, for my part, I dissent from the starveling and nipcheese performances of modern funerals. It is most true that a hole in the sand, or a coral-reef, full fathom five, has been at many times my likeliest Grave; but I have left it nevertheless in my Will—which let those who come after me dispute if they dare—that I may be buried as a Gentleman of long descent, with all due Blacks, and Plumes, and Lights, and a supper for my friends, and mourning cloaks for six poor men.

Why the doctors should have remained in the house jangling and glozing in the very lobby of Death, and eating of cold meats and drinking of sweet wine in the parlour, after the breath was out of the body of their patient and patroness, it passes me to say; as well should a player tarry upon the Stage long after the epilogue has been spoken, the curtain lowered, and the lights all put out. Yet were Pall Mall and Warwick Lane faithful, not only unto the death, but beyond it, to Hanover Square. A coachful of these grave gentlemen were bidden to the burial, although it was probable that words would run so high among them as for wigs to be tossed out of the windows. And although it is but ill fighting and base fence to draw upon a foe in a coach, I think (so bitter are our Physicians against one another) that they would make but little ado in breaking their blades in halves and stabbing at one another crosswise as they sat, with their handkerchiefs for hilts.

It was on the eighth night after her demise, and at half-past nine of the clock, that my Grandmother was Buried. I was dressed early in the afternoon in a suit of black, full trimmed, falling bands of white cambric, edged, and a little mourning sword with a crape knot, and slings of black velvet. Then Mrs. Talmash knotted round my neck a mourning cloak that was about eight times too large for me, and with no gentle hand flattened on my head a hat bordered by heavy sable plumes. On the left shoulder of my cloak there was embroidered in gold and coloured silks a little escocheon of arms; and with this, in my child-like way, my fingers hankered to play; but with threats that to me were dreadful, and not without sundry nips and pinches, and sly clouts, I was bidden to be still, and stir not from a certain stool apportioned to me in the great Withdrawing-room. Not on this side of the tomb shall I forget the weary, dreary sense of desolation that came over me when, thus equipped, or rather swaddled and hampered in garments strange to me, and of which I scarcely knew the meaning, I was left alone for many hours in a dismal room, whose ancient splendour was now all under the eclipse wrought by the undertakers. And I pray that few children may so cruelly and suddenly have their happiness taken away from them, and from pampered

E

darlings become all at once despised and friendless out-
casts.

By and by the house began to fill with company; and one
that was acting as Groom of the Chambers, and marshalling
the guests to their places, I heard whisper to the Harbinger,
who first called out the names at the Stair-head, that Clarencieux, king-at-arms (who was then wont to attend the funerals
of the Quality, and to be gratified with heavy fees for his
office; although in our days 'tis only public noblemen, gene-
rals, ambassadors, and the like, who are so honoured at their
interment, only undertaker's pageantry being permitted to the
private sort)—that Clarencieux himself might have attended
to marshal the following, and proclaim the Style of the Departed; but that it was ordered by Authority that, as in
her life her name and honours had been kept secret, so likewise in her death she was to remain an Unknown Lady.
How such a reticence was found to jump with the dictates
of the law, which required a registry of all dead persons in
the parish-books, I know not; but in that time there were
many things suffered to the Great which to the meaner kind
would have been sternly denied; and, indeed, I have since
heard tell that sufferance even went beyond the concealment
of her Name, and that she was not even buried in woollen,—
a thing then very strictly insisted upon, in order to encourage
the staple manufactures of Lancashire and the North,—and
that, either by a Faculty from the Arches Court, or a winking
and conniving of Authority, she was placed in her coffin in
the same garb in which she had lain in state. Of such sorry
mocks and sneers as to the velvet of her funeral coffer being
nearer Purple than Crimson in its hue, and of my mourning
cloak being edged with a narrow strip of a Violet tinge,—as
though to hint in some wise that my Grandmother was foregathered, either by descent or by marital alliance with
Royalty,—I take little account. 'Tis not every one who is
sprung from the loins of a King who cares to publish the
particulars of his lineage, and John Dangerous may perchance
be one of such discreet men.

The doctors had been so long in the house that their names
and their faces were familiar to me, not indeed as friends, but
as that kind of acquaintance one may see every day for twenty
years, and be not very grieved some morning if news comes that
they are dead. Such an eye-acquaintance passes my windows

every morning. I know his face, his form, his hat and coat, the very tie of his wig and the fashion of his shoe-buckle; but he is no more to me than I am haply to him, and there would be scant weeping, I opine, between us if either of us were to die. So I knew these doctors and regarded them little, wondering only why they ate and drank so much, and could so ill conceal their hatred as to be calling foul names, and well-nigh threatening fisticuffs, while the corse of my Grandmother was in the house. But of the body of those who were bidden to this sad ceremony, I had no knowledge whatsoever. For aught I knew, they might have been players or bullies and Piccadilly captains, or mere undertaker's men dressed up in fine clothes; yet, believe me, it is no foolish pride, or a dead vanity that prompts me to surmise that there were those who came to my Grandmother's funeral who had a Claim to be reckoned amongst the very noblest and proudest in the land. Beneath the great mourning cloaks and scarves, I could see diamond stars glistening, and the brave sheen of green and crimson ribbons. I desire in this particularity to confine myself strictly to the Truth, and therefore make no vain boast of a Blue Ribbon being seen there, thus denoting the presence of a Knight of the most noble Order of the Garter. I leave it to mine enemies to lie, and to cowardly Jacks to boast of their own exploits. This brave gathering was not void of women; but they were closely veiled and impenetrably shrouded in their mourning weeds, so that of their faces and their figures I am not qualified to speak; and if you would ask me that which I remember chiefly of the noble gentlemen who were present, I can say with conscience, that beyond their stars and ribbons, I was only stricken by their monstrous and portentous Periwigs, which towered in the candle-light like so many great tufts of plumage atop of the Pope's Baldaquin, which I have seen so many times staggering through the great aisles of St. Peter's at Rome.

Your humble servant, and truly humble and forlorn he was that night, was placed at the coffin's head; it being part of that black night's sport to hold me as Chief Mourner; and, indeed, poor wretch, I had much to mourn for. The great plumed hat they had put upon me flapped and swaled over my eyes so as almost to blind me. My foot was for ever catching in my great mourning cloak, and I on the verge of tripping myself up; and there was a hot smoke sweltering from the tapers, and a dreadful smell of new black cloth and sawdust and beeswax, that was like to have suffocated me. Infinite was the relief when two of the ladies attired in black, who had sat on either side of me, as though to guard me from running away, lifted me gently each under an armpit, and held me up so that I could see the writing on the coffin-plate, which was of embossed silver and very brave to view.

"Can you read it out, my little man?" a deep rich voice as of a lady sounded in mine ears.

I said, with much trembling, "that I thought I could spell out the words, if time and patience were accorded me."

"There is little need, child," the voice resumed. "I will read it to thee;" and a black-gloved hand came from beneath her robe, and she took my hand, and holding my fore-finger not ungently made me trace the writing on the silver. But I declare that I can remember little of that Legend now, although I am impressed with the belief that my kinswoman's married name was not mentioned. That it was merely set forth that she was the Lady D—, whose maiden name was A. G., and that she died in London in the 90th year of her age, King George I. being king of England. And then the smoke of the tapers, the smell of the cloth and the wax, and the remembrance of my Desolation, were too much for me, and I broke out into a loud wail, and was so carried fainting from the room; being speedily, however, sufficiently recovered to take my place in the coach that was to bear us Eastward.

We rode in sorrowful solemnity till nigh three o'clock that morning; but where my Grandmother was buried I never knew. From some odd hints that I afterwards treasured up, it seems to me that the coaches parted company with the Hearse somewhere on the road to Harwich; but of this, as I have averred, I have no certain knowledge. In sheer fatigue I fell asleep, and woke in broad daylight in the great state-bed at Hanover Square.

CHAPTER THE FIFTH.

In the morning, the wicked people into whose power I was
now delivered came and dragged me from my bed with fierce
thumps, and giving me coarse and rude apparel, forced me to
dress myself like a beggar boy. I had a wretched little frock
and breeches of gray frieze, ribbed woollen hose and clouted
shoes, and a cap that was fitter for a chimney-sweep than a
young gentleman of Quality. I was to go away in the Wagon,
they told me, forthwith, to School; for my Grandmother—if
I was indeed any body's Grandson—had left me nothing,
not even a name. Henceforth I was to be little Scrub, little
Ragamuffin, little boy Jack. All the unknown Lady's property, they said, was left to Charities and to deserving Servants. There was not a penny for me, not even to pay for
my Schooling; but, in Christian mercy, Mrs. Talmash was
about to have me taught some things suitable for my new
degree, and in due time have me apprenticed to some rough
Trade, in which I might haply—if I were not hanged, as she
hinted pretty plainly, and more than once—earn an honest
livelihood. Meanwhile I was to be taken away in the Wagon,
as though I were a Malefactor going in a Cart to Tyburn.

I was taken down-stairs, arrayed in my new garments of
poverty and disgrace, and drank in a last long look at my
dear and old and splendid Home. How little did I think
that I should ever come to look upon it again, and that it
would be my own House—mine, a prosperous and honoured
old man! The undertaker's men were busied in taking down
the rich hangings, and guzzling and gorging, as was their
wont, on what fragments remained of the banquetings and
carousals of Death, which had lasted for eight whole days.
All wretched as I was, I should—so easily are the griefs of
childhood assuaged by cates and dainties—have been grateful
for the wing of a chicken or a glass of Canary; but this was
not to be. John a'Nokes and John a'Styles were now more
considered than I was, and I was pushed and bandied about
by fustian knaves and base mechanics, and made to wait for

full half an hour in the hall, as though I had been the by-
blow of a Running Footman promoted into carrying of a
link.

'Twas Dick the Groom that took me to the Wagon.
Many a time he had walked by the side of my little pony,
trotting up the Oxford Road. He was a gross unlettered
churl, but not unkind ; and I think remembered with something like compunction the many pieces of silver he had had
from his Little Master.

"It's mortal hard," he said, as he took my hand, and
began lugging me along, "that your grandam should have
died and left you nothing. 'Tis all clear as Bexley ale in a
yard-glass. Lawyers ha' been reading the will to the gentlefolks, and there's nothing for thee, poor castaway."

I began to cry, not because my Grandmother had disin-
herited me, but because this common horse-lout called me a
"castaway," and because I knew myself to be one.

"Don't fret," the groom continued ; "there'll be greet
enough for thee when thou'rt older ; for thou'lt have a hard
time on't, or my name's not Dick Snaffle."

We had a long way to reach the Wagon, which started
from a Tavern called the "Pillars of Hercules," right on the
other side of Hyde Park. I was desperately tired when we
came thither, and craved leave to sit on a bench before the
door, between the Sign-post and the Horse-trough. So low
was I fallen. A beggar came alongside of me, and as I dozed
tried to pick my pocket. There was nothing in it—not even
a crust; and he hit me a savage blow over the mouth because
I had nothing to be robbed of. Anon comes Dick Snaffle,
who, telling me that the Saddler of Bawtry was hanged for
leaving his liquor, and that he had no mind for a halter while
good ale was to be drunk, had been comforting himself within
the tavern; and he finding me all blubbered with grief at the
blow I had gotten from the beggar, fetches him a sound kick ;
and so the two fell to fighting, till out comes the tapster,
raving at Tom Ostler to duck the cutpurse cadger in the
Horse-trough. There was much more sport out of doors in
my young days than now.

At last the Wagon, for which we had another good hour
to wait, came lumbering up to the Pillars of Hercules ; and
after the Wagoner had fought with a Grenadier, who wanted
to go to Brentford for fourpence, and would have stabbed the

man with his bayonet had not his hand been stayed, the
Groom took me up, and put me on the straw inside. He
paid the Wagoner some money for me, and also gave into his
keeping a little bundle, containing, I suppose, some change
of raiment for me, saying that more would be sent after me
when needed; and so, handing him too a letter, he bade me
Godd'en, and went on his way with the Grenadier, a Sweep,
and a Gipsy woman, who was importunate that he should
cross her hand with silver, in order that he might know all
about the great Fortune that he was to wed, as Tom Phil-
brick did in the ballad. And this was the way in which the
Servants of the Quality spent their forenoons when I was
young.

As the great rumbling chariot creaked away westward,
there came across my child-heart a kind of consciousness that
I had been Wronged, and Cheated out of my inheritance.
Why was I all clad in laces and velvet but yesterday, and
to-day appareled like a tramping pedlar's foster-brat? Why
was I, who was used to ride in coaches, and on pony-back,
and on the shoulder of my own body-servant, and was called
"Little Master," and made much of, to be carted away in a
vile dray like this? But what is a child of eight years old to
do? and how is he to make head against those who are older
and wickeder than he? I knew nothing about lawyers, or
wills, or the Rogueries of domestics. I only knew that I had
been foully and shamefully Abused since my dear Grand-
parent's death; and in that wagon, I think, as I lay tumbling
and sobbing on that straw, were first planted in me those
seeds of a Wild, and sometimes Savage, disposition that have
not made my name to be called "Dangerous" in vain.

We were a small and not a very merry company under
the wagon tilt. There was a Tinker, with all his accoutrements of pots and kettles about him, who was lazy, as most
Tinkers are when not at hard work, and lay on his back
chewing straw, and cursing me fiercely whenever I moved.
There was a Welsh gentleman, very ragged and dirty, with a
wife raggeder and dirtier than he. He was addressed as
Captain, and was bound, he said, for Bristol, to raise soldiers
for the King's Service. He beat his wife now and then,
before we came to Hounslow. There was the Tinker's dog,
a great terror to me; for although he feigned to sleep, and to
snore as much as a Dog can snore, he always kept one little

red eye fixed upon me, and gave a growl and made a Snap
whenever I turned on the straw.   There was the Wagoner's
child that was sickly, and continually cried for its mammy;
and lastly there was a buxom servant-maid, with a little
straw hat and cherry ribbons over a Luton lace mob, and
a pretty flowered gown pulled through the placket-holes, and
a quilted petticoat, and silver buckles in her shoes, and black
mits, who was going home to see her Grandmother at Stoke
Pogis,—so she told me, and made me bitterly remember that
I had now no Grandmother,—and was as clean and bright
and smiling as a new pin, or the milkmaids on May morning
dancing round the brave Garlands that they have gotten
from the silversmiths in Cranbourn Alley.   She sat prettily
crouched up on her box in a corner; and so, with the Tinker
among his pots and kettles, the Welsh Captain and his Lady
on sundry bundles of rags, the sickly child in a basket, the
Tinker's dog curled up in his Master's hat, I tossing on the
straw, and a great rout of crates of crockery, rolls of cloth,
tea and sugar, and other London merchandise, which the
Wagoner was taking down West, as a return cargo for the
eggs, poultry, butcher's meat, and green stuff that he had
brought up, made altogether such a higgledypiggledy that
you do not often see in these days, when Servant-maids come
up by Coach—my service to them!—and disdain the Wagon,
and his Worship the Captain wears a fine laced coat and a
cockade in his hat,—who but he!—and travels post.

   The Maid who was bound on a visit to her Grandmother
was, I rejoice to admit, most tenderly kind to me.   She
combed my hair, and wiped away the tears that besmirched
my face.   When the Wagon halted at the King's Arms,
Kensington, she tripped down and brought me a flagon of
new milk with some peppermint in it; and she told me
stories all the way to Hounslow, and bade me mind my book,
and be a good child, and that Angels would love me.   Likewise that she was being courted by a Pewterer in Panyer
Alley, who had parted a bright sixpence with her—she
showed me her token, drawn from her modest bodice, and
who had passed his word to Wed, if he had to take to the
Road for the price of the Ring—but that was only his fun-
ning, she said,—or if she were forced even to run away from
her Mistress, and make a Fleet Match of it.   It was little, in
good sooth, that I knew about courtships or Love-tokens or

Fleet Matches; but I believe that a woman, for want of a better gossip, would open her Love-budget to a Baby or a Blind Puppy, and I listened so well that she kissed me ere we parted, and gave me a pocketful of cheese-cakes.

It was quite night, and far beyond Hounslow, when I was dozing off into happy sleep again, that the Wagon came to a dead stop, and I awoke in great fright at the sound of a harsh voice asking if the Boy Jack was there. I was the "Boy Jack;" and the Wagoner coming to the after part of the tilt with his lantern, pulled me from among the straw with far less ado than if I had been the Tinker's dog.

I was set down on the ground before a tall man with a long face and an ugly little scratch wig, who had large boots with straps over his thighs, like a Farmer, and swayed about him with a long whip.

"Oh, this is the boy, is it?" said the long man. "A rare lump to lick into shape, upon my word."

I was too frightened to say aught; but the Wagoner muttered something in the long man's ear, and gave him my bundle and money and the letter; and then I was clapped up on a pillion behind the long man, who had clomb up to the saddle of a vicious horse that went sideways; and he, bidding me hold on tight to his belt, for a mangy young whelp as I was, began jolting me to the dreadful place of Torture and Infernal cruelty which for six intolerable months was to be my home.

This man's name was Gnawbit, and he was my Schoolmaster. I was delivered over to him, bound hand and foot, as it were, by those hard-hearted folk (who should have been most tender to me, a desolate orphan) in Hanover Square. His name was Gnawbit, and he lived hard by West Drayton.

We are told in Good Books about the Devil and his Angels; but sure I think that the Devil must come to earth sometimes, and marry and have children : whence the Gnawbit race. I don't believe that the man had one Spark of Human Feeling in him. I don't believe that any tale of Man or Woman's Woe would ever have wrung one tear from that cold eye, or drawn a pang from that hard heart. I believe that he was a perfectly senseless, pitiless Brute and Beast, suffered, for some unknown purpose, to dwell here above, instead of being everlastingly kept down below, for the purpose of Tormenting. I was always a Dangerous, but

I was never a Revengeful man. I have given mine enemy to eat when he was a-hungered, and to drink when he was athirst. I have returned Good for Evil very many times in this Troubled Life of mine, exposed as it has been always to the very sorest of temptations; but I honestly aver, that were I to meet this Tyrant of mine, now, on a solitary island, I would mash his Hands with a Club or with my Feet, if he strove to grub up roots; that were I Alone with him, wrecked, in a shallop, and there were one Keg of Fresh Water between us, I would stave it, and let the Stream of Life waste itself in the gunwales while I held his head down into the Sea, and forced him to swallow the brine that should drive him Raving Mad. But this is unchristian, and I must go consult Doctor Dubiety.

Flesh and Blood! Have you never thought upon the Wrongs your Pedagogue has wrought upon you, and longed to meet that Wretch, and wheal his flesh with the same instrument with which he whealed you, and make the Ruffian howl for mercy? Mercy, quotha! did he ever show you any? A pretty equal match it was, surely! You a poor, weak starveling of a child shivering in your shoes, and ill-nurtured by the coarse food he gave you, and he a great, hulking, muscular villain, tall and long-limbed, and all-powerful in his wretched Empire; while you were so ignorant as not to know that the Law, were he discovered (but who was to denounce him?), might trounce him for his barbarity. Ah! brother Gnawbit, if I had ever caught you on board a good ship of mine! Aha! knave, if John Dangerous would not have dubbed himself the sheerest of asses, had he not made your back acquainted with nine good tails of three-strand cord, with triple knots in each, and the brine-tub afterwards. I will find out this Gnawbit yet, and cudgel him to the death. But, alas, I rave. He must have been full five-and-forty years old when I first knew him, and that is nigh sixty years agone. And at a hundred and five the cruellest Tyrant is past cudgelling.

This man had one of the prettiest houses that was to be seen in the prettiest part of England. The place was all draped in ivy, and roses, and eglantine, with a blooming flower-garden in front, and a luscious orchard behind. He had a wife too who was Fair to see,—a mild, little woman, with blue eyes, who used to sit in a corner of her parlour,

and shudder as she heard the boys shrieking in the schoolroom. There was an old infirm Gentleman that lodged with
them, that had been a Captain under the renowned Sir
Cloudesley Shovel and Admiral Russell, and could even, so
it was said, remember, as a sea-boy, the Dutch being in the
Medway, in King Charles's time. This Old Gentleman seemed
the only person that Gnawbit was afraid of. He never inter-
fered to dissuade him from his brutalities, nay seemed rather
to encourage him therein, crying out as the sounds of torture
reached him, "Bear it! bear it! Good again! Make 'em
holloa! Make 'em dance! Cross the cuts! Dig it in!
Rub in the brine! Oho! Bear it, brave boys; there's nothing
like it!" Yet was there something jeering and sarcastic in
his voice that made Gnawbit prefer to torture his unhappy
scholars when the Old Gentleman was asleep,—and even then
he would sometimes wake up and cry out, "Bear it!" from
the attic, or when he was being wheeled about the neighbourhood in a sick man's chair.

The first morning I saw the Old Gentleman he shook his
crutch at me, and cried, "Aha! another of 'em! Another
morsel for Gnawbit. More meat for his market. Is he
plump? is he tender? Will he bear it? Will he dance?
Oho! King Solomon for ever." And then he burst into
such a fit of wheezing laughter that Mrs. Gnawbit had to
come and pat him on the back and bring him cordials; and
my Master, looking very discomposed, sternly bade me betake
myself to the schoolroom.

After that, the Old Gentleman never saw me without
shaking his crutch and asking me if I liked it, if I could
bear it, and if Gnawbit made my flesh quiver. Of a truth he
did.

Why should I record the sickening experience of six
months' daily suffering. That I was beaten every day was
to be expected in an Age when blows and stripes were the
only means thought of for instilling knowledge into the minds
of youth. But I was alone, I was friendless, I was poor.
My master received, I have reason to believe, but a slender
Stipend with me, and he balanced accounts by using me with
greater barbarity than he employed towards his better paying
scholars. I had no Surname, I was only "Boy Jack;" and
my schoolfellows put me down, I fancy, as some base-born
child, and accordingly despised me. I had no pocket-money.

I was not allowed to share in the school-games. I was bidden to stand aside when a cake was to be cut up. God help me ! I was the most forlorn of little children. Mrs. Gnawbit was as kind to me as she dared be, but she never showed me the slightest favour without its bringing me (if her husband came to hear of it) an additionally cruel Punishment.

There was a Pond behind the orchard called Tibb's hole, because, as our schoolboy legend ran, a boy called Tibb had once cast himself thereinto, and was drowned, through dread of being tortured by this Monster. I grew to be very fond of standing alone by the bank of this Pond, and of looking at my pale face in its cool blue-black depth. It seemed to me that the Pond was my friend, and that within its bosom I should find rest.

I was musing in this manner by the bank one day when I felt myself touched on the shoulder. It was the crutch of the Old Gentleman, who had been. wheeled hither, as was his custom, by one of the boys.

"You go into the orchard and steal a juicy pear," said the Old Gentleman to his attendant. "Gnawbit's out, and I won't tell him. Leave me with Boy Jack for five minutes, and then come back.—Boy Jack," he continued, when we were alone, "how do you like it ?"

"Like what, sir ?" I asked humbly.

"All of it, to be sure :—the birch, the cane, the thong, the ferula, the rope's-end,—all Gnawbit's little toys ?"

I told him, weeping, that I was very, very unhappy, and that I would like to drown myself.

"That's wrong, that's wicked," observed the Old Gentleman with a chuckle ; "you mustn't drown yourself, because then you'd lose your chance of being hanged. Gregory has as much right to live as other folks."*

I did not in the least understand what he meant, but went on sobbing.

"I tell you what it is," pursued the Old Gentleman : "you mustn't stop here, because Gnawbit will skin you alive if you do. He's bound to do it; he's sworn to do it. He half-skinned Tibb ; and was going to take off the other half, when Tibb drowned himself like a fool in this hole here. He was

---

* In my youth ancient persons as frequently spoke of the hangman as "Gregory"—and he was so named at the trial of the Regicides in 1660-61—as by his later title of "Jack Ketch."—J. D.

a fool, and should have followed my advice and run away. 'Tibb,' I said, 'you'll be skinned. Bear it, but run away. Here's a guinea. Run!' He was afraid that Gnawbit would catch him : and where is he now? Skinned, and drowned into the bargain. Don't you be a Fool. You Run while there's some skin left. Gnawbit's sworn to have it all, if you don't. Here's a guinea, and run away as fast as ever your legs can carry you."

He gave me a bright piece of gold and waved me off, as though I were to run away that very moment. I submissively said that I would run away after school was over, but asked him where I should run to.

"I'm sure I don't know," the Old Gentleman said somewhat peevishly. "That's not my business. A boy that has got legs with skin on 'em, and doesn't know where to run to, is a Jackass.—Stop!" he continued, as if a bright idea had just struck him ; "did you ever hear of the Blacks?"

"No, sir," I answered.

"Stupid oaf! Do you know where Charlwood Chase is!"

"Yes, sir; my schoolfellows have been nutting there, and I have heard them speak of it."

"Then you make the best of your way to Charlwood Chase, and go a-nutting there till you find the Blacks; you can't miss them ; they're everywhere. Run, you little Imp. See! the time's up, and here comes the boy who stole the juicy pear." And the boy coming up, munching the remains of one of Gnawbit's juiciest pears, my patron was wheeled away, and I have never seen him from that day to this.

That very night I ran away from Gnawbit's, and made my way towards Charlwood Chase to join the "Blacks," although who those "Blacks" were, and whereabouts in the Chase they lived, and what they did when they were there, I had no more definite idea than who the Emperor Prester John or the Man in the Moon might be.

CHAPTER THE SIXTH.

THE HISTORY OF MY GRANDFATHER, WHO WAS SO LONG KEPT A PRISONER IN ONE OF THE KING'S CASTLES IN THE EAST COUNTRY.

AT the time when his Majesty Charles II. was so happily restored to the throne of these kingdoms, there was, and had been, confined for upwards of ten years, in one of his Majesty's Castles in the eastern part of this kingdom, a certain Prisoner. His Name was known to none, not even to the guards who kept watch over him, so to speak, night and day,—not even to the gaoler, who had been told that he must answer with his Head for his safe custody, who had him always in a spying, fretful overlooking, and who slept every night with the keys of the Captive's cell under his pillow. The Castle where he lay in hold has been long since levelled to the earth, if, indeed, it ever had any earth to rest upon, and was not rather stayed upon some jutting fragment of Rock washed away at last by the ever-encroaching sea. Nay, of its exact situation I am not qualified to tell. I never saw the place, and my knowledge of it is confined to a bald hearsay, albeit of the Deeds that were done within its walls, I can affirm the certitude with Truth. From such shadowy accounts as I have collected, the edifice would seem to have consisted but of a single tower or donjon-keep very strong and thick, and defying the lashings of the waves, almost as though it were some Pharos or other guide to mariners. It was surrounded by a low stone wall of prodigious weight of masonry, and was approached from the mainland by a drawbridge and barbican. But for many months of the year there was no mainland within half a mile of it, and the King's Castle could only be reached by boats. Men said that the Sun never shone there but for ten minutes before and ten minutes after a storm, and there were almost always storms lowering over or departing from that dismal place. The Castle was at least two miles from any human habitation; for the few fishermen's cabins, made of rotten boats, hogsheads nailed together, and the like, which had pitifully nestled under the lee of the Castle in old time, had been rigorously demolished to their last crazy timber when the Prisoner was brought there. At a respectful distance only, far in, and yet but a damp little islet in the midst of the fens, was permitted to linger on, in despised obscurity, a poor swamp of some twenty houses that might, half in derision and half in civility, be called a Village. It had a church without a steeple, but with a poor Stump like the blunted wreck of some tall ship's mainmast. The priest's wages were less than those of a London coal-porter. The poor man could get no tithes, for there were no tithes to give him. Three parts of his glebe were always under water, and he was forced to keep a little school for his maintenance, of which the scholars could pay him but scant fees, seeing that it was always a chance whether their parents were dead of the Ague, or Drowned. Yet there was a tavern in the village, where these poor, shrinking, feverish, creatures met and drank and smoked and sang their songs, contriving now and again to smuggle a few kegs of spirits from Holland, and baffle the riding-officers in a scamper through the fens. They were a simple folk, fond of telling Ghost-Stories, and with a firm belief in charms to cure them from the Ague. And, with an awe whose intensity was renewed each time the tale was told, they whispered among themselves as to that Prisoner of Fate up at the Castle yonder. What this man's Crime had been, none could tell. His misdeed was not, it was whispered, stated in the King's Warrant. The Governor was simply told to receive a certain Prisoner, who would be delivered to him by a certain Officer, and that, at the peril of his life, he was to answer for his safe custody. The Governor, whose name was Ferdinando Glover, had been a Captain of Horse in the late Protector Oliver's time ; but, to the surprise of all men, he was not dismissed at his Majesty's Restoration, but was continued in his command, and, indeed, received preferment, having the grade of a Colonel on the Irish establishment. But they did not fail to tell him, and with fresh instances of his severity, that he would answer with his head for the safe keeping of his Prisoner.

Of this strange Person it behoves me now to speak. In the year 1660, he appeared to be about seven-and-thirty years of age, tall, shapely, well-knit in his limbs, which captivity had rather tended to make full of flesh than to waste away ; for there were no yards, nor spacious outlying walls to this Castle ; and but for a narrow ledge that ran along the surrounding border, and where he was but rarely suffered to walk, there were no means for him to take any exercise whatever. He wore his own hair in full dark locks, which Time and Sorrow had alike agreed to grizzle. Strong lines marked his face, but age had not brought them there. His eye was dim, but more with watching and study than with the natural failing of vital forces.

So he had been in this grim place going on for twelve years, without a day's respite, without an hour's enlargement. True, he wore no fetters, and was treated with a grave and stately Consideration ; but his bonds were not less galling, and the iron had not the less entered into his soul. The Order was, that he was to be held as a Gentleman, and to be subjected to no grovelling indignities or base usage. But the Order was (for a long time, and until another Prisoner, hereafter to be named, received a meed of Enlargement) like-wise as strict that, save his keepers, he should see no living soul. "And it is useless," wrote a Great Lord to the Governor once, when it was humbly submitted to him that the Prisoner might need spiritual consolation and have solace to his soul by conferring with poor Parson Webfoot yonder,—" it is useless," said that nobleman, "for your charge to see any black gown, under pretext that he would Repent ; for, albeit, though I know not his crime more than the babe unborn, I have it from his Majesty's own gracious word of mouth, that what he has done cannot be repented of ; therefore you are again commanded to keep him close, and to let him have speech neither of parson nor of peasant." Which was duly done. But Colonel Glover, not untouched by that curiosity inherent to mankind, as well as womankind, took pains to cast about whether this was not one who had a hand in com-passing the death of King Charles I. ; and this coming, in some strange manner (through inquiries he had made in London), to the ears of Authority, he was distinctly told that his prisoner was not one of those bold bad men who, misled by Oliver Cromwell, had signed that fatal Warrant :—the names and doom of the Regicides being now all well known, as having suffered or fled from Justice, or being in hold, as Mr. Martyn was. So Colonel Glover, being well assured that what was done was for the King's honour, and for the well-being of his Estates, and that any other further search-ing or prying might cost him his place, if they did not draw him within the meshes of the law against Misprison of

Treason, forbore to vex himself or Authority further on matters that concerned him not, and so was content to guard his Prisoner with greater care than ever. The Castle was garrisoned by but twelve men, and of these six were invalids and matrosses; but the other six were tall and sturdy veterans, who had been indeed of Oliver's Life-guard, and were now confirmed in their places, and with the pay, not of common soldiers, but of private gentlemen, by the King's own order. Their life was dreary enough, for they could hold but little comradeship with the invalids, whom they dubbed "gray-beards, drivellers, and kill-joys." But they had a guard-room to themselves, where they diced and drank, and told their ruffian stories, and sang their knavish catches, as is the manner, I suppose, for all soldiers to do in all countries, whether in camps or in cities. But their duty was withal of the severest. The invalids went snugly to bed at nine of the clock, or thereabouts, but the veritable men-of-war kept watch and ward all night, turn and turn about, and even when they slept took their repose on a bench, which was placed right across the Prisoner's door.

This much-enduring man — for surely no lot could be harder than his — to be thus, and in the very prime and vigour of manhood, cooped up in a worse than gaol, wherein for a long time he was even denied the company of captives as wretched as he,—this slave to some Mightier Will and Sterner Fate than, it would seem, mortal knowledge could wot of, bore his great Distress with an unvarying meekness and calm dignity. With him, indeed, they did as they listed, using him as one that was as Clay in the hands of the Potter; but, not to the extent of one tetchy word or froward movement, did he ever show that he thought his imprisonment unjust, or the bearing of those who were set over him cruel. And this was not an abject stupor or dull indifference, such as I have marked in rogues confined for life in the Bagnios of the Levant, who knew that they must needs pull so many strokes and get so many stripes every day, and so gave up battling with the World, and grinned contumely at their gaolers or the visitors who came sometimes to point at them and fling them copper money. In the King's Prisoner there was a philosophic reserve and quietness that almost approached content; and his resignation under suffering was of that kind that a Just Man may feel who

F

knows he is upon the ground, and that, howsoever his enemies push at him, he cannot fall far. He never sought to evade the conditions of his captivity or to plead for its being lightened. The courtesies that were offered to him, in so far as the Governor was warranted in offering such civilities, he took as his due; but he never craved a greater indulgence or went one step in word or in deed to obtain a surcease from his harsh and cruel lot.

He would rise at six of the clock both in winter and summer, and apply himself with great ardour to his private devotions and to good studies until eight, when his breakfast, a tankard of furmenty and a small measure of wine, was brought him. And from nine until noon he would again be at his studies, and then have dinner of such meats as were in season. From one to three he was privileged to walk either on the narrow strip of masonry that encompassed his prison-house, and with a soldier with his firelock on hip following his every step, or else to wander up and down in the various chambers of the Castle, still followed by a guard. Now he would tarry awhile in the guard-room, and stand over against the soldiers' table, his head resting very sadly against the chimney, and listen to their wild talk, which was, however, somewhat hushed and shaped to decency so long as he abided there. And anon he would come into the Governor's apartment, and hold Colonel Glover for some moments in grave discourse on matters of history, and the lives of Worthy Captains, and sometimes upon points and passages of Scripture, but never upon any thing that concerned the present day. For, beyond the bounds of the place in which he was immured, what should he know of things of instant moment, or of the way the world was wagging? By permission, the Colonel had told him that Oliver was no more, and that Richard, his son, was made Protector in his stead. Then, at the close of that weak and vain shadow of a Reign, and after the politic act of my Lord Duke of Albemarle (Gen. Monk), who made his own and the country's fortune, and Nan Clarges'* to boot, at one stroke, the Pri-

---

* A woman of very mean belongings, whose parents lived, I have heard, somewhere about the Maypole in the Strand, and who was promoted to high station, being Monk's Duchess, but to her death of a coarse and brutish carriage, and shamefully given to the drinking of strong waters.—J. D.

soner was given to know that schism was at an end, and that the King had come to his own again. Colonel Glover must needs tell him; for he was bidden to fire a salvo from the five pieces of artillery he had mounted, three on his outer wall, and two at the top of his donjon-keep, to say nothing of hoisting the Royal Standard, which now streamed from the pole where erst had floated the rag that bore the arms of the Commonwealth of England.*

"I am glad," the Prisoner said, when they told him. "I hope this young man will make England happier than did his father before him." But this was after he was in hopes of getting some company in his solitude, and when he was cheerfuller.

It was about midway in his imprisonment when another Captive was brought to the King's Castle; but it was not until close upon the Restoration of King Charles II. that the two Prisoners were permitted to come together. The second guest in this most dolorous place was a Woman, and that Woman was my Grandmother, Arabella Greenville.

There is no use in disguising the fact that, for many months after the failure of her attack on the Protector, the poor Lady had been as entirely distraught as was her fate after the death of the Lord Francis, and that to write her Life during this period would be merely penning the chronicle of a continued Frenzy. It were merciful to draw a veil over so sad and mortifying a scene—so well brought up as she had been, and respected by all the Quality,— but in pursuit of the determination with which I set out, to tell the Truth, and all the Truth, I am forced to confess that my Grandmother's Ravings were of the most violent, and that of her thoroughly demented state there could be no doubt. So far, indeed, did the unhappy creature's Abandonment extend, that those who were about her could with difficulty persuade her to keep any Garments upon her body, and were forced with Stripes and Revilings to force to a decorous carriage the gentle Lady who had once been the very soul and mirror of Modesty. But in process of time these dreadful furies and rages left her, and she became calm. She was still beautiful, albeit her comeliness was now of a chastened and saddened order, and, save her eye, there was no light or sparkle in her face.

* A very glorious rag, nevertheless.—ED.

When her health and mind were healed, so far as earthly
skill could heal them,—it being given out, I am told, to her
kindred that she had died mad in the Spinning House at
Cambridge : but she had never been further than the house
of one Dr. Empson at Colchester, who had tended her during
her distraction,—my Grandmother was brought to the King's
Castle in the East, and for a long time lay incarcerate in a
lower chamber of the keep, being not allowed even that
scant exercise which was permitted to the Prisoner above,
and being waited upon and watched night and day by the
Governor's Daughter, Mistress Ruth Glover, who at night
slept in a little closet adjoining my Grandmother's chamber.
The girl had a tongue, I suppose, like the rest of her sex,—
and of our sex too, brother,—and she would not have been
eighteen, of a lively Disposition, and continually in the society of a Lady of Birth and accomplishments, now more
than ten years her senior, without gossiping to her concerning all that she knew of the sorry little world round about
her.   It was not, however, much, or of any great moment,
that Ruth had to tell my Grandmother.   She could but
hold her in discourse of how the Invalid Matrosses had the
rheumatism and the ague ; how the Life-guard men in their
room diced and drank and quarrelled, both over their dice
and their drink ; how the rumour ran that the poverty-
stricken habitants of the adjoining village had, from long
dwelling among the fens, become as web-footed as the wild-
fowl they hunted ; and how her Father, who had been for
many years a widower, was harsh and stern with her, and
would not suffer her to read the romances and playbooks,
some half-dozen of which the Sergeant of the Guard had
with him.   She may have had a little also to say about the
Prisoner in the upper story of the Keep—how his chamber
was all filled with folios and papers ; how he studied and
wrote and prayed ; and during his two hours' daily liberty
wandered sadly and in a silent manner about the Castle.
For this was all Mistress Ruth had to tell, and of the Prisoner's name, or of his Crime, she was, perforce, mum.

These two Women nevertheless shaped all kinds of feverish Romances and wild conjectures respecting this unknown
man above stairs.   Arabella had told her own sad story to
the girl, whom—though little better than a waiting-woman—
she had made, for want of a better bower-maiden, her Con-

fidante. I need not say that oceans of Sympathy, or the accepted Tokens thereof, I mean Tears, ran out from the eyes of the Governor's Daughter when she heard the History of the Lord Francis, of the words he spoke just before the musketeers fired their pieces at him, and of another noble speech he made two hours before he suffered, when the Officer in command, compassionating his youth and parts, told him that if he had any suit, short of life, to prefer to the Lord General, he would take upon himself to say that it should be granted without question ; whereon quoth my Lord Francis, "I will not die with any suit in my mouth, save to the King of kings." On this, and on the story of the Locket, and of his first becoming acquainted with Arabella, of his sprightly disguise as a Teacher, with the young squire at Madam Desaguiliers' school at Hackney, of his Beauty and Virtues and fine manners and extraordinary proficiency in Arts and Letters and the Exercises of Chivalry, —of these and a thousand kindred things the two women were never tired of talking. And, indeed, if one calls to mind what vast Eloquence and wealth of words two loving hearts can distil from a Bit of Ribbon or a Torn Letter, it is not to be wondered at that Arabella and Ruth should find their Theme inexhaustible—so good and brave as had been its Object, now dead and cold in the bloody trench at Hampton yonder, and convert it into a perpetually welling spring of Mournful Remembrances.

Arabella had taken to her old trick of Painting again, and in the first and second year of her removal to the Castle executed some very creditable performances. But she never attempted either the effigies of her Lover or of the Protector, and confined herself to portraitures of the late martyred King, and of the Princes now unjustly kept from their inheritance.

It was during the Protectorate of Richard Cromwell (that mere puppet-play of Power) that the watch kept on the prisoners in the King's Castle grew for a time much less severe and even lax. Arabella was suffered to go out of her chamber, even at the very hours that the Prisoner above was wandering to and fro. The guards did not hinder their meeting ; and, says Colonel Ferdinando Glover, one day to his daughter, "I should not wonder if, some of these days, Orders were to come down for me to set both my birds free

from their cage. That which Mrs. Greenville has done, you
and I know full well, and I am almost sorry that she did
not succeed."

"Oh, father !" cries Mistress Ruth, who was of a very
soft and tender nature, and abhorred the very idea of bloodshed ; so that, loving Arabella as she did with all her heart,
she could not help regarding her with a kind of Terror when
she remembered the deed for which she was confined.

"Tush, girl," the Colonel makes answer, "'tis no Treason
now to name such a thing. Oliver's dead, and will eat no
more bread ; and I misliked him much at the end, for it is
certain that he betrayed the Good Old Cause, and hankered
after an earthly crown. As for this young Popinjay, he will
have more need to protect himself than these Kingdoms.
And I think that if your father is to live on the King's
wages, it had better be on the real King's than the false
one."

"And do you think, father, that King Charles will come
to his own again ?" asks Ruth, in a flutter of delight ; for Arabella had made her a very Royalist at heart.

"I think what I think," replies the Colonel, with his
stern look ; "but whatever happens, it is not likely, it seems
to me, that we shall have our prisoners here much longer.
That is to say :—Mrs. Greenville, for what she hath done,
can scarcely be distasteful to those who loved not Oliver.
But for my other bird,—who can tell ?—He may have raised
the very Devil for aught I know."

"Do you think that he also tried to kill the Protector?"
Ruth asks timidly, and just hazarding a Surmise that had
oft been mooted betwixt Arabella and herself.

"Get thee to thy chamber, and about thy business,
wench," the Colonel says, quite storming. "Away, or I will
lay my willow wand about thy shoulders. Is there nothing
but killing of Protectors, forsooth, for thy silly head to be
filled with?" And yet I incline to think that Mr. Governor
was not of a very different mind to his daughter ; for away
he hies to his chamber, and falls to reading Colonel Titus'
famous book, *Killing no Murder*, and, looking anon on his
Prisoner coming wandering down a winding staircase, says
softly to himself, "He looks like one, for all his studious
guise, who could do a Bold Deed at a pinch."

This Person, I should have said, wore, winter and sum-

mer, a plain black shag gown untrimmed, with camlet
netherstocks, and a smooth band. And his Right Hand
was always covered with a glove of Black Velvet.

By and by came, as I have related, the news of his Majesty's Restoration and fresh Strict Orders for the keeping of
the Prisoner. But though he was not to see a clergyman,—
and for all that prohibition he saw more than one before
he came out of Captivity,—a certain Indulgence was now
granted him. He was permitted to have free access to
Mrs. Arabella Greenville, and to converse freely with her
at all proper times and seasons.

But that I know the very noble nature of my Grandmother, and am prepared, old as I am, to defend her fame
even to taking the heart's blood of the villain that maligned
her, I might blush at having to record a fact which must
needs be set down here. Ere six months had passed, there
grew up between Mrs. Greenville and the Prisoner a very
warm and close friendship, which in time ripened into the
tenderest of attachments. That her love for her dead Frank
ever wavered, or that she ever swerved for one moment in
her reverence for his memory, I cannot and I will not believe ; but she nevertheless looked with an exceeding favour
upon the imprisoned man, and made no scruple of avowing
her Flame to Ruth. This young person did in time confide
the same to her father, who was much concerned thereat,
he not knowing how far the allowance of any love-passages
between two such strangely assorted suitors might tally with
his duty towards the King and Government. Nor could he
shut his eyes to the fact that the Prisoner regarded Mrs.
Greenville first with a tender compassion (such as a father
might have towards his child), next with an ardent sympathy, and finally—and that very speedily too—with a
Feeling that had all the Signs and the Portents of Love.
These two unfortunate People were so shut out from the
world, and so spiritually wedded by a common Misery and
discomfort, that their mere earthly coming together could
not be looked upon but as natural and reasonable ; for Mrs.
Greenville was the only woman upon whom the Prisoner
could be expected to look,—he being, beyond doubt, one of
Gentle Degree, if not of Great and Noble Station, and therefore beyond aught but the caresses of a Patron with such a
simple maid as Ruth Glover, whose father, although of some

military rank, was, like most of the Captains who had served under the Commonwealth (witness Ireton, Harrison, Hacker, and many more) of exceeding mean extraction.

That love-vows were interchanged between this Bride and Bridegroom of Sorrow and a Dark Dungeon almost, I know not; but their liking for each other's society—he imparting to her some of his studies, and she playing music, with implements of which she was well provided, to him of an afternoon —had become so apparent both to the soldiers on guard and servants, even to the poor Invalid Matrosses wheezing and shivering in their buff-coats, that Colonel Glover, in a very flurry of uncertainty, sent post haste to Whitehall to know what he was to do—whether to chamber up Mrs. Greenville in her chamber, as of aforetime, or confine the Prisoner in one of the lower vaults in the body of the rock, with so many pounds-weight of iron on his legs. For Colonel Glover was a man accustomed to use strong measures, whether with his family or with those he had custody over.

No answer came for many days; and the Governor had almost begun to think his message to be forgotten, when one summer evening (A.D. 1661) a troop of horse were seen galloping from the Village towards the Castle. The Drawbridge, which was on the ordinary kept slung, was now lowered; and the captain of the troop passing up to the barbican, gave Colonel Glover a sealed packet, and told him that he and his men would bivack at the bridge-foot (for the fens were passable at this season) until one who was expected at nightfall should come. Meat and drink were sent for, and the soldiers, dismounting, began to take tobacco and rail against the Castle in their brutal fashion—shame on them!—as an old mangy rat-trap.

Colonel Glover went up into his chamber in extreme disturbance. He had opened the packet and conned its contents; and having his daughter to him presently, and charging her, by her filial duty, to use discretion in all things that he should confide to her, tells her that his Majesty the King of England, France, and Ireland was coming to the Castle in a strictly Disguised habit that very evening.

There was barely time to make the slightest of preparations for this Glorious Guest; but what there was, and of the best of Meat, and Wine, and Plate, and hangings, and candles in sconces, was set out in the Governor's chamber, and ordered as handsomely as might be for his Majesty's coming. About eight o'clock—the villagers being given to understand that only some noble commander is coming to pass the soldiers in the Castle in review—arrived two lackeys, with panniers and saddle-bags, and a French varlet, who said he was, forsooth, a cook, and carried about with him a whole elaboratory of stove-furnaces, pots and pans, and jars of sauces and condiments. Monsieur was quickly at work in the kitchen, turning all things topsy-turvy, and nearly frightening Margery, the old cook, who had been a baggage-wagon sutler at Naseby in the Great Wars, into fits. About half-past ten a trumpet was heard to wind at the bridge-foot, and a couple of horses came tramping over the planks, making the chains rattle even to the barbican, where their riders dismounted.

The King, for it is useless to make any further disguise about him—although the Governor deferred falling on his knees and kissing his hand until he had conducted him to his own chamber—was habited in strict incognito, with an uncurled wig, a flap-hat, and a horseman's coat over all. He had not so much as a hanger by his side, carrying only a stout oak walking-staff. With him came a great lord, of an impudent countenance, and with a rich dress beneath his cloak, who, when his Master was out of the room, sometimes joked with, and sometimes swore at, poor little Ruth, as, I grieve to say, was the uncivil custom among the Quality in those wild days. The King supped very copiously, drinking many beakers of wine, and singing French songs, to which the impudent Lord beat time, and sometimes presumed to join in chorus. But this Prince was ever of an easy manner and affable complexion, which so well explains the Love his people bore him. All this while the Governor and Ruth waited at table, serving the dishes and wine on their knees; for they would suffer no mean hirelings to wait upon their guests.

As the King drank—and he was a great taker of wine— he asked a multitude of questions concerning the Prisoner and Mrs. Greenville, to all of which Colonel Glover made answer in as plain a manner as was consistent with his deep loyalty and reverence. Soon, however, Colonel Glover found that his Majesty was paying far more attention to the bottle than to his conversation, and, about one in the morning, was conducted, with much reverence, to the Governor's own sleeping-chamber, which had been hastily prepared. His

Majesty was quite Affable, but Haggard visibly. The impudent Lord was bestowed in the chamber which had been Ruth's, before she came to sleep so near Mrs. Greenville; and it is well he knew not what a pretty tenant the room had had, else would he have doubtless passed some villanous pleasantries thereupon.

The King, who was always an early riser, was up betimes in the morning ; and on Colonel Glover representing to him his sorrow for the mean manner in which he had of necessity been lodged, answered airily that he was better off there than in the Oak, or in Holland, without a styver in his pocket; "Although, oddsfish !" quoth his Majesty, "this Castle of mine seems fitter to harbour wild-ducks than Christians." And then nothing would suit his Majesty but to be introduced to Mrs. Greenville, with whom he was closeted two whole hours.

He came forth from her chamber with his dark, saturnine face all flushed. "A brave woman !—a bold woman !" he kept saying. "An awful service she was like to have done me ; and all to think that it was for love of poor Frank." For this Prince had known the Lord Francis well, and had shown him many favours.

"And now, good Master Governor," the King continued, but with quite another expression on his countenance, "we will see your Man Captive, if it shall so please you." And the two went up-stairs.

This is all I am permitted to tell in this place of what passed between King Charles the Second and the Prisoner in the upper chamber :—

"You know me !" the King said, sitting over against him at the table, and scanning his face with dark earnestness.

"You are Charles Stuart, second of the name on the throne of England."

"You know I am in the possession of your secret—of the King's Secret ; for of those dead it was known but to Oliver, as of those living it is now only known to yourself and to me."

"And the young Man, Richard ?"

"He never knew it. His father never trusted him so far. He had doubts and suspicions, that was all."

"Thank God !" said the prisoner.

"What was Oliver's enmity towards you, that he should immure you here all these years ?"

"I had served him too well. He feared lest the Shedder of Blood should become the Avenger of Blood."

"Are you sorry?"

"Sorry!" cried the Prisoner, with a kind of scream. "Had he a thousand lives, had I a thousand hands, I would do the same deed to-morrow." And he struck the right hand that was covered with the velvet glove with cruel violence on to the oaken table.

CHAPTER THE SEVENTH.

I AM BRED UP IN VERY BAD COMPANY, AND (TO MY SHAME) HELP TO KILL
THE KING'S DEER.

I LAY all that night in a little Hole by the side of a Bank,
just as though I had been a Fox-cub. I was not in much
better case than that Vermin, and I only marvel that my
Schoolmaster did not come out next day to Hunt me with
horses and hounds. Hounds!—The Black Fever to him!—
he had used me like a Hound any time for Six Months past;
and often had I given tongue under his Double Thonging.
Happily the weather was warm, and I got no hurt by sleeping
in the Hole. 'Tis strange, too, what Hardships and Hazards
of Climate and Excess we can bear in our Youth, whereas in
middle life an extra Slice gives us a Surfeit, and another cup
turns our Liver to Touchwood; whilst in age (as I know to
my sorrow) we dare scarcely venture our shoe in a Puddle for
fear of the Chills and Sciatica. In the morning I laved my
face in a Brook that hurtled hard by; but waited very fear-
fully until Noon ere I dared venture forth from my covert. I
had filled my pockets with Fruit and Bread (which I am
afraid I did not come very honestly by, and indeed admit that
Gnawbit's Larder and Orchard found me in Provender), and
was so able to break my fast. And my Guinea, I remembered,
was still unchanged. I had a dim kind of impression that I
was bound to Charlwood Chase, to join the Blacks, of whom
the Old Gentleman had spoken; but I was not in any Hurry
to get to my Goal. I was Free, albeit a Runaway, and felt all
the delights of Independence. You whose pleasures lie in
Bowers, and Beds, and Cards, and Wine, can little judge of
the Ease felt by him who is indeed a Beggar and pursued,
but is at Liberty. I remember being in hiding once with a
Gentleman Robber, who had, by the aid of a File and a
Friend, contrived to give the Galleys leg-bail, and who for
days afterwards was never tired of patting and smoothing
his ancles, and saying, "'Twas there the shackles galled me
so." Poor rogue! he was soon afterwards laid by the heels
and swung; for there is no Neck Verse in France to save a
Gentleman from the Gallows.

Towards evening my gall began to grate somewhat with the sense of mine own utter loneliness ; and for a moment I Wavered between the resolve to go Forward, and a slavish prompting to return to my Tyrant, and suffer all the torments his cruelty could visit me with. Then, as a middle course, I thought I would creep back to my kennel and die there ; but I was happily dissuaded from such a mean surrender to Fortune's Spites through the all-unknowing agency of a Bull, that, spying me from afar off where he was feeding, came thundering across two fields and through a shallow stream, routed me up from my refuge, and chased me into the open. I have often since been thankful to this ungovernable Beast (that would have Tossed, and perchance Gored me sorely, had he got at me), and seldom, in later life, when I have felt weak and wavering in the pursuit of a profitable purpose, have I failed to remember the Bull, and how he chased me out of Distempered Idleness into Activity.

The Sun had begun to welk in the west by the time I had mustered up enough courage to come into the High Road, which I had an uncertain idea stretched away from Gnawbit's house, and towards Reading. But suddenly recalling the Danger of travelling by the Highway, where I might be met by Horsemen or Labouring persons sent in quest of me,—for it did not enter my mind that I was too worthless a scholar to be Pursued, and that Gnawbit was, 'tis likely enough, more Pleased than sorry to be Rid of me,—I branched off from the main to the left; so walking, as it seemed to me, many miles. I grew grievously hungry. No more Bread or Apples remained in my pouch ; but I still had my Guinea, so I deemed, and resolved that if I came upon any House of Entertainment, I would sup. For indeed, while all Nature round me seemed to be taking some kind of Sustenance, it was hard that I, a Christian, should go to bed (or into another Fox-hole, for bed I had none, and yet had slept in my time in a grand chamber in Hanover Square) with an empty belly. The Earth was beginning to drink up the dews, like an insatiate toper as she is. I passed a flock of sheep biting their hasty supper from the grass ; and each one with a little cloud of gnats buzzing around it, that with feeble stings, poor insects, were trying for their supper too. And 'tis effect we have upon one another. The birds had taken home their worm-cheer to the little ones in the nests,

and were singing their after-supper songs, very sweetly but
drowsily. 'Twas too late in the year for the Nightingale,—
that I knew,—but the jolly Blackbird was in full feather and
voice ; and presently there swept by me a great Owl, going
home to feast, I will be bound, in his hollow tree, and with
nothing less than a Field Mouse for his supper, the rascal.
'Twas a wicked imagining, but I could not help thinking, as
I heard the birds carolling so merrily,—and how they keep
so plump upon so little to eat is always to me a marvel, until
I remember with what loving care Heaven daily spreads their
table from Nature's infinite ordinary,—how choice a Refection
a dish of birds' eggs, so often idly stolen and blown hollow
by us boys, would make.   The feathered creatures are a forgiving folk ; and 'tis not unlikely that the Children in the
Wood had often gone birds'-nesting : but when they were
dead, the kindly Red Jerkins forgave all their little maraud-
ings, and covered them with leaves, as though the children
had strewn them crumbs or brought them worms from
January to December.   Gnawbit was a wretch who used to
kill the Robins, and for that, if for naught else, he will
surely howl.
      By and by, when darkness was coming down like a play-
house curtain, and the Northern wagoner up yonder—how
often have I watched him at sea !—was yoking his seven
cart-mares to the steadfast star, I came upon a Man—the first
I had seen since the Old Gentleman bade me begone with
my Guinea, and join the Blacks.   This Man was not walking
or running, nay nor sitting nor lying as Lazars do in hedges.
But he tumbled out of the quicket as it were, and came to
me with short leaps, making as though he would Devour me.
We schoolboys had talked often enough about Claude Duval
and the Golden Farmer, and I set this Dreadful Being down
at once as a Highwayman ; so down I went Plump on my
knees and Roared for mercy, as I was wont to do to Gnawbit,
till I learnt that no Roaring would make him desist from his
brutish purpose.   It was darkish now, and I well-nigh fancied
the Man was indeed my wicked Master, for he had an up-
lifted weapon in his hand ; but when he came nearer to me,
I found that it was not a cane nor a thong, but a Great Flail,
which he whirled over his head, and then brought down on
the ground with a Thwack, making the Night Flies dance.
      " You Imp of mischief," said the man, as he seized me by

the collar and shook me roughly, "what are you doing here, spying on honest folks? Speak, or I'll brain you with this Flail."

I thought it best to tell this terrible man the Truth.

"If you please, sir," I answered, trembling, "I've run away."

"Run away from where, you egg?"

"From Gnawbit's, sir."

"And who the pest is Gnawbit, you hempen babe?"

"My schoolmaster, sir."

"Ha! that's good," the Man replied, loosening his hold somewhat on my collar. "And what did you run away for?"

I told him in broken sentences my short Story—of my Sufferings at School, at least, but never saying a word about my being a little Gentleman, and the son of a Lady of Quality in Hanover Square.

"And where are you going?" the Man asked, when I had finished.

I told him that I was on my way to Charlwood Chase to join the Blacks. And then he asked me whether I had any Money, whereto I answered that I had a Guinea; and little doubting in my Quaking Heart but that he would presently Wrench it from me, if haply he were not minded to have Meal as well as Malt, and brain me as he had threatened. But he forbore to offer me violence, and, quite releasing his hold, said,

"I suppose you'd like some supper."

I said that I had not broken my fast for many hours, and was dead a-hungered.

"And wouldn't mind supping with the Blacks in Charlwood Chase, eh?" he continued.

I rather gave him to understand that such was not only my Wish but my Ambition.

"Come along to the Blacks, then," said the Man. "*I'm one of 'em.*"

He drew a Lantern from under his garments as he spoke, and letting out the Light from the slide, passed it over, and up and down, his Face and Figure. Then did I see with Horror and Amazement that both his Countenance and his Raiment were all smirched and bewrayed with dabs and patches of what seemed soot or blackened grease. It was a once white Smock or Gaberdine that made the chief part of his apparel; and this, with the black patches on it, gave him a Pied appearance fearful to behold. There was on his head what looked like a great bundle of black rags; and tufts of hair that might have been pulled out of the mane of a wild horse grew out from either side of his face, and wreathed its lower half.

"Come along," repeated the Man; "we'll blacken you bravely in time, my Chicken-skin."

And so he grasped my hand in his,—and when I came to look at it afterwards, I found it smeared with sable, and with great black finger-marks upon it,—and led me away. We journeyed on in the Dark—for he had put up his Lantern—for another good half hour, he singing to himself from time to time some hoarse catches of song having reference to some "Billy Boys," that I conjectured were his companions. And so we struck from by-lane into by-lane, and presently into a Plantation, and then through a gap in a Hedge, and through a Ditch full of Brambles, which galled my legs sorely. I was half asleep by this time, and was only brought to full wakefulness by the deep baying as of a Dog some few yards, as it seemed, from us.

The Lantern's light gleamed forth again; and in the circle of Clear it made I could see we were surrounded by tall Trees that with their long crooked Arms looked as though they would entwine me in deadly embraces.

"Hist!" the man said very low. "That's surely Black Towzer's tongue." And to my huge dismay he set up a sad responsive Howl, very like unto that of a Dog, but not at all akin to the voice of a Man.

The answer to this was a whistle, and human speech, saying,

"Black Jowler!"

"Black Towzer, for a spade Guinea!" my companion made answer; and in another moment there came bounding towards us another fellow in the same blackened masquerade as he, and with another Lantern. He had with him, besides, a shaggy hound that smelt me suspiciously and prowled round me, growling low, I shivering the whiles.

"What have we here?" asked the Second Black; for I made no doubt now but that my Company were of that Confederacy.

"Kid loose," replied he who was to take me to supper.

"Given the keepers the slip, and run down by Billy Boys' park. Aha!" and he whispered his comrade ruffian.

Out went the Lanterns again, and he who answered to the name of Jowler tightened his grasp, and bade me for a young Tyburn Token quicken my pace. So we walked and walked again, poor I as sore as a pilgrim tramping up the Hill to Louth—which I have many times seen in those parts —with shards in his shoes. Then it must come, forsooth, to more whistling; and the same Play being over, we had one more Lantern to our Band, and one more Scurvy Companion as Black as a Flag,* who in their kennel Tongue was Mungo. And by and by we were joined by Surly, and Black Tom, and Grumps; and so with these five Men, who were pleased to be called as the Beasts are, I stumbled along, tired, and drowsy, and famishing, and thinking my journey would never come to an end.

Surely it must have been long past midnight when we made a halt; and all the five lanterns being lit, and making so many dancing wheels of yellow, I found that we were still encircled by those tall trees with the twining arms. And Jowler—for it is useless to speak of my conductor according to Human Rule—gave me a rough pat on the shoulder, and bade me cheer up, for that I should have my supper very soon now. All five then joined in a whistle so sharp, so clear, and so well sustained, that it sounded well-nigh melodious; and to this there came, after the lapse of a few seconds, the noise as of a little peevish Terrier barking.

"True as Touchwood," cried Black Jowler. "In, Billy Boys, and hey for fat and flagons."

With this he takes me by the shoulders, telling me to fear naught, and spend my money like a gentleman, and bundles me before him till we came to something hard, as board. This I presently found was a door; and in an instant I was in the midst of a kind of Tavern parlour, all lighted up with great candles stuck into lumps of clay, and face to face with the Fattest Woman I ever saw in my life.

"Mother Moll Drum," quoth my conductor, "save you, and give me a quart of three threads, or I faint. Body o' me, was ever green plover so pulled as I was."

The Fat Woman he called Mother Moll Drum was to all

---

* "*My* Flag" in the original Ms.; but I put it down as a slip of the pen, and altered it.—G. A. S.

seeming in no very blessed temper; for she bade Jowler go hang for a lean polecat, and be cursed meanwhile, and that she would draw him naught.

"Come, come, Mother," Jowler said, making as though to appease her, "what be these tantrums? Come, draw; for I am as thirsty as an hour-glass, poor wretch, that has felt sand run through his gullet any time these twenty years."

"Draw for yourself, rogue," says Mother Drum; "there's naught I'll serve you with, unless, indeed, I were bar-woman at St. Giles's Pound, and had to froth you your last quart, as you went up the Heavy Hill to Tyburn."

"We shall all go there in time—good time," breaks in a deep solemn voice, drawn somehow through the nose, and coming from the Man-Dog they called Grumps; "meanwhile, O greasy woman, let the beverage our brother asked for be drawn, and I, even Grumps, will partake thereof, and ask a blessing."

"Woman yourself!" cries Moll Drum, in a rage. "Woman yourself, and T— in your teeth, and woman to the mother that bore you, and sat in the stocks for Lightness! Who are you, quotha, old reverend smock with the splay foot? Come up, now, prithee, Bridewell Bird! You will drink, will you? I saw no dust or cobwebs come out of your mouth. Go hang, you moon-calf, false faucet, you roaring horse-courser, you ranger of Turnbull, you dull malt-house with a mouth of a peck and the sign of the swallow above."

By this time Mother Drum was well-nigh out of breath, and panted, and looked so hot, that they might have put her up by Temple Bar on Queen Bess's birthnight for a Bonfire, and so saved Tar Barrels. And as she spoke she brandished a large Frying Pan, from which great drops of hot grease—smelling very savoury by the way—dropped on to the sanded floor. The other Blacks seemed in nowise disturbed by this Dispute, but were rather amused thereby, and gathered in a ring round Jowler and Grumps and the Fat Woman laughing.

"Never mind, Mother Drum," quoth one; "she was a pig-woman once in Bartlemy Fair, and lost her temper through the heat of a coal-fire roasting porkers. Was't not hot, Mother Drum? was not Tophet a kind of cool cellar to it?"

It was Surly who spoke, and Mother Drum turns on him in a rage.

"You lie, you pannierman's by-blow!" she cried; "you bony muck-fowl, with the bony back sticking out like the acc of spades on the point of a small sword! you lie, Bobchin, Changeling, Horseleech! 'Slid, you Shrovetide Cutpurse, I'll scald your hide with gravy, I will!"

"Ware the pan, ware the pan!" all the Blacks cried out; for the Good Woman made a flourish as though she would have carried out her threat; whereupon my Man-Dog, Jowler, thought it was time to interpose, and spoke.

"There's no harm in Mother Drum, but that her temper's as hot as her pan, and we are late to supper. Come, Mother, Draw for us, and save you still. I'll treat you to burnt brandy afterwards."

"What did he call me Pig-Woman for?" she grumbled, but still half mollified. "What if I did waste my youth and prime in cooking of porkers in a booth; I am no cutpurse. I, I never shoved the tumbler for tail-drawing or poll-snatching on a levee-day.* But I will draw for you, and welcome my guests of the game."

"And Supper, good Moll, Supper," added Jowler.

"An you had not hindered me, it would have been ready upstairs. There are more upstairs besides you that hunger after the fat and the lean. But can you sup without a cook? Will vension run off the spit ready roasted, think you, like the pigs in Lubberland, that jump down your throat, and cry *wee wee?*"

She began to bustle about, and summoned, by the name of Cicely Grip—adding thereto the epithet of "faggot"—a stout serving-lass, who might have been comely enough, but whose face and hands were very nearly as black as those of the Man-Dog's. This wench brought a number of brown jugs full of beer, and the Blacks took to drinking with much zest. Then Jowler, who seemed a kind of lieutenant, in some authority over them, gave the word of command to "Peel;" and they hastened to leave the room, which was but a mean sort of barn-like chamber, with bare walls, a wattled roof, and a number of rough wooden tables and settles, all littered with

* Madam Drum, so far as I can make out the *argot* of the day, here insinuated that her opponent had been corrected at the cart's tail for stealing swords out of the scabbards, and conveying wigs from the heads of their owners; two crimes which have become obsolete since the Quality have ceased to wear swords and periwigs.—G. A. S.

jugs and Tobacco-pipes. So I and the Fat Woman and Jowler, Cicely Grip having betaken herself to the kitchen, were
left together.

" Cicely will dish up, Mother Drum," he says ; " you have
fried collops enow for us, I trow ; and if more are wanted for
the Billy Boys, you can to your pan again. You began your
brandy pottage too early to-night, Mother. Let us have no
more of your vapours twixt this and day-break, prithee. What
would Captain Night say ?"

" Captain Night be hanged !"

" He will be hanged, as our brother Surly has it. in good
time. I doubt it not. Meanwhile, order must be kept at
the Stag o' Tyne. Get you and draw the dram I promised
you : and, Mother, wash for me this little lad's face and
hands, that he may sit down to meat with us in a seemly
manner."

" Who the Clink is he ?" asked Mother Drum, eyeing me
with no very Great Favour.

" He says he is little Boy Jack;" answered Mr. Jowler
gravely. " We will give him another name before we have
done with him. Meantime he has a guinea in his pocket to
pay his shot. and that's enough for the fat old Alewife of the
Stag o' Tyne."

" Fat again !" muttered Mother Drum. " Is it a 'Sizes
matter to be full of flesh ? I be fat indeed," she answered
with a sigh. "and must have a chair let out o' the sides for
me, that these poor old hips may have play And I, that
was of so buxom a figure."

" Never mind your Figure, Mother," remarked my Conductor. "but do my bidding. I'll e'en go and peel too ;" and
without more ado he leaves us.

Mother Drum went into her kitchen and fetched forth a
Tin Bowl full of hot suds, and with these she washed me as
she had been directed.   I bore it all unresistingly—likewise
a scrubbing with a rough towel. Then, when my hair was
kempt with an old Felting comb, almost toothless, I felt refreshed and hungrier than ever. But Mother Drum never
ceased to complain of having been called fat.

" Time was, my smooth-faced Coney," she said, " that I
was as lithe and limber as you are, and was called Jaunty
Peg. And now poor old Moll cooks collops for those that
are born to dance jigs in chains for the north-east wind to

play the fiddle to. Time was when a whole army followed me, when I beat the drum before the great Duke."

" What Duke ?" I asked, looking up at her great red face.

" What Duke, milksop ! Why, who should I mean but the Duke that won Hochstedt and Ramilies :—the Ace of Trumps, my dear, that saved the Queen of Hearts, the good Queen Anne, so bravely. What Duke should I mean but John o' Marlborough ?"

" I have seen *him*," I said, with childish gravity.

" Seen him ! when and where, loblolly boy ? You're too young to have been a drummer."

" I saw him," I answered, blushing and stammering ; " I saw him when—when I was a little Gentleman."

" Lord save us !" cries Mother Drum, bursting into a jolly laugh. " A Gentleman ! since when, your Lordship, I pray ? But we're all Gentlefolks here, I trow ; and Captain Night's the Marquis of Aylesbury Jail. A Gentleman ! oho !"

Hereupon, and which, to my great relief, quitted me of the perturbation brought on by a Rash Admission, there came three knocks from above, and Mother Drum said hurriedly, "Supper, supper ;" and opening a side-door, pushes me on to a staircase, and tells me to mount, and pull a reverence to the company I found at table.

Twenty steps brought me to another door I found on the jar, and I passed into a great room with a roof of wooden joists, and a vast table in the middle set out with supper. There was no table-cloth ; but there were plenty of meats smoking hot in great pewter dishes. I never saw, either, so many bottles and glasses on one board in my life ; and besides these, there was good store of great shining Flagons, carved and chased, which I afterwards knew to be of Solid Silver.

Round this table were gathered at least Twenty Men ; and but for their voices I should never have known that five among them were my companions of just now. For all were attired in a very brave Manner, wore wigs and powder and embroidered waistcoats ; although, what I thought strange, each man dined in boots, with a gold-laced hat on his head, and his Hanger by his side, and a brace of Pistols on the table beside him. Yet I must make two exceptions to this rule. He whom they called Surly had on a full frizzed wig and a cassock and bands, that, but for his rascal face, would

have put me in mind of the Parson at St. George's Hanover
Square, who always seemed to be so angry with me. Surly
was Chaplain, and said Grace, and ate and drank more than
any one there. Lastly, at the table's head sat a thin, pale,
proper kind of a man, wearing his own hair long in a silken
club, dressed in the pink of Fashion, as though he were bidden
to a birthday, with a dandy rapier at his side, and instead of
Pistols, a Black Velvet Visor laid by the side of his plate.
He had very large blue eyes and very fair hair. He might
have been some thirty-five years old, and the guests, who
treated him with much deference, addressed him as Captain
Night.

Mr. Jowler, whose hat had as brave a cock as any there,
made me sit by him ; and, with three more knocks and the
Parson's Grace, we all fell to supper. They helped me plentifully, and I ate my fill. Then my friend gave me a silver
porringer full of wine-and-water. It was all very good ; but
I knew not what viands I was eating, and made bold to ask
Jowler.

" 'Tis venison, boy, that was never shot by the King's
keeper," he answered. "But, if you would be free of Charlwood Chase, and wish to get out yet with a whole skin, I
should advise you to eat your meat and ask no questions."

I was very much frightened at this, and said no more
until the end of Supper. When they had finished, they fell
to drinking of Healths, great bowls of Punch being brought
to them for that purpose. The first toast was the King, and
that fell to Jowler.

" The King !" says he, rising.

" Over the water ?" they ask.

" No," answers Jowler. " The King every where. King
James, and God bless him."

" I wont drink *that*," objects the Chaplain. " You know
I am a King George man."

" Drink the Foul Fiend, an' you will," retorts the Pro-
poser. " You'd be staunch and true either way. Now, Billy
Boys, the King."

And they fell to tumbling down on their knees, and drinking His Majesty in brimming bumpers. I joined in the ceremony perforce, although I knew nothing about King James,
save that Monarch my Grandmother used to speak about,
who Withdrew himself from these kingdoms in the year 1688;

and at Church 'twas King George they were wont to pray for, and not King James. And little did I ween that, in drinking this Great Person on my knees, I was disobeying the Precept of my dear dead Kinswoman.

"I have a bad foot," quoth Captain Night, "and cannot stir from my chair; but I drink all healths that come from loyal hearts."

Many more Healths followed. The Chaplain gave the Church, "and confusion to Old Rapine, that goes about robbing chancels of their chalices, and parsons of their dues, and the very poor-box of alms." And then they drank "Vert and Venison," and then, "A black face, a white smock, and a red hand." And then they betook themselves to Roaring choruses, and Smoking and Drinking galore, until I fell fast asleep in my chair.

I woke up not much before Noon the next day, in a neat little chamber very cleanly appointed; but found to my surprise that, in addition to my own clothes, there was laid by my bedside a little Smock or Gaberdine of coarse linen, and a bowl full of some sooty stuff that made me shudder to look at. And my Surprise was heightened into amazed astonishment when, having donned my own garments, and while curiously turning over the Gaberdine, there came a knock, and anon stepped into the room that same comely Servant-maid that had ridden with us in the Wagon six months since, on that sad journey to school, and that had been so kind to me in the way of new milk and cheesecakes.

She was very smartly dressed, with a gay flowered apron, and a fly-cap all over glass-beads, like so many Blue-bottles. And she had a gold brooch in her stomacher, and fine thread hose, and red Heels to her shoes.

She was as kind to me as ever, and told me that I was among those who would treat me well, and stand my friends, if I obeyed their commands. And I, who, I confess, had by this time begun to look on the Blacks and their Ways with a kind of Schoolboy glee, rose, nothing loth, and donned the Strange Accoutrements my entertainers provided for me. The girl helped me to dress, smiling and giggling mightily the while; but, as I dressed, I could not help calling her by the name she had given me in the Wagon, and asking how she had come into that strange Place.

"Hush, hush!" says she. "I'm Marian now, Maid Ma-

rian, that lives with Mother Drum, and serves the Gentlemen Blacks, and brings Captain Night his morning Draught.
None of us are called by our real names at the Stag o' Tyne,
my dear. We all are in No-man's-land."

"But where is No-man's-land, and what is the Stag o'
Tyne?" I asked, as she slipped the Gaberdine over my
head.

"No-man's-land is just in the left-hand top Corner of
Charlwood Chase, after you have turned to the left, and gone
as far forward as you can by taking two steps backwards for
every one straight on," answers the saucy hussy. "And the
Stag o' Tyne's even a Christian House of Entertainment that
Mother Drum keeps."

"And who is Mother Drum?" I resumed, my eyes opening wider than ever.

"A decent Alewife, much given to grease, and that cooks
the King's Venison for Captain Night and his Gentlemen
Blacks."

"And Captain Night,—who is he?"

"Ask me no questions, and I'll tell you no lies," she
makes reply. "Captain Night is a Gentleman every inch of
him, and as sure as Tom o' Ten Thousand."

"And the Gentlemen Blacks?"

"You're mighty particular," quoth she, regarding me with
a comical look. "Well, my dear, since you are to be a Black
yourself, and a Gentleman to boot, I don't mind telling you.
The Gentlemen Blacks are all Bold Hearts, that like to kill
the King's Venison without a Ranger's Warrant, and to eat
of it without paying Fee nor Royalty, and that drink of the
very best—"

"And that have Dog-whips to lay about the shoulders of
tattling minxes and curious urchins," cries, to my dismay, a
voice behind us, and so to us—by his voice at least—Captain
Night, but in his body no longer the same gay spark that I
had seen the night before, or rather that morning early. He
was as Black, and Hairy, and Savage-looking as any—as
Jowler, or any one of that Dark Gang; and in no way
differed from them, save that on the middle finger of his
Right Hand there glittered, from out all his Grease and Soot,
a Great Diamond Ring.

"Come," he cries, "Mistress Nimble Tongue, will you be
giving your Red Rag a gallop yet, and Billy Boys waiting to

break their Fast? Despatch, and set out the boy, as I bade you."

"I am no kitchen-wench, I," answers the Maid of the Wagon, tossing her head. "Cicely o' the Cinders yonder will bring you to your umble-pie, and a Jack of small-beer to cool you, I trow. Was it live Charcoal or Seacoal embers that you swallowed last night, Captain, makes you so dry this morning?"

"Never mind, Goody Slack Jaw," says Captain Night. "I shall be thirstier anon from listening to your prate. Will you hurry now, Gadfly, or is the sun to sink before we get hounds in leash?"

Thus admonished, the girl takes me by the arm, and, without more ado, dips a rag in the pot of black pigment, and begins to smear all my hands, and face, and throat, with dabs of disguising shade. And, as she bade me do the same to my Garment, and never spare Soot, I fell to work too, making myself into the likeness of a Chimney-boy, till they might have taken me into a nursery to Frighten naughty children.

Captain Night sat by himself on the side of the bed, idly clicking a pistol-lock till such time as he proceeded to load it, the which threw me into a cold tremor, not knowing but that it might be the Custom among the Gentlemen Blacks to blow out the brains in the morning of those they had feasted over-night. Yet, as there never was Schoolboy, I suppose, but delighted in Soiling of his raiment, and making himself as Black as any Sweep in Whetstone Park, so did I begin to feel something like a Pleasure in being masqueraded up to this Disguise, and began to wish for a Pistol such as Captain Night had in his Hand, and such a Diamond Ring as he wore on his finger.

"There!" cries the Maid of the Wagon, when I was well Blacked, surveying me approvingly. "You're a real imp of Charlwood Chase now. Ugh! thou young Rig! I'll kiss you when the Captain brings you home, and good soap and water takes off those mourning weeds before supper-time."

She had clapped a great Deerskin cap on my head, and giving me a friendly pat, was going off, when I could not help asking her in a sly whisper what had become of the Pewterer of Panyer Alley.

"What! you remember him, do you?" she returned, with

a half-smile and a half-sigh. " Well, the Pewterer's here, and as black as you are."

" But I thought you were to wed," I remarked.

" Well!" she went on, almost fiercely, " cannot one wed at the Stag o' Tyne? We have a brave Chaplain down-stairs, —as good as a Fleet Parson any day, I wuss."

" But the Pewterer?" I persisted.

" I'll hang the Pewterer round thy neck!" she exclaimed, in a pet. " The Pewterer was unfortunate in his business, and so took to the Road; and thus we have all come together in Charlwood Chase. But ask me no more questions, or Captain Night will be deadly angry. Look, he fumes already."

She tripped away saying this, and in Time, I think; for indeed the Captain was beginning to show signs of impatience. She being gone, he took me on his knee, all Black as I was, and in a voice kind enough, but full of authority, bade me tell him all my History and the bare truth, else would he have me tied neck and heels and thrown to the fishes.

So I told this strange Man all :—of Hanover Square, and my earliest childhood. Of the Unknown Lady, and her Behaviour and conversation, even to her Death. Of her Funeral, and the harsh bearing of Mistress Talmash and the Steward Cadwallader unto me in my Helplessness and Loneliness. Of my being smuggled away in a Wagon and sent to school to Gnawbit, and of the barbarous cruelty with which I had been treated by that Monster. And finally, of the old Gentleman that used to cry, " Bear it! bear it!" and of his giving me a Guinea, and bidding me run away.

He listened to all I had to say, and then putting me down,

" A strange story," he thoughtfully remarks, " and not learnt out of the story-books either, or I sorely err. You have not a Lying Face, my man. Wait a while and you'll wear a Mask thicker than all that screen of soot you have upon you now." But in this he was mistaken; for John Dangerous ever scorned deception, and through life has always acted fair and above-board.

" And that Guinea," he continued. " Hast it still?"

I answered that I had, producing it as I spoke, and that I was ready to pay my Reckoning, and to treat him and the others, in which, meseems, there spoke less of the little Run-

away Schoolboy that had turned Sweep, than of the Little
Gentleman that was wont to be a Patron to his Grandmother's lacqueys in Hanover Square.

"Keep thy piece of Gold," he answers, with a smile.
"Thou shalt pay thy footing soon enough. Or wilt thou
go forth with thy Guinea and spend it, and be taken by
thy Schoolmaster to be whipped, perchance to death!"

I replied that I had the much rather stay with him and
the Gentlemen.

"The less said of the 'Gentlemen' the better. However,
'tis all one : we are all Gentlemen at the Stag o' Tyne. Even
thou art a Gentleman, little Ragamuff."

"I am a Gentleman of long descent ; and my fathers have
fought and bled for the True King; and Norman blood's
better than German puddle-mud," I replied, repeating well-
nigh Mechanically that which my dear Kinswoman had said
to me and Instilled into me many and many a time. In my
degraded Slavery, I had *well*-nigh forgotten the proud old
words ; but only once it chanced that they had risen up un-
bidden, when I was flouted and jeered at as Little Boy Jack
by my schoolmates. Heaven help us, how villanously cruel
are children to those who are of their own age and Poor and
Friendless ! What is it that makes young hearts so Hard ?
The boys Derided and mocked me more than ever for that
I said I was a Gentleman ; and by and by comes Gnawbit,
and beats me black and blue—ay and gory too—with a furze-
tub, for telling of Lies, as he falsely said, the Ruffian.

"Well," resumed Captain Night, "thou shalt stay with
us, young Gentleman. But weigh it soberly, boy," he continued. "Thou art old enough to know black from white,
and brass from gold. Be advised ; know what we Blacks are.
We are only Thieves that go about stealing the King's Deer
in Charlwood Chase."

I told him that I would abide by him and his Company ;
and with a grim smile he clapped me on the shoulder, and
told me that now indeed I was a Gentleman Black, and
Forest Free.

CHAPTER THE EIGHTH

THE END OF MY ADVENTURES AMONG THE BLACKS.

WERE I to give vent to that Garrulity which grows upon us Veterans with Gout and the Gravel, and the kindred Ailments of Age, this Account of my Life would never reach beyond the record of Boyhood. For from the first Flower of my freshest childhood to the time that I became toward to the more serious Business of this World, I think I could set down Day by Day, and well-nigh Hour by Hour, all the things that have occurred to me. How is it that I preserve so keen a Remembrance of a little lad's joys and sorrows, when I can scarcely recall how many times I have suffered Shipwreck in later age, or tell how many Sansfoy Miscreants, caring neither for Heaven or man a Point, I have slain? Nay, from what cause does it proceed that I, upon whom the broken reliques of my Schoolmaster's former Cruelty are yet Green, and who can conjure up all the events that bore upon Running away into Charlwood Chase, even to the doggish names of the Blacks, their ribald talk, and the fleering of the Women they had about them, find it sore travail to remember what I had for dinner yesterday, what friends I conversed with, what Tavern I supped at, what news I read in the Gazette? But 'tis the knowledge of that overweening Craving to count up the trivial Things of my Youth that warns me to use despatch, even if the chronicle of my after-doings be but a short summary or sketch of so many Perils by Land and Sea. And for this manner of the remotest things being the more distinct and dilated upon, let me put it to a Man of keen vision, if whirling along a High Road in a rapid carriage, he has not marked, first, that the Palings and Milestones close by have passed beneath him in a confused and jarring swiftness; next, that the Trees, Hedges, &c. of the middleplan (as the limners call it) have moved slower and with more Deliberation, yet somewhat Fitfully, and encroaching on each other's outlines; whereas the extreme distance in Clouds, Mountains, far-off Hill-sides, and the like, have seemed remote, indeed, but stationary, clear, and unchangeable; so that you could count the fissures in the

hoar rocks, and the very sheep still feeding on the smooth
slopes, even as they fed fifty years ago? And who (let his
later life have been ever so fortunate) does not preferably
dwell on that sharp prospect so clearly yet so light looming
through the Long Avenue of years?

It was not, I will frankly admit, a very righteous beginning to a young life to be hail-fellow well-met with a Gang
of Deer-stealers, and to go careering about the King's Forest
in quest of Venison which belonged to the Crown. Often
have I felt remorseful for so having wronged his Majesty
(whom Heaven preserve for the safety of these distraught
kingdoms!); but what was I, an' it please you, to do? Little
Boy Jack was just Little Boy Beggar; and for want of proper
Training he became Little Boy Thief. Not that I ever pil-
fered aught. I was no Candle-snuffer filcher, and, save in
the matter of Fat Bucks, the rest of our Gang were, indeed,
passing honest. Part of the Venison we killed (mostly with
a larger kind of Bird-Bolt, or Arbalest Crossbow, for through
fear of the keepers we used as little powder and ball as possible) we ate for our Sustenance; for rogues must eat and
drink as well as other folks. The greater portion, however,
was discreetly conveyed, in carts covered over with garden-
stuff, to the market-towns of Uxbridge, Windsor, and Reading, and sold, under the coat-tail as we called it, to Higglers
who were in our secret. Sometimes our Merchandise was
taken right into London, where we found a good Market with
the Fishmongers dwelling about Lincoln's Inn, and who as
they did considerable traffic with the Nobility and Gentry,
of whom they took Park Venison, giving them Fish in exchange, were not likely to be suspected of unlawful dealings,
or at least were able to make a colourable pretext of Honest
Trade to such Constables and Market Conners who had a
right to question them about their barterings. From the
Fishmongers we took sometimes money and sometimes rich
apparel—the cast-off clothes, indeed, of the Nobility, birthday suits or the like, which were not good enough for the
Players of Drury Lane and Lincoln's Inn, forsooth, to strut
about in on their tragedy boards, and which they had therefore bestowed upon their domestics to sell. For our Blacks
loved to quit their bewrayed apparel at supper-time, and to
dress themselves as bravely as when I first tasted their ill-
gotten meat at the Stag o' Tyne. From the Higglers, too, we

would as willingly take Wine, Strong Waters, and Tobacco,
in exchange for our fat and lean, as money : for the Currency
of the Realm was then most wofully clipped and defaced,
and our Brethren had a wholesome avoidance of meddling
with Bank Bills. When, from time to time, one of us ventured to a Market-town, well made-up as a decent Yeoman or
Merchant's Rider, 'twas always payment on the Nail and in
sounding money for the reckoning. We ran no scores, and
paid in no paper.

It was long ere I found out that the Wagon in which I
had travelled from the Hercules' Pillars, to be delivered over
to Gnawbit, was conducted by one of the most trusted Confederates of our Company; that he took Venison to town for
them, and brought them back the Account in specie or needments as they required. And although I am loth to think
that the pretty Servant Maid was altogether deceiving me
when she told me she was going to see her Grandmother,
I fancy that she knew Charlwood Chase, and the gentry that
inhabited it, as well as she knew the Pewterer in Panyer
Alley. He went a-pewtering no more, if ever he had been
'prentice or done journey-work for that trade, but was neither
more nor less than one of the Blacks, and Mistress Slyboots,
his Flame, kept him company. Although I hope, I am sure,
that they were Married by the Chaplain; for, rough as I am,
I had ever a Hatred of Unlawful Passions, and when I am
summoned on a Jury, always listen to the King's Proclamation against Vice and Immorality with much gusto and savour.

I stayed with the Blacks in Charlwood Chase until I
grew to be a sturdy lad of twelve years of age. I went out
with them and followed their naughty courses, and have
stricken down many a fat Buck in my time. Ours was the
most jovial but the most perilous of lives. The Keepers
were always on our track ; and sometimes the Sheriff would
call out the Posse Comitatis, and he and half the beef-fed
tenant-farmers of the country-side would come horsing and
hoofing it about the glades to catch us. For weeks together
in each year we dared not keep our rendezvous at the Stag,
but were fain to hide in Brakes and Hollow Trees, listening
to the pursuit as it grew hot and heavy around us ; and often
with no better Victuals than Pig's-meat and Ditch-water.
But then the search would begin to lag ; and two or three of
the great Squires round about being well terrified by letters

written in a liquid designed to counterfeit Blood, with a great Skull and Cross-bones scrawled at the bottom, the whole signed "Captain Night," and telling them that if they dared to meddle with the Blacks their Lives should pay for it, we were left quiet for a season, and could return to our Haunt, there to feast and carouse according to custom. Nor am I slow to believe that some of the tolerance we met with was due to our being known to the County Gentry as stanch Tories, and as stanch detesters of the House of Hanover (I speak, of course, of my companions, for I was of years too tender to have any politics). We never killed a Deer but on the nearest tree some one of us out with his Jack-knife and carved on the bark of it, "Slain by King James's order;" or, if there were no time for so long a legend, or the Beast was stricken in the Open, a simple K. J. (which the Hanover Rats understood well enough, whether cut in the trunk or the turf) sufficed. The Country Gentlemen were then of a very furious way of thinking concerning the Rights of the present Illustrious House to the Throne; but Times do alter, and so likewise do Men's Thoughts and Opinions, and I dare swear there is no Brunswicker or Church-of-England man more leal at this present writing than John Dangerous.

Captain Night, to whom I was a kind of Page or Henchman, used me with much tenderness. Whenever at supper the tongues grew too loosened, and wild talk, and of the wickedest, began to jingle among the bottles and glasses, he would bid me withdraw, and go keep company for a time with Mistress Slyboots. Captain Night was a man of parts and even of letters; and I often wondered why he, who seemed so well fitted to Shine even among the Great, should pass his time among Rogues, and take the thing that was not his. He was often absent from us for many days, sometimes for nigh a month; and would return sunburnt and travel-stained, as though he had been journeying in Foreign Parts. He was always very thoughtful and reserved after these Gaddings about; and Mistress Slyboots, the Maid, used to say that he was in Love, and had been playing the gallant to some fine Madam. But I thought otherwise: for at this season it was his custom to bring back a Valise full to the very brim of letters and papers, the which he would take Days to read and re-read, noting and seemingly copying some, but burning the greater portion. At this season he would refrain from joining

the Gang, and honourably foreswore his share of their plunder, always giving Mother Drum a broad piece for each
night's Supper, Bottle, and Bed. But when his pressing
business was over, no man was keener in the chase, or
brought down the quarry so skilfully as Captain Night. He
loved to have me with him, to talk to and Question me ; and
it was one day, after I had told him that the Initial letter D
was the only clue to my Grandmother's name, which I had
seen graven on her Coffin-plate, he must needs tell me that if
she were Madam (or rather the Lady) D—, I must needs, as a
Kinsman, be D— too, and that he would piece out the name,
and call me Dangerous. So that I was Little Boy Jack no
more, and John Dangerous I have been from that day to this.
Not but what my Ancestry and Belongings might warrant
me in assuming another title, than which—so far as lineage
counts—Bourbon or Nassau could not rank much higher.
But the name of Dangerous has pleased me alway ; it has
stood me in stead in many a hard pass, and I am content to
abide by it now that my locks are gray, and the walls of this
my battered old tenement are crumbling into decay.

'Twas I alone that was privileged to stay with Captain
Night when he was doing Secretary's work among his papers ;
for, save when Mistress Slyboots came up to him—discreetly
tapping at the door first, you may be sure—with a cup of ale
and a toast, he would abide no other company. And on such
days I wore not my Black Disguisement, but the better
clothes he had provided for me,—a little Riding Suit of red
drugget, silver-laced, and a cock to my hat like a Military
Officer,—and felt myself as grand as you please. I never
dared speak to him until he spoke to me ; but used to sit
quietly enough sharpening bolts or twisting bow-strings, or
cleaning his Pistols, or furbishing up his Hanger and Belt, or
such-like boyish pastime-labour. He was careful to burn
every paper that he Discarded after taking it from the
Valise ; but once, and once only, a scrap remained uncon-
sumed on the hearth, the which, with my ape-like curiosity
of half-a-score summers, I must needs spell over, although I
got small good therefrom. 'Twas but the top of a letter, and
all the writing I could make out ran,

" MY DEAR "   "St. Germains, August 12th.

and here it broke off, and baffled me.

Whenever Captain Night went a hunting, I attended upon him; but when he was away, I was confided to the care of Jowler, who, albeit much given to brabble in his liquor, was about the most discreet (the Chaplain always excepted) among the Gang. In the dead season, when Venison was not to be had, or was nothing worth for the Market if it had been killed, we lived mostly on dried meats and cured salmon; the first prepared by Mother Drum and her maid, the last furnished us by our good friends and Chapmen the Fishmongers about Lincoln's Inn. And during this same Dead Season, I am glad to say that my Master did not suffer me to remain idle; but, besides taking some pains in tutoring me himself, moved our Chaplain, all of whose humane letters had not been washed out by burnt Brandy or fumed out by Tobacco (to the use of which he was immoderately given), to put me through a course of daily instruction. I had had some Latin beaten into me by Gnawbit, when he had nothing of more moment to bestir himself about, and had attained a decent proficiency in reading and writing. Under the Chaplain of the Blacks, who swore at me grievously, but never, under the direst forbidding, laid finger on me, I became a current scholar enough of my own tongue, with just such a little smattering of the Latin as helped me at a pinch in some of the Secret Dealings of my later career. But Salt Water has done its work upon my Lilly's Grammar; and although I yield to no man in the Faculty of saying what I mean, ay, and of writing it down in good plain English ('tis true that of your nominatives and genitives and stuff, I know nothing), I question if I could tell you the Latin for a pair of riding-boots.

There was a paltry parcel of books at the Stag o' Tyne, and these I read over and over again at my leisure. There was a History of the Persecutions undergone by the Quakers, and Bishop Sprat's Narrative of the Conspiracy of Blackhead and the others against him. There was Foxe's Martyrs, and God's Revenge against Murder (a very grim tome), and Mr. Daniel Defoe's Life of Moll Flanders, and Colonel Jack. These, with two or three Play-books, and a Novel by Mrs. Aphra Behn (very scurrilous), a few Ballads, and some ridiculous Chap-books about Knights and Fairies and Dragons, made up the tattered and torn library of our house in Charlwood Chase. 'Twas good enough, you may say, for a nest of

H

Deer-stealers. Well, there might have been a worse one; but these, I can aver, with English and Foreign newspapers and letters, and my Bible in later life, have been all the reading that John Dangerous can boast of. Which makes me so mad against your fine Scholars and Scribblers, who, because they can turn verse and make Te-to-tum into Greek, must needs sneer at me at the Coffee House, and make a butt of an honest man who has been from one end of the world to the other, and has fought his way through it to Fortune and Honour.

I was in the twelfth year of my age when a great change overtook me in my career. Moved, as it would seem, to exceeding Anger and implacable Disgust by the carryings-on of Captain Night and his merry men in Charlwood Chase, the King's Ministers put forth a Proclamation against us, promising heavy Blood Money to any one who would deliver us, or any one member of the Gang, into the hands of Authority. This Proclamation came at first to little. There was no sending a troop of horse into the Chase, and the husbandmen of the country-side were too good Friends of ours to play the Judas. We were not Highway Robbers. Not one of our band had ever taken to or been taken from the Road. Rascals of the Cartouche and Macheath kidney we Disdained. We were neither Foot-pads nor Cutpurses, nay, nor Smugglers nor Rick-burners. We were only Unfortunate Gentlemen, who much did need, and who had suffered much for our politics and our religion, and had no other means of earning a livelihood than by killing the King's Deer. Those peasants whom we came across Feared us, indeed, as they would the very Fiend, but bore us no malice; for we always treated them with civility, and not rarely gave them the 'Umbles and other inferior parts of the Deer, against their poor Christenings and Lyings-in. And through these means, and some small money presents our Captain would make to their wives and callow brats, it came to pass that Mother Drum had seldom cause to brew aught but the smallest beer for morning drinking; for though we had to pay for our Wine and Ardent Drinks, the cellar of the Stag o' Tyne was always handsomely furnished with barrels of strong ale, which Lobbin Clout or Colin Mayfly, the Hind or the Plough-churl, would bring us secretly by night in their Wains for gratitude.

I know not where they got the Malt from, but there was narrow a fault to find with the Brew. I recollect its savour now with a sweet tooth, condemned as I am to the inky Hog's-wash which the Londoners call Porter; and indeed it is fit for Porters to drink, but not for Gentlemen. These Peasants used to tremble all over with terror when they came to the Stag o' Tyne; but they were always hospitably made welcome, and sent away with full gizzards, ay, and with full heads too, and by potions to which the louts were but little used.

We had no fear of treachery from these Chawbacons, but we had Enemies in the Chase nevertheless. Here dwelt a vagabond tribe of Bastard Verderers and Charcoal-burners, savage, ignorant, brutish Wretches, as superstitious as the Manilla Creoles. They were one-half gipsies, and one-half, or perhaps a quarter, trade-fallen whippers-in and keepers that had been stripped of their livery. They picked up their sorry crust by burning of charcoal, and carting of dead wood to farmers for to consume in their ingles. Now and again, when any of the Quality came to hunt in the Chase, the Head Keeper would make use of a score or so of them as beaters and rabble-prickers of the game; but nine months out of the twelve they rather starved than lived. These Charcoal-burners hated us Blacks, first, because in our sable disguise we rather imitated their own Beastly appearance—for the varlets never washed from Candlemas to Shrovetide; next, because we were Gentlemen; and lastly, because we would not suffer them to catch Deer for themselves in pit-falls and springes. Nay, a True Gentleman Black meeting a "Coaley," as we called the Charcoal fellows, with so much as a hare, a rabbit, or a pheasant with him, let alone venison, would ofttimes give him a sackful of sore bones to carry as well as a game-bag. No "Coaley" was ever let to slake his thirst at the Stag o' Tyne. The poor wretches had a miserable hovel of an inn to their own part on the western outskirts of the Chase, a place by the sign of the Hand and Hatchet, where they ate their rye-bread and drank their sour Clink, when they could muster coppers enough for a two-penny carouse.

This Proclamation, of which at first we made light, was speedily followed by a real live Act of Parliament, which is yet, I have been told, Law, and is known as the "Black

Act."* The most dreadful punishments were denounced against us by the Houses of Lords and Commons, and the Blood Money was doubled. One of the most noted Thief-takers of that day—almost as great a one as Jonathan Wild —comes down post, and sets up his Standard at Reading, as though he had been King William on the banks of the Boyne. With him he brings a mangy Rout of Constables and Bailiff's Followers, and other kennel-ranging vagabonds ; and now nothing must serve him but to beg of the Commanding Officer at Windsor (my Lord Treherne) for a loan of two companies of the Foot Guards, who, nothing loth for field-sport and extra pay, were placed, with their captain and all—more shame for a Gentleman to mix in such Hangman's work !— under Mr. Thief-taker's orders. He and his Bandogs, ay, and his Grenadiers, might have hunted us through Charlwood Chase until Doomsday but for the treachery of the "Coaleys." 'Twas one of their number,—named, or rather nicknamed, "the Beau," because he washed his face on Sunday, and was therefore held to be of the first fashion,—who earned eighty-pounds by revealing the hour when the whole Gang of Blacks might be pounced upon at the Stag o' Tyne. The infamous wretch goes to Aylesbury,—for our part of the Chase was in the county of Bucks,—and my Thief-taking gentleman from Reading meets him—a pretty couple ; and he makes oath before Mr. Justice Cribfee (who should have set him in the Stocks, or delivered him over to the Beadle for a vagrant) ; and after a fine to-do of Sheriff's business and swearing-in of special constables, the end of it was, that a whole Rout of them, Sheriff, Javelin-men, and Headboroughs and all, with the Grenadiers at their back, came upon us unawares one moonlight night as we were merrily supping at the Stag.

'Twas no use showing Fight perhaps, for we were undermanned, some of us being away on the scent, for we suspected some foul play. The constables and other clodhopping Alguazils were all armed to the teeth with Bills and Blunderbusses, Pistols and Hangers ; but had they worn all the weapons in

---

* See the Statutes at Large. The Black Act was repealed mainly through the exertions of Sir James Macintosh, early in the present century. Under its clauses the going about "disguised or blackened in pursuit of game" was made felony without benefit of clergy; the punishment thereof death.—ED.

the Horse Armoury in the Tower, it would not have saved them from shivering in their shoes when "Hard and sharp" was the word, and an encounter with the terrible Blacks had to be endured. We should have made mince-meat of them all, and perhaps hanged up one or two of them outside the inn as an extra signpost. But we were not only unarmed, we were overmatched, my hearties. There were the Redcoats, burn them! How many times in my life have I been foiled and baffled by those miscreated men-machines in scarlet blanketing! No use in a stout Heart, no use in a strong Hand, no use in a sharp Sword, or a pair of barkers with teeth that never fail, when you have to do with a Soldier. Do! What are you to do with him? There he is, with his shaven face and his hair powdered, as if he were going to a fourpenny fandango at Bagnigge Wells. There he is, as obstinate as a Pig, and as firm as a Rock, with his confounded bright firelock, bayonet, and crossbelts. There he is, immovable and unconquerable, defying the boldest of Smugglers, the bravest of Gentlemen Rovers, and, by the Lord Harry, *he eats you up*. Always give the Redcoats a wide berth, my dear, and the Grenadiers more than all.

Unequal as were the odds, with all these Roaring Dragons, in scarlet baize, on our trail, we had still a most desperate fight for it. While the mob of Constables kept cowering in the bar-room down-stairs, crying out to us to surrender in the King's name,—I believe that one poor creature, the Justice of Peace, after getting himself well walled up in a corner with chairs and tables, began to quaver out the King's Proclamation against the Blacks,—the plaguy Soldiers came blundering up both pair of stairs, and fell upon us Billy Boys tooth and nail. 'Slid! my blood simmers when I think of it. Over went the tables and settles! Smash went trenchers and cups and glasses! Clink-a-clink went sword-blades and bayonets! "And don't fire, my lads!" cries out the Soldier-officer to his Grannies. "We want all these rogues to hang up at Aylesbury Gaol."

"Rogue yourself, and back to your Mother!" cries Captain Night, very pale; but I never saw him look Bolder or Handsomer. "Rogue in your Tripes, you Hanover Rat!" and he shortens his sword and rushes on the Soldier-officer.

The Grenadier Captain was brave enough, but he was but a smock-faced lad fresh from the Mall and St. James's Guard-

room, and he had no chance against a steady practised Swords-
man and Forest Blood, as Captain Night was. We all thought
he would make short work of the Soldier-officer. He had him
in a corner, and the Chaplain, a-top of whom was a Grenadier
trying to throttle or capture him, or both, exclaims, "Give
him the grace-blow, my dear; give it him under' the fifth
rib !" when Captain Night cries, "Go home to your mother,
Milksop !" and he catches his own sword by the hilt, hits his
Enemy a blow on the right wrist enough to numb it for a
month, twists his fingers in his cravat, flings him on one side,
and right into the middle of a punch-bowl, and then, upon
my word, he, himself, jumps out of Window, shouting out,
"Follow me, little Jack Dangerous !"

I wished for nothing better, and had already my leg on
the sill, when two great hulking Grenadiers seized hold of
me. 'Twas then, for the first time, that I earned a just claim
and title to the name of Dangerous; for a little dirk I was
armed with being wrested from me by Soldier number one,
who eggs-on his comrade to collar the young Fox-cub, as he
calls me, I seize a heavy Stone Demijohn full of brandy, and
smash it goes on the head of Soldier number two. He falls
with a dismal groan, the blood and brandy running in equal
measure from his head, and the first Soldier runs his bayonet
through me.

Luckily, 'twas but a flesh-wound in the flank, and no
vital part was touched. It was enough for me, however, poor
Urchin,—enough to make me tumble down in a dead faint;
and when I came to myself, I found that I had been removed
to the bar-room down-stairs, where I made one of nineteen
Blacks, all prisoners to the King for stealing his Deer, and
all bound hand and foot with Ropes.

"Never mind their hurting your wrists, young Hemp-
seed," chuckled one of the scaldpated constable rogues who
was guarding us. "You'll have enough to tighten your gullet
after 'Sizes, as sure as eggs is eggs."

"Nay, brother Grimstock, the elf's too young to be
hanged," puts in another constable, with somewhat of a
charitable visage.

"Too young !" echoed he addressed as Grimstock. "'Twas
bred in the bone in him, the varmint, and the Gallows Fever
will come out in the flesh. Too young ! he was weaned on
rue, and rode between his Father's legs (that swung) i' the

cart to Tyburn, and never sailed a cockboat but in Execution Dock. My tobacco-box to a tester an' he dance not on nothing if he comes to holding up his hand before Judge Blackcap, that never spared but one in the Calendar, and then 'twas by Mistake."

These were not very comfortable news for me, poor manacled wretch; and with a great bayonet-wound in my side to boot, that had been but clumsily dressed by a village Leech, who was, I suspect, a Farrier and Cow Doctor as well. But I have always found, in this life's whirligig, that when your Case is at the worst (unless a Man indeed Dies, when there is nothing more to be done), it is pretty sure to mend, if you lie quiet and let things take their chance. I could not be much worse off than I was, wounded and friendless and a captive; and so I held my tongue, and let them use me as they would. Some scant comfort was it, however, to find, when the battle-field was gone over, that, besides the Grenadier whose crown we had cracked, another had been pistoled by Jowler, and lay mortally wounded, and Groaning Dismally. Poor Jowler himself would never pistol Foe more. He was dead; for the Men of War, furious at our desperate Resistance, at the worsting of their fine-feathered officer (who was mumbling of his bruised hand as a down-trodden Hound would its paw, and cursing meanwhile, which Dogs use not to do), and driven to Mad Rage by the escape of Captain Night, had fired pell-mell into a Group of which Jowler made one, and so killed him. A bullet through his brain set him clean quit of all indictments under the Black Act, before our Sovereign Lord the King. Likewise was it a matter of rejoicing for our party that, after long seeking the Traitor Coaley, the wretched "Beau" was found duly strangled, and completely a corpse on the staircase. There was something curious about the manner of justice coming to this villain. The Deed had been done with no weapon more Lethal than an old Stocking; yet so tightly was it tied round his false neck, that it had to be cut off piecemeal, and even then the ribs of the worsted were found to be Imbedded, and to have made Furrows in his flesh. Now it is certain that we Blacks had not laid about us with old Wives' hose, any more than we had lunged at our enemies with knitting-needles. There, however, was Monsieur Judas, as dead as a Dolphin two hours on deck. Lord, what an ugly countenance had the losel when they came to wash the charcoal off him! As to who had forestalled the Hangman in his office, no certain testimony could be given. I have always found at Sea, when any doubts arise as to the why and the wherefore of a gentleman's death, that the best way to settle accounts is to fling him overboard; but on dry land your plaguy Dead Body is a sore Stumbling Block and Impediment, always turning up when it is not Wanted, and bringing other Gentlemen into all kinds of trouble. Crowner's Quest was held on the " Beau ;" and I only wonder that they did not bring it in murder against Me. The jury sat a long time without making up their minds, till the Parish constable ordered them in a bowl of Flip, upon which they proceeded to bring in a verdict of Wilful Murder against some person or persons unknown. I can scarcely, to this day, bring myself to suspect my pretty maid, that should have married the Pewterer, of such a bold Act, and the rather believe that it was the girl Grip and her Mistress that worked off the Spy and Traitor between them. Not that Mother Drum would have needed any assistance in the mere doing of the thing. She was a Mutton-fisted woman, and as strong in the forearm as a Bridewell correctioner.

O, the dreary journey we made that morning to Aylesbury! The Men Blacks were tied back to back, and thrown into such carts as could be pressed into the service from the farmsteads on the skirts of the Chase. One of the constables must needs offer, the Scoundrel, to take horse and go borrow a cartload of fetters from the gaoler at Reading; but he was overruled, and Ropes were thought strong enough to confine us. There was no chance, alas, of any rescue; for those of our comrades who had been fortunate enough through absence to avoid capture, had doubtless by this time scent of the Soldiers, and there was no kicking against those bright Firelocks and Bayonets. Yet had there been another escape. Cicely Grip and Mother Drum were taken, but the pretty maid I loved so for her kindness to me when I was Forlorn had shown a clean pair of heels, and was nowhere to be found. Good luck to her, I thought. Perchance she has met with Captain Night, and they are Safe and Sound by this time, and off to Foreign Parts. For in all this I declare I saw nothing Wrong, and held, in my baby logic, that we Blacks had all been very harshly entreated by the Constables and Redcoats, and that it was a shame to use us so. Mother Drum, the Wench, and my poor wounded Self, were put into one cart together, and through Humanity, a Sergeant (for the Constables would not have done it) bade his men litter down some straw for us to lie upon. There was a ragged Tilt too over the cart; and thinks I, in a Gruesome manner, "The first time you rode on straw under a Tilt, Jack, you were going to school, and now, 'ifegs, you are going to be Hanged." For it was settled on all sides, and even he with the Charitable Countenance came to be of that mind at last, that my fate was to die by the Cord.

"Why," says one, "you've half-brained Corporal Foss with the Demijohn; never did liquor get into a pretty man's head so soon and so deep. They'll stretch your neck for this, my poult,—they will."

The Sergeant interposing, said that perhaps, if interest were made for me, I might be spared an Indictment, and let to go and serve the King as a Drummer till I was old enough to carry a firelock. But at this the soldiers shook their heads; for Captain Poppingjay, their officer, was, it seems, still in a towering rage at having had his fine-lady's hand so wofully mauled by Captain Night, and vowed vengeance against the whole crew of poachers and their whelp, as he must needs be Polite enough to call me.

This Fine Gentleman had been provided with a Horse by the Sheriff, and, as he rode by the cart where I and Drum and the Girl were jogging on, he spies me under the Tilt, and in his cruel manner makes a cut at me with his riding wand, calling me a young spawn of Thievery and Rebellion.

"You coward," I cried in a passion; "you daren't do that if my hands were loose, and I hadn't this baggonet-wound in me."

"Shame to hit the boy," growled the charitable Constable, who was on horseback too.

The Soldier-officer turned round quickly to see who had spoken; but the Sergeant, who watched him, pointed with his halbert to the Constable, and he returned the Captain's glance with a sturdy mien. So my Fine Gentleman reins-in his beast and lets us pass, eyeing his hand, which was all wrapped up in Bandages, and muttering that it was well none of his own fellows had given him this sauciness.

The day was a dreadful one. How many times our train

halted to bait I know not ; but this I know, that I fainted
often from Agony of my wound and the uneasy motion of my
carriage.   It is a wonder that I ever came to my journey's
end alive, and in all likelihood never should, but for the
unceasing . care and solicitude of the two poor women who
were with me, Prisoners like myself, but full of merciful
kindness for one who was in a sorer strait than they.   By
earnest pleading did Mother Drum persuade the Head Constable—who, the nearer we got to gaol the more authority he
took, and the less he seemed to think of our soldier escort—
to allow her hands to be unbound that she might minister
unto me ; and also did she obtain so much grace as for some
of the Money belonging unto her, and which had been seized
at the Stag o' Tyne, to be spent in buying of a bottle of
brandy at one of our halting-places, with which she not only
comforted herself and her afflicted Maid, but, mingling it
with water, cooled my parched tongue and bathed my forehead.

Brandy was the only medicament this good soul knew ;
and more lives, she averred, had been saved by Right Nantz
than lost by bad B. W ; but still brandy was not precisely
the kind of physic to give a Patient who before Sundown
was in a Raging Fever.   But 'twas all one to the Law ; and
coming at last to my journey's end, we were all, the wounded
and the whole, flung into Gaol to answer for it at the 'Sizes.

CHAPTER THE NINTH.

I AM VERY NEAR BEING HANGED.

OUR prison was surely the most loathsome hole that Human beings were ever immured in. It was a Horrible and Shameful Place, conspicuous for such even in those days, when every prison was a place of Horror and Shame. 'Twas one of the King's Prisons,—one of His Majesty's Gaols,—the county had nothing to do with it; and the Keeper thereof was a Woman. Say a Tigress rather; but Mrs. Macphilader wore a hoop and lappets and gold ear-rings, and was dubbed "Madam" by her Underlings. Here you might at any time have seen poor Wretches chained to the floor of reeking dungeons, their arms, legs, necks even, laden with irons, themselves abused, beaten, jeered at, drenched with pailfuls of foul water, and more than three-quarter starved, merely for not being able to pay Garnish to the Gaoleress, or comply with other her exorbitant demands. Fetters, indeed, were common and Fashionable Wear in the Gaol. 'Twas pleaded that the walls of the prison were so rotten through age, and the means of guarding the prisoners—for they could not be always calling in the Grenadiers—so limited, that they must needs put the poor creatures in the bilboes, or run the chance of their escaping every day in the week. Thus it came to pass, even, that they were tried in Fetters, and sometimes could not hold up their hands (weakened besides by the Gaol Distemper), at the bidding of the Clerk of the Arraigns, for the weight of the Manacles that were upon them. And it is to the famous and admirable Mr. John Howard that we owe the putting down of this last Abomination.

We lay so long in this dreadful place before a Gaol Delivery was made, that my wound, bad as it was, had ample time to heal, leaving only a great indented cicatrix, as though some Giant had forced his finger into my flesh, and of which I shall never be rid. Two more of our Gang died of the Gaol Fever before Assize time; one was so fortunate as to break prison, file the irons off his legs, and get clear away; and another (who was always of a Melancholy turn) hanged himself one morning, in a halter made from slips of his

blanket knotted together. The rest of us were knocked
about by the Turnkeys, or abused by the Gaoleress, Mrs.
Macphilader, pretty much as they liked. We were, however,
not so badly off as some of the poor prisoners—sheep-stealers,
footpads, vagrom men and women, and the like, or even as
some of the poor Debtors—many of whom lay here incarcerate
years after they had discharged the Demands of their Creditors against them, and only because they could not pay
their Fees. We Blacks were always well supplied with
money; and money could purchase almost any thing in a
prison in those days. Roast meats, and wine and beer and
punch, pipes and tobacco, and playing cards and song-books,
—all these were to be had by Gentlemen Prisoners; the
Gaoleress taking a heavy toll, and making a mighty profit
from all these luxurious things. But there was one thing
that money could not buy, namely, cleanly lodging; for the
State Room, a hole of a place very meanly furnished, where
your great Smugglers or ruffling Highwaymen were sometimes lodged, at a guinea a day for their accommodation, was
only so much better than the common room in so far as the
prisoner had bed and board to himself; but for nastiness and
creeping things—which I wonder, so numerous were they,
did not crawl away with the whole prison bodily: but 'tis
hard to find those that are unanimous, even Vermin. For
all that made the Gaol most thoroughly hateful and dreadful,
there was not a pin to choose between the State Room, the
Common Side, and the Rat's Larder, Clink, or Dark Dungeon, where the Poor were confined in wantonness, and the
Stubborn were kept sometimes for punishment; for Madam
Gaoleress had a will of her own, and would brook no incivi-
lities from her lodgers; so sure is it, that falling out one day
on the disputed question of a bottle of Aquavitæ on which
toll had not been paid, she calls one of the Turnkeys and
bids him clap Mother Drum into the Stocks (that stood in
the Prison Yard) for an hour or two, for the cooling of her
temper. But this had just the contrary effect; for the
whilom Hostess of the Stag o' Tyne, enraged at the Indignity
offered to her, did so bemaul and bewray Madam Macphilader
with her tongue, shaking her fist at her meanwhile, that the
Gaoleress in a fury clawed at least two handfuls of M.
Drum's hair from her head, not without getting some smart
clapperclawing in the face: whereupon she cries out " Mur-

ther" and " Mutiny" and " Prisonrupt," and sends post-haste for Justice Palmworm, her gossip indeed, and one of those trading magistrates that so disgraced our bench before Mr. Henry Fielding the writer stirred up Authority to put some order therein. The Justice comes; and he and the Gaoleress, after cracking a bottle of mulled port between them, poor Mother Drum was brought up before his Worship for mutinous conduct. The Justice would willingly have compounded the case, for Lucre was his only love; but 'twas vengeance the Gaoleress hankered after; and the end of it was, poor Mother Drum was triced up at the post that was by the Stocks, and had a dozen and a half from a cat with indeed but three tails, but that, I warrant, hurt pretty nigh as sharply as nine would have done in weaker hands; for 'twas the Gaoler that played the Beadle and laid on the Scourge.

At length, when I was quite tired out, and, knowing nothing of the course of Law, began to think that we were doomed to perpetual imprisonment, His Majesty's Judges of Assize came upon the circuit, and those whom the Fever and Want and the Duresse of their Keeper had spared were put upon their trial. By this time I was thought well enough, though as gaunt as a hound, to be put in the same Gaolbird's trim as my companions; so a pair of Woman's fetters —ay, my friends, the Women wore fetters in those days— were put upon me; and the whole of us, all shackled as we were, found ourselves, one fine Monday morning, in the Dock, having been driven thereinto very much after the fashion of a flock of sheep. The Court was crowded, for the case against the Blacks had made a prodigious stir; and the King's Attorney, the most furious Person for talking a Fellow-creature's Life away that ever I remember to have seen or heard, came down especially from London to prosecute us. Neither he nor His Lordship the Judge, in his charge to the Grand Jury, had any but the worst of words to give us; and folks began to say that this would be another Bloody Assize; that the Shire Hall had need to be hung with scarlet, as when Jeffreys was on the bench; and that as short work would be made of us as of the Rebels in the West. And I did not much care, for I was sick of lying in hold, amidst Evil Odours, and with a green wound. It came even to whispering that of one of us at least would be made a Gibbeting-in-chains matter for killing the Grenadier, if that

Act could be fixed on any particular Black. And half in jest, half in earnest, the Woman-keeper told me on the morning of the Assizes that, young as I was (not yet twelve years of age), my bones might rattle in a birdcage in the midst of Charlwood Chase; for if I could brain one Grenadier, I could kill another. But yet, being so weary of the Life, I did not much Care.

It was still somewhat of a Relief to me to come into the Dock, and look upon State and Rich Clothes (in which I have always taken a Gentleman-like pleasure), in the stead of all the dirt and squalor which for so long had been my surrounding. There were the Judges all ranged, a Terrible show, in their brave Scarlet Robes and Fur Tippets, with Great Monstrous Wigs, and the King's Arms behind them, under a Canopy, done in Carver's work, gilt. They frowned on us dreadfully when we came trooping into the Dock, bringing all manner of Deadly pestilential Fumes with us from the Gaol yonder, and which not all the rue, rosemary, and marjoram strewn on the Dock-ledge, nor the hot vinegar sprinkled about the Court, could mitigate. The middle Judge, who was old, and had a split lip and a fang protruding from it, shook his head at me, and put on such an Awful face, that for a moment my scared thoughts went back to the Clergyman at St. George's, Hanover Square, that was wont to be so angry with me in his Sermons. Ah, how different was the lamentable Hole in the which I now found myself, cheek by jowl with Felons and Caravats, to the great red-baize Pew in which I had sat so often a Little Gentleman! He to the right of the middle Judge was a very sleepy gentleman, and scarcely ever woke up during the proceedings, save once towards one of the clock, when he turned to his Lordship (whom I had at once set down as Mr. Justice Blackcap, and was in truth that Dread Functionary), saying, " Brother, is it dinner-time?" But his Lordship to the left, who had an old white face like a sheep, and his wig all awry, was of a more placable demeanour, and looked at me, poor luckless Outcast, with some interest. I saw him turn his head and whisper to the gentleman they told me was the High Sheriff, and who sat on the Bench alongside the Judges, very fine, in a robe and gold chain, and with a great sheathed sword behind him, resting on a silver goblet. Then the High Sheriff took to reading over the Calendar, and shrugged his shoulders, whereupon I indulged in some Hope. Then he leans over to Mr. Clerk of the Arraigns, pointing me out, and seemingly asking him some question about me; but that gentleman hands him up a couple of parchments, and my quick Ear (for the Court was but small) caught the words, " There are two Indictments against him, Sir John." Whereupon they looked at me no more, save with a Stern and Sorrowful Gravity; and the Hope I had nourished for a moment departed from me. Yet then, as afterwards, and as now, I found (although then too babyish to reason about it), that, bad as we say the World is, it is difficult to come upon Three Men together in it but that one is Good and Merciful.

I feel that my disclaimer notwithstanding the Bark of my Narrative is running down the stream of a Garrulous talkativeness; but I shall be more brief anon. And what would you have? If there be any circumstances which should entitle a man to give chapter and verse, they must surely be those under which he was Tried for his Life.

The first day we only held up our hands, and heard the Indictment against us read. Some of us who were Moneyed had retained Counsellors from London to cross-question the witnesses; for to speak to the Jury in aid of Prisoners, who could not often speak for themselves, the Gentlemen of the Law were not then permitted. And this I have ever held to be a crying Injustice. There was no one, however, not so much as a Pettifogger, to lift tongue, or pen, or finger, to save little Jack Dangerous from the Rope. My Protector, Captain Night, was at large; Jowler, my first friend among the Blacks, was dead; and, as Misery is apt to make men Selfish, the rest of my companions had entirely forgotten how friendless and deserted I was. But, just as we were going back to Gaol, up comes to the spikes of the Dock a Gentleman with a red face, and a vast bushy powdered wig, like a cauliflower in curls. He wore a silk cassock and sash, and was the Ordinary; but he had forgotten, I think, to come into the Prison and read prayers to us. He kept those ministrations against such time as the Cart was ready, and the Tree decked with its hempen garland. This gentleman beckons me, and asks if I have any Counsellor. I told him, No; and that I had no Friends ayont Mother Drum, and she was laid up, sick of a pair of sore shoulders. He goes back to the Bench and confers with the Gentlemen, and by and by the Clerk of the Arraigns calls out that, through the Humanity of the Sheriff, the prisoner John Dangerous was to have Counsel Assigned to him. But it would have been more Humane, I think, to have let the Court and the World know that I was a poor neglected Castaway, knowing scarcely my right Hand from my left, and that all I had done had been in that Blindfoldedness of Ignorance which can scarcely, I trust, be called Sin.

Back, however, we went to Gaol, and a great Rout there was made that night by Mrs. Macphilader for the payment of all arrears of Fees and Garnish to her ; for, you see, being a prudent Woman, she feared lest some of the prisoners should be Acquitted, or Discharged on Proclamation. And our Gang of Blacks, for whose aid their friends in ambush— and they had friends in all kinds of holes and corners, as I afterwards discovered to my surprise—had mostly bountifully come forward, did not trouble themselves much about the peril they were in, but bestowed themselves of making a Roaring Fight. And hindered by none in Authority,—for the Gaolers and Turnkeys in those days were not above drinking, and smoking, and singing, and dicing with their charges,—they did keep it up so merrily and so roaringly, that the best part of the night was spent before drowsiness came over Aylesbury Gaol.

Then the next day to Court, and there the Judges as before, and Sir John the High Sheriff, and the Counsel for the Crown and for us, and twelve honest gentlemen in a box by themselves, that were of the Petty Jury, to try us ; and, I am ashamed to say, a great store of Ladies, all in ribbons and patches and laces and fine clothes, that sate some on the Bench beside the Judges, and others in the body of the Court among the Counsel, and stared at us miserable objects in the Dock as though we had been a Galantee Show. It is some years now since I have entered a Court of Criminal Justice, and I do hope that this Indecent and Uncivil Behaviour of well-bred Women coming to gaze on Criminals for their diversion has utterly given way before the Benevolence and good taste of a polite Age.

When, at the last, I was told to plead, and at the bidding of an Officer of the Court, who stood underneath me, had pleaded Not Guilty, and had been asked how I would be tried, and had answered, likewise at his bidding, " By God and my Country," and when after that the Clerk of the

Arraigns had prayed Heaven—and I am sure I needed it, and thanked him heartily at the time, kind Gentleman, thinking that he meant it, and not knowing that it was a mere Legal Form—to send me a good Deliverance,—the Judge bids me, to my great surprise, to Stand By. I thought at first that they were going to have Mercy on me, and would have down on my knees in gratitude to them. But it was not so; and the sleepy old Judge, suddenly waking up, told me that there were two Indictments against me, and that I should have the honour of being tried separately. Goodness save us! I was looked upon as one of the most desperate of the Gang, and was to be tried, not only under the Black Act, but that, not having the fear of God before my eyes, but being moved by the instigation of the Devil, I had, against the Peace of our Sovereign Lord the King, attempted feloniously to kill, slay, and murder one John Foss, a Corporal in His Majesty's Regiment of Grenadier Foot-guards, by striking him, the said John Foss, over the back, breast, hips, loins, shoulders, thighs, legs, feet, arms, and fingers, with a certain deadly weapon, to wit, with a demijohn of Brandy.

I was put back and kept all day in the prison. At evening came in my comrades, and from them I learnt that the case had gone dead against them from the beginning, that the Jury had found them guilty under the Statute without leaving the box ; and that, as the felony was one without the benefit of Clergy, Judge Blackcap had put on a wig as black as his name, and sentenced every man Jack of them to be hanged on the Monday week next following.

So then it came to my turn to be tried. The ordeal on the first Indictment was very short ; for, at the Judge's bidding, the Jury acquitted me of trying to murder Corporal Foss before I had been ten minutes in the dock. I did not understand the proceedings in the least at that time ; but I was told afterwards that the clever legal gentlemen who had drawn up the Indictment against me, while very particularly setting down the parts of the body on which I might have struck Corporal Foss, omitted to specify the one place, namely, his head, on which I did hit him. Counsel for the Crown endeavoured, indeed, to prove that a splinter from the broken demijohn had grazed the corporal's finger, but the evidence for this fell dead. And, again, it coming out that I was arraigned as John Danger, whereas I had

I

given the name of John Dangerous, to which I had perhaps
no more right than to that of the Pope of Rome, the Judge
roundly tells the Jury that the Indictment is bad in law, and
I was forthwith acquitted as aforesaid.

But I was not scot-free.   There was that other Indictment under the Black Act; and in that, alas, there was no
flaw.   The Solemn Court freed itself, to be sure, of the
Mockery of finding a child under twelve years Guilty of the
attempted murder of a Grenadier six feet high; but no less
did the witnesses swear, and the Judge sum up, and Counsel
for the Crown insist, and my Counsel feebly deny, and the
Jury at last fatally find against me, that I had gone about
armed and Disguised by night, and wandered up and down
in the King's Forests, and stolen his Deer, and Goodness
can tell what besides; and so, being found guilty, the middle
Judge puts on his black cap again, and tells me that I am to
be hanged on Monday week by the neck.

He did not say anything about my youth, or about my
utter loneliness, or about the evil examples which had
brought me to this Pass.   Perhaps it was not his Duty,
but that of the Ordinary, to tell me so.   The Hanging was
his department, the praying belonged to his Reverence.
They led me back to prison, feeling rather hot and sick
after the words I had listened to about being "hanged by
the neck until I was dead," but still not caring much; for I
could not rightly understand why all these fine gentlemen
should be at the pains of Butchering me merely because I
had run away from school (being so cruelly entreated by
Gnawbit), and, to save myself from starvation, had joined
the Blacks.

Being to Die, it seemed for the first time to occur to
them that I was not as the rest of the poor souls that were
doomed to death, and that it behoved them to treat me
rather as a lamb that is doomed for the slaughter than as a
great overgrown Bullock to be knocked down by the Butcher's Pole-axe.   So they put me away from the rest of my
companions, and bestowed me in a sorry little chamber,
where I had a truckle-bed to myself.   Dear old Mother
Drum, being still under disgrace, was not suffered to come
near me.   Her trial, with that of Cicely Grip, for harbouring
armed and disguised men, under the Black Act, which was
likewise a felony, was not to come on till the next session.

I believe that the Great Gentlemen at Whitehall were, for a long time after my conviction, in a mind for Hanging me. 'Twas thought a small matter then to stretch the neck of a Boy of Twelve, and children even smaller than I had worn the white Nightcap, and smelt the Nosegay in the Cart. Indeed, I think the Ordinary wanted me to be Finished according to Law, that he might preach a Sermon on it, and liken me to one of the Children that mocked the Prophet, and so was eaten up by the She-Bears that came out of a Wood. When I think on the Reverend and Pious Persons who now attend our Criminals in their last unhappy Moments, and strive to bring them to a Sense of their Sins, it gives me the Goose-flesh to remember the Profane and Riotous Parsons who, for a Mean Stipend, did the contemned work of Gaol Chaplains in the days I speak of. Even while the Hangman was getting into proper Trim, and fashioning his tools for the slaughter, these callous Clergymen would be smoking and drinking with the keepers in the Lodge, talking now of a Main at Cocks and now of him who was to suffer on the Morrow, fleering and jesting, with the Church Service in one sleeve of their cassock and a Bottle Screw or a Pack of Cards in the other. And the Condemned persons, too, did not take the matter in a much more serious light. They had their Brandy and Tobacco even in their Dismal Hold, and thought much less of Mercy and Forgiveness than of the ease they would have from their Irons being stricken off, or the comfort they would gain from a last bellyful of Meat. I have not come to be sixty-eight years of age without observing somewhat of the Things that have passed around me ; and one of the best signs of the Times in which I live (and due in great part to the Humane and Benignant complexion of his Majesty) is the falling off in bloodthirsty and cruel Punishments. If a Dozen or so are hanged after each Gaol Delivery at the Old Bailey, and a score or more whipped or burnt in the Hand, what are such workings of justice compared with the Waste of Life that was used to be practised under the two last monarchs ? At home 'twas all pressing to death those who would not plead, hanging, drawing, and quartering (how often have I sickened to see the pitch-seethed members of my Fellow-creatures on the spikes of Temple Bar and London Bridge !), taking out the entrails of those convict of Treason (as witness Colonel

Towneley, Mr. Dawson, and many more unfortunate gentlemen on Kennington Common), to say nothing of the burning
alive of women for petty treason,—and to kill a husband or
coin a groat were alike Treasonable,—the Scourging of the
same wretched creatures in Public till the blood ran from
their shoulders and soaked the knots of the Beadle's lash ;
the cartings, brandings, and dolorous Imprisonments which
were then inflicted for the slightest of offences. Why, I have
seen a man stand in the Pillory in the Seven Dials (to be
certain, he was a secure scoundrel), and the Mob, not satisfied, must take him out, strip him to the buff, stone him, cast
him down, root up the pillory, and trample him under foot,
till, being rescued by the constables, he has been taken back
to Newgate, and has died in the Hackney Coach conveying
him thither.

Oh, 'tis woe to think of the Horrors that were then
done in the name of the Law and Justice, not only in this
country but in Foreign Parts,—with their Breakings on the
Wheel, Questions Ordinary and Extraordinary, Bastinadoes,
Carcans, Wooden horses, Burning alive too (for vending of
Irreligious Books), and the like Barbarities. Let me tell you
likewise, that, for all the evil name gotten by the Spanish
and Portuguese Inquisitions,—for which I entertain, as a
Protestant, due Detestation and Abhorrence,—the darkest
deeds ever done by the so-called Holy Office in their Torture
Chambers were not half so cruel as those performed with the
full cognisance and approbation of authority, in open places,
and in pursuance of the sentence of the Civil Judges. But a
term has come to these wickednesses. The admirable Mr.
Howard before named (whom I have often met in my travels,
as he, good man, with nothing but a Biscuit and a few Raisins
in his pocket, went up and down Europe Doing Good, smiling
at Fever and tapping Pestilence on the cheek),—this Blessed
Worthy has lightened the captive's fetters, and cleansed his
dungeon, and given him Light and Air. Then I hear at the
Coffee House that the great Judge, Sir William Blackstone,
has given his caveat against the Frequency of Capital Punishment for small offences ; and as His Majesty is notoriously
averse from signing more than six Death Warrants at once
(the old King used to say at council, in his German-English,
" Vere is de Dyin' speech man dat hang de Rogue for me ?"
meaning the Recorder with his Report, and seeming, in a sort,

eager to despatch that awful Business, of which the present Prince is so Tender), I think that we have every cause to Bless the Times and Reign we live in. For surely 'tis but affected Softness of Heart, and Mock, Sickly Sentiment, to maintain that Highwaymen, Horse-stealers, and other hardened villains, do not deserve the Tree, and do not righteously Suffer for their misdeeds ; or that wanton women do not deserve bodily correction, so long as it be done within Bridewell Walls, and not in front of the Sessions House, for the ribald Populace to stare at. Truly our present code is a merciful one, although I do not hold that the ·Extreme Penalty of the law should be exacted for such offences as cutting down growing trees, forging hat-stamps, or stealing above the value of a Shilling ; nevertheless crime must be kept under, that is certain.*

At all events, they didn't hang John Dangerous. For a time, as I have said, the Great Gentlemen at Whitehall hesitated. I have heard that Justice Blackcap, being asked to intercede for me, did, with a scurril jest, tell Mr. Secretary that I was a young Imp of the Evil One, and that a little Hanging would do me no harm. Five, indeed, of my miserable companions were put to death, at different points on the borders of Charlwood Chase, and one, the unlucky Chaplain, met his fate before the door of the Stag o' Tyne. The rest of the Blacks, of whom, to my joy, I shall have no further occasion to speak, were sent to be Slaves in the American Plantations.

I had lain in the Gaol more than a month after my Sentence, when Mr. Shapcott, a good Quaker Gentleman of the place (who had suffered much for Conscience' sake, and was very Pitifully inclined to all those who were in Affliction), began to take some interest in my unhappy Self; calling me a strayed Lamb, a brand to be snatched from the burning, and the like. And he, by the humane connivance of the Mayor and other Justices, was now permitted to have access unto me, and to conciliate the Keeper, Mrs. Macphilader, by

---

* Captain Dangerous, it will be seen, was, in regard to our criminal code, somewhat in advance of the ideas of his age ; but he was scarcely on a level with those of our own, and, I think, would have perused with some surprise the speeches of Mr. Ewart and the *Vacation Thoughts on Capital Punishments* of the late Mr. Commissioner Phillips.—G. A. S.

money-presents, to treat me with some kindness. Also he brought me many Good Books, in thin paper covers; the which, although I could understand but very little of their Saving Truths, yet caused me to shed many Tears, more Sweet than Bitter, and to acknowledge, when taxed with it in a Soothing way, that my former Manner of Life had been most Wicked. But I should do this good man foul injustice, were I to let it stand that his benevolence to me was confined to books. He and (ever-remembered) Mistress Shapcott, his Meek and Pious Partner, and his daughter, Wingrace Shapcott (a tall and straight young woman, as Beautiful as an Angel), were continually bringing me Comforts and Needments, both in Raiment and Food. It churns my Old Heart now to think of that Beautiful Girl, sitting beside me in my dank Prison Room, the tears streaming from her mild eyes, calling me by Endearing names, and ever and anon taking my hand in hers, and sinking on her knees to the sodden floor (with no thought of soiling her kirtle), while with profound Fervour she prayed for the conversion of errant Me. Sure there are Hearts of Gold among those Broadbrims and their fair straight-laced Daughters. Many a Merchant's Money-bags I have spared for the sake of Mr. Barzillai Shapcott (late of Aylesbury). Many a Fair Woman have I intermitted from my Furious Will in remembrance of the good that was shown me, in the old time, by that pale, straight-gowned Wingrace yonder, with her meek Face and welling Eyes. Of my deep and grievous Sins they told me enow, but they forbore to Terrify me with Frightful Images of Unforgiving Wrath; speaking to me of Forgiveness alway, rather than of Torment. And once, when I had gotten, through favour of the Keeper, Mr. Drelincourt his book on Death (and had half-frightened myself into fits by reading the Apparition of Mrs. Veal), these good people must needs take it from me, telling me that such strong meat was not fit for Babes, and gave me in its place a pretty little chapbook, called "Joy for Friendly Friends." But that I am old and battered, and black as a Guinea Negro with sins, I would go join the Quakers now. Never mind their broad-brims, and theeing and thouing. I tell you, man, that they have hearts as soft as toast-and-butter, and that they do more good in a day than my Lord Bishop (with his coach-horses, forsooth!) does in a year. And oh, the pleasure of devalising

one of these Proud Prelates, as I—that is, some of my Friends
—have done scores of times!

Nothing would suit the good Shapcotts but that I should
write in mine own hand a Petition to the King's Majesty.
The Magistrates, who now began to take some interest in me,
were for having it drawn up by their Town Clerk, and me
only to put my Mark to it; for they would not give a poor
little Hangdog of a Black any credit of Clergy. But being
told that I could both read and write, after a Fashion, it was
agreed that I was to have myself the scrivening of the Document ; they giving me some Forms and Hints for beginning
and ending, and bidding me con my Bible, and choose such
texts as I thought bore on my Unhappy Condition. And
after Great Endeavours and many painful days, and calling
all my little Scholarship under my Grandmother, the kind
old schoolmistress of Foubert's Passage, Gnawbit (burn him !),
and Captain Night, I succeeded in producing the following.
I give it word for word as I wrote it, having kept a copy ;
but I need not say that, as a Gentleman of Fortune, my
Style and Spelling are not now so Barbarous and Uncouth.

This was my Petition to His Majesty :

"The Humble Pettyshon of Jon Dangerous now a prisinner under
centense off Deth in His Maggesty's Gayle at Alesbury to His
Maggesty Gorge by the grease of God King of Grate Briton
Frans and Eyearland Deffender off the Fathe Showeth That yore
Petetioner which I am Unfortunate cnuff to be mixed up in this
business Me and the others wich have suffered was Cast by the
Jewry and Justis Blackcapp he ses that as a Warming and Egg-
sample i am to be Hanged by the Nek till you are Ded and the
Lord have Mercy upon his Soul Great Sur your Maggesty the
Book ses that wen the wicked man turneth away from his Wickedness wich he have committed and doeth that wich is Lawful and
Rite he shall save his Sole alive   Therefore deer Great Sur wich
a repreive would fall like Thunder upon a Contrite Hart and am
most sorrowful under the Black Act wich it is true I took the
deere but was led to it Deere Sur wich Mungo and others was
repreeved at the Tree and sent to the Plantations but am not
twelve yeeres old And have always been a Prottestant Great Sur
i shall be happy to serve his Maggesty by see or land and if the
Grannydeere he had not Vexed me but had no other way being
in a Korner and all Fiting and so i up with the demmyjon which
i hoap he is better   And your Petishioner will ever pray your
Maggesty's loving Subject and Servant

JON DANGEROUS

My Granmother was a Lady of Quality and lived in her own
House in Hannover Squair and was used after her Deth very

cruelly by one Mistress Tallmash and Kadwalladcr which was the
Stoard and was sent in a Waggin like a Beggar   Deere Sur Mr.
Gnawbit he used me shameful wich I was Blak and Blue and the
Old Gentleman he ses you Run away ses he into Charwood chaise
and join the Blacks   Deere Sur this is All which Captain Nite
would swear but as eloped   I am now lying here many weekes
Deere Sur I shood like to be hanged in Wite for I am Innocent
leastways of meaning to kill the Grannydeere"

This was a Curious kind of Schoolboy letter.   Different I
take it from those one gets from a Brother, asking for a
Crown, a Pony, or a Plumcake.   But my Schools had been
of the hardest, and this was *my* Holiday letter.

When the Mayor read it, he burst out a-laughing, and
says that no such Thieves' Flash must be sent to the Foot of
the Throne.   But Mr. Shapcott told him that he would not
have one word altered; that he would not even strike out
the paragraph where I had been irreverent enough to quote
a Text (and spell it badly) ; and that what I had written, and
naught else, should go to the King.   He took it to London
himself, and His Majesty being much elated by some suc-
cesses in Germany, and the Discovery of a Jacobite Plot, and
moved moreover by the intercession of a Foreign Lady, that
was his Favourite, and who vowed that the little Deer-Stealer's
Petition was Monstrous Droll, and almost as good as a Play,
—His Majesty was graciously pleased to remit my Sentence,
on condition of my transporting myself for life to His Majesty's Plantations in North America.

As to my transporting "myself," that was a Fiction.   I
was henceforth as much a Slave to my own Countrymen as
I was in after days to the Moors.   The Shapcotts would
willingly have provided me with the means of going to the
uttermost ends of the World, but that was not the way the
thing was to be done.   Flesh and Blood were bought and
sold in those days, and it did not much matter about
the colour.   By that strange Laxity which then tempered
the severity of the Laws, I was permitted, for many days
after my Fate was settled, to remain in a kind of semi-En-
largement.   I suppose that Mr. Shapcott gave bail for me;
but I was taken into his Family, and treated with the most
Loving Kindness, till the fearful intelligence came that I,
with two hundred other Convicts, had been "Taken up" for
Transportation by Sir Basil Hopwood, a rich Merchant and
Alderman of London, who paid a certain Sum a head for us

to the King's Government for taking us to America, where he might make what profit he pleased, by selling our wretched Carcasses to be Slaves to the Planters.

Oh, the terrible Parting ! but there was no other Way, and it had to be Endured. My kind friends made me up a packet of Necessaries for the Voyage, and with a Heavy Heart I bade them farewell. These good people are all Dead ; but their woman-servant, Ruth, a pure soul, of great Serenity of Countenance, still lives ; and every Christmas does the Carrier convey for me to Aylesbury a Hamper full of the Good Things of this Life, and Ten Golden Guineas. And I know that this Good and Faithful Servant (who has been well provided for) just touches the Kissing-crust of one of the Pies my Lilias has made for her, and that she goes straight with the rest, Money and Cakes, to the Gaol, and therewith relieves the Debtors (whom Heaven deliver out of their Captivity !). And it is more seemly that she rather than I should do this thing, seeing that there are those who will not believe that after a Hard Life a man can keep a fleshy heart, and who would be apt to dub me Hypocrite if these Doles came from me directly.

CHAPTER THE TENTH.

ON SUNDRY MY ADVENTURES FROM THE TIME OF MY GOING ABROAD UNTIL
MY COMING TO MAN'S ESTATE (WHICH WAS ALL THE ESTATE I HAD).

A STRANGE Nursing-mother—rather a Step-mother of the
Stoniest sort—was this Sir Basil Hopwood, Knight and
Alderman of London, that contracted with the Government
to take us Transports abroad. Sure there never was a man,
on this side the land of Horseleeches, that was so Hungry
after money. Yet was his avarice not of the kind practised
by old Audley, the money-scrivener of the Commonwealth's
time; or Hopkins, the wretch that saved candles' ends and
yet had a thousand wax-lights blazing at his Funeral; or Guy
the Bookseller, that founded the Hospital in Southwark; or
even old John Elwes, Esquire, the admired Miser of these
latter days. Sir Basil Hopwood was the rather of the same
complexion of Entrails with that Signor Volpone whom we
have all seen—at least such of us as be old Boys—in Ben
Jonson's play of the *Fox.* He money-grubbed, and Money-
clutched, and Money-wrung, ay, and in a manner Money-
stole, that he might live largely, and ruffle it among his
brother Cits in surpassing state and splendour. He had been
Lord Mayor; and on his Show-day the Equipments of chivalry had been more Sumptuous, the Banners more varied,
the Entertainment at Saddlers' Hall,—where the Lord Mayor
was wont to hold his Feast before the present Mansion House
was built, the ancient Guildhall in King Street being then
but in an ill condition for banquet,—Hopwood's Entertainment, I say, had been more plentifully provided with Marrow-
bones, Custards, Ruffs and Reeves, Baked Cygnets, Malmsey,
Canary, and Hippocras, than had ever been known since the
days of Sir Robert Clayton, the Merry Mayor, who swore
that King Charles the Second should take t'other bottle.
He was a Parliament man, too, and had a Borough in his
Pocket,—more's the shame,—besides one to serve him as a
cushion to sit on.

This enormously rich man had a fine House in Bishopsgate Street, with as many rogues in blue liveries as a Rotterdam Syndic that has made three good ventures in Java.

When we poor wretches, chained together, had been brought
up in Carts from Aylesbury to London, on our way to be Embarked, nothing would serve this Haughty and Purse-proud
Citizen but that our ragged Regiment must halt before his
peddling Palace ; and there the varlets in blue that attended
upon him brought us out Loaves and Cheese, and Blackjacks
full of two-thread Beer, which, with many disdainful gestures
and uncivil words, they offered to our famished lips.   And
my Lady Hopwood, and the fine Madams her daughters,—all
laced and furbelowed, and with widows' and orphans' tears,
and the blood-drops of crimped seamen and kidnapped children, twinkling in their Stomachers for gems,—were all set at
their Bowery window, a pudding-fed chaplain standing bowing
and smirking behind them, and glozing in their ears no doubt
Praises of their exceeding Charity and Humanity to wretches
such as we were.   But this Charity, Jack, says I to myself,
is not of the Shapcott sort, and is but cast metal after all.
My troth, but we wanted the Bread and Cheese and Swipes :
for we had had neither Bite nor Sup since we left Aylesbury
Gaol seven-and-twenty hours agone.   So, after a while, and
the mob hallooing at us for Gallows-birds, and some Ruffians
about the South-Sea House pelting us with stones,—for Luck,
as they said,—we were had over London Bridge,—where with
dreadful admiration I viewed the Heads and Quarters of
Traitors, all shimmering in the coat of pitch i' the Sun, over
the North Turret,—and were bestowed for the night in the
Borough Clink.   And hither we were pursued by the Alderman's Agents, who straightway began to drive Unholy Bargains with those among us that had Money.   Now 'twas selling them Necessaries for the voyage at exorbitant rates ; or
promising them, for cash in hand, to deliver them Luxuries,
such as Tobacco, playing-cards, and strong waters, at the
Port of Embarkation.   Now 'twas substituting Light for
Heavy Fetters, if the Heaviness could be Assuaged by Gold ;
and sometimes even negotiations were carried so far as for
the convicted persons to give Drafts of Exchange, to be
honoured by their Agents in London, so soon as word came
from the Plantations that they had been placed in Tolerable
Servitude, instead of Agonising Slavery.   For although there
was then, as there is now, a convenient Fiction that a Felon's
goods became at once forfeit to the Crown, I never yet knew
a Felon (and I have known many) that felt ever so little

difficulty in keeping his property, if he had any, and disposing of it according to his own Good Will and Pleasure.

The Head Gaoler of the Borough Clink—I know not how his Proper official title ran—was a colonel in the Foot Guards, who lived in Jermyn Street, St. James's, and transacted most of his High and Mighty business either at Poingdestre's Ordinary in St. Alban's Place, or at White's Chocolate House, to say naught of the Row, or the Key in Chandos Street. Much, truly, did he concern himself about his unhappy Captives. His place was a Patent one, and was worth to him about Fifteen Hundred a year, at which sum it was farmed by Sir Basil Hopwood; who, in his turn, on the principle that "'tis scurvy money that won't stick to your fingers," underlet the place to a company of Four Rogues, who gave him Two Thousand for it, which they managed to swell into at least Three for themselves by squeezing of Poor Prisoners, and the like crying Injustices. 'Twas Aylesbury Gaol over again, with the newest improvements and the Humours of the Town added to it. So, when Sir Basil Hopwood took up a cargo of cast persons for Transportation, his underlings of the Borough Clink were only too glad to harbour them for a night or two, making a pretty profit out of the poor creatures. For all which, I doubt it not, Sir Basil Hopwood and his scoundrelly Myrmidons are, at this instant moment, Howling.

This place was a prison for Debtors as well as Criminals, and was to the full as Foul as the Tophet-pit at Aylesbury yonder. I had not been there half an hour before a Lively companion of a Gentleman Cutpurse, with a wrench at my kerchief, a twist at my arm (which nearly Broke it in twain), and a smart Blow under my Lower Jaw, robs me of the packet of comforts (clothing, pressed beef, sugar, comfits, and the like) which my kind friends at Aylesbury had given me. The Rascal comes to me a few minutes afterwards with a packet of Soap and a Testament, which he had taken from my Bundle, and returns them to me with a Grin, telling me that it was long since his Body had felt need of the one or his Soul of the other. And yet I think they would have profited considerably (pending a Right Cord) by the application of Both. So I in a corner, to moan and whimper at my Distressed condition.

A sad Sunday I spent in the Clink,—'twas on the Monday

we were to start,—although, to some other of my companions, the Time passed jovially enough. For very many of the Relations and Friends of the Detained Persons came to visit them, bringing them money, victuals, clothing, and other Refreshments. 'Twas on this day I heard that one of us, who was cast for Forgery, had been offered a Free Pardon if he could lodge Five Hundred Pounds in the hands of a Person who had Great Influence near a Great Man.

Late on the Sunday afternoon, Sir Basil Hopwood came down in his coach, and with his chaplain attendant on him. We Convicts were all had to the Grate, for the Knight and Alderman would not venture further in, for fear of the Gaol Fever; and he makes us a Fine Speech about the King's Mercy,—which I deny not,—and his own Infinite Goodness in providing for us in a Foreign Land. The which I question. Then he told us how we were to be very civil and obedient on the voyage to those who were set over us, refraining from cursing, swearing, gaming, or singing of profane songs, on pain of immediate and smart chastisement; and having said this, and the chaplain having given us his Benediction, he gat him gone, and we were rid of so much Rapacious and Luxurious Hypocrisy. We lay in the yard that night, wrapped in such extra Garments as some of us were Fortunate enough to have; and I sobbed myself to sleep, wishing, I well remember, that it might never be Day again, but that my Sorrows might all be closed in by the Merciful Curtain of Eternal Night.

So on the Monday morning we were driven down—a body of Sir Basil Hopwood's own company of the Trainbands guarding us—to Shayler's Stairs, near unto the church of St. Mary Overy; and there—we were in number about a hundred —put on board a Hoy, which straightway, the tide being toward, bore down the river for Gravesend.

By this time I found that, almost insensibly, as it were, I had become separated from my old companions, the Blacks, and that I was more than ever Alone. The greatest likelihood is, that Authority deemed it advisable to break up, for good and all, the Formidable Confederacy they had laid hold of, and to prevent those Dangerous Men from ever again making Head together. But my whole Life was but a kind of Shifting and uncertain Vision, and I took little note of the personages with whom I came in contact, till looking around

me, in a dull listlessness about the Hoy, I found myself,
cheek by jowl, with a motley crew, seemingly picked up hap-
hazard from all the gaols in England. But 'twas all one to
me, and I did not much care. Such a Stupor of Misery
came over me, that for a time I almost forgot my good
Quaker Friends, and the lessons they had taught me; that I
felt myself once more drifting into being a Dangerous little
brute; and that seeing the Master of the Hoy, a thirsty-
looking man, lifting a great stone-bottle to his lips, I longed
to serve him as I had served Corporal Foss with the demijohn
of Brandy in the upper chamber of the Stag o' Tyne.

We landed not at Gravesend, but were forthwith removed
to a bark called *The Humane Hopwood*, in compliment, I
suppose, to Sir Basil, and which, after lying three days in
the Downs, put into Deal to complete her complement of
Unfortunate Persons. And I remember that, before making
Deal, we saw a stranded Brig on the Goodwins, which was
said to be a Leghorner, very rich with oil and silks; round
which were gathered,—just as you may see obscene Birds of
Prey gathered round a dead carcass, and picking the Flesh
from its bones,—at least a score of luggers belonging to the
Deal Boatmen. These worthies had knocked holes in the
hull of the wreck, and were busily hauling out packages and
casks into their craft, coming to blows sometimes with axes
and marlin-spikes as to who should have the Biggest Booty.
And it was said on Board that they would not unfrequently
decoy by false signals, or positively haul, a vessel in distress
on to those same Goodwins,—in whose fatal depths so many
tall Ships lie Engulfed,—in order to have the Plunder of her,
which was more profitable than the Salvage, that being in the
long-run mostly swallowed up by the Crimps and Longshore
Lawyers of Deal and other Ports, who were wont to buy
the Boatmen's rights at a Ruinous Discount. Salvage Men,
indeed, these Boatmen might well be called; for when I was
young it was their manner to act with an extreme of Savage
Barbarity, thinking far less of saving Human Life than of
clutching at the waifs and strays of a Rich Cargo. And then
up would sheer a Custom-House cutter or Revenue Pink, the
skipper and his crew fierce in their Defence of the Laws of
the Land, the Admiralty Droits, and their own twentieths;
and from Hard blows with fists and spikes, matters would
often come to the arbitrament of cutlasses and firearms; so

that Naval Engagements of a Miniature kind have often raged between the Deal Boatmen and the King's Officers. Surely the world was a Hard and a Cruel and a Brutal one, when I was young—bating the Poor-Laws, which were tenderer than now; for now that I am old the Gazettes are full of the Tender Valour and Merciful Devotion of the Deal Boatmen, who, in the most tempestuous weather, will leave their warm beds, their wives and bairns, and put off, with the Sea running mountains high, to rescue Distraught Vessels and the Precious Lives that are within them. The Salvage Men of my time were brave enough, but they were likewise unconscionable rogues.

The wind proved false to us at Deal, and we had to wait a weary ten days there. Captain Handsell was our commander. He was a man who knew but one course of proceeding. 'Twas always a word and a blow with him. By the same token the blow generally came first, and the word that followed was sure to be a bad one. The Captain of a Ship, from a Fishing Smack to a Three-Decker, was in those days a cruel and merciless Despot. 'Twas only the size of his ship and the number of his Equipage that decided the question whether he was to be a Petty Tyrant or a Tremendous One. His Empire was as undisputed as that of a Schoolmaster. Who was to gainsay him? To whom, at Sea, could his victims appeal? To the Sharks and Grampuses, the Dolphins and the Bonettas? He was privileged to beat, to fetter, to starve, to kick, to curse his Seamen. Even his Passengers trembled at the sight of this Bashaw of Bluewater; for he had Irons and Rations of Mouldy Biscuit for them too, if they offended him; and many a Beautiful and Haughty Lady, paying full cabin-passage, has bowed down before the wrath of a vulgar Skipper, who, at home, she would have thought unworthy to Black her Shoes, and who would be seething in the revelry of a Tavern in Rotherhithe, while she would be footing it in the Saloons of St. James's. Yet for a little time, at the outset of his voyage, the Skipper had his superior; the Bashaw had a Vizier who was bigger than he. There was a Terrible Man called the Pilot. He cared no more for the Captain than the Archbishop of Canterbury cares for a Charity-Boy. He gave him a piece of his Mind whenever he chose, and he would have his own Way, and had it. It was the delight of the Seamen to see their Tyrant and Bully degraded for a time under the supreme authority of the Pilot, who drank the Skipper's rum; who had the best Beef and Burgoo at the Skipper's table; who wore, if he was so minded, the Skipper's tarpaulin; who used the Skipper's telescope, and thumbed his charts, and kicked his Cabin-boy, and swore his oaths, till, but for the fear of the Trinity House, I think the Skipper would have been mighty glad to fling him over the taffrail. But the reign of this Great Mogul of Lights and Points and Creeks soon came to an end. A River Pilot was the lesser evil, a Channel Pilot was the greater one; but both were got rid of at last. Then the Skipper was himself again. He would drink himself blind with Punch in the forenoon, or cob his cabin-boy to Death's door after dinner for a frolic. He could play the very Devil among the Hands, and they perforce bore with his capricious cruelty; for there is no running away from a Ship at Sea. Jack Shark is Gaoler, and keeps the door tight. There is but one way out of it, and that is to Mutiny, and hey for the Black Flag and a Pirate's Free and Jovial Life!* But Mutiny is Hanging, and Piracy is Hanging, and Gibbeting too; and how seldom it is that you find Bold Hearts who have Stuff enough in them to run the great risk! As on sea, so it is on land. That Ugly Halter dances before a man's eyes, and dazes him away from the Firmest Resolve. For how long will Schoolboys endure the hideous Enormities of a Gnawbit before they come to the Supreme Revolt of a Barring-out! And for how long will a People suffer the mad tyranny of a Ruler, who outrages their Laws, who strangles their Liberties, who fleeces and squeezes and tramples upon them, before they take Heart of Grace, and up Pike and Musket, and down-derry-down with your Ruler, who is ordinarily the basest of Poltroons, and runs away in a fright so soon as the first Goose is bold enough to cry out that the Capitol *shall* be saved!

Nothing of this did I think aboard *The Humane Hopwood*. I was too young to have any thought at all, save of rage and anguish when it pleased Captain Handsell, being in a cheerful mood, to belabour me, till I was black and blue, with a rope's end. At the beginning of the voyage I was put into the hold, ironed, with the rest of the convicts, who

---

* Captain Dangerous! Captain Dangerous!—Ed.

were only permitted to come on deck twice a day, morning
and evening, for a few Mouthfuls of Fresh air; who were fed
on the vilest biscuit and the most putrid water, getting but a
scrap of fat pork and a dram of Rum that was like Fire twice
a week, and who were treated, generally, much like Negroes
on the Middle Passage. But by and by,—say after ten days;
but I took little account of Time in this floating Purgatory,
—Captain Handsell has me unironed; and his cabin-boy, a
poor weakly little lad, that could not stand much beating,
being dead of that and a flux, and so thrown overboard without any more words being said about it—(he was but a little
Scottish castaway from Edinburgh, who had been kidnapped
late one night in the Grass Market, and sold to a Greenock
skipper trading in that line for a hundred pound Scots—not
above eight pounds of our currency)—and there is no Crowner's Quest at sea, I was promoted to the Vacant Post. I was
Strong enough now, and the Wound in my arm gave me no
more pain; and I think I grew daily stronger and more
hardened under the shower of blows which the Skipper very
liberally dealt out to me; I hardly know with more plenitude
when he was vexed, or when he was pleased. But I was not
the same bleating little Lamb that the wolfish Gnawbit used
to torture. No, no; John Dangerous's apprenticeship had
been useful to him. Even as college-lads graduate in their
Latin and Greek, so I had graduated upon braining the
Grenadier with the demijohn. I could take kicks and cuffs,
but I could likewise give them. And so, as this Roaring
Skipper made me a Block to vent his spite upon, I would
struggle with, and bite, and kick his shins till sometimes
we managed to fall together on the cabin-floor and tumble
about there,—pull he, pull I, and a kick together!—till the
Watch would look down the skylight upon us, grinning,
and chuckle hoarsely that old Belzey, as they called their
commander (being a diminutive for Beelzebub), and his
young Imp were having a tussle. Thus it came about that
among these unthinking Seamen I grew to be called Pug
(who, I have heard, is the Lesser Fiend), or Little Brimstone,
or young Pitch-ladle. And then I, in my Impish way,
would offer to fight them too, resenting their scurril nick-
names, and telling them that I had but one name, which was
Jack Dangerous.

The oddest thing in the world was that the Skipper,

Ungovernable Brute as he was, seemed to take a kind of
liking for me through my Resistance to him.

"What a young Tiger-cub it is!" he would say sometimes, swaying about his Rope's End, as if undecided whether to hit me or not. "Lie down, Rawbones! Lie down,
Tearem!"

"You go to hit me again," I would cry, all hot and
flurried; "I'll mark you, I will, you Tarpaulin Hedgehog!"

Then in a Rage he would make a Rush at me, and Welt
me sorely; but oftener he would Relent, and opening his
Locker would give me a slice of Sausage, or a white Biscuit,
or a nip of curious Nantz.

At last he gave up maltreating me altogether. "If you'd
been of the same kidney as Sawney M'Gillicuddy," he said,
speaking of the poor little Scottish lad who Died, "I'd have
made you food for fishes long ago. 'Slid, my younker, but
they should 'a had their meat tender enough, or there's no
vartue in hackled hemp for a lacing! But you've got a
Heart, my lad; and if you're not hanged before you're out of
your Teens, you'll show the World that you can Bite as well
as Bark some of these days."

So I became a prime Favourite with Captain Handsell;
and, in the Expansion of his Liking towards me, he began to
give me instruction in the vocation in which a portion of my
life has since (with no small distinction, though I say it that
should not) been passed. Of scientific Navigation this very
Rude and Boorish person knew little, if any thing; but as a
Practical Seaman he had much skill and experience. Indeed, if the Hands had not enjoyed a lively Faith in the
solid sea-going Qualities of "Foul-Weather Bob," as they
called him when they did not choose to give him his de-
moniacal appellation, they would have Mutinied, and sent
him, Lashed to a grating, on a voyage of Discovery at least
twice in every Twenty-Four Hours. For he lead them a
most Fearful Life.

I had imparted to him that I was somewhat of a scholar,
and that Captain Night had taught me something besides
stealing the King's Deer. There was a Bible on Board,
which the Skipper never read,—and read, indeed, he was
scarcely able to do,—but which he turned to the unseemly
use, when he had been over-cruel to his crew, of swearing
them upon it, that they would not inform against him when

they got into port. For this was an odd medley of a man, and had his moments of Remorse for evil-doing, or else of Fear as to what might be the Consequences when he reached a Land where some degree of Law and Justice were recognised. At some times he would propitiate his crew with donatives of Rum, or even of Money; but the next day he would have his Cruelty Fit on again, and use his men with ten times more Fierceness and Arbitrary Barbarity. But to this Bible and a volume of Nautical Tables our Library was confined; and as he troubled himself very little about the latter, I was set to read to him sometimes after dinner from the Good Book. But he was ever coarse and ungovernable, and would have no Righteous Doctrine or Tender Precepts, but only took delight when I read to him from the Old Scriptures the stories of the Jews, their bloody wars, and how their captains and men of war slew their Thousands and Tens of Thousands in Battle. And with shame I own that 'twas these Furious Narratives that I liked also; and with exceeding pleasure read of Joshua his victories, and Samson his achievements, and Gideon how he battled, and Agag how they hewed him to pieces. Little cockering books I see now put forth, with pretty decoying pictures, which little children are bidden to read. Stories from the Old Testament are dressed up in pretty sugared language. Oh, you makers of these little books! oh, you fond mothers who place them so deftly in your children's hands! bethink you whether this strong meat is fit for Babes. An old Man, whose life has been passed in Storms and Stratagems and Violence, not innocent of blood-spilling, bids you beware! Let the children read that other Book, its Sweet and Tender Counsels, its examples of Mercy and Love to all Mankind. But if I had a child five or six years old, would I let him fill himself with the horrible chronicles of Lust, and Spoliation, and Hatred, and Murder, and Revenge? " Why shouldn't I torture the cat?" asks little Tommy. " Didn't the man in the Good Book tie blazing Torches to the foxes' tails?" And little Tommy has some show of reason on his side. Let the children grow up; wait till their stomachs are strong enough to digest this potent victual. It is hard indeed for one who has been a Protestant alway to have to confess that when such indiscreet reading is placed in children's hands, those crafty Romish ecclesiastics speak not altogether foolishly when they tell us that the mere Word slayeth. But on this point I am agreed to consult Doctor Dubiety, and to be bound by his decision.

In so reading to the Skipper every day, I did not forget to exercise myself in that other art of Writing, and was in time serviceable enough to be able to keep, in something like a rational and legible form, the Log of *The Humane Hopwood*, which heretofore had been a kind of cabalistic Register, full of blots, crosses, half-moons, and zigzags, like the chalk score of an unlettered Ale-wife. And the more I read (of surely the grandest and simplest language in the world), the more I discovered how ignorant I was of that essential art of Spelling, and blushed at the vile manner in which the Petition I had written to the King of England was set down. And before we came to our voyage's end, I had made a noticeable improvement in the Curious Mystery of writing Plain English.

One day as the Skipper was taking Tobacco (for he was a great Smoker), he said to me, "Jack, do you know what you are, lad?"

"Your cabin-boy," I answered; "bound to fetch and carry: hempen wages, and not much better treated than a dog."

"You lie, you scum," Captain Handsell answered pleasantly. "You go snacks with me in the very best, and your beef is boiled in my own copper. But 'tisn't that I mean. Do you know how you hail on the World's books? what the number of your mess in Life is?"

"Yes," I replied; "I'm a Transport. Was to have been hanged; but I wrote out a Petition, and the Gentlemen in London gave it to the King, God bless him!"

"Vastly well, mate!" continued the Captain. "Do you know what a Transport is?"

"No; something very bad, I suppose; though I don't see that he can be much worse off than a cabin-boy that's been cast for Death, and lain in gaol with a bayonet-wound he got from a Grenadier,—let alone having been among the Blacks, and paid anigh to Death by Gnawbit,—when he was born a Gentleman."

"You lie again. To be a Transport is worse than aught you've had. Why, a cat in a furnace without claws is an Angel of bliss along of a Transport! You're living in a land of beans and bacon now, in a land of milk and honey and

new rum. Wait till you get to Jamaica. The hundred and
odd vagabonds that I've got aboard will be given over to the
Sheriff at Port Royal, and he'll sell 'em by auction; and for
as long as they're sent across the herring-pond they'll be
slaves, and worse than slaves, to the planters; for the black
Niggers themselves, rot 'em! make a mock of a Newgate
bird. Hard work in the blazing sun, scarce enough to eat to
keep body and soul together, the cat-o'-nine-tails every day,
with the cow-hide for a change; and, when your term's out,
not a Joe in your pocket to help you to get back to your own
country again. That's the life of a Transport, my hearty.
Why, it's worse cheer than one of my own hands gets here on
shipboard!"

"I think I'd rather be hanged," I said, with something
like a Trembling come over me at the Picture the Skipper had
drawn.

"I should rather think you would; but such isn't your
luck, little Jack Dangerous. What would you say if I was
to tell you that you ain't a Transport at all?"

I stammered out something, I know not what, but could
make no substantial reply.

"Not a bit of it," continued Captain Handsell, who by
this time was getting somewhat Brisk with his afternoon's
Punch. "Hang it, who's afraid? I like thee, lad. I'm off
my bargain, and don't care a salt herring if I'm a loser by
a few broad pieces in not sticking to it. I tell thee, Jack,
thou'rt Free, as Free as I am; leastways if we get to Jamaica
without going to Davy Jones's Locker; for on blue water no
man can say he's Free. No; not the Skipper even."

And then he told me, to my exceeding Amazement and
Delight, of what an Iniquitous Transaction I had very nearly
been made the victim. It seems that although the Pardon
granted me after the Petition I had sent to his Majesty was
conditional on my transporting myself to the Plantations,
further influence had been made for me in London,—by
whom I knew not then, but I have since discovered,—and
on the very Day of the arrival of our condemned crew in
London, an Entire and Free Pardon had been issued for
John Dangerous, and lodged in the hands of Sir Basil Hopwood at his House in Bishopsgate Street. Along with this
merciful Document there came a letter from one of his Majesty's principal Secretaries of State, in which directions were

given that I was to be delivered over to a person who was my Guardian. And that I was in no danger of being again given up to the villains Cadwallader and Talmash, or their Instrument Gnawbit, was clear, I think, from what Captain Handsell told me :—That the Person bringing the letter—the Pardon itself being in the hands of a King's Messenger—had the appearance, although dressed in a lay habit, of being a Foreign Ecclesiastic. The crafty Extortioner of a Knight and Alderman makes answer that I had not come with the other Transports to London, but had been left sick at Brentford, in the care of an agent of his there ; but he entreats the Foreign Person to go visit Newgate, where he had another gang of unhappy persons for Transportation, and see if I had arrived. And all this while the wretch knew that I was safely clapped up in the yard of the Borough Clink. And the Foreign Person being met at the Old Bailey by one of Hopwood's creatures, this Thing takes him to walk on the leads of the Session House, praying him not to enter the gaol, where many had lately been stricken with the Distemper, and by and by up comes a Messenger all hot as it seemed with express riding,—though his sweat and dust were all Forged,— and says that a gang of Ruffians have broken up the Cage of Brentford, where, for greater safety, the Boy Dangerous had been bestowed ; that these Ruffians were supposed to be the remnant of the Blacks of Charlwood Chase who had escaped from capture ; and that they had stolen away the Boy Dangerous, and made clear off with him. And, indeed, it was a curious circumstance that Brentford Cage was that day broken into (the Times were very Lawless), and a Strange Boy taken out therefrom. But Hopwood had artfully separated me from the Blacks who were in Newgate, and placed me among a stranger mob of riffraff in the Borough Clink. The Newgate Gang were in due time taken, not to Gravesend, but straight away from the Pool to Richmond in Virginia ; whereas I was conveyed to Gravesend and Deal, and shipped off to Jamaica in *The Humane Hopwood.* And what do you think was the object of this Humane Scoundrel in thus sequestrating the King's Pardon and robbing me of my liberty, and perhaps of the occasion of returning to the state of a Gentleman, in which I was Born? 'Twas simply to kidnap me, and make a wretched profit of twenty or thirty pounds,—the Commander of his Ship going him half in the adventure,—by selling me in the West Indies, where white boys not being Transports were then much in demand, to be brought up as clerks and cash-keepers to the Planters. Sure there was never such a Diabolical Plot for so sorry an end; but a vast number of paltry conspiracies, carried out with Infernal Cunning and Ingenuity, had made, in the course of years, Sir Basil Hopwood rich and mighty, a Knight and Alderman, Parliament man and ex-Lord Mayor. To carry out these designs was just part of the ordinary calling of a Ship-master in those days. 'Twas looked upon as the simplest matter of business in the world. To kidnap a child was such an every-day deed of devilry, that the slightest amount of pains was deemed sufficing to conceal the abominable thing. And thus the Foreign Person saw with dolorous Eyes the convoy of convicts take their departure from Newgate to ship on board the Virginian vessel at St. Katherine's Stairs, while poor little Jack Dangerous was being smuggled away from Gravesend to Jamaica.

And to Jamaica I should have gone to be sold as a Slave, but for the strange occurrence of the Captain taking a liking to me. He dared not have kept me among the convicts, as the Sheriff at Port Royal would have had a List in Duplicate of their names sent out by a fast-sailing King's Ship; for the Government at Home had some faint Suspicion of the prevailing custom of Kidnapping, and made some Feeble Attempts to stop it. But he would have kept me on board as a shipboy till the Auction of the Transports was over, and then he would have coolly sold me, for as much as I would fetch, to some Merchant of Kingston or Port Royal, who was used to deal in flesh and blood, and who, in due course, would have transferred me, at a profit, to some up-country planter.

"But that shall never be, Jack my hearty," Captain Handsell exclaimed, when, after many more pipes of Tobacco and rummers of Punch, he had explained these wonderful things to me. "I shall lose my half share in the venture, and shall have to tell a game lie to yonder old Skin-a-flea-for-the-hide-and-fat in London; but what o' that? I tell thee I won't have the sale of thy flesh and blood on my conscience. No slave shall you be, forsooth. I have an aunt at Kingston, as honest a woman as ever broke biscuit, although she has got a dash of the tar-brush on her mug, and she shall take charge of thee; and if thou wert a gentleman born, I'll be hanged if thou sha'n't be a gentleman bred."

It would have been more fitted to the performance of this Honourable and Upright Action towards one that he had no motive at all in serving (in Fact. his Interest lay right the other way), that I should be able to chronicle a sensible Reformation in my Commander's bearing and conduct towards others ; but, alas, that I am unable to do ; the truth being that he continued, unto the very end of our voyage, to be towards the Hands the same brutal and merciless Tyrant that he had once, in the days of his Rope's-End Discipline, been towards me. 'Twas Punch and Cobbing, Tobacco and Ugly Words, from the rising of the Sun until the setting of the same. And for this reason it is (having seen so many Contradictions in Human character) that I am never surprised to hear of a Good Action on the part of a very Bad Man, or of a Bad Action done by him who is ordinarily accounted a very Good one.

The Humane Hopwood was a very bad Sailer,—being. in truth, as Leaky an old Tub as ever escaped breaking-up for Fire-Wood at Lumberers' Wharfs,—and we were seven weeks at Sea before we fell in with a trade-wind, and then setting every Rag we could hoist, went gaily before that Favourable breeze, and so cast anchor at Port Royal in the island of Jamaica.

Captain Handsell was as good as his word. Not a syllable did he say to the Sheriff of Kingston about my not being a Transport, or being, indeed, in the Flesh at all in those parts ; for he argued that the Sheriff might have some foregatherings with the Knight and Alderman of Bishopsgate Street by correspondence, and that the Wealthy Extortioner might make use of his credit in the Sugar Islands to do me. some day or another, an ill turn. But he had me privily on shore when the Transports had all been assigned to different task-masters ; and in due time he introduced me to his Aunt, his Brother's Wife indeed (and I believe he had come out to the Island with an Old-Bailey Passport ; but Rum and the climate had been too strong for him, and he had so Died and left her a Widow).

She was by right and title, then, Mistress Handsell, with the Christian name of Sarah ; but among the coloured people of Kingston she went by the name of Maum Buckey, and, among her more immediate intimates, as "Yaller Sally." And, although she passed for being very Wealthy, I declare that she was nothing but a Washerwoman. This Washing Trade of hers, however, which she carried on for the King and Merchants' ships that were in Harbour, and for nearly all the rich Merchants and Traders of Kingston, brought Maum Buckey in a very pretty penny ; and not only was her tub commerce a brisk ready-money business, but she had two flourishing plantations—one for the growing of Coffee, and the other of Sugar—near the town of Savannah de la Mar. Moreover, she had a distillery of Rum and Arrack in Kingston itself, and every body agreed that she must be very well to do in the world. She was an immensely fat old Mulatto woman, on the wrong side of Fifty when I knew her, and her Mother had been a slave that had been the Favourite House-keeper to the English Governor, who, dying, left her her Freedom, and enough Money to carry on that Trade of cleansing clothes which her Daughter afterwards made so profitable.

Maum Buckey and I speedily became very good friends. She was proud of her relationship with a white Englishman —a right go-down Buckra as she called him—who commanded a ship, and besides recommended her to other gentlemen in his way for a Washerwoman ; and although she took care to inform me, before we had been twenty-four hours acquainted, that her Husband, Sam Handsell, had been a sad Rascal, who would have drunk all her Money away, had he not Timeously drunk himself to death, she made me the friend-liest welcome, and promised that she would do all she could for me, "the little piccaninny buckra," who was set down by Mr. Handsell as being the son of an old Shipmate of his that had met with misfortunes. After a six-weeks' stay in the island, and *The Humane Hopwood* getting Freight in the way of Sugar, Captain Handsell bade me good-by, and set sail with a fair wind for Bristol, England. I never set Eyes upon him again. You see, my Friends, that this is no cunningly-spun Romance, in which a character disappears for a Season, and turns up again, as pat as you please, at the end of the Fourth Volume ; but a plain Narrative of Facts, in which the Personages introduced must needs Come and Go precisely as they Came and Went to me in Real Life. I have often wished, when I had Power and Riches, to meet

with and show my Gratitude to the rough old Sea-Porpoise
that used to Rope's-End me so, and was so tearing a Tyrant
to his Hands, and yet in a mere fit of kind-heartedness played
the Honest Man to me, when All Things seemed against
me, and rescued John Dangerous from a Foul and Wicked
Trap.

Maum Buckey had a great rambling house—it had but
one Storey, with a Piazza running round, but a huge number
of Rooms and Yards—in the suburbs of Kingston.   There
did I take up my abode.   She had at least twenty Negro
and Mulotter Women and Girls that worked for her at the
Washing, and at Starching and Ironing, for the Mill was
always going with her.   'Twas wash, wash, wash, and wring,
wring, wring, and scrub, scrub, scrub, all day and all night
too, when the harbour was full of ships.   Not that she ever
touched Soapsuds or Flat-iron or Goffering-stick herself.   She
was vastly too much of a Fine Lady for that, and would loll
about in a great chair,—one Negro child fanning her with
a great Palmetto, and another tickling the soles of her feet,—
sipping her Sangaree as daintily as you please.   She was the
most ignorant old creature that ever was known, could neither
read nor write, and made a sad jumble of the King's English
when she spoke ; yet, by mere natural quickness and rule-
of-thumb, she could calculate to a Joe how much a Ship-
master's Washing-Bill came to.   And when she had settled
that according to her Scale of Charges, which were of the
most Exorbitant Kind, she would Grin and say, " He dam
ship, good consignee ;" or, " He dam ship, dam rich owner ;
stick him on 'nother dam fi' poun' English, my chile ;" and
for some curious reason or another, 'twas seldom that a ship-
master cared to quarrel with Maum Buckey's Washing-Bills.
She, being so unlettered, had been compelled to engage all
manner of Whites who could write and read—now Transports, now Free—to keep her accounts, and draw her necessary writings ; but it was hard to tell which were the greatest
Rogues, the Convicts whose term was out, or the Free Gentlemen who had come out without a pair of iron garters to
their hose.   In those days all our plantations, and Jamaica
most notably, were full of the very Scum and Riffraff of our
English towns.   'Twas as though you had let Fleet Ditch,
dead dogs and all, loose on a West-India Island.   That
Ragged Regiment which Falstaff in the Play would not

march through Coventry with were at free quarters in Jamaica, leave alone the regular garrison of King's Troops, of which the private men were mostly pickpockets, poachers, and runaway serving-men, who had enlisted to save themselves from a merry-go-round at Rope Fair; and the officers the worst and most deboshed Gentlemen that ever wore his Majesty's cockade, and gave themselves airs because they had three-quarters of a yard of black ribbon crinked up in their hats. Captain This, who had been kicked out of a Charing-Cross coffee-house for pocketing a Punch-ladle while the drawer was not looking; Lieutenant That, who had been caned on the Mall for cheating at cards; and Ensign 'Tother, who had been my lord's valet, and married his Madam for enough cash to buy a pair of colours withal. Military gentlemen of this feather used to serve in the West Indies in those days, and swagger about Kingston as proud as peacocks, when every one of them had done that at home they should be cashiered for. Maum Buckey would not have to do with these light-come-light-go gallants. "Me wash for Gem'n Ship-Cap'n, Gem'n Marchant, Gem'n Keep-store," she would observe; "me not wash for dam Soger-officer."

Her Sugar Plantation was in charge of a shrewd North-countryman, against whom, save that he was a runaway bankrupt from Hull in England, there was nothing to say. Her Coffee Estate was managed by an Irishman that had married, as he thought, a great Fortune, but found the day after his wedding that she was but a fortune-hunter like himself, and had at least three husbands living in divers parts of the world. And finally, the Distillery had for overseer one, an Englishman, that had been a Horse Couper, and a runner for the Crimps at Wapping, and a supercargo that was not too honest,—albeit he had to keep his accounts pretty square with Maum Buckey, than whom there never was a woman who had a keener Eye for business or a finer Scent for a Rogue.

She made me her Bookkeeper for the Washing Department. 'Twas not a very dignified Employment for one that had been a young Gentleman, but 'twas vastly better than the Fate of one who, but for a mere Accident, might have been a young Slave. So I kept Maum Buckey's Books, teaching myself how to do so featly from a Ready Reckoner and Accomptant's Assistant (Mr. Cocker's), which I bought at a Bookstore in Kingston. The work was pretty hard, and the old Dame of the Tub kept me tightly enough at it ; but when work was over she was very kind to me, and we had the very best of living : ducks and geese and turkeys and pork (of which the Mulotter women are inordinately fond, although I never could reconcile to myself how their stomachs, in so hot a climate, could endure so Luscious a Food); fish of the primest from the Harbour of Port Royal, lobsters and crabs and turtle (which is as cheap as Tripe with us, and so plentiful, that the Niggers will sometimes disdain to eat it, though 'tis excellent served as soup in the creature's own shell, and a most digestible Viand); to say nothing of bananas, shaddock, mango, plantains, and the many delicious fruits and vegetables of that Fertile Colony ; where, if the land-breeze in the morning did not half choke you with harsh dust, and the sea-breeze in the afternoon pierce you to the marrow with deadly chills, and if one could abstain from surfeits of fruits and over-drinking of the too abundant ardent spirits of the country, a man might live a very jovial kind of life. However, I was young and healthy, and, though never a shirk of my glass in after-day, prudently moderate in my Potations. During four years that I passed in the island of Jamaica (one of the brightest jewels in the British Crown, and as Loyal, I delight to say, as I am myself), I don't think I had the Yellow Fever more than three times, and at last grew as tough as leather, and could say Bo to a land-crab (how many a White Man's carcass have those crabs picked clean at the Palisadoes !), as though I feared him no more than a Green Goose.

It may be fitting here that I should say something about that Abominable Curse of Negro Slavery, which was then so Familiar and Unquestioned a Thing in all our Colonies, that its innate and Detestable Wickedness was scarcely taken into account in men's minds. Speaking only by the Card, and of that which I saw with my own eyes, I don't think that Maum Buckey was any crueller than other slave-owners of her class ; for 'tis well known that the Mulotter women are far more severe task-mistresses than the Whites. But, Lord, Whites and coloured people, who in the West Indies are permitted, when free, to own their fellow-creatures who are only a shade darker in colour than they, left little to choose betwixt on the score of cruelty. When I tell you that I

have seen Slave Women and Girls chained to the washing-
tub, their naked bodies all one gore of blood from the lashes
of the whip; that on the public wharf at Kingston I have
seen a Negro man drawn up by his hands to a crane used
for lifting merchandise, while his toes, that barely touched
the ground, were ballasted with a thirty-pound weight, and,
in that Trim, beaten with the Raw Hide or with Tamarind-
Bushes till you could lay your two fingers in the furrows
made by the whip (with which expert Scourgineers boast
they can lay deep ruts in a Deal Board), or else I have seen
the poor Miserable Wretch the next day lying on his face on
the Beach, and a Comrade taking the prickles of the Tama-
rind Stubs, which are tempered in the Fire, and far worse
than English Thornbushes, out of his back;—you may
imagine that 'twas no milk-and-water Regiment that the
slaves in the West Indies had to undergo at the hands of
their Hard masters and mistresses. Also, I have known
slaves taken to the Sick-House or Hospital, so dreadfully
mangled with unmerciful correction as for their wounds to be
one mass of putrefaction, and they shortly do give up the
Ghost; while, at other times, I have seen unfortunate creatures that had been so lacerated, both back and front, as to
be obliged to crawl about on All Fours. Likewise have I
seen Negro men, Negro women, yea, and Negro children,
with iron collars and prongs about their necks; with logs
riveted to their legs, with their Ears torn off, their Nostrils
slit, their Cheeks branded, and otherwise most frightfully
Mutilated. Item, I have known at the dinner-table of a
Planter of wealth and repute, the Jumper, or Public Flogger,
to come in and ask if Master and Missee had any commands
for him; and, by the order of the Lady of the House, take
out two Decent Women that had been waiting at Table, and
give them fifty lashes apiece on the public parade, every
stroke drawing Blood and bringing Flesh with it, and they,
when all was over, embracing and thanking him for their
Punishment, as was the custom of the Colony.* Item, within my own knowledge have I been made familiar with many

* That which I have made Captain Dangerous relate in fiction
will be found narrated, act for act, and nearly word for word, in the
very unromantic evidence given before the first parliamentary committee on slavery and the slave-trade moved for by Mr. Clarkson.—
ED.

acts of the Deepest Barbarity. Mistresses, for Jealousy or Caprice, pouring boiling-water or hot melted Sealing-Wax on their slave-girls' flesh after they have suffered the worst Tortures of the whip; and white Ladies of Education rubbing Cayenne-pepper into the eyes of Negroes who had offended them, or singeing the tenderest parts of their limbs with sticks of fire. And of one horrid instance have I heard of Malignant and Hellish revenge in Two Ladies who were Sisters (and bred at a Fine Boarding-School in England), who, having a spite against a yellow woman that attended on them, did tie her hands and feet, and so beat her nearly to death with the heels of their slippers; and not satisfied with that, or with laving her gashed body with Vinegar and Chillies, did send for a Negro man, and bid him, under threats of punishment, strike out two of the Victim's teeth with a punch, which, to the shame of Human Womanhood, was done.

But enough of these Horrors:—not the worst that I have seen, though, in the course of my Adventures; only I will not further sicken you with the Recital of the Sufferings inflicted on the Wretched Creatures by Ladies and Gentlemen, who had had the first breeding, and went to Church every Sunday. I have merely set down these dreadful things to work out the theory of my Belief, that the World is growing Milder and more Merciful every day; and that the Barbarities which were once openly practised in the broad sunshine, and without e'er a one lifting finger or wagging tongue against them, are becoming rarer and rarer, and will soon be Impossible of Commission. The unspeakable Miseries of the Middle Passage (of which I have been an eye-witness) exist no more; really Humane and Charitable Gentlemen, not such False Rogues and Kidnappers as your Hopwoods, are bestirring themselves in Parliament and elsewhere to better the Dolorous Condition of the Negro; and although it may be a Decree of Providence that the children of Ham are to continue always slaves and servants to their white brethren, I see every day that men's hearts are being more and more benevolently turned towards them, and that laws, ere long, will be made to forbid their being treated worse than the beasts that perish.

CHAPTER THE ELEVENTH.

THUS in a sultry colony, among Black Negroes and their cruel Taskmasters, and I the clerk to a Mulotter Washerwoman, did I come to be full sixteen years of age, and a stalwart Lad of my inches. But for that Fate, which from the first irrevocably decreed that mine was to be a Roving Life, almost to its end, I might have continued in the employ of Maüm Buckey until Manhood overtook me. The Dame was not unfavourable towards me; and, without vanity, may I say that, had I waited my occasion, 'tis not unlikely but that I might have married her, and become the possessor of her plump Money-Bags, full of Moidores, pilar Dollars, and pieces of Eight. Happily I was not permitted so to disparage my lineage, and put a coffee-coloured blot on my escutcheon. No, my Lilias is no Mulotter Quartercaste. 'Twas my roving propensity that made me set but little store by the sugar-eyes and Molasses-speech which Madam Soapsuds was not loth to bestow on me, a tall and likely Lad. I valued her sweetness just as though it had been so much cane-trash. With much impatience I had waited for the coming back of my friendly skipper, that he might advise me as to my future career. But, as I have already warned the Reader, it was fated that I was to see that kindly shipmaster no more. Once, indeed, the old ship came into Port Royal, and right eagerly did I take boat and board her. But her name had been changed from *The Humane Hopwood* to *The Protestant Pledge*. She was in the Guinea trade now, and brought Negroes, poor souls! to slave in our Plantations. The Mariner that was her commander had but dismal news to tell me of my friendly Handsell. He, returning to the old country, had it seems a Mighty Quarrel with his Patron—and my Patron too, forsooth!—Villain Hopwood. Whether he had reproached him with his treachery to me or not, I know not; but it is certain that both parted full of Wrath and High Disdain, and each swearing to be the Ruin of the other. But Gold had, as it has always in a Mammon-ridden world, the longest, strongest pull. Devil Hopwood found it easy to get the better of a

poor unlettered tarpaulin, that knew well enough the way
into a Wapping Alehouse, but quite lost himself in threading
the mazes of a great man's Antechamber.   'Tis inconceivable
how much dirty work there was done in my young days between Corinthian columns and over Turkey carpets, and under
ceilings painted by Verrio and Laguerre.   Sir Basil, I believe,
went to a great man, and puts a hundred guineas into the
hands of his Gentleman—by which I mean his Menial Servant, save that he wore no Livery ; but there's many a Base
wretch hath his soul in plush, and the Devil's aigulets on
his heart.   How much out of the Hundred my Lord took,
and how much his Gentleman kept, it serves not to inquire.
They struck a Bargain, and short was the Time before Ruin
came swooping down on Captain Handsell.   He had gone
into the Channel trade ; and they must needs have him ex-
chequered for smuggling brandies and lace from St. Malo's.
Quick on this follows a criminal Indictment, from which, as
a Fool, he flies ; for he might at least have threatened to say
damaging things of Brute Basil in the dock, and have made
terms with him before trial came on.   And then he must
needs take command of a miserable lugger that fetched and
carried between Deal and Dunquerque—the old, old, sorry,
tinpot business of kegs of strong waters, and worse contraband in the guise of Jacobite despatches.   To think of brave
men's lives being risked in these twopenny errands, and a
heart of Oak brought to the gallows, that clowns may get
drunk the cheaper, or traitors—for your Jacobite conspirators
were but handy-dandy Judases, now to King James and now
to King George—exchange their rubbishing ciphers the easier!
It drives me wild to think of these pinchbeck enterprises.   If
a man's tastes lead him towards the Open, the Bold, and the
Free, e'en let him ship himself off to a far climate, the hotter
the better, where Prizes are rich, and the King's writ in
Assault and Battery runneth not, — nor for a great many
other things ayont Assault and Battery,—and where, up a
snug creek, of which he knows the pilotage well, he may
give a good account of a King's ship when he finds her.   He
who does anything contrair to English law within five hundred leagues of an English lawyer or an English law-court is
a very Ass and Dolt.   Fees and costs will have their cravings ;
and from the process-server to the Hangman all will have
their due.   Give me an offing, where there is 'no law but that

of the strong hand and the bold Heart. Any sharks but land-sharks for John Dangerous. I never see a parchment-visaged, fee-clutching limb of the law but I long to beat him, and, if I had him on blue water, to trice him up higher than ever he went before. But for a keg of brandy! But for a packet of treason-papers! Shame! 'tis base, 'tis idiotic. And this did the unlucky Handsell find to his cost. I believe he was slain in a midnight affray with some Riding Officers of the Customs close unto Deal, about two years after his going into a trade that was as mean as it was perilous.

So no more Hope for me from that quarter. The skipper of *The Protestant Pledge* would have retained me on board for a Carouse; but I had too much care for my Head and my Liver for such pranks, and went back, as dolefully as might be, to keep Maum Buckey's washing-books. I chafed at the thought that I could do no more. I told her the grim news I had heard of her brother-in-law, whereat she wept somewhat; for where Whites were concerned she was not a hard-hearted woman. But she cheered up speedily, saying that Samhe had come to as sorry an end, and that she supposed there was but one way with the Handsells, Rum and Riot being generally their Ruin.

As it is one of the failings of youth not to know when it is well off, and to grow A-weary even of continued prosperity, I admit that the life I led palled upon me, and that I longed to change it. But it was not, all things considered, so very unpleasant a one. True, the employment was a sorry one, and utterly beneath the dignity of a Gentleman, such as bearing fardels in the streets or unloading casks and bales at the wharf, for instance. But it is in man's nature never to be satisfied, and when he is well, to long to be better, and so, by force of striving, to tumble into a Hole, where indeed he is at the Best, for he is Dead. At this distance of time, though I have many comforts around me,—Worldly Goods, a Reputable name, my Child, and her Husband,—I still look back on my old life in Jamaica, and confess that Providence dealt very mercifully with me in those bygone days. For I had enough to eat and to drink, and a Mistress who, though Passionate and Quarrelsome enough by times, was not unkind. If she would swear, she would also tender gentle Language upon occasion; and if she would throw things,

L

she was not backward in giving one a dollar to heal one's
pate. An odd life it was, truly. There was very little of
that magnificence about the town of Port Royal in my days
which I have heard the Creoles to boast about. It may have
been handsome enough in the Spaniard's Reign, or in King
Charles the Second's ; but I have heard that its most comely
parts had been swallowed up by an Earthquake, and, when I
remember it, the Main thoroughfare was like nothing half so
much as the Fag End of Kent Street in the Borough, where
the Broom-men live. As for public scavengers—humane at
least—there were none ; for that salutary practice of putting
rebellious Blacks into chain-gangs, and making them sweep
the streets,—which might be well done in London with
Pickpockets and the like trash, to their souls' health and the
benefit of the Body-politic,—did not then obtain. The only
way of clearing the offal was by the obscene birds that flew
down from the hills ; Messieurs the landcrabs, who were
assuredly the best scavengers of all, not stirring beyond the
palisadoes. Some things were very cheap, but others inordinately dear. Veal was at a prodigious price ; and 'twas a
common saying, that you could buy Four children in England
cheaper than you could one calf in Jamaica. But for the
products and dishes of the colony, which I have elsewhere
hinted at, all was as low-priced as it was abundant. What
droll names did they give, too, unto their fish and flesh and
fowl ! How often have you in England heard of Crampos,
Bonettas, Ringrays, Albacoras, and Sea-adders, among fish ;
of Noddies and Boobies and Pitternells and Sheerwaters
among birds ? And Calialou Soup, and Pepperpot to break
your Fast withal in the morning, and make you feel, ere you
got accustomed to that Fiery victual, like a Salamander for
some hours afterwards.

Now and then also, with some other young white folks
with whom I had stricken up acquaintance,—clerks, store-
keepers, and the like,—would we seek out the dusky beauties
of the town in their own quarters, and shake a leg at their
Dignity Routs, Blackamoor Drums, and Pumpkin-Faced
Assemblies, or by what other name the poor Black wretches
might choose to call their uproarious merry-makings. There,
in some shed, all hustled together as a Moorfields Sweetener
does luck in a bag, would be a mob of men and women Negroes, all dressed in their bravest finery, although little of it

was to be seen either on their Backs or their Feet, the Head
being the part of their Bodies which they chiefly delight to
ornament. Such ribbons and owches, such gay-coloured rags
and blazing tatters, would they assume, and to the Trips and
Rounds played to them by some Varlet of a black fiddler,
with his hat at a prodigious cock, and mounted on a Tub,
like unto the sign of the Indian Bacchus at the Tobacconist's,
would they dance and stamp and foot it merrily—with plenty
of fruit, salt fish, pork, roasted plantain, and so forth, to regale themselves withal, not forgetting punch and sangaree—
quite forgetful, poor mercurial wretches, for the time being
of Fetters and the Scourge and the Driver that would hurry
them to their dire labour the morrow morn. Surely there
never did exist so volatile, light-spirited, feather-brained a
race as these same Negro Blacks. They will whistle and
crack nuts, ay and dance and sing to the music of the Fiddle or the Banjar an hour after the skin has been half flayed
off their backs. They seem to bear no particular Malice to
their Tormentors, so long as their weekly rations of plantain,
yam, or salt fish, be not denied them, and that they have
Osnaburgs enow to make them shirts and petticoats to cover
themselves withal. Give them but these, and their dance
at Christmas time, with a kind word thrown to them now
and again, just as you would fling a marrow-bone to a dog,
and they will get along well enough in slavery, almost
grinning at its Horrors and making light of its unutterable
Woes. I never saw so droll a people in my life. Nor is it
the less astonishing thing about them that, beneath all this
seeming lightheartedness and jollity, there often lies smoul-
dering a Fire of the Fiercest passion and blackest revenge.
The dark-skinned fellow who may be flapping the flies
away from you in the morning, and bearing your kicks and
cuffs as though they were so many cates and caresses, may,
in the evening, make one in a circle of Heathen monsters
joined together to listen to the Devilish Incantations of the
Obeah man,—to mingle in ceremonies most hideous and
abominable, and of which perhaps that of swearing eternal
Hatred to the White Race over a calabash that is made out
of the skull of a new-born Babe, and filled with Dirt, Rum,
and Blood mixed together, is perchance the least horrid.
And yet I don't think the unhappy creatures are by nature
either treacherous, malicious, or cruel. 'Tis only when the

fit seizes them. Like the Elephants, the idea suddenly
comes over them that they are wronged—that 'tis the White
Man who has wrought them all these evils ; and that they
are bound to Trample him to pieces without more ado.
But 'tis all done in a capricious cobweb-headed manner ;
and on the morrow they are as quiet and good-tempered
as may be. Then, just as suddenly, will come over them a
fit of despondency, or dark, dull, brooding Melancholy. If
they are at sea, they will cast themselves into the waves
and swim right towards the sharks, whose jaws are yawn-
ing to devour them. If they are on dry land, they will,
for days together, refuse all food, or worse still, go dirt-
eating, stuffing themselves with clay till they have the *mal
d'estomac*, and so die ; this *mal*, of which our English
stomach-ache gives no valid translation (which must prove
my excuse for placing here a foreign word), being, with the
Yaws, their most frequent and fatal complaint. Of a less
perplexing nature also are their fits of the Sulks, when, for
more than a week at a time, they will remain wholly mute
and intractably obstinate, folding their arms or squatting on
their hams, and refusing either to move or speak, whatsoever
threats may be uttered or enforced against them, and setting
no more store by the deep furrowing cuts of the Cowhide
whip (that will make marks in a deal board, if well laid on,
the which I have often seen) than by the buzzings of a
Shambles Fly. They had many ways of treating these fits
of the sulks in my time, all of them cruel, and none of them
successful. One was, to set the poor wretches in the stocks
or the bilboes, rubbing chillies into their eyes to keep them
from going to sleep. Another was a dose of the Fire-cane,
as it was called, which was just a long paddle, or slender
oar, pierced with holes at the broadest part, with the which
the patient being belaboured, a blister on the flesh rose to
each hole of the Paddle. A curious method, and one much
followed ; but the Negroes sulked all the more for it. There
was a Dutchwoman from Surinam, who had brought with
her from that plantation of the Hollanders that highly Ingenious Mode of Torment known as the "Spanso Bocko."*
The manner of it was this. You took your Negro and tied
him wrists and ankles, so bending him into a neat curve.

* Vide Stedman's *Surinam.*

Then, if his spine did not crack the while, you thrust a stake
between his legs, and having thus comfortably Trussed him,
pullet fashion, you laid him on the ground one side upwards,
and at your leisure scarified him from one cheek to one heel
with any instrument of Torture that came handy. Then he
(or she, it did not at all matter in the Dutchwoman's esteem),
being one gore of welts and gashes, was thought to be Done
enough on one side, and consequently required Doing t'other.
So one that stood by to help just took hold of the stake and
turned the Human Pullet over, and then he was so thoroughly basted as sometimes to be Done a little too much,
often dying on the spot from that Rib wasting. Oh, it was
rare sport! I wonder whereabouts in the nethermost Hell
the cunning Dutchman is now who first devised this torment; also the Dutchwoman who practised it? I can fancy
Signor Beelzebub and his Imps taking a keen delight in
their application of the Spanso Bocko. The which I never
knew cure a Negro of the sulks. They would force back
their tongues into their gullets while the torment was going
on, determined not so much as to utter a moan, and, having
a peculiar Art that way, brought by them from their own
country, would often contrive to suffocate themselves and
Expire. Their own country! That is what one of the
miserable beings said when, being threatened with torment
of a peculiarly outrageous nature, he flung himself into a
cauldron of boiling sugar, and was scalded to death on the
instant. Let me not omit to mention while I am on this
chapter of Brutality—wreaked by Christian men upon poor
Heathen savages, for many of them were not many weeks
from Guinea and Old Calabar, where they had been worship-
ping Mumbo Jumbo, and making war upon one another
in their own Pagan fashion—that I have known Planters
even more refined in their cruelty. They would make their
slaves drink salt water, and then set them out in the hot
sun tied to the outside posts of the Piazza. The end of
that was, that they went Raving Mad, gnawing their
Tongues and poor blubberous Lips to pieces* before they
died. Another genius, who was a proficient in his Humani-
ties, and quite of a classic frame of mind in his cruelties, bethought himself of a mode of Torture much practised among

* Dean of Myddelton's Evidence, Clarkson's Committee.

the Ancient Persians, and so must needs smear the body of
an unhappy Negro all over with molasses. Then, binding
him fast to a stake in the open, the flies and mosquitoes
got at him,—for he was kept there from one morning until
the next,—and he presently gave up the Ghost. But nothing that I ever saw or heard of during the time of my
living in the Western Indies, could equal the Romantic
Torture, not so much invented as imported, by a Gentleman Merchant who had lived among the islands of the
Grecian Archipelago, and whose jocose humour it was to
imprison his women slaves in loose garments of leather, very
tightly secured, however, at the wrists, neck, and ankles.
In the same garments, before fastening round the limbs of
the victims, one or more infuriated cats were introduced ;
the which ferocious animals, playfully disporting themselves
in their attempt to find a point of egress, would so up and
tear, and mangle, and lacerate, with their Terrible claws,
the flesh of the sufferers, that not all the Brine-washing or
pepper-pod-rubbing in the world, afterwards humanely re-
sorted to on their release from their leathern sepulchre,
would save them from mortification. There was a com-
pleteness and gusto about this Performance that always
made me think my Gentleman Merchant from the Greek
Islands a very Great Mind. The mere vulgar imitations of
his Process which, in times more Modern, I have heard of
—such as taking an angry cat by the tail and drawing its
claws all abroad down the back of a Negro strapped on to a
plank, so making a map of all the rivers in Tartarus from
his neck to his loins—are, in my holding, beneath contempt.
There is positive Genius in that idea of shutting-up the cats
in a hide-bound prison, and so letting them work their own
wills on the inner walls ; and I hope my Gentleman Merchant has as warm a niche in Signor Beelzebub's Temple of
Fame, as the Great Dutch Philosopher who first dreamt of
the Spanso Bocko.

Before I left the island of Jamaica, there befell me an adventure which I may briefly narrate. It being the sickly
season and very few ships in port, Maum Buckey's business
was somewhat at a stand-still, and with little difficulty I obtained from her a fortnight's holiday. I might have spent it
with no small pleasure, and even profit, at one of her up-
country plantations, or at the Estate of some other Planter ;

for I had friends and to spare among the white Overseers and Bookkeepers ; and although the Gentry—that is to say, the Enriched Adventurers, who deemed themselves such—were of course too High and Mighty to associate with one of my Mean Station, I was at no loss for companions among those of my own degree. So, bent upon a frolic, and being by this time a good Rider and a capital shot, I joined a band of wild young Slips like myself, to go up the country hunting the miserable Negroes that had Marooned, as it was called. These Maroons were runaway slaves who had bid a sudden good-by to Bolts and shackles, whips and rods, and shown their Tyrants a clean pair of heels, finding their covert in the dense jungles that covered the mountain slopes, where they lived on the wild animals and birds they could shoot or snare, and sometimes making descents to the nearest plantations, thence to carry off cattle, ponies, or pigs, or whatever else they could lay their felonious hands upon. These were the Blacks again, you will say, with a vengeance, and at many Thousand Miles' distance from Charlwood Chase : but those poor varlets of Deerstealers in England never dreamt of taking Human Life, save when defending their own, in a fair stand-up Fight ; whereas the Maroons had no such scruples, and spared neither age, nor sex, nor Degree—that had a white skin—in their bloodthirsty frenzy. The Savage Indians in the American plantations, who will swoop down on some peaceful English settlement, slaying, scalping, and Burning up men, women, and children,—with other Horrors and Outrages not to be described in decent terms,—are just on a par with these blacks Maroons. Now and again would be found among them some Household Runaways, or Field Hands born into slavery on the Plantations,—and these were most useful in acting as spies or scouts ; but as a rule the Head Men and Boldest Villains among the Maroons were Savage Negroes, just fresh from Africa, on whom the bonds of servitude had sate but for a short time, and who in the jungle were as much at Home as though they were in their native wilds again. Of great stature, of prodigious strength, amazing Agility, and astounding natural cunning, these creatures were as ferocious as Wild Baboons that had lived among civilised mankind just long enough to learn the Art of firing off a Gun and wielding a cutlass, instead of brandishing a Tree-branch or heaving a Cocoa-nut. They were without Pity ; they were without knowledge that theirs was a cut-throat, nay a cannibal trade. The white man had made war on them, and torn them from their Homes, where they were happy enough in their Dirt and Grease, their War-paint, and their idolatrous worship of Obeah and Bungey. 'Twas these Men-monsters that we went to hunt. The Planters themselves were somewhat chary of dealing with them; for the cruelties which the Maroons inflicted on those who fell into their power were Awful alone to contemplate, much more so to Endure; but they were glad enough when any gang of young Desperadoes of the meaner white sort—which, speaking not for myself, I am inclined to believe the Meanest and most Despicable of any sort or condition of Humanity—would volunteer to go on a Maroon Hunt. We were to have a Handsome Recompense, whether our enterprise succeeded or failed; but were likewise stimulated to increased exertion by the covenanted promise of so many dollars—I forget how many now—for every head of a Maroon that we brought at our saddlebows to the place of Rendezvous. And so we started one summer morning, some twenty strong, all young, valiant, and not over-scrupulous, armed, I need scarcely say, to the teeth, and mounted on the rough but fleet ponies of the country.

A train of Negroes on whom we could Depend—that is, by the strict application of the law of Fear, not Kindness, and who stood in such Terror of us, and of our ever-ready Thongs, Halters, Pistols, and Cutlasses, as scarcely to dare call their souls their own—followed us with Sumpter mules well laden with provisions, kegs of drink, both of water and ardent, and additional ammunition. I was full of glee at the prospects of this Foray, vowed that it was a hundred times pleasanter than making out Maum Buckey's washing-books, and hearing her scold her laundry-wenches; and longed to prove to my companions that the Prowess I had shown at twelve—ay, and before that age, when I brained the Grenadier with the Demijohn—had not degenerated now that I was turned sixteen, and far away from my own country. So we rode and rode, who but we, and dined gaily under spreading trees, boasting of the brave deeds we would do when we had tracked the black Marooning Vagabonds to their lair. At which those Negro servants upon whom we could depend grinned from ear to ear, and told us in their lingo that they " oped we would sav Dam black negar tief out, and burn his

Fader like canebrake." "'Tis strange," I thought, "that these creatures have not more compassion for their fellows whom we are hunting." To be sure, they were mostly of the Household breed, between whom and the fresh-imported Negroes held to field-service there is little sympathy. It escaped me to tell you that we had with us yet more powerful and Trustworthy auxiliaries than either our arms, our Horses, or our servants; being none other than nine couples of ferocious Bloodhounds, of a breed now extinct in Jamaica, and to be found only at this present moment, I believe, in the island of Cuba. These animals, which were of a terrible Ferocity and exquisitely keen scent, were kept specially for the purpose of hunting Maroons,—such are the Engines which Tyrannical Slavery is compelled to have recourse to,—and were purposely deprived of food beyond that necessary for their bare sustenance, that they might more fully relish the Recompense that awaited them when they had hunted down their prey.

Gaily we went on our Road rejoicing, now by mere bridle-paths, and now plunging our hardy little steeds right through the bristling underwood, when there burst upon us one of those terrible Tornadoes, or Tempests of wind and rain, so common in the Western Indies. The water came down in great solid sheets, drenching us to the skin in a moment; the sky was lit-up for hundreds of miles round by huge blasts of lurid fire; the wind tore great branches off trees, and hurled them across the bows of our saddles, or battered our faces with their soaked leaves or sharp prickles. The very Dogs were blinded and baffled by this tremendous protest of nature; and in the very midst of the storm there broke from an ambuscade a band of Maroons, three times as strong as our own, who fell upon us like incarnate Demons as they were. Our hounds had found their scent long before,—just after dinner, indeed,—and we had been following it for some two hours; —even now it was Reeking close upon us, but we little deemed how Near. I suppose that those Negro Rascals, whom we had trusted so implicitly, and on whom we thought that we could Depend so thoroughly, had Betrayed us. This was the second time in my short Life that I had fallen into an Ambuscade; and, lo, each time the "Blacks" had been mixed up with my misadventure.

These naked Maroons cared nothing about the Storm, whose torrents ran off their well-oiled carcasses like water off a Duck's back. There was a very Devil of a fight. 'Twas every one for himself, and the Tempest for us all. The Runaways were well armed, and besides could use their teeth and nails to better advantage than many a doughty Fighting man can use his weapons, and clawed and tore at us like Wild Beasts. I doubt not we should have got the worst of it but that we were Mounted,—and a Man on horseback is three times a Footman in a Hand-to-Hand encounter; and again, that our good friends the bloodhounds, that had been scared somewhat at the outset, recovered their self-possession, and proceeded each to pin his Maroon, and to rend him to pieces with great deliberation. In the end, that is to say, after about twenty-seven minutes' sharp tussling, Dogs, Horses, and Men were victorious; and, as we surveyed the scene of our Triumph, the storm had spent its fury. The black clouds cleared away as suddenly as they had darkled upon us; the Golden Sun came out, and the dreadful scene was lit up in Splendour. Above, indeed, it was all Beauty and Peace, for Nature cannot be long Angry. The trees all seemed stemmed and sprayed with glistering jewels; the moisture that rose had the tints of a hundred Rainbows; the long grass flashed and waved; the many birds in the boughs began to sing Hymns of Thankfulness and Joy. But below, ah, me! what a Dreadful scene of blood and Carnage, and Demoniac revenge, there was shown! Of our band we had lost three Killed; five more were badly Wounded; and there was not one of us but had some Hurt of greater or lesser seriousness. We had killed a many of the Maroons; and the two or three that had escaped with Life, albeit most grievously gashed, were speedily put out of their misery. Had we been seeking for Runaway house-servants, we might have taken prisoners; but with a wild African Maroon this is not serviceable. The only thing that you can do with him, when you catch him, is to kill him.

The Dead Bodies of our unfortunate companions were laid across the sumpter mule's back; but when we came to look for our train of dependable Negroes, we found that all save three had fled. These did so very strongly protest their Innocence, and plead their abiding by us as a proof thereof, that I felt half inclined to hold them blameless. There were those among us, however, who were of a far different opinion, and were for lighting a fire of branches and Roasting them into confession. But there was a Scotch gentleman among us by the name of Macgillicuddy, who, being of a Practical turn (as most of his countrymen are, and, indeed, Edinburgh in Scotland is about the most Practical town that ever I was in), pointed out that we were all very Tired, and needed Refreshment and Repose; that the task of Torturing Negroes gave much trouble and consumed more time ("Aiblins it's douce wark," quoth the Scotch gentleman); that all the wood about was sopped with wet (and a "Dry Roast's best," said the Scotch Gentleman); and finally, that the thing could be much better done at home, where we had proper Engines and Instruments for inflicting Exquisite Agony, and proper Slaves to administer the same. So that for the nonce, and for our own Convenience, we were Merciful, and promised to defer making necessary Inquisition, by means of Cowhide, Tamarind-bush, and Fire-cane, until our return to the Rendezvous.

I should tell you that I got a Hurt in my hand from a kind of short Chopper or Tommyhawk that one of the Savages carried. 'Twas fortunately my left hand, and seeming but a mere scratch, I thought little or nothing about it. But at the end of the second day it began to swell and swell to a most alarming size and tumorous discoloration, the inflammation extending right up my arm, even to my shoulder. Then it was agreed on all sides that the blade of the Tommyhawk with which I had been stricken must have been anointed with some subtle and deadly Poison, of which not only the Maroons but the common Household and Town Negroes have many, preparing them themselves, and obstinately refusing, whether by hope of Reward or fear of punishment, to reveal the secret of their components to the Whites. I had to rest at the nearest Plantation to our battle-field; and the Planter—who had been a captain in the Chevalier de St. George's service (the old one), that had come out here, after the troubles of 1715, a Banished man, but had since been Pardoned, and had taken to Planting, and grown Rich—was kind enough to permit me to be taken into his house and laid in one of his own Guest-chambers, where I was not only tended by his own Domestics, but was sometimes favoured with the Attention and sympathy of his angelic Wife, a young woman of most charming countenance and lively manners, most cheerful, pious, and Humane, taking great care of her slaves, physicking them frequently, reading

to them little paper books written by persons of the Noncon-
forming persuasion,—a kind of doctrine that I never could
abide,—and never suffering them to be whipped upon a Sunday.   However, I grew worse ; whereupon one Mr. Sprague,
that set up for surgeon, but was more like a Boatswain turned
Landsman than that, or than a Horse, came to me, and was
for cutting off my arm, to prevent mortification.   There were
two obstacles in the way of this operation's performance ; the
first being that Mr. Sprague had no proper instruments by
him beyond a fleam and a syringe, with which, and with
however good a will, you can scarcely sever a Man's limb
from his Body ; and the next, that Mr. Sprague was not
sober.   Love for a young widow had driven him to drinking,
it was said ; but I think it was more the Love of Liquor to
which his bibulous backslidings were owing.   'Twas lucky
for me that he had nor saw nor torniquet with him.   It is
true that he departed in quest of some Carpenter's Tools,
which he declared would do the job quite as well ; but, again
to my good luck, the carpenter was as Rare a pottlepot as he,
and they two took to boiling rum in a calabash and drinking
of it, and smoking of Tobacco, and playing at Skimming Dish
Hob, Spie the Market, Shove-halfpenny, Brag, Put, and Dilly
Dally, and other games that reminded them of the old country, for days and nights together ; so that the old Negro
woman that belonged to the carpenter, seeing them gambling
and drinking in the morning just as she had left them drinking and gambling the overnight, stared with amazement like
a Mouse in a Throwster's mill.   And by the time they had
finished their Rouse I was, through Heaven's kindness and
the sagacity of a Negro nurse named Cubjack, cured.   This
woman, it is probable, knew the secret of the Poison from
the bitter effects of which I was suffering.   At all events, she
took me in hand, and by warm fomentations and bathings,
and some outward applications of herbs and anointed bandages,
reduced the swelling and restored my hand to its proper Form
and Hue.   At the end of the week I was quite cured, and
able to resume my journey back to Kingston.   I did not fail
to express my gratitude to the hospitable Planter and his
Lady, and I gave the Nurse Cubjack half a dollar and a silver
tobacco-stopper that had been presented to me by Maum
Buckey.
        As a perverse destiny would have it, this Tobacco-stopper,

this harmless trinket, was the very means of my losing my situation, and parting in anger from my Pumpkin-faced Patroness. Although I was, even at the present dating, but a raw lad, she took it into her head to be jealous of me, and all about this silver pipe-stopper. She vowed I had given it away to some Quadroon lass up country; she would not hearken to my protests of having bestowed it upon the nurse who had saved my life; and indeed when, at my instance, inquiries were made, Cubjack's replies did not in any way bear out my statement. The unhappy creature, who had probably sold my Tobacco-stopper for a few joes, or been deluded out of it by the Obeah Man, and was afraid of a flogging if discovery were made thereof, positively denied that I had given her anything beyond the half-dollar. You see that these Negroes have no more idea of the pernicious quality of the Sin of Lying, than has a white European shopkeeper deluding a Lady into buying of a lustring or a paduasoy; and see what similar vices there are engendered among savages and Christian folks by opposite causes.

We had a fearful war of words together, Maum Buckey and myself. She was a bitter woman when vexed, and called me "beggar buckra," "poor white trash," "tam lily thief," and the like. Whereat I told her plainly that I had no liking for her lackered countenance, and that she was a mahogany-coloured, slave-driving, old curmudgeon, that in England would be shown about at the fairs for a penny a peep. At the which she screamed with rage, and threw at me a jug of sangaree. Heavy enough it was; but the old lady had not so good an Aim as I had when I brained the Grenadier with the demijohn.

We had little converse after that. There were some wages due, and these she paid me, telling me that I might "go to de Debbil," and that if she ever saw me again, she hoped it would be to see me hanged. I could have got Employment, I doubt not, in Jamaica, or in some other of the islands; but I was for the time sick of the Western Indies, and was resolved, come what might, to tempt my fortune in Europe. A desire to return to England first came over me; nor am I ashamed to confess that, mingled with my wish to see my own country once more, was a Hope that I might meet the Traitorous Villain Hopwood, and tell him to his teeth what a false Deceiver I took him to be. You see how bold a lad can be when he has turned the corner of sixteen ; but 'twas always so with John Dangerous.

Some difficulty, nay, considerable obstacles, I encountered in obtaining a ship to carry me to Europe. The vindictive yellow woman, with whom (through no fault of my own, I declare) I was in disfavour, did so pursue me with her Animosity as to prejudice one Sea Captain after another against me ; and it was long ere any would consent to treat with me, even as a Passenger. To those of my own nation did she in particular speak against me with such virulence, that in sheer despite I abandoned for the time my intention of going to England, and determined upon making for some other part of Europe, where I might push my fortune. And there being in port early in the winter a Holland ship, named the *Gebrüder*, which was bound for Ostend, I struck a bargain with the skipper of her, a decent man, whose name was Van Pjerboom, and prepared to leave the colony, in which I had passed over four years of my Eventful Life. Some friends who took an interest in me,—the " bright English lad," as they called me,—and who thought I had been treated by Maum Buckey with some unnecessary degree of Harshness, made up a purse of money for me, by which I was enabled to pay my Passage Money in advance, and lay-in a stock of Provisions for the voyage ; for, save in the way of Schnapps, Cheeses, and Herrings, the Holland ships were at that time but indifferently well Found. When everything was paid, I found that I had indeed but a very small Surplus remaining ; but there was no other way, and I bade adieu to the Island of Jamaica, as I thought, for ever.

CHAPTER THE TWELFTH.

OF WHAT BEFELL ME IN THE LOW COUNTRIES.

I LANDED, after a long and tedious voyage, at the Town of Ostend, it being the Spring time of the year 1729, with Youth, Health, a strong Frame, and a comely Countenance (as they told me), indeed, but with just two Guineas in my pouch for all my Fortune. Many a Lord Mayor of London has begun the World, 'tis said, with a yet more slender Provision (I wonder what Harpy Hopwood had to begin with?) and Eighteenpence would seem to be the average of Capital Stock for an Adventurer that is to heap-up Riches. Still I seemed to have made my Start in Life's Voyage a great many times, and to have been very near ending with it more than once — witness the Aylesbury Assizes. Thus I felt rather Despondency than Hope at being come almost to manhood, and but to a beggarly Estate of Two-and-forty shillings. "But," said I, "courage, Jack Dangerous; thou hast strong legs and a valorous Stomach; at least thou needst not starve (bar cutpurses) for two-and-forty days; thou hast a knowledge of the French tongue" (which I picked up from a Huguenot emigrant from Languedoc, who was a Barber at Kingston, and taught me for well-nigh nothing), "and art cunning of Fence. Be the world thine Oyster, as the Playactor has it, and e'en open it with thy Spadapoint." In this not unwholesome frame of mind I came out of the ship *Gebrüder*, and set foot on the Port with something like a Defiance of Fortune's scurvy tricks fermenting within me.

The Ship Master recommended me to a very cleanly Tavern, by the sign of the Red Goose, kept in the Ganz-Straet, by a widow woman named Giessens. 'Twas Goose here, Goose there, and Goose everywhere, so it seemed with this good Frau; for she served Schiedam at the sign of the Goose, and she lived in Goose Street. She had herself a long neck and a round body and flat feet, going waddling and hissing about the house, a-scolding of her maids, like any Michaelmas matron among the stubble; not to forget her children, of whom she had a flock, waddling and hissing in their little way too, and who were all as like goslings as

Sherris is like Sack. Little would have lacked for her to give me hot roast goose to my dinner, and goose-pie for supper, and some unguent of goose-grease to anoint my Pate withal, had it chanced to be broken; and truly if I had lived under the sign of the Goose for many days, I might have taken to waddling and hissing too in my own Generation, and have been in time as brave a goose as any of them. Here there was a civil enough company of Seafaring men, Mates, Pilots, Supercargoes, and the like, with some Holland traders, and, if I mistake not, a few Smugglers that had contraband dealings in Cambrics, Steenkirks, Strong waters, and Point of Bruxelles. These last worthies did I carefully avoid ; for since my Boyish Mischances I had imbibed a wholesome fear of hurting the King's Revenue, or meddling in any way with his Prerogative. " Well out of it, Jack Dangerous," I said. "Touch not His Majesty's Deer, nor His Majesty's Customs, and there shall be no sense of a tickling in thy windpipe when thou passest a post that is like unto the sign of the Tyburn Tavern." 'Tis astonishing how gingerly a man will walk who has once been within an ace of dancing upon nothing.

There is a mighty quantity of Sand and good store of Mud at Ostend, and a very comforting smell of fish ; and so the High Dutch gentry, who, poor souls, know very little about the sea, and see no more salt water from Life's beginning unto its end than is contained within the compass of a pickling-tub, do use the place much for Bathing, and brag about their Dips and Flounderings, crying out, *Die Zee ist mein Lust*, in their plat Deutsch, as though they had all been born so many Porpoises. I would walk upon a morning much upon the Ramping-Parts, or Fortifications of the Town, watching whole caravans of Bathers, both of High and Low Dutch Gentry, coming to be dipped, borne into the Sea by sturdy Fellows that carried them like so many Sacks of Coals, and who would Discharge them into shallows with little more Ceremony than they would use in shooting such a Cargo of Fuel into a cellar. " When my Money is gone," thought I, "I may earn a crust by the like labour." But then I bethought me that I was a Stranger among them ; that they might be Jealous of me ; and, indeed, when I imparted my design to the Widow-woman Giessens, who was beholden to me, she said, for that I had warned her how poor a guest I was growing, she told me that much interest was needed to obtain one of these Bather's places—almost as much, forsooth, as is wanted to get the berth of a Tide-waiter in England, and these rascals were always waiting for the tide. Something like a Patent had to be humbly sued for, and fat fees paid to Syndies and Burgomasters, for the fine Privilege of sousing the gentry in the Brine. The good woman offered me Credit till I should find employment, and did so vehemently press a couple of Guilders upon me to defray my present charges, that I had not the heart to refuse, although I took care to avise her that my prospects of being able to repay her were as far off as the Cape of Good Hope.

It chanced one morning that I was walking out of the Town, by the side of the Sea below the fortified parts to the Norrard. 'Twas fine and calm enough, and there was not so much Swell as to take a Puppy off his swimming legs; but suddenly I heard a great Outcry and Hubbub, and perceived some ten feet from me in the Water, the head of a Man convulsed with Terror, and who was crying out with all his might that he was Drowning, that he should never see his dear Mamma again, and that all his Estate would go to the Heir-at-Law, whom, as well as he could, for screeching and spluttering, he Cursed heartily in the English tongue. I wondered how he could be in such a Pother, seeing that he was so close to shore, and that moreover there were those nigh unto him who could have helped him if they had had a Mind to it. Close upon him was a Fat gentleman in a clergyman's cassock and a prodigious Fluster, who kept crying out, "Save him! Save him!" but budged not a foot to come to his assistance himself; and, but a dozen yards or so, was a Flemish Fellow, one of the Bathers, who, so far as I could make out from his shaking his head and crying out, "nicht" and "Geld,"—the rest of his lingo was Greek to me,—did refuse to save the Gentleman unless he had more Money given him. For these Bathing-men were a most Mercenary Pack. In a much shorter time than it has taken me to put this on Paper I had off coat and vest, kicked off my shoes, and struck into the water. 'Twas of the shallowest, and I had but to wade towards him who struggled. When I came anigh him, he must even catch hold of me, clinging like Grim Death or a Barnacle to the bottom of a Barge, very nearly Dragging me down. But I

was happily strong; and so, giving him with my disengaged
arm a sound Cuff under the ear, the better to Preserve his
Life, I seized him by the waist with the other, and so
dragged him up high, if not dry, unto the Sandy Shore.
And a pretty sight he looked there, dripping and Shivering, although the Sun shone Brightly, and he well nigh
Blue with Fright.

What do you think the first words were that my Gentleman uttered so soon as he had got his tongue clear of
Salt and Seaweed?

"You villain!" he cries to me, "you have assaulted me.
Take witness, Gentlemen, he hath stricken me under the
Ear.   I will have him in the King's Bench for Battery.
Mr. Hodge, you saw it; and you leave me this day week
for allowing your Patron to be within an inch of Drowning."

I was always of a Hot Temper, and this cavalier treatment of me after my Services threw me into a Rage.

"Why, you little half-boiled Shrimp," I bawled out, "I
have a mind to clout you under t'other Ear, that Brothers
may not complain of Favour, and e'en carry you to where I
found you."

The Gentleman in the cassock began to break out in ex-
cuses, saying that his Patron would reward me, and that he
was glad that an Englishman had been by to rescue a Person of Quality from such great Peril, when that Flanders
Oaf yonder—the extortionate villain—would not stir a
finger to help him unless he had half a guilder over and
above his fee.

"Let him dry and dress himself," I said, in Dudgeon;
"and if he be not civil to a Countryman, who is as good as
he, I will kick him back to his Inn, and you too."

"A desperate youth!" murmured the Clergyman, as he
handed his Patron a great bundle of towels; "and very
meanly clad."

I walked away a few paces while the gentleman dried
and dressed himself.   Had I obeyed the Promptings of Pride,
I should have gone on my ways and left him to his likings;
but I was exceeding Poor, and thought it Foolish to throw
away the chance of receiving what his Generosity might
bestow upon me.   The Bathing-Man, who had been already
paid his Fee, had the impudence to come up and ask for
more "Geld,"—for minding the gentleman's clothes, as I

gathered from the speech of the clergyman, who understood Flemish. He was, however, indignantly refused, and, not relishing, perchance, the likelihood of a scuffle with three Englishmen, straightway decamped.

By and by the Gentleman was dressed, and a very smart appearance he made in a blue shag frock laced with silver, a yellow waistcoat bound with black velvet, green paduasoy breeches, red stockings, gold buckles, an ivory hilt to his sword, and a white feather in his hat. I have no mind to write out Tailors' accompts, but I do declare this to be the exact Schedule of his Equipment. Under the hat, which had a kind of Sunday Marylabonne cock to it, there bulged out a mighty White Periwig of fleecy curls, for all the world like the coat of a Bologna Poodle Dog, and in the middle of his Wig there peeped out a little hatchet face, with lantern jaws, and blue gills, and a pair of great black eyebrows, under which glistened a pair of inflamed eyes. He was not above five feet three inches, and his fingers, very long and skinny, went to and fro under his Point ruffles like a Lobster's Feelers. The Chaplain, who waited upon him as a Maid would on a lardy-dardy woman of Fashion, handed my Gentleman a very tall stick with a golden knob at the end on't, and with this, and a laced handkerchief and a long cravat, which he had likely bought at Mechlin, and a Snuff-box in the lean little Paw that held not the cane, he looked for all the world like one of my Grandmother's Footmen who had run away and turned Dancing Master.

" This, young man," said the Chaplain, making a low bow as he spoke to the comical Image before him, " is Bartholomew Pinchin, Esquire, of Hampstead. Make your reverence, sirrah !"

" Make a reverence to a Rag-doll !" I answered, with a sneer. " He hath left his twin brother beyond sea. I know him, and he is a Barbary Ape."

" The rogue is insolent," says B. Pinchin, Esq., clutching tighter at his tall cane, but turning very white the while. " I must batoon him into better manners."

" What !" I cried in a great voice, making a step towards him, for my blood was up. I would but have tweaked the little creature's Ears; but he, for a surety, thought I had a mind to Murder him. I do aver that he fell upon his knees, and with most piteous Accents and Protestations en-

treated me, for the sake of his Mamma, to spare his life, and
he would give me all I asked.

I was quite bewildered, and turning towards the Parson,
asked if his master was Mad ; to which he made answer,
with some Heat, that he was no Master of his, but his
Honoured Friend and Gracious Patron ; whereupon the little
Spark must go up to him, whimpering and cuddling about
him, and beseeching him to save him from the Tall Rogue,
meaning me.

" Body o' me, man," I exclaimed, scarcely able to keep
from laughing, " I mean you no harm. I am a young Englishman, lately come from the Plantations, and seeking employment. I see you struggling yonder and like to give up
the ghost, and I pull you out ; and then you call me Rogue
and charge me with striking of you. Was it cramp or cow-
ardice that made you bawl so ? Give me something to drink
better manners to you, and I will leave you and this reverend
gentlemen alone."

The Parson bowed his head with a pleased look when I
called him Reverend and a Gentleman, and, in an under-tone,
told his Patron that I was a civilly behaved youth, after all.
But the Poltroon with the white wig was not out of his
Pother yet. He had risen to his feet with a patch of sand
on each knee, and as the Chaplain wiped it off with a kerchief, he blubbered out that I wanted to rob him.

The Clergyman whispered in his ear—perhaps that I was
a Dangerous-looking Fellow, and might lose my temper anon
to some tune ; for my Whippersnapper approaches me, and,
in a manner Civil enough, tells me that he is much obliged
for what I had done for him. " And you will take this,"
says he. I will be shot if he did not give me an English Groat.

" You can readily get English coin changed in the town,"
he observed with a smirk, as in sheer bewilderment I gazed
upon this paltry doit.

I was desperately minded to Fling it at him, knock him
and the Chaplain down, and leave the precious pair to pick
themselves up again ; but I forbore. " Well," I said, " if
that's the value you put upon your life, I can't grumble at
your Guerdon. I suppose that shrivelled little carcass of
yours isn't worth more than fourpence. I'll e'en change it in
town, and buy fourpennyworth of Dutch cheese, and you
shall have the parings for nothing to send to your Mamma

as a gift from foreign parts. Good morning to you, my noble Captain." And so saying I walked away in a Fume of Wrath and Contempt.

I was idling, that same afternoon, along the Main street of Ostend, very much in the Dumps, and thinking of going down to the Port to seek a cook's place from some Ship Master, for I was not yet Qualified to engage as an Able-bodied Mariner, when I met the Chaplain again, this time alone, and coming out of a pastryman's shop. I would have passed him, as holding both him and his master in Disdain, but he Arrested me, and beckoned me into an Entry, there to have some Speech.

" My Patron is somewhat quick and hasty, and was uncommonly flustered by his mischance this morning," quoth the Rev. Mr. Hodge. " Nor perhaps did he use you as liberally as he should have done. Here is a golden guilder for you, honest man."

I thanked him, and as I pouched it told him that I would have taken no Money at all for a service which every man is bound to render to his Fellow-creature, but that I was sorely pressed for Money. On this, he asked my name and belongings. The name I gave him, at the which he winced somewhat ; but of my history I did not care to enlighten him further beyond broadly stating that I had come from the Plantations, where I had been used to keep Accompts, and that I was an Orphan, and had no friends in England, even if I possessed the means to return thither.

" I think I can find you a place," the chaplain replied, when I had finished. " 'Twill not be a very handsome one, but the work is little and light. Would it meet your purpose, now, to attend on a gentleman ?"

" It depends," I replied, " on what kind of a Gentleman he is."

" A Gentleman of landed Estate," quoth the parson, quite pat. " An English gentleman, now travelling for his Diversion, but will, in good time, settle down in England, to live on his Acres in a Handsome manner, and be a justice of peace and of the Quorum."

" Do you mean your Squire of Hampstead, yonder ?" I answered, pointing my thumb over my shoulder, as though in the direction where I had met his Reverence and his Patron that morning.

" I do," responds Mr. Hodge.

" Bartholomew Pinchin, of Hampstead, Esquire, eh ?" I continued.

" Exactly so."

" Then," I went on, raising my voice, and giving a furious glance at my companion, " I'll see Bartholomew Pinchin boiled, and I'll see Bartholomew Pinchin baked, and his Esquireship to boot, before I'll be his servant.   He, a mean, skulking, pinchbeck hound ! Tell him I'm meat for his master, and that he has no service, body or lip, of mine."

" Tut, tut, you foolish lad," said Mr. Hodge, not in the least offended.   " What a wild young colt it is, and how impatient ! For all your strapping figure, now, I doubt whether you are twenty years of age."

I answered with something like a Blush, that I was not yet seventeen.

" There it is—there it is," the Chaplain took me, chuckling.   " As I thought.   A mere boy.   A very lad.   Not come to years of discretion yet, and never will, if he goes on raging in this manner.   Hearken to me, youngster.   Don't be such a fool as to throw away a good chance."

" I don't see where it is yet," I observed sulkily, yet sheepishly ; for there was a Good-natured air about the Chaplain that overcame me.

" But I do," he rejoined.   " The good chance you have is of getting a comfortable place, with a smart livery—"

" I won't wear a livery," I cried, in a heat.   " I'll be no man's lacquey ; I'm a gentleman."

" So was Adam," retorted Mr. Hodge, " and the very first of the breed ; but he had to wear a livery of fig-leaves for all that, and so had his wife Eve.   Come, 'tis better to don a land-jerkin, and a hat with a ribbon to't, and be a Gentleman's Gentleman, with regular Wages and Vails, and plenty of good Victuals every day, than to be starving and in rags about the streets of a Flemish town."

" I'm not starving ; I'm not in rags," I protested, with my Proud stomach.

" But you will be the day after to-morrow.   The two things always go together.   Come, my young friend, I'll own that Bartholomew Pinchin, Esquire, is not generous."

" Generous !" I exclaimed ; " why, he's the meanest little hunks that ever skinned a flea for the hide and fat.

Didn't he give me fourpence this morning for saving his life ?"

" And didn't you tell him that his life wasn't worth more than a groat ?" asked the Chaplain, with a sly grin ; "besides insulting him on the question of Dutch cheese (to which he has an exquisite aversion), into the bargain ?"

" That's true," I replied, vanquished by the Parson's logic.

" There, then," his Reverence went on. " Bartholomew Pinchin Esquire's more easily managed than you think for. Do you prove a good servant, and it shall be my duty to make him show himself a good master to you. But I must have no further parley with you here, else these Papistical Ostenders will think that you are some Flemish lad (for indeed you have somewhat of a foreign air), and I a Lutheran Minister striving to convert you. Get you back to your Inn, good youth. Pay your score, if you have one ; and if you have not, e'en spend your guilder in treating of your companions, and come to me at nine of the clock this evening at the Inn of the Three Archduchesses. Till then, fare you well."

It must be owned that his Reverence's proposals were fair, and that his conversation was very civil. As I watched him trotting up the Main Street, his Cassock bulging out behind, I agreed with myself that perhaps the most prudent thing I could do just at present would be to put my gentility in my pocket till better times came round. There was a Spanish Don, I believe, once upon a time, who did very nearly the same thing with his sword.

At the appointed time I duly found myself at the sign of the Three Archduchesses, which was the bravest Hostelry in all Ostend, and the one where all the Quality put up. I asked for Bartholomew Pinchin, Esquire, in the best French that I could muster ; whereupon the drawer, who was a Fleming, and, I think, spoke even worse French than I did, asked me if I meant the English Lord who had the grand suite of apartments looking on the courtyard. I was fit to die of laughing at first to hear the trumpery little Hampstead squire spoken of as a lord ; but Prudence came to my aid again, and I answered that such was the personage I came to seek ; and, after not much delay, I was ushered into the presence of Mr. Pinchin, whose Esquiredom — and proud

enough he was of it—I may now as well Drop. I found him
in a very handsome apartment, richly furnished, drinking
Burgundy with his chaplain, and with a pack of cards alongside the bottles, and two great wax candles in sconces on
either side. But, as he drank his Burgundy, he ceased not
to scream and whimper at the expense he was being put to
in having such a costly liquor at his table, and scolded Mr.
Hodge very sorely because he had not ordered some thin
Bordeaux, or light Rhine wine. " I'm drinking guineas," he
moaned, as he gulped down his Gobbets; "it'll be the ruin
of me. A dozen of this is as bad as a Mortgage upon my
Titmouse Farm. What'll my mamma say? I shall die in
the poor-house." But all this time he kept on drinking;
and it was not glass and glass about with him, I promise you,
for he took at least three bumpers full to his Chaplain's one,
and eyed that reverend personage grudgingly as he seized
his opportunity, and brimmed up the generous Red Liquor
in his tall-stemmed glass. Yet the Chaplain seemed in no
way discountenanced by his scanty allowance, and I thought
that, perchance, his Reverence liked not wine of Burgundy.

They were playing a hand of piquet when I was introduced; and they being Gentlefolks, and I a poor humble
Serving Man that was to be, I was bidden to wait, which I
did very patiently in the embrasure of a window, admiring
the great dark tapestried curtains as they loomed in indistinct
gorgeousness among the shadows. The hand of piquet was
over at last, and Mr. Pinchin found that he had lost three
shillings and sixpence.

" I can't pay it, I can't pay it," he said, making a most
rueful countenance. " I'm eaten out of house and home,
and sharped at cards besides. It's a shame for a Parson to
play foul,—I say foul, Mr. Hodge. It's a disgrace to the
cloth to bring your wicked card-cheating practices to devalise
an English gentleman who is travelling for his diversion."

" We'll play the game over again, if you choose, Worthy
Sir," the Chaplain answers quite quietly.

" Yes, and then you'll win seven shillings of me. You've
sworn to bring me to beggary and ruin. I know you swore
it when my mamma sent you abroad with me. O, why did
I come to foreign parts with a wicked, guzzling, gambling,
chambering Chaplain, that's in league with the very host
and the drawers of this thieving inn against me—that burns

me a guinea a night in wax candles, and has had a freehold farm out of me in Burgundy wine."

" I've had but two glasses the entire evening," the Chaplain pleaded, in a voice truly that was meek ; but I thought that, even at the distance I stood from him, I could see the colour rising in his cheek.

" O, you have, you have," went on Squire Bartholomew, who, if not half Mad, was certainly more than three parts Muzzy ; " you've ruined me, Mr. Hodge, with your cards and your candles and your Burgundy, and Goodness only knows what else besides."

The Chaplain could stand it no longer, and rose in a Rage.

" I wish all the candles and the cards were down your throat," he cried ; " nearly all the wine is there already. I wish they'd choke you. I wish they were all in the pit of your stomach, and turned to hot burning coals. What shall I do with you, you cadaverous little jackanapes ? The Lout did well this morning—" (I was the Lout, by your leave) " to—to liken thee to one, for thou art more monkey than man. But for fear of staining my cassock, I'd—I'd—"

He advanced towards him with a vengeful air, clenching his fist, as well as I could see, as he approached. Surely there never was such a comical character as this Bartholomew Pinchin. 'Tis the bare truth, that, as the enraged parson came at him, this Gentleman of broad acres drops down again on his marrow-bones, just as I had seen him on the sands in the morning ; and lifting up his little skinny hands towards the ceiling, begins yelling and bawling out louder than ever.

"Spare my life ! spare my life !" he cried. " Take my watch and trinkets. Take my Gold Medal of the Pearl of Brunswick Club. Take the diamond solitaire I wear in my great Steenkirk on Sundays. Go to my Banker's, and draw every penny I've got in the world. Turn me out a naked, naked Pauper ; but oh, Mr. Hodge, spare my life. I'm young. I've been a sinner. I want to give a hundred Pounds to Lady Wackerbarth's charity school. I want to do every body good. Take my gold, but spare my life.—Oh, you tall young man in the corner there, come and help an English gentleman out of the hands of a murtherous Chaplain."

" Why, you craven cur, you," puts in the Chaplain, bending over him with half-poised fist, yet with a kind of half-

amusement in his features, don't you know that the Tall
young Man, as you call him, is the poor English lad who
saved your worthless little carcass from drowning this morning, and whom you offered to recompense with a Scurvy
Groat."

"I'll give him forty pound, I will," blubbered Mr. Pinchin,
still on his knees. "I'll give him fifty pounds when my
Midsummer rents come in, only let him rescue me from the
jaws of the roaring lion. Oh, my Mamma! my mamma!"

"Come forward, then, young man," cried the Chaplain,
with a smile of disdain on his good-humoured countenance,
"and help this worthy and courageous gentleman to his legs.
Don't be afraid, Squire Barty. *He* won't murder you."

I advanced in obedience to the summons, and putting a
hand under either armpit of the Squire, helped him on to his
feet. Then, at a nod of approval, I set him in the great arm-
chair of Utrecht velvet. Then I pointed to the bottle on the
table, and looked at Mr. Hodge, as though to ask whether
he thought a glass of Burgundy would do the patient good.

"No," said the Chaplain. "He's had enough Burgundy.
He'd better have a flask of champagne to give him some
spirits. Will you drink a flask of champagne, Squire?" he
continued, addressing his patron in a strangely authoritative
voice.

"Yes," quoth the little man, whose periwig was all Awry,
and who looked, on the whole, a most doleful figure,—"yes,
if you please, Mr. Hodge."

"Vastly pretty! And what am I to have? *I* think I
should like some Burgundy."

"Any thing," murmured the discomfited Squire; "only
spare me—"

"Tush! your life's in no danger. *We'll* take good care
of it. And this most obliging English youth,—will your
Honour offer him no refreshment? What is he to have?"

"Can he drink beer?" asked the Squire, in a faint voice,
and averting his head as though the having to treat me was
too much for him.

"Can you drink beer?" echoed the Chaplain, looking at
me, but shaking his head meanwhile, as if to warn me not to
consent to partake of so cheap a beverage.

"It's very cheap," added Mr. Pinchin very plaintively.
"It isn't a farthing a glass; and when you get used to it, it's

better for the inwards than burnt brandy. Have a glass of
beer, good youth.—Kind Mr. Hodge, let them bring him a
glass of Faro."

"Hang your faro! I don't like it," I said bluntly.

"What will you have, then?" asked the Squire, with a
gasp of agony, and his head still buried in the chair-cushion.
It seemed that the chaplain's lips, as he looked at me,
were mutely forming the letters W I N E. So I put a
bold front upon it, and said,

"Why, I should like, master, to drink your health in a
bumper of right Burgundy with this good Gentleman here."

"He will have Burgundy," whimpered Mr. Pinchin, half
to the chair-cushion, and half to his periwig. "He will have
Burgundy. The ragged, tall young man will have Burgundy
at eight livres ten sols the flask. Oh, let him have it, and let
me die! for he and the Parson have sworn to my Mamma to
murder me and have my blood, and leave me among Smugglers,
and Papistry, and Landlords who have sworn to ruin me in
waxen candles."

There was something at once so ludicrous, and yet so
Pathetic, in the little man's lamentations, that I scarcely
knew whether to laugh or to cry. His feelings seemed so
very acute, and he himself so perfectly sincere in his moan-
ings and groanings, that it were almost Barbarity to jeer at
him. The Chaplain, however, was, to all appearance, accustomed to these little Comedies; for, whispering to me that it
was all Mr. Pinchin's manner, and that the young Gentleman
meant no harm, he bade me bestir myself and hurry up the
servants of the House to serve supper. So not only were the
champagne and the Burgundy put on table,—and of the
which there was put behind a screen a demiflask of the same
true vintage for my own private drinking,—("And the
Squire will be pleased, when he comes to Audit the score, to
find that you have been content with Half a bottle. 'Twill
seem like something saved out of the Fire," whispers the
Chaplain to me, as I helped to lay the cloth),—not only
were Strong Waters and sweet Liquors and cordials provided,
especially that renowned stomachic the Maraschyno, of which
the Hollanders and Flemings are so outrageously fond, and
which is made to such perfection in the Batavian settlements
in Asia, but a substantial Repast likewise made its appearance, comprising Fowl, both wild and tame, and hot and cold,

a mighty pasty of veal and eggs baked in a Standing Crust, some curious fresh sallets, and one of potatoes and salted herrings flavoured with garlic—to me most villanously nasty, but much affected in these amphibious Low Countries. So, the little Squire being brought to with a copious draught of champagne,—and he was the most weazened little Bacchus I ever knew, moistening his ever-dry throttle from morning until night,—he and the chaplain sate down to supper, and remained feasting until long past midnight. So far as the Parson's part went, it might have been called a Carouse as well as a Feast, for his Reverence took his Liquor, and plenty of it, with a joviality of Contentment which it would have done your Heart good to see, drinking "Church and King," and then "King and Church," so that neither Institution should have cause to grumble, and then giving the Army, the Navy, the Courts of Quarter Sessions throughout England, Newmarket and the horses, not forgetting the Jockeys, the pious memory of Dr. Sacheverell, at which the Squire winced somewhat, for he was a bitter Whig, with many other elegant and appropriate sentiments. In fact, it was easy to see that his reverence had known the very best of company; and when at one of the clock he called for a Bowl of Punch, which he had taught the Woman of the House very well how to brew, I put him down as one who had sate with Lords,—ay and of the Council too, over their Potations. But the Behaviour of Bartholomew Pinchin, Esq., was, from the beginning unto the end of the Regale, of a piece with his former extraordinary and Grotesque conduct. After the champagne, he essayed to sing a song to the tune of "Cold and Raw," but, failing therein, he began to cry. Then did he accuse me of having secreted the Liver-Wing of a Capon, which, I declare, I had seen him devour not Five Minutes before. Then he had more Drink, and proposed successively as Toasts his Cousin Lady Betty Heeltap, daughter to my Lord Poddle; a certain Madame Van Foorst, who I afterwards discovered to be the keeper of a dancing Ridotto on the Port at Antwerp; then the Jung-frau, or serving wench, that waited upon us, who had for name Babette; and lastly his Mamma, whom, ten minutes afterward, he began to load with Abuse, declaring that she wished to have her Barty shut up in a madhouse, in order that she might enjoy his Lands and Revenues. And then he fell to computing the cost of the supper, swearing that it would Ruin him, and making his old complaints about those eternal wax candles. Then, espying me out, he asks who I am, challenges me to fight with him for a Crown, vows that he will delate me to the English Resident at Brussels for a Jacobite spy, tells me that I am an Honest Fellow, and, next to Mr. Hodge, the best friend he ever had in the world, and falls down at last stupefied. Whereupon, with the assistance of the Flemish Drawer, I carried my new master up to bed.

CHAPTER THE THIRTEENTH.

I MAKE THE GRAND TOUR, AND ACQUIRE SOME KNOWLEDGE OF THE POLITE WORLD.

FOR I had decided that he was to be my Master. "I can bear with his strange ways," I said to myself. "John Dangerous has seen stranger, young as he is; and it will go hard if this droll creature does not furnish forth some sport, ay and some Profit too before long." For now that I had put my Gentility in my pocket, I began to remember that Hay is a very pleasant and toothsome thing for Fodder, to say nothing of its having a most pleasant odour, and that the best time to make hay was while the sun did shine.

After I had assisted in conveying the Little Man to bed, I came down to the Saloon, finding there Mr. Hodge, who was comforting himself with a last bumper of punch before seeking bed.

"Well, Youth," he accosts me, "have you thought better of your surly, huffing manner of this morning and this afternoon?"

I told him that I had, and that I desired nothing better than to enter forthwith into the service of Bartholomew Pinchin, Esquire, of Hampstead.

"That's well," says his Reverence, nodding at me over his punch. "You've had your supper behind yon screen, haven't you?"

I answered, "Yes, and my Burgundy likewise."

"That you mustn't expect every day," he continues, "but only on extraordinary occasions such as that of to-night. What the living is like, you have seen. The best of fish, flesh, and fowl, and plenty of it. As to your Clothes and your Wages, we will hold discourse of that in the morning; for 'twill take your Master half the morning to beat you down a penny a Month, and quarrel with a Tailor about the cheapest kind of serge for your Livery. Leave it to me, however, and I'll engage that you have no reason to complain either of one or the other. What did you say your name was, friend? As for Recommendations, you have none to Give, and I seek not any from you. I will be content to take your character from your Face and Speech."

I began to stammer and bow and thank his Honour's Reverence for his good opinion.

"Don't thank me before you're asked," answers Mr. Hodge, with a grin. "The academy of compliments is not held here. By your speech you have given every sign of being a very Saucy Fellow, and, to judge from your face, you have all the elements in you of a complete Scoundrel."

I bowed, and was silent.

"But your name," he pursued, "that has escaped me."

I answered Respectfully, that I had used to be called John Dangerous.

"Tut, tut!" Mr. Hodge cried out hastily. "Fie upon the name! John is all very well; but Dangerous will never do. Why, our Patron would think directly he heard it that you were bent on cutting his throat, or running away with his valaise."

I submitted, again with much respect, that it was the only name I had.

"Well, thou art a straightforward youth," said the Chaplain good-humouredly, "and I will not press thee to take up an alias. John will serve excellently well for the present; and if more be wanted, thou shalt be John D. But understand that the name of Dangerous is to remain a secret between me and thee and the Post."

"With all my heart," I cried, "so long as the Post be not a gallows."

"Well said, John D.," murmured Mr. Hodge, upon whom by this time the punch had taken some little effect. "A good Lad, John. And now thou mayst help me up to bed."

And so I did, for his Reverence had begun to stagger. Then a pallet was found for me high up in the Roof of the Inn of the Three Archduchesses. I forebore to grumble, for I had been used from my first going out into the world to Hard Lodging. And that night I slept very soundly, and dreamt that I was in the Great Four-post Bed at my Grandmother's in Hanover Square.

Never had a Man, I suppose, in this Mortal World, ever so droll a master as this Bartholomew Pinchin, of Hampstead, Esquire. 'Tis Tame, and may be Offensive, for me to be so continually telling that he wrote himself down *Armiger*,

after my Promise to forego for the future such recapitulation
of his Title; but Mr. Pinchin was himself never tired of
dubbing himself Esquire, and you could scarcely be five
Minutes in his company without hearing of his Estate, and
his Mamma, and his Right to bear Arms. I, who was by
birth a Gentleman of Long Descent, could not forbear Smiling
from time to time (in my Sleeve, be it understood, since I
was a Servant at Wages to him) at his ridiculous Assumptions. And there are few things more Contemptible, I take
it, than for a Man of really good Belongings, and whose
Lineage is as old as Stonehenge (albeit, for Reasons best
known to Himself, he permits his Pedigree to lie Perdu),
to hear an Upstart of Yesterday Bragging and Swelling that
he is come from this or from that, when we, who are of the
true Good Stock, know very well, but that we are not so
ill-mannered as to say so, that he is sprung from Nothing at
all. I think that if the Heralds were to make their Journeys
now, as of Yore, among the Country Churchyards, and hack
out from the Headstones the sculptured·cognisances of those
having no manner of Right to them, the Stone-Masons about
Hyde Park Corner would all make Fortunes from the orders
that would be given to them for fresh Tombs. Not a mealy-
mouthed Burgess now, whose great-grandfather sold stocking-
hose to my Lord Duke of Northumberland, but sets himself
up for a Percy; not a supercilious Cit, whose Uncle married
a cast-off waiting-woman from Arundel Castle, but vaunts
himself on his alliance with the noble house of Howard;
not a starveling Scrivener, whose ancestor, as the playwright
has it, got his Skull cracked by John of Gaunt for crowding
among the Marshalmen in the Tilt Yard, but must pertly
Wink and Snigger, and say that the Dukedom of Lancaster
would not be found extinct if the Right Heir chose to come
Forward. Since that poor young Lord of the Lakes was
attainted for his part in the Troubles of the 'Fifteen, and lost
his head on Tower Hill (his vast Estates going to Greenwich
Hospital), I am given to understand that every man in Cumberland or Westmoreland whose name happens to be Ratcliffe
(I knew the late Mr. Charles Ratcliffe, that Suffered with a
red Feather in his Hat, very well), must give himself out to
be titular Earl of Derwentwater, and Importune the Government to reverse the Attainder, and restore him the Lands of
which the Greenwich Commissioners have gotten such a tight

Hold; and as for Grandchildren of the byblows of King
Charles II., good lack! to hear them talk of the "Merry
Monarch," and to see them draw up their Eyebrows into
the Stuart Frown, one would think that every Player-Woman
at the King's or the Duke's House had been as favoured in
her time as Madam Eleanour Gwyn.

Thus do I no more believe that Mr. Bartholomew Pinchin
was cousin to Lady Betty Heeltap, or in any manner connected with the family of my Lord Poddle (and he was only
one of the Revolution Peers, that got his coronet for Ratting
at the right moment to King William III.), than that he
was the Great Mogul's Grandmother. His gentlemanly extraction was with him all a Vain Pretence and silly outward
show. It did no very great Harm, however. When the
French adventurer Poirier asked King Augustus the Strong
to make him a Count, what said his Majesty of Warsaw and
Luneville? "That I cannot do," quoth he; "but there is
nothing under the sun to prevent thee from calling thyself
a Count, if the humour so please thee." And Count Poirier,
by Self-Creation, he straightway became, and as Count Poirier
was knouted to Death at Moscow for Forging of Rubles
Assignats. Pinchin was palpably a Plebeian; but it suited
him to be called and to call himself an Esquire; and who
should gainsay him? At the Three Archduchesses at Ostend
indeed, they had an exceeding sensible Plan regarding Titles
and Precedence for Strangers, which was found to answer
admirably well. He who took the Grand Suite, looking upon
the courtyard, was always held to be an English Lord. The
tenant of the floor above him was duly esteemed by the
Drawers and Chamberlains to be a Count of the Holy Roman
Empire; a quiet gentleman, who would pay a Louis a day
for his charges, but was content to dine at the Public Table,
was put down as a Baron or a Chevalier; those who occupied the rooms running round the galleries were saluted Merchants, or if they chose it, Captains; but, in the gardens
behind the Inn, there stood a separate Building, called a
Pavilion, most sumptuously appointed, and the Great Room
hung with the Story of Susannah and the Elders in Arras
Tapestry; and he who would pay enough for this Pavilion
might have been hailed as an Ambassador Plenipotentiary, as
a Duke and Peer of France, or even as a Sovereign Prince
travelling incognito, had he been so minded. For what will

N

not Money do?   Take our English Army, for instance, which
is surely the Bravest and the Worst Managed in the whole
World.   My Lord buys a pair of colours for the Valet that
has married his Leman, and forthwith Mr. Jackanapes struts
forth an Ensign.   But for his own Son and Heir my Lord
will purchase a whole troop of Horse; and a Beardless Boy,
that a month agone was Birched at Eton for flaws in his
Grammar, will Vapour it about on the Mall with a Queue à
la Rosbach, and a Long Sword trailing behind him, as a full-
blown Captain of Dragoons.

I believe Pinchin's father to have been a Tailor.   There
is no harm in the Craft, honestly exercised; but since the
world first Began nine Tailors have made a Man; and you
cannot well see a knight of the shears without asking in your
own mind where he has left his Eight brethren.   Bartholomew Pinchin looked like a Tailor, talked like a Tailor, and
thought like a Tailor.   Let it not, however, be surmised that
I have any mind to Malign the Useful Churls who make our
Clothes.   Many a time have I been beholden to the strong
Faith and Generous Belief of a Tailor when I have stood
in need of new Apparel, and have been under momentary
Famine of Funds for the Payment thereof.   Those who are
so ready to sneer at a Snip, and to cast Cabbage in his
teeth, would do well to remember that there are Seasons in
Life when the Goose (or rather he that wields it) may save,
not only the Capitol, but the Soldier who stands on Guard
within.   How doubly Agonising is Death when you are in
doubt as to whence that Full Suit of Black needed on the
Funeral Night will arrive!   What a tremor comes over you
when you remember that this Day Week you are to be Married, and that your Wedding Garment is by no means a cer-
tainty!   What a dreadful Shipwreck to your Fortune menaces you when you are bidden to wait on a Great Man who
has Places to give away, and you find that your Velvet Coat
shows the Cord!   'Tis in these Emergencies that the brave
Confidence of the Tailor is distilled over us like the Blessed
Dew from Heaven; for Trust, when it is really needed, and
opportunely comes, is Real Mercy and a Holy Thing.

About my master's Wealth there was no doubt.   Lord
Poddle, although a questionable cousin of his, would have
been glad to possess his spurious kinsman's acres.   I should
put down the young Esquire's income as at least Twenty

Hundred Pounds a year. His Father had been, it cannot be questioned, a Warm Man ; but I should like to know, if he was veritably, as his Son essayed to make out, a Gentleman, how he came to live in Honey-Lane Market, hard by Cheapside. Gentlemen don't live in Honey-Lane Market. 'Tis in Bloomsbury, or Soho, or Lincoln's Inn, or in the parish of St. George, Hanover Square, that the real Quality have their habitations. I shall be told next that Gentlefolks should have their mansions by the Bunhouse at Pimlico, or in the Purlieus of Tyburn Turnpike. No ; 'twas at the sign of the Sleeveboard, in Honey-Lane Market, that our Patrician Squire made his money. The estate at Hampstead was a very fair one, lying on the North side, Highgate way. Mr. Pinchin's Mamma, a Rare City Dame, had a Life Interest in the property, and, under the old Gentleman's will, had a Right to a Whole Sum of Ten Thousand Pounds if she married again. Thus it was that young Bartholomew was always in an agony of Terror to learn that his mamma had been seen walking on a Sunday afternoon in Gray's-Inn Gardens, or taking Powdered Beef and Ratafia at the tavern in Flask Walk, or drinking of Syllabubs at Bellasise ; and by every post he expected to hear the dreadful intelligence that Madam Pinchin had been picked up as a City Fortune by some ruffling Student of the Inns of Court, some Irish Captain, or some smart Draper that, on the strength of a new Periwig and a lacquered hilt to his Sword, passes for a Macarony. 'Tis not very romantic to relate, but 'tis no less a fact, that the Son and the Mother hated one another. You who have gone through the World and watched it, know that these sad unnatural loathings between Parents and Children, after the latter have grown up, are by no means uncommon. To me it seems almost impossible that Estrangement and Dislike—nay absolute Aversion —should ever engender between the Mother and the Daughter that as a Babe hath hung on her Paps (or should have been so Nurtured, for too many of our Fashionable Fine Dames are given to the cruelly Pernicious Practice of sending their Infants to Nurse almost the very next Week after they are Born, thus Divorcing themselves from the Joys of Tender Affection, and drying-up the very Source and Fontinel of Natural Endearments ; from which I draw the cause of many of the harsh cold Humours and Uncivil Vapours that do reign between the Great and their children). You may cry Haro

upon me for a Cynic or Doggish Philosopher; but I relate
my Experiences, and the Things that have stricken my Mind
and Sense. I do know Ladies of Quality that hate their
Daughters, and would willingly Whip them, did they dare
do so, Grown Women as they are, for Spite. I do know Fathers, Men of Parts and Rank, forsooth, jealous of their Sons,
and that have kept the Youngsters in the Background, and
even striven to Obscure their Minds that they might not cross
the Paternal Orbit. And has it not almost passed into a proverb, that my Lord Duke's Natural and most Inveterate Enemy
is my Lord Marquis, who is his Heir? But not to the World
of Gold and Purple are these Jealousies and Evil Feelings
confined. You shall find them to the full as Venomous in
hovels, where pewter Platters are on the shelves, and where
Fustian and Homespun are the only wear. Down in the West
of England, where a worthy Friend of mine has an Estate, I
know a Shepherd tending his flocks from sunrise—ay, and before the Sun gets up—until sundown. The honest man has
but half-a-dozen shillings a week, and has begotten Fourteen
Children. He is old now, and feeble, and is despised by his
Progeny. He leads at Home the sorriest of Lives. They
take his wages from him, and, were it not for a lump of fat
Bacon which my friend's Servants give him now and again
for Charity's sake, he would have nothing better to eat from
Week's End to Week's End than the hunch of Bread and the
morsel of Cheese that are doled forth to him every morning
when he goes to his labour. Only the other day, his sixth
daughter, a comely Piece enough, was Married. The poor
old Shepherd begs a Holiday, granted to him easily enough,
and goes home at Midday instead of Even, thinking to have
some part in the Wedding Rejoicings, the which his last
week's wages have gone some way to furnish forth. I promise
you that 'tis a fine Family Feast that he comes across. What
but ribs of Beef and Strong Ale—none of your Harvest Clink
—and old Cyder and Plum-pudding galore! But his Family
will have none of his company, and set the poor old Shepherd
apart, giving him but an extra lump of Bread and Cheese to
regale himself withal. 'Twas he who told the Story to my
Friend, from whom I heard it. What, think you, was his
simple complaint, his sole Protest against so much Cruelty
and Injustice? He did not rush into the Feasting Room and
curse these Ingrates; he did not trample on this Brood that

he had nurtured, and that had turned out worse in their Un-
thankfulness than Vipers: no, he just sat apart, wringing of
his Hands, and meekly wailing, "What, a weddin', and narrer
a bit o' puddin'—narrer a bit, a bit o' puddin' !" The poor
soul had set his head on a slice of dough with raisins in it,
and even this crumb from their Table was denied him by his
Cubs. 'Tis a brave thing, is it not, Neighbour, to be come
to Threescore Years, and to have had Fruitful Loins, and to
be Mocked and Misused by those thou hast begotten? How
infinitely better do we deem ourselves than the Cat and Dog,
and yet how often do we imitate those Dumb Beasts in our
own degree! fondling them indeed when they are Kittens
and Puppies, but fighting Tooth and Nail with them when
they be full grown. But there is as much to be said on the
one side as on the other; and for every poor old Lear wandering up and down, pursued by the spite of Goneril and
Regan, shall you find a Cordelia whose heart is broken by her
Sire's Cruelty.

We did not long abide in Ostend. Presently my master
grew tired of the Town, as he did of most Things, and longed
for change. He had no better words for the Innkeepers,
Merchants, and others who attended him than to call them
a parcel of Extortionate Thieves, and to vow that they were
all in a conspiracy for robbing and bringing him to the Poor
House. He often did us the honour to accuse us of being
in the Plot; and many a time I felt inclined to resent his
Impertinence and to cudgel the abusive little man soundly;
but I was wise, and held my Tongue and my Hand as well.
Following the Chaplain's advice, and humouring this little
Man-monkey in all his caprices, I found that he was not so
bad a master after all, and that when he was Drunk, which
was almost always, he could be generous enough. When he
was sober and bewailed his excessive Expenditure, our policy
was to be Mum, or else to Flatter him; and so no bones
were broken, and I was well clad and fed, and always had
a piece of gold in my pouch, and so began to Feel my Feet.

We visited most of the towns in the Low Countries, then
under the Austrian rule, enjoying ourselves, with but little
occasion for repining. Now our travelling was done on
Horseback, and now, when there was a Canal Route, by
one of those heavy, lumbering, jovial old boats called Treyck-
shuyts. I know not whether I spell the word correctly, for

in the Languages albeit fluent enough, I could never be accurate; but of the pleasant old vessels themselves I shall ever preserve a lively recollection. You made a bargain with the Master before starting, giving him so many guilders for a journey, say between Ghent and Bruges, the charge amounting generally to about a Guinea a day for each Gentleman passenger, and half the sum for a servant. And the Domestic's place on the fore-deck and in the fore-cabin was by no means an unpleasant one; for there he was sure to meet good store of comely Fraws, and Jungfraws comelier still, with their clean white caps, Linsey-woolsey petticoats, wooden shoes, and little gold crosses about their necks. Farmers and labouring men and pedlars, with now and then a fat, smirking Priest or two, who tried Hard to Convert you, if by any means he discovered you to be a Heretic, made up the complement of passengers forward; but I, as a servant, was often called aft, and had the pick of both companies, with but light duties, and faring always like a Fighting Cock. For no sooner was our Passage-Money paid than it became my duty to lay-in a Great Stock of Provisions for the voyage, my master disdaining to put up with the ordinary country Fare of dried fish, salted beef, pickled cabbage, hard-boiled eggs, faro-Beer, Schiedam, and so forth, and instructing me, under Mr. Hodge's direction, to purchase Game, Venison, Fruit, Vegetables, Preserves, Cheeses, and other condiments, with a sufficient number of flasks of choice wine, and a little keg of strong cordial, for fear of Accidents. And aboard the Treyckshuyt it was all Singing and Dancing and Carding and drinking of Toasts. The quantity of Tobacco that the country people took was alarming, and the fumes thereof at first highly displeasing to Mr. Pinchin; but I, from my sea education, and the Time I had passed in the Western Indies, was a seasoned vessel as to tobacco; and often when my Master had gone to his cabin for the night was permitted to partake of a Puff on deck with the Reverend Mr. Hodge, who dearly loved his Pipe of Virginia. The Chaplain always called me John D.; and indeed by this time I seemed to be fast losing the character as well as the name of Dangerous. My life was passed in the Plenitude of Fatness; and I may say almost that I was at Grass with Nebuchadnezzar, and had one Life with the beasts of the field; for my days were given up to earthly indulgences, and I was no better than a stalled ox. But the old perils and troubles of my career were only Dormant, and ere long I was to become Jack Dangerous again.

A year passed away in this eating and drinking, dozy, lazy kind of life. I was seventeen years of age, and it was the autumn of the year '29. We were resting for a time—not that Master, Chaplain, or Man ever did much to entitle them to repose—at the famous watering-place of Spa, close to the German Frontier. We put up at the Silver Stag, where we were entertained in very Handsome Style. Spa, or the Spaw, as it was sometimes called, was then one of the most Renowned Baths in Europe, and was attended by the very Grandest company. Here, when we arrived, was my Lord Duke of Tantivy, an English nobleman of the very Highest Figure, accompanied by my Lady Duchess, the Lord Marquis of Newmarket, his Grace's Son and Heir, who made Rare Work at the gaming tables, with which the place abounded; the Ladies Kitty and Bell Jockeymore, his daughters; and attended by a Numerous and sumptuous suite. Here also did I see the famous French Prince de Noisy-Gevres, then somewhat out of favour at the French Court for writing of a Lampoon on one of his Eminence the Cardinal Minister's Lady Favourites; the Great Muscovite Boyard Stchigakoff, who had been here ever since the Czar Peter his master had honoured the Spaw with his presence; and any number of Foreign Notabilities, of the most Illustrious Rank, and of either sex. Money was the great Master of the Ceremonies, however, and he who had the Longest Purse was bidden to the Bravest Entertainments. The English of Quality, indeed (as is their custom, which makes 'em so hated by Foreigners), kept themselves very much to themselves, and my Lord Duke of Tantivy's party, with the exception of the Marquis of Newmarket, who was good enough to Borrow a score of gold pieces from us, and to Rook us at cards now and then, took not the slightest notice of my poor little Master, who was dying to be introduced into Polite Society, and spread abroad those fictions of his cousinage to Lady Betty Heeltap and my Lord Poddle every where he went; but the French and German Magnificoes were less Haughty, and were glad to receive an English Traveller who, when his Vanity was concerned, would spend his cash without stint. We drank a great deal of the Water of the Spaw, and uncommonly nasty it was, making it a Thing of vital necessity to take the Taste of it out of our Mouths as soon as might be with Wine and Strong Waters.

From the Spaw we went by easy Stages to Cologne, a dirty, foul-smelling place, but very Handsome in Buildings, and saw all that was to be seen, that is to say, the churches, which Abound Greatly. The Jesuits' Church is the neatest, and this was shown us in a very complaisant manner, although 'tis not the custom to allow Protestants to enter it. Our Cicerone was a bouncing young Jesuit, with a Face as Rosy as the sunny side of a Katherine Pear ; but it shocked me to hear how he indulged in Drolleries and Railleries in the very edifice itself. He quizzed both the Magnificence and Tawdriness of the Altars, the Images of the Saints, the Rich Framing of the Relics, and all he came across, seeming no more impressed by their solemnity than the Verger Fellow in Westminster Abbey when he shows the Waxwork to a lot of Yokels at sixpence a head. "Surely," I thought, "there must be something wrong in a Faith whose Professors make so light of its ceremonies, and turn Buffoons in the very Temples ;" nor could I help murmuring inwardly at that profusion of Pearls, Diamonds, and Rubies bestowed on the adornment of a parcel of old Bones, decayed Teeth, and dirty Rags. A Fine English Lady, all paint and Furbelows, who was in the church with us, honestly owned that she coveted St. Ursula's great Pearl Necklace, and, says she, "'Tis no sin, and not coveting one's neighbour's goods, for neither St. Ursula nor the Jesuits are any Neighbours of mine ;" and as for my Master, he stared at a Great St. Christopher, mighty fine in Silver, and said that it would have looked very well as an Ornament for a Cistern in his garden at Hampstead.

From Cologne to Nuremberg was five days, travelling post from Frankfort ; and here we observed the difference between the Free Towns of Germany and those under the government of petty Absolute Princes. The streets of Nuremberg are well built, and full of People ; the shops are loaded with Merchandise, and commonly Clean and Cheerful. In Cologne and Wurtsburg there was but a sort of shabby finery : a number of dirty People of Quality sauntered out ; narrow nasty streets out of repair ; and above half of the common Sort asking Alms. Mr. Hodge, who would have his jest, compared a Free Town to a handsome, clean Dutch

Burgher's wife, and a Petty Prince's capital to a poor Town Lady of Pleasure, painted and ribboned out in her Head-dress, with tarnished Silver-lace shoes, and a ragged Under Petticoat—a miserable mixture of Vice and Poverty.

Here at Nuremberg they had Sumptuary Laws, each man and woman being compelled to dress according to his Degree, and the Better sort only being licensed to wear Rich suits of clothes. And, to my thinking (though the Putting it in Practice might prove somewhat inconvenient), we should be much better off in England if some such laws were made for the moderation and restraining of Excess and Extravagance in Apparel. As folks dress nowadays, it is impossible to tell Base Raff from the Highest Quality. What with the cheapness of Manufactured goods, and the pernicious introduction of imitation Gold and Silver lace, you shall find Drapers' apprentices, Tavern drawers, and Cook wenches, making as Brave a Figure on Sundays as their masters and mistresses; and many a young Spark has been brought to the Gallows, and many a poor Lass to Bridewell or the Spital, through an over Fondness for cheap Finery, and a crazy conceit for dressing like their betters.

Nuremberg hath its store of Churches and Relics, and the like; and even the Lutherans, who are usually thought to be so strict and severe in the adornment of their Temples, have in one of 'em a large Cross fairly set with jewels. But this is nothing to the Popish High Church, where they have at least a score of Saints, all dressed out in laced clothes, and fair Full-bottomed Wigs plentifully powdered. Here did we come across a Prince Bishop of one of the Electoral German Towns, travelling with a Mighty Retinue of Canons and Priests, and Assessors and Secretaries, and a long train of Mules most richly caparisoned, with a guard of a hundred Musketeers, with violet liveries and Mitres broidered on their cartouch-boxes, to keep the Prince Bishop from coming to harm. My Master dined with this Reverend Personage, although Mr. Hodge, to maintain the purity of his cloth, kept aloof from any such Papistical entertainment; but I was of the party, it being my duty to wait behind the Squire's chair. We dined at two of the clock on very rich meats, high spiced, as I have usually found Princes and Bishops to like their victuals (for the Plainer sort soon Pall on their Palates); and after dinner there was a Carousal, which lasted

well nigh till bed-time. His Episcopal Highness's Master of
the Horse (though the title of Master of the Mules, on which
beasts the company mostly rode, would have better served
him) got somewhat too Merry on Rhenish about Dusk, and
was carried out to the stable, where the Palefreneers littered
him down with straw, as though he had been a Horse or a
Mule himself; and then a little fat Canon, who was the
Buffoon or Jack Pudding of the party, sang songs over his
drink which were not in the least like unto Hymns or Can-
ticles, but rather of a most Mundane, not to say Loose, order
of Chant. His Highness (who wore the Biggest Emerald
ring on his right Forefinger, over his glove, that ever I saw)
took a great fancy to my Master, and at Parting pledged him
in choice Rhenish in the handsomest fashion, using for that
purpose a Silver Bell holding at least a Pint and a half
English. Out of this Bell he takes the clapper, and holding
it mouth upwards, drains it to the health of my Master, then
fixes the clapper in again, Topsy-turvies his goblet, and rings
a peal on the bell to show that he is a right Skinker. My
Master does the same, as in Duty Bound, and mighty Flustered he got before the Ringing-time came; and then the
little Fat Canon that sang the songs essayed to do the same,
but was in such a Quandary of Liquor, that he spills a pint
over Mr. Secretary's lace bands, and the two would have
fallen to Fisticuffs but for his Episcopal Highness (who
laughed till his Sides Shook again) commanding that they
should be separated by the Lacqueys. This was the most
jovial Bishop that I did meet with; and I have heard that
he was a good kind of man enough to the Poor, and not a
harsh Sovereign to his subjects, especially to the Female
Part who were fortunate enough to be pretty; but young
as I was, and given to Pleasures, I could not help lifting
up my Hands in shocked Amazement to see this Roystering
kind of life held by a Christian Prelate. And it is certain
that many of the High Dutch Church Dignitaries were at
this time addicted to a most riotous mode of living. 'Twas
thought no scandal in a Bishop to Drink, or to Dice, or to
gallivant after Damosels; but woe be to him if he Dared to
Dance, for the Shaking of a Leg (that had a cassock over it)
was held to be a most Heinous and Unpardonable Sin.

Next to Ratisbon, where Mr. Pinchin was Laid up with
a Fever brought on by High Living, and for more than Five

Weeks remained between Life and Death, causing both to
Mr. Hodge and myself the Greatest Anxiety; for, with all
his Faults and Absurd Humours, there was something about
the Little Man that made us Bear with him. And to be in
his Service, for all his capricious and passing Meannesses,
was to be in very Good Quarters indeed. He was dreadfully
frightened at the prospect of Slipping his Cable in a Foreign
Land, and was accustomed, during the Delirium that accompanied the Fever, to call most piteously on his Mamma,
sometimes fancying himself at Hampstead, and sometimes
battling with the Waves in the Agonies of the cramp, as I
first came across him at Ostend. When he grew better, to
our Infinite Relief, the old fit of Economy came upon him,
and he must needs make up his mind to Diet himself upon
Panada and Mint Tea, taking no other nourishment until his
Doctor tells him that if he did not fall to with a Roast
chicken and a flask of White Wine, he would sink and Die
from pure Exhaustion. After this he began to Pick up a bit,
and to Relish his Victuals; but it was woful to see the countenance he pulled when the Doctor's Bill was brought him,
and he found that he had something like Eighty Pounds
sterling to pay for a Sickness of Forty Days. Of course he
swore that he had not had a tithe of the Draughts and Mixtures that were set down to him,—and he had not indeed
consumed them bodily, for the poor little Wretch would
have assuredly Died had he swallowed a Twentieth Part of
the Vile Messes that the Pill-blistering Gentleman sent in;
but Draughts and Mixtures had all duly arrived, and we in
our Discretion had uncorked them, and thrown the major
part of their contents out of window. We were in league,
forsooth (so he said) with the Doctor to Eat and Ruin him,
and 'twas not till the latter had threatened to appeal to the
Burgomaster, and to have us all clapped up in the Town
Gaol for roving adventurers (for they manage things with a
High Hand at Ratisbon), that the convalescent would consent
to Discharge the Pill-blisterer's demands; and, granting even
that all this Muckwash had been supplied, the Doctor must
have been after all an Extortioner, and have made a Smart
Profit out of that said Fever; for he presses a compliment of
a silver snuff-box on the Chaplain, giving me also privately
a couple of Golden Ducats; nor have I any doubt that the
Innkeeper had also his commission to receive for recommend-

ing a Doctor to the sick Englishman, and was duly satisfied by Meinheer Bolus.

There was the Innkeeper's bill itself to be unpouched, and a mighty Pother there was over each item, Mr. Pinchin seeming to think that because he had been sick, it was our Duty to have laid abed too, swallowing naught but Draughts and Slops. Truth was, that we should not have been Equal to the task of Nursing and Tending so difficult a Patient had we not taken Fortifying and Substantial Nourishment and a sufficiency of Wholesome Liquor; not making merry, it is true, with indecent revelry, but Bearing up with a Grave and Reverent countenance, and taking our Four Meals a day, with Refreshing Sups between whiles. And I have always found that the vicinage of a Sick Room is apt to make one exceeding Hungry and Thirsty, and that a Moribund, albeit he can take neither Bite nor Sup himself, is, in his surroundings, the cook's best Friend, and the Vintner's most bountiful Patron.

Coming to his health again, Mr. Pinchin falls nevertheless into a state of Dark Melancholy and Despondency, talking now of returning to England, and ending his days there, and now entertaining an even Stranger Fancy that had come over his capricious mind. We had nursed him during his sickness according to the best of our Capacity, but felt nevertheless the want of some Woman's hand to help us. Now all the Maids in the House were mortally afraid of the Fever, and would not so much as enter the Sick Man's apartment, much less make his bed; while, if we had not taken it at our own Risk to promise the Innkeeper Double Fees for lodging, the cowardly knave would have turned us out, Neck and Crop, and we should have been forced to convey our poor Sufferer to a common Hospital. But there was in this City of Ratisbon a convent of Pious Ladies who devoted themselves wholly (and without Fee or Reward for the most part) to works of Mercy and Charity; and Mr. Hodge happening to mention my Master's State to the English Banker—one Mr. Sturt, who was a Romanist, but a very civil kind of man —he sends to the convent, and there comes down forthwith to our Inn a dear Good Nun that turned out to be the most zealous and patient Nurse that I have ever met with in my Travels. She sat up night and day with the Patient, and could scarcely be persuaded to take ever so little needful Rest

and Refreshment. When she was not ministering to the
sufferer's wants, she was Praying, although it did scandalise
Mr. Hodge a little to see her tell her Beads; and when Mr.
Pinchin was well enough to eat his first slice of chicken, and
sip his first beaker of white wine, she Clapped her Hands for
joy, and sang a little Latin Hymn.   When it came to her
dismissal, this Excellent Nun (the whole of whose Behaviour
was most touchingly Edifying) at first stoutly refused to
accept of any Recompense for her services (which, truly, no
Gold, Silver, or Jewels could have fitly rewarded); and I am
ashamed to say that my Master, who had then his Parsimo-
nious Nightcap on, was at first inclined to take the Good
Sister at her Word.   Mr. Hodge, however, showed him the
Gross Ingratitude and Indecorum of such a proceeding, and,
as was usual with him, he gave way, bellowing, however, like
a Calf when the Chaplain told him that he could not in Decency do less than present a sum of Fifty Ducats (making
about Forty Pounds of our Money) to the convent; for per-
sonal or private Guerdon the Nun positively refused to take.
So the Money was given, to the great delectation of the
Sisterhood, who, I believe, made up their minds to Sing
Masses for the bountiful English Lord as they called him,
whether he desired it or not.

Sorry am I to have to relate that so Pleasant and Moving
an Incident should have had any thing like a Dark side.
But 'tis always thus in the World, and there is no Rose without a Thorn.   My master, thanks to his Chaplain, and, it
may be, likewise to my own Humble and Respectful Representations while I was a-dressing of him in the Morning, had
come out of this convent and sick-nurse affair with Infinite
credit to himself and to the English nation in general.   Every
where in Ratisbon was his Liberality applauded; but, alas,
the publicity that was given to his Donation speedily brought
upon us a Plague and Swarm of Ravenous Locusts and Blood-
suckers.   There were as many convents in Ratisbon as plums
in a Christmas porridge; there were Nuns of all kinds of
orders, many of whom, I am afraid, no better than they should
be; there were Black Monks and Gray Monks and Brown
Monks and White Monks, Monks of all colours of the Rain-
bow, for aught I can tell.   There were Canons and Chapters
and Priories and Brotherhoods and Sisterhoods and Ecclesi-
astical Hospitals and Priors' Almonries and Saints' Guilds

without end. Never did I see a larger fry of holy men and
women, professing to live only for the next world, but making
the very best of this one while they were in it. A greasy,
lazy, worthless Rabble-Rout they were, making their Religion
a mere Pretext for Mendicancy and the worst of crimes. For
the most part they were as Ignorant as Irish Hedge School-
masters; but there were those among them of the Jesuit,
Capuchin, and Benedictine orders; men very subtle and
dangerous, well acquainted with the Languages, and able to
twist you round their Little Fingers with False Rhetoric and
Lying Persuasions.

These Snakes in the grass got about my poor weak-
minded Master, although we, as True Protestants and
Faithful Servants, did our utmost to keep them out;
but if you closed the Door against 'em, they would come in
at the Keyhole; and if you made the Window fast, they
would slip down the Chimney; and, with their Pernicious
Doctrines, Begging Petitions, and Fraudulent Representations,
did so Badger, Bait, Beleaguer, and Bully him, that the poor
Man knew not which Way to Turn. They too did much
differ in their Theology, and each order of Friars seemed to
hold the strong opinion that all who wore cowls cut in
another shape than theirs, or shaved their pates differently,
must Infallibly Burn; but they were of one Mind in tugging
at Mr. Pinchin's Purse-strings, and their cry was ever that of
the Horse-Leech's Three Daughters—"Give, give!"

Thus they did extract from him Forty Crowns in gold
for Redeeming out of Slavery among the Sallee Rovers ten
Citizens of Ratisbon fallen into that doleful captivity; although I do, on my conscience, believe that there were not
five native-born men in the whole city who had ever seen
the Salt Sea, much less a Sallee Rover. Next was a donation
for a petticoat for this Saint, and a wig for that one; a score
of Ducats for a School, another for an Hospital for Lepers;
until it was Ducats here and Ducats there all day long. Nor
was this the worst; for my Master began to be Troubled in
the Spirit, and to cry out against the Vanities of the World,
and to sigh after the Blessedness of a Life passed in Seclusion
and Contemplation.

"I'll turn Monk, I will," he cried out one day; "my Lord
Duke of Wharton did it, and why should not I?"

"Monk, and a Murrain to them, and Mercy to us all!"

says Mr. Hodge, quite aghast. "What new Bee will you put under your Bonnet next, sir?"

"You're a Heretic," answers Mr. Pinchin. "An Anglican Heretic, and so is my knave John here. There's nothing like the old Faith. There's nothing like Relics. Didn't I see a prodigious claw set in gold only yesterday in the Barnabite Church, and wasn't that the true and undoubted relic of a Griffin?"

"Was the Griffin a Saint?" asks the Chaplain humbly.

"What's that to you?" retorts my Master. "You're a Heretic, you're a Scoffer, an Infidel! I tell you that I mean to become a Monk."

"What, and wear peas in your shoes! nay, go without shoes at all, and leave off cutting your toe-nails?" quoth the Chaplain, much irate. "Forsake washing and the Thirty-nine Articles! Shave your head, and forswear the Act of Settlement! Wear a rope girdle and a rosary instead of a handsome sword with a silver hilt at your side! Go about begging and bawling of paternosters! Was it for this that I, a Clergyman of the Church of England, came abroad with you to keep you in the True Faith and a Proper respect for the Protestant Succession?" Mr. Hodge had quite forgotten the value of his Patron's favour, and was growing really angry. In those days men would make sacrifices for conscience' sake.

"Hang the Protestant Succession, and you too!" screams Mr. Pinchin.

"Jacobite, Papist, Warming Pan!" roars the Chaplain, "I will delate you to the English Envoy here, and you shall be laid by the heels as soon as ever you set foot in England. You shall swing for this, sir!"

"Leave the Room!" yells Mr. Pinchin, starting up, but trembling in every limb, for he was hardly yet convalescent of his Fever.

"I won't," answers the sturdy Chaplain. "You wretched rebellious little Ape, I arrest you in the King's name and Convocation's. I'll teach you to malign the Act of Settlement, I will!"

Whenever Mr. Hodge assumed a certain threatening tone, and began to pluck at his cassock in a certain manner, Mr. Pinchin was sure to grow frightened. He was beginning to looked scared, when I, who remembering my place as a servant had hitherto said nothing, ventured to interpose.

" Oh, Mr. Pinchin !" I pleaded, " think of your Mamma
in England. Why, it will break the good lady's heart if you
go Romewards, Sir. Think of your estate. Think of your
tenants and the Commission of the Peace, and the duties of a
Liveryman of the City of London."

I knew that I had touched my Master in a tender part, and
anon he began to whimper, and cry about his Mamma, who,
he shrewdly enough remarked, might cause his Estate to be
sequestrated under the Act against Alienation of Lands by
Popish Recusants, and so rob the Monks of their prey. And
then, being soothingly addressed by Mr. Hodge, he admitted
that the Friars were for the greater part Beggars and Thieves ;
and before supper-time we obtained an easy permission from
him to drive those Pestilent Gentry from the doors, and deny
him on every occasion when they should be impudent enough
to seek admission to his presence.

We were no such high Favourites in Ratisbon after this ;
and I believe the Jesuits denounced us to the Inquisition at
Rome,—in case we should ever go that way,—that the Capu-
chins cursed us, and the Benedictines preached against us.
The Town Authorities began also to look upon us with a cold
eye of suspicion ; and but for the sojourn of an English
Envoy in Ratisbon (we had diplomatic agents then all over
the Continent, and very little they did for their Money save
Dance and Intrigue), the Burgomaster and his Councillors
might have gotten up against us what the French do call *une
querelle d'Allemand*, which may be a Quarrel about Any thing,
and is a Fashion of Disagreeing peculiar to the Germans, who
may take offence at the cock of your Hat or the cut of your
Coat, and make either of them a State affair.   Indeed, I
believe that some Imprudent Expressions, made use of by my
Master on seeing the Horrible Engines of Torture shown to
the curious in the vaults of the castle, were very nearly being
construed into High Treason by the unfriendly clerical party,
and that an Information by the Stadt-Assessor was being
actually drawn up against him, when, by much Persuasion
coupled with some degree of gentle Violence, we got him
away from Ratisbon altogether.

CHAPTER THE FOURTEENTH.

From Ratisbon we travelled down the River Danube, in a very pleasant and agreeable manner, in a kind of Wooden House mounted on a flat-bottomed Barge, and not unlike a Noah's Ark. 'Twas most convenient, and even handsomely laid out, with Parlours, and with Drawing Rooms, and Kitchens and Stoves, and a broad planked Promenade over all, railed in, and with Flowering Plants in pots by the sides, quite like a garden. They are rowed by twelve men each, and move with an almost Incredible Celerity; so that in the same day one can Delight one's Eye with a vast Variety of Prospects; and within a short space of time the Traveller has the diversion of seeing a populous City adorned with magnificent Palaces, and the most Romantic Solitude, which appear quite Apart from the commerce of Mankind, the banks of the Danube being exquisitely disposed into Forests, Mountains, Vineyards rising in Terraces one above the other, Fields of Corn and Rye, great Towns, and Ruins of Ancient Castles. Now for the first time did I see the Cities of Passau and of Lintz, famous for the retreat of the Imperial Court when Vienna was besieged by the Great Turk, the same that John Sobieski, King of Poland, timeously Defeated and put to Rout, to the great shame of the Osmanlis, and the Everlasting Glory of the Christian arms.

And now for Vienna. This is the capital of the German Emperor, Kaiser, or Cæsar as he calls himself, and a mighty mob of under-Cæsars or Archdukes he has about him. In my young days the Holy Roman Empire was a Flourishing concern, and made a great noise in the world; but now people do begin to speak somewhat scornfully of it, and to hold it in no very great Account, principally, I am told, owing to the levelling Principles of the Emperor Joseph the Second, who, instead of keeping up the proper State of Despotic Rule, and filling his Subjects' minds with a due impression of the Dreadful Awe of Imperial Majesty, has taken to occupying himself with the affairs of mean and common persons,—such as Paupers, Debtors, Criminals, Orphans, Mechanics, and the

o

like,—quite turning his back on the Exalted Tradition of undisputed power, and saying sneeringly, that he only bore
Crown and Sceptre because Royalty was his Trade.   This they
call a Reforming Sovereign; but I cannot see what good comes
out of such wild Humours and Fancies.   It is as though my
Lord Duke were to ask his Running Footman to sit down
at table with him; beg the Coachman not to trouble himself about stable work, but go wash the carriage-wheels and
currycomb the Horses himself; bid my Lady Duchess and his
Daughters dress themselves in Dimity Gowns and Mob caps,
while Sukey Mops and Dorothy Draggletail went off to the
Drawing-room in Satin sacks and High-heeled shoes; and, to
cap his Absurdities, called up all his Tenants to tell them that
henceforth they were to pay no Rent or Manor Dues at the
Court Leet, but to have their Farms in freehold for ever.
No; it is certain the World cannot go on without Authority,
and that too of the Smartest.   What would you think of a
ship where the Master Mariner had no power over his crew,
and no license to put 'em in the Bilboes, or have 'em up at
the gangway to be Drubbed soundly when they deserved it?
And these Reforming Sovereigns, as they call 'em, are only
making, to my mind, Rods for their own Backs, and Halters
for their own Necks.   Where would the Crown and Majesty
be now, I wonder, if His Blessed Majesty had given way to
the Impudent Demands of Mr. Washington and the American
Rebels?*

The Streets of Vienna, when I first visited that capital,
were very close and narrow—so narrow, indeed, that the
fine fronts of the Palaces (which are very Grand) can scarcely
be seen.   Many of 'em deserve close observation, being truly
Superb, all built of Fine White Stone, and excessive high,
the town being much too little for the number of its inhabitants.   But the Builders seem to have repaired that Misfortune by clapping one town on the top of another, most of
the Houses being of Five and some of Six Stories.   The
Streets being so narrow, the rooms are all exceeding Dark,
and never so humble a mansion but has half a dozen families
living in it.   In the Handsomest even all Ranks and Con-

---

* Had Captain Dangerous written his memoirs a few years later,
he might have found cause to alter his opinion respecting the wisdom
of George III, in refusing to grant the American demands.

ditions are Mingled together pellmell. You shall find Field-Marshals, Lieutenants, Aulic Councillors, and Great Court Ladies divided but by a thin partition from the cabins of Tailors and Shoemakers ; and few even of the Quality could afford a House to themselves, or had more than Two Floors in a House—one for their own use, and another for their Domestics. It was the Dead Season of the year when we came to this City, and so, at not so very enormous a rate, we got a suite of six or eight large rooms, all inlaid, the Doors and Windows richly carved and gilt, and the Furniture such as is rarely seen but in the Palaces of Sovereign Princes in other countries ; the Hangings in finest tapestry in Brussels, prodigious large looking-glasses in silver frames (in making which they are exceeding Expert) ; fine Japan Tables, Beds, Chairs, Canopies, and Curtains of the richest Genoa Damask or Velvet, almost covered with gold lace or embroidery. The whole made Gay by Pictures, or Great Jars of Porcelain ; in almost every room large lustres of pure Crystal ; and everything as dirty as a Secondhand Clothes dealer's booth in Rag Fair.

We were not much invited out at Vienna, the very Highest Quality only being admitted to their company by the Austrians, who are the very Haughtiest and most exclusive among the High Dutch, and look upon a mere untitled Englishman as Nobody (although he may be of Ten Times better blood than their most noble Raggednesses). A mean sort, for all their finely furnished palaces, and wearing mighty foul Body Linen. The first question they ask, when they Hear that a Stranger desires to be Presented to them, is, " Is he Born ?" The query having nothing to do with the fact of his nativity, but meaning (so I have been told), " Has he five-and-thirty Quarterings in his Coat-of-Arms ?" And if he has but four-and-thirty (though some of their greatest nobles have not above Four or Five Hundred Pounds a year to live on), the Stranger is held to be no more Born than if he were an Embryo : and the Quality of Vienna takes no more notice of him than of the Babe which is unborn.

Truly, it was the Dead Season, and we could not have gone to many Dinners and Assemblies, even if the Aristocracy had been minded to show hospitality towards us. There were Theatres and Operas, however, open, which much delighted my Master and myself (who was privileged to attend him), although the Reverend Mr. Hodge stayed away for conscience' sake from such Profane amusements, comforting himself at home over a Merry Book and a Bottle of Erlauer, which is an Hungarian wine, very dark and Rough, but as strong as a Bullock, and an excellent stomachic. Nothing more magnificent than the Operas then performed at the Gardens of the Favorite, throwing the Paris and London houses utterly into the shade, and I have heard that the Habits, Decorations, and Scene Paintings, cost the Emperor Thirty Thousand Pound Sterling. And to think of the millions of poor ragged wretches that must have been taxed, and starved, and beaten, and robbed, and skinned alive, so to speak, before His Majesty's pleasures would be paid for.* The Stage in this Favorite Garden was built over a large canal, and at the beginning of the Second Act divided (as in our own Theatre hard by Sadler's Wells) into Two Parts, discovering the water, on which there immediately came from different parts two little Fleets of gilded vessels, that gave the impression (though ludicrously incorrect in their Riggings and Manœuvres) of a Sea-fight. The story of the Opera was, if I remember right, the Enchantments of Alcina ; an entertainment which gave opportunity for a great Variety of Machines and changes of the Scene, which were performed with surprising swiftness. No House could hold such large Decorations. But the Ladies all sitting in the open air, exposed them to much inconvenience ; for there was but one Canopy for the Imperial Family ; and the first night we were there, a shower of Rain coming on, the Opera was broken off, and the Company crowded away in such confusion that we were almost squeezed to Death.

If their Operas were thus productive of such Delectable Entertainment (abating the Rain and crowding), I cannot say much for their Comedies and Drolls, which were highly Ridiculous. We went to the German Playhouse, and saw the Story of Amphitryon very scurvily represented. Jupiter falls in love out of a peep-hole in the clouds in the beginning, and the end of it was the Birth of Hercules. It was very pitiful to see Jove, under the figure of Amphitryon, cheating a Tailor of a laced coat, and a Banker of a bag of Money, and a Jew of a Diamond Ring, with the like Rascally Subterfuges ; and Mercury's usage of Sosia was little more digni-

---

* And yet Captain Dangerous is a stanch opponent of Reform.—Ed.

fied. And the play was interlarded with very gross expressions and unseemly gestures, such as in England would not be tolerated by the Master of the Revels, or even in France by the Gentleman of the Chamber having charge over the Theatres, but at which the Viennese Quality, both Male and Female, did laugh Heartily and with much Gusto.

Memorandum. As some of the Manners then existing have passed away (in this sad changeful age, when everything seems melting away like Cowheel Jelly at a Wedding Feast), I have set down for those curious in such matters that the Vienna Dames were squeezed up in my time in gowns and gorgets, and had built fabrics of gauze on their Heads about a yard high, consisting of Three or Four Stories, fortified with numberless yards of heavy Ribbon. The foundation of this alarming structure was a thing they called a *Bourle*, which was exactly of the same shape and kind—only four times Bigger—as those Rolls which our Milkmaids make use of to fix their Pails upon. This machine they covered with their own hair, with which they mixed a great deal of False; it being a Particular and Especial Grace with them to have their Heads too large to go into a moderate-sized Tub. Their Hair was prodigiously powdered to conceal the mixture, and so set out with numerous rows of Bodkins, sticking out three or four Inches on each side, made of Diamonds, Pearls, Green, Red, and Yellow Stones, that it certainly required as much Art and Experience to carry the load upright as to dance on May-day with the Garland that the Dairy Wenches borrow (under good security) from the Silversmiths in Cranbourn Alley. Also they had Whalebone Petticoats, outdoing ours by several yards in circumference. Vastly Ridiculous were these Fashions—think you not so, good Sir or Madam, as the case may be? And yet, may I be whipped, but much later in the present century I have seen such things as hoops, tours, and toupees, not one whit less Ridiculous.

The Empress, a sweet pretty lady, was perforce obliged to wear this Habit; but with the other Female Grandees it only served to increase their natural Ugliness. Memorandum: that at Court (whither we went not, being "unborn," but heard a great deal of it from hearsay) a Game called Quinze was the Carding most in vogue. Their drawing-rooms are different from those in England, no Man Creature entering them but the old Grand-Master, who comes to announce to the Empress the arrival of His Imperial Majesty the Cæsar. Much gravity and Ceremony at these Receptions, and all very Formal, but decent. The Empress sits in a great easy-chair; but the Archduchesses are ranged on chairs with tall, straight Backs, but without arms; whilst the other Ladies of the Court (poor things) may stand on one Leg, or lean against sideboards, to rest themselves as they choose; but Sit Down they Dare not. This is the same Discipline, I believe, that still prevails, and so I speak of it in the present tense. The Table is entirely set out, and served by the Empress's Maids of Honour (who put on the very dishes and sauces), Twelve young Ladies of the First Quality, having no Salary but their chamber at court (like our Maids at the Montpelier by Twitnam), where they live in a kind of Honourable Captivity, not being suffered to go to the Assemblies or Public Places in Town, except in compliment to the Wedding of a Sister Maid, whom the Empress always presents with her picture set in Diamonds. And yet, for all their Strict confinement, I have heard fine Accounts of the goings-on of these noble Ladies. The first three of them are called "Ladies of the Key," and wear little golden keys at their sides. The Dressers are not at all the figures they pretend to in England, being looked upon no otherwise than as downright Chambermaids.

So much of the State and Grandeur of Vienna, then the most considerable city in Germany, though now Berlin, thanks to the Genius of its Puissant Monarch, has Reared its head very high. It was, however, my cruel Fate to see something more of the Capital of the Holy Roman Empire, and that too in a form that was of the unpleasantest. You see that my Master and the Chaplain and I (when we had been some Weeks in town, and through the interest of the English Bankers had gotten admission into some Society not quite so exclusive as the People who wanted to know whether you were "born") went one afternoon to an Archery Festival that was held in the garden of the Archchancellor's Villa, Schönbrunn (now Imperial property). 'Twas necessary to have some kind of Introduction; but that, if you stood well in the Banker's Books, was not very Difficult; and, invited or not, you had to pay a golden Ducat to the Usher of Ceremonies (a preposterous creature, like the Jack of Diamonds in his dress), that brought your ticket to your lodgings. So away we went to Schönbrunn, and at a Respectful distance were privileged to behold two of the young Archduchesses all dressed, their Hair full of jewels, and with bows and arrows in their hands; while a little way off were placed three oval pictures, which were the marks to be shot at. The first was a Cupid, filling a bottle of Burgundy, with the motto " *Cowards may be brave here.*" The second Fortune, holding a garland, with the motto " *Venture and Win.*" The third a Sword with a Laurel Wreath at the point, and for legend, " *I can be vanquished without shame.*" At t'other end was a Fine Gilded Trophy all wreathed with flowers, and made of little crooks, on which were hung rich Moorish Kerchiefs (which were much affected by the Viennese, a people very fond of gay and lively colours), tippets, ribbons, laces, &c. for the small prizes. The Empress, who sat under a splendid canopy fenced about by musketeers of the Life Guard, gave away the first prize with her own hand, which was a brave Ruby Ring set with Diamonds in a gold snuffbox. For the Second prize there was a little Cupid, very nicely done out in amethysts, and besides these a set of fine Porcelain, of the kind they call Eggshell (for its exceeding Tenderness and Brittleness), with some Japan trunks, feather-fans, and Whimwhams of that order. All the men of quality in Vienna were spectators; but only the ladies had permission to shoot. There was a good background of burghers and strangers, and in the rear of all a Mob that drank beer and scrambled for Kreutzers, that the officers of the Guard who were keeping the Barriers would now and then throw among them for their Diversion's sake. And all behind it was like a Fair, set out with Booths, where there was shooting and drinking and Gaming, just at one's ease; for I have ever found that in the most Despotic countries the Mobile have a kind of Rude License accorded them; whereas in States where there is Freedom Authority gives a man leave to Think, but very carefully ties his hands and feet whenever he has a mind to a Frisk. My Master was in very good spirits that day (having quite recovered his health), and for a time wanders about the Tents, now treating the common people, and now having a bumper with Mr. Hodge. We had tickets for the second ring, but not for the Inner one, where the Quality were stand-

ing; but just before the shooting of the great Match for
the Empress's ruby ring, Mr. Pinchin, into whose head some
of the bubbles from the white Hungarian had begun to mount,
begins to brag about his gentle extraction, and his cousinage
to Lady Betty Heeltap and my Lord Poddle. He vows that
he is as well "born" as any of the rascaille German Sausage
gorgers (as he calls them), and is as fit to stand about Royalty
as any of them. The Chaplain, who was always a discreet
man, tried hard to persuade him against thrusting himself
forward where his company was not desired; but Mr. Pinchin
was in that state in which arguing with a man makes him
more obstinate. Away he goes, the Chaplain prudently with-
drawing into a Booth; but I, as in Duty bound, followed
my Master, to see that he got into no mischief. But alas,
the Mischief that unhappy little Man speedily contrived to
entangle himself within !

By dint of a Florin here and a Florin there, the adventurous Squire succeeded in slipping through the row of
Guards who separated the outer from the inner Ring, who,
from the richness of his Apparel (for he was dressed in his
very Best), may perhaps have mistaken him for some Court
Nobleman who had arrived late. He had got within the
charmed circle indeed (I being a few paces behind him), and
was standing on Tiptoe to take a full stare at one of the young
Archduchesses who was bending her bow to shoot at Cupid,
when up comes an old Lord with a very long white face like
a Sheep, with a Crimson Ribbon across his breast, and a long
white staff in his hand atop of which was a Golden Key. He
first asks my Master in German what he wants there, at least
so far as I could understand; to which the Squire, not being
versed in the Tongues of Almaine (and, indeed, High Dutch
and Low Dutch are both very Base Parlance, and I never
could master 'em), answers, "*Non comprenny*," which was
his general reply when he was puzzled in the Foreign Lingos.
Then the old Lord, with a very sharp voice and in French,
tells him that he has no Business there, and bids him begone.
Mr. Pinchin could understand French, though he spoke it
but indifferently; but he, being fairly Primed, and in one of
his Obstinate Moods, musters up his best parleyvoo, and tells
the Ancient with the Golden Key (and I saw that he had
another one hung round his neck by a parcel chain, and conjectured him to be a High Chamberlain at least) to go to the

Devil. (I ask pardon for this word.) Hereupon my Lord
with the Sheep's countenance collars him, runs his white
stick into his visage, so that the key nearly puts his eye out,
and roars for the Guard. Then Mr. Pinchin, according to
his custom when he has gotten himself into a pother, begins
to squeal for Me, and the Chaplain, and his Mamma, to help
him out of it. My blood was up in a moment; I had not
had a Tussle with any one for a long time. "Shall I, who
have brained an English Grenadier, sneak off before a rabble-
rout of Sauerkraut Soldiers?" I asked myself, remembering
how much Stronger and Older I had grown since that night.
"Here goes, Jack Dangerous!" and away I went into the
throng, wrenched the white staff from the old Lord's hand,
made him unhand my Master, and drawing his Sword for him
(he being too terrified to draw it himself), grasped him firmly
by the arm, and was preparing to cut a way back for both of
us through the crowd. But 'twas a mad attempt. Up came
the Guard, every man of them Six Foot high, and for all they
were Sauerkraut Soldiers, pestilent Veterans who knew what
Fighting meant. When I saw their fixed Bayonets, and
their Mustachios curling with rage, I remembered a certain
Scar I had left after a memorable night in Charlwood Chase.
We were far from our own country, and there was no Demijohn of Brandy by; so, though it went sorely against my
Stomach, there was no help for it but to surrender ourselves
at once Prisoners of War. Prisoners of War, forsooth!
They treated us worse than Galley Slaves. Our hands were
bound behind us with cords, Halters were put about our
necks, and, the Grenadiers prodding us behind with their
Bayonets,—the Dastards, so to prick Unarmed Men!—we
were conducted in ignominy through the rascal Crowd, which
made a Grinning, Jeering, Hooting lane for us to pass to the
Guardhouse at the Entrance of the Gardens. The Officer of
the Guard was at first for having both of us strapped down
to a Bench as a preliminary measure to receive two hundred
Blows apiece with Willow Rods in the small of our backs,
which is their usual way of commencing Judicial proceedings,
when up comes the old Lord in a Monstrous Puff and Flurry,
and says that by the Empress's command no present Harm is
to be done us; but that we are to be removed to the Town
Gaol till the Cæsar's pleasure respecting us shall be known.
Her Majesty, however, forgot to enjoin that we were not to

be fettered ; so the Captain of the Guard he claps on us the
heaviest Irons that ever Mutineers howled in ; and we, being
flung into a kind of Brewer's Dray, and accompanied by a
Strong Guard of Horse and Foot, were conveyed to Vienna,
and locked up in the Town Gaol.

Luckily Mr. Hodge speedily got wind of our misfortune,
and hied him to the British Ambassador, who, being fond of
a Pleasant Story, laughed heartily at the recital. He promised to get my Master off on payment of a Fine or something
of that sort ; and as for me, he was good enough to opine that
I might think myself Lucky if I escaped with a sound dose
of the Bastinado once a week for three months, and a couple
of years or so in Irons. The Chaplain pleaded for me as well
as for my Master as hard as he could ; and his Excellency
frowned and said, that the Diversions of a Gentleman might
run a little Wild sometimes and no harm done ; but that the
Insolence of Servants (which was a growing evil) must be
restrained. "At all events, I'll see what I can do," he condescended to explain. "At all events, the Fellow can't fare
very badly for a sound Beating, and perhaps they will let him
off when he has had cudgelling enough." So he calls for his
Coach, and goes off to Court.

CHAPTER THE FIFTEENTH.

OF PARIS (BY THE WAY OF THE PRISON AT VIENNA), AND OF MY COMING
BACK FOR A SEASON TO MY OWN COUNTRY, WHERE MY MASTER, THE
CHAPLAIN, AND I PART COMPANY.

THE Fox in the Fable, so my Grannum (who had a ready
Memory for those Tales) used to tell me, when he first saw
the Lion was half dead with Fright. The Second View only
a little Dashed him with Tremour; at the Third he durst
salute him Boldly; and at the Fourth Rencounter Monsieur
Reynard steals a Shin Bone of Beef from under the old
Roarer's Nose, and laughs at his Beard. This Fable came
back to me, as with a Shrug and a Grin (somewhat of the
ruefulest) I found myself again (and for no Base Action I
aver) in a Prison Hold. I remembered what a dreadful Sickness and Soul-sinking I had felt when doors of Oak clamped
with Iron had first clanged upon me; when I first saw the
Blessed Sun made into a Quince Tart by the cross-bars over
his Golden face; when I first heard that clashing of Gyves
together which is the Death Rattle of a man's Liberty. But
now! Gaols and I were old Acquaintances. Had I not lain
long in the dismal Dungeon at Aylesbury? Had I not swel-
tered in the Hold of a Transport Ship? I was but a Youth;
but I felt myself by this time a Parcel Philosopher. The first
thing a man should do when he gets into Gaol, is to ask himself whether there is any chance of his being Hanged. If he
have no Sand Blindness, or Gossamer dancing of Threepenny
cord before his eyes, why then he had e'en better eat and
drink, and Thank God, and hope for the Best. "They won't
Hang me," I said cheerfully enough to myself, when I was
well laid up in Limbo. The Empress is well known to be a
merciful Lady, and will cast the ermine of Mercy over the
Scarlet Robe of Stern Authority. Perhaps I shall get my Ribs
basted. What of that? Flesh is flesh, and will Heal. They
cannot beat me so sorely as I have seen done (but never of
myself Ordered but when I was compelled) to Negro Slaves.
If they fine me, my Master must Pay. Here I am by the
Heels, and until I get out again, what use is there in fretting?
Lady Fortune has played me a scurvy trick; but may she not

to-morrow play as roguish a one to the Sheepfaced old Chamber Lord with the golden Key, or any other smart Pink-an-eye Dandiprat that hangs about the Court? The Spoke which now is highest in her Wheel may, when she gives it the next good Twist, be undermost as Nock. So I took Courage, and bade Despair go Swing for a dried Yeoman Sprat as he is.

I being a Servant, and so unjustly accounted of Base Degree by these Sour Cabbage gorging and Sourer Beer swilling High Dutch Bed-Pressers, was put into the Common Ward with the Raff; while my Master was suffered, on payment of Fees, to have better Lodgings. Gaolers are Gaolers all over the world, and Golden Fetters are always the lightsomest. We were some Sixty Rascals (that is to say, Fifty-Nine scoundrels, with one Honest Youth, your Humble Servant) in the Common Room, with but one Bed between us ; this being, indeed, but a Raised Wooden Platform, like that you see in a Soldiers' Guard Room. They brought us some Straw every day, and littered us down Dog Fashion, and that was all we had for Lodging Gear. It mattered little. There was a Roof to the Gaol that was weather-tight, and what more could a Man want?—until things got better at least.

Which they speedily did ; and neither Master nor Man came to any very great harm. 'Twas a near touch though ; and the safety of Jack Dangerous's bones hung for days, so I was afterwards told, by the merest thread. They deliberated long and earnestly about my case among themselves. It was even, I believe, brought before the Aulic Council ; but, after a week's confinement, and much going to and fro between the English Ambassador and the Great ones of the Court, Mr. Pinchin had signified to him that he might procure his Enlargement by paying a Fine of Eight Hundred Florins, which was reckoned remarkably cheap, considering his outrageous behaviour at the Shooting match. Some days longer they thought fit to detain Me ; but my Master, after he regained his liberty, came to see me once and sometimes twice a day ; and, through his and Mr. Hodge's kindness, I was supplied with as good Victuals and Drink as I had heretofore been accustomed to. Indeed, such abundant fare was there provided for me, that I had always a superfluity, and I was enabled to relieve the necessities and fill the bellies of many poor Miserable Hungry creatures, who otherwise must have starved; for 'twas the custom of the Crown only to allow their Captives a few Kreutzers, amounting to some twopence-farthing a day English, for their subsistence. The Oldest Prisoner in the Ward, whom they called Father of the Room, would on this Bare Pittance take tithe and toll often in a most Extortionate manner. Then these Gaol birds would fall to thieving from one another, even as they slept; and if a man was weak of Arm and Feeble of Heart, he might go for a week without touching a doit of his allowance, and so might Die of Famine, unless he could manage to beg a little filthy Cabbage Soup, or a lump of Black Bread, from some one not wholly without Bowels of Compassion.

But I had not been here more than a month when the instances of my master at length prevailed, and I too was enlarged; only some Fifty Florins being laid upon me by way of fine. This mulct was paid perforce by Mr. Pinchin; for as 'twas through his mad folly, and no fault of my own, that I had come to Sorrow, he was in Justice and Equity bound to bear me harmless in the Consequences. He was fain, however, to make some Demur, and to Complain, in his usual piteous manner, of being so amerced.

"Suppose you had been sentenced to Five Hundred Blows of a Stick, sirrah,"—'twas thus he put the case to me, logically enough,—"would you have expected me to pay for thee in carcass, as now I am paying for thee in Purse?"

"Circumstances alter cases," interposes Mr. Hodge in my behalf. "Here is luckily no question of Stripes at all. John may bless his Stars that he hath gotten off without a Rib Roasting; and to your Worship, after the Tune they have made you dance to, and the Piper you have paid, what is this miserable little Fine of Fifty Florins?" So my Master paid; and Leaving another Ten Florins for the poor Losels in the Gaol to drink his health in, we departed from that place of Durance, thinking ourselves, and with reason, very well out of it.

Servants are not always so lucky when they too implicitly obey the behests of their Masters, or, in a hot fever of Fidelity, stand up for them in Times of Danger or Desperate Affrays. Has there not ever been brought under your notice that famous French Law Case, of the Court Lady,—the Dame de Liancourt, I think she was called,—against whom another Dame had a Spite, either for her Beauty, or her Wit, or her

Riches' sake? She, riding one day in her Coach-and-Six by
a cross-road, comes upon the Dame de Liancourt, likewise
in her Coach-and-Six, both ladies having the ordinary complement of Running Footmen. My Lady who had the Spite
against her of Liancourt whispers to her Lacqueys; and these
poor Faithful Rogues, too eager to obey their Mistress's commands, ran to the other coach-door, pulled out that unlucky
Dame de Liancourt, and then and there inflicted on her that
shameful chastisement which jealous Venus, as the Poetry
books say, did, once upon a time, order to poor Psyche;
and which, even in our own times, so I have heard, Madame
du Barry, the last French King's Favourite, did cause Four
Chambermaids to inflict on some Lady about Versailles with
whom she had cause of Anger. At any rate, the cruel and
Disgraceful thing was done, the Dame sitting in her coach
meanwhile clapping her hands. O, 'twas a scandalous thing!
The poor Dame de Liancourt goes, Burning with Rage and
Shame, to the Chief Town of the Province, to lodge her complaint. The matter is brought before the Parliament, and
in due time it goes to Paris, and is heard and reheard, the
Judges all making a Mighty to-do about it; and at last, after
some two years and a half's litigation, is settled in this wise.
My Lady pays a Fine and the Costs, and begs the Dame de
Liancourt's pardon. But what, think you, becomes of the two
poor Lacqueys that had been rash enough to execute her
Revengeful Orders? Why, at first they are haled about from
one gaol to another for Thirty Months in succession, and then
they are subjected to the question, Ordinary and Extraordinary
—that is to say, to the Torture; and at last, when my Lady
is paying her fine of 10,000 livres, I think, or about Four
Hundred Pounds of our Money, the Judges at Paris pro-
nounce against these two poor Devils of Footmen,—that were
as innocent of any Malice in the Matter as the Babe that is
unborn, and only Did what they were Told,—that one is to be
Hanged in the Place de Grève, and the other banished to the
Galleys, there to be chained to the Oar for life. A fine Encouragement truly for those who think that, for good Victuals
and a Fine Livery, they are bound to obey all the Humours
and Caprices, even to the most Unreasonable and most Arbitrary, of their Masters and Mistresses.

We were in no great Mood, after this Affair was over,
to remain in Vienna. Mr. Pinchin did at first propose jour-

neying through the Province of Styria by Gratz, to a little
town on the sea-coast called Trieste,—that has much grown
in importance during these latter days,—and so crossing the
Gulf to Venice; but he abandoned this Scheme. His health
was visibly breaking; his Funds, he said, were running low;
he was more anxious about his Mamma than ever; and 'twas
easy to see that he was half-weary and half-afraid of the
Chaplain and Myself, and that he desired nothing Half so
Much as to get Rid of us Both. So we packed up, and resumed our Wanderings, but in Retreat instead of Advance.
We passed, coming back, through Dresden, where there are
some fine History Pictures, and close to which the Saxon
Elector had set up a great Factory for the making of painted
Pottery Ware : not after the monstrous Chinese Fashion, but
rather after the Mode practised with great Success at our own
Chelsea. The manner of making this Pottery was, however,
kept a high State Secret by the government of the then Saxon
Elector; and no strangers were, on any pretence, admitted
to the place where the Works were carried on; so of this we
saw nothing; and not Sorry was I of the privation, being
utterly Wearied and palled with much gadding about and
Sight-seeing. So post to Frankfort, where there were a many
Jews; and thence to Mayence; and from thence down the
grand old River Rhine to the City of Cologne; whence, by
the most lagging stages I did ever know, to Bruxelles. But
we stayed not here to see the sights—not even the droll little
statue of the Mannikin (at the corner of a street, in a most
unproper attitude; and there is a Group quite as unseemly
in one of the Markets, so I was told, although at that time
we were fain to pass them by), which Mannikin the burgesses
of Bruxelles regard as a kind of tutelary Divinity, and set
much greater store by than we do by our London Stone, or
little naked boy in Panyer Alley. But it is curious to mark
what strange whimwhams these Foreigners run mad after.

At Bruxelles my Master buys an old Post Carriage—cost
him Two Hundred and Fifty Livres, which was not dear;
and the wretched horses of the country being harnessed
thereto, we made Paris in about a week afterwards. We
alighted at a decent enough kind of Inn, in the Place named
after Lewis the Great (an eight-sided space, and the houses
handsome, though not so large as Golden Square). There
was a great sight the day after our coming, which we could

not well avoid seeing. This was the Burial of a certain great nobleman, a Duke and Marshal of France, and at the time of his Decease Governor of the City of Paris. I have forgotten his name; but it does not so much matter at this time of day, his Grace and Governorship being as dead as Queen Anne. The Burial began on foot, from his house, which was next door but one to our Inn, and went first to his Parish Church, and thence, in coaches, right to the other end of Paris, to a Monastery, where his Lordship's Family Vault was. There was a prodigious long procession of Flambeaux; Friars, white, black, and gray, very trumpery, and marvellous foul-looking;—no plumes, banners, scutcheons, led horses, or open chariots,—altogether most mean obsequies. The march began at eight in the evening, and did not end till four o'clock the next morning, for at each church they passed they stopped for a Hymn and Holy Water. And, by the way, we were told that one of these same choice Friars, who had been set to watching the body while it lay in state, fell asleep one night, and let the Tapers catch fire of the rich Velvet Mantle, lined with Ermine and powdered over with gold Flower-de-Luces, which melted all the candles, and burnt off one of the feet of the Departed, before it wakened him.

It was afterwards my fortune to know Paris very well; but I cannot say that I thought much of the place on first coming to it. Dirt there was everywhere, and the most villanous smells that could be imagined. A great deal of Show, but a vein of Rascal manners running through it all. Nothing neat or handsomely ordered. Where my Master stood to see the Burial Procession, the balcony was hung with Crimson Damask and Gold; but the windows behind him were patched in half-a-dozen places with oiled paper. At dinner they gave you at least Three Courses; but a third of the Repast was patched up with Sallets, Butter, Puff-paste, or some such miscarriages of Dishes. Nothing like good, wholesome, substantial Belly Timber. None but Germans, and other Strangers, wore fine clothes; the French people mainly in rags, but powdered up to their eyebrows. Their coaches miserably horsed, and rope harnessed; yet, in the way of Allegorics on the panels, all tawdry enough for the Wedding of Cupid and Psyche. Their shop-signs extremely laughable. Here some living at the Y Gue; some at Venus's Toilette; and others at the Sucking Cat. Their notions of

Honour most preposterous. It was thought mighty dishonourable for any that was a Born Gentleman not to be in the Army, or in the King's Service, but no dishonour at all to keep Public Gaming Houses; there being at least five hundred persons of the first Quality in Paris living by it. You might go to their Houses at all Hours of the Night, and find Hazard, Pharaoh, &c. The men who kept the gaming-tables at the Duke of Gesvres' paid him twelve guineas a night for the privilege. Even the Princesses of the Blood were mean enough to go snacks in the profits of the banks kept in their palaces. I will say nothing more of Paris in this place, save that it was the fashion of the Ladies to wear Red Hair of a very deep hue; these said Princesses of the Blood being consumedly carroty. And I do think that if a Princess of the Blood was born with a Tail, and chose to show it, tied up with Pea-Green Ribbon, through the Placket-hole of her Gown, the Ladies, not only in France, but all over the World, would be proud to sport Tails with Pea-Green Ribbons,—or any other colour that was the mode,—whether they were Born with 'em or not.

Nothing more that is worthy of Mention took place until our leaving Paris. We came away in a calash, that is, my Master and the Chaplain, riding at their Ease in that vehicle, while I trotted behind on a little Bidet, and posted it through St. Denis to Beauvais. So on to Abbeville, where they had the Impudence to charge us Ten Livres for three Dishes of Coffee, and some of the nastiest Eau de Vie that ever I tasted; excusing themselves, the Rogues, on the score that Englishmen were scarce nowadays. And to our great Relief, we at last arrived at Calais, where we had comfortable Lodgings, and good fare, at a not too exorbitant rate. Here we had to wait four days for a favourable Wind; and even then we found the Packet Boat all taken up for Passengers, and not a place on board to be had either for Love or Money. As Mr. Pinchin was desperately pressed to reach his Native Land, to wait for the next boat seemed utterly intolerable to him; so, all in a Hurry, and being cheated, as folks when they are in a Hurry must needs be, we bargained for a Private Yacht to take us to Dover. The Master would hear of nothing less than five-and-twenty guineas for the voyage, which, with many Sighs and almost Weeping, my poor Little Master agrees to give. He might have recouped himself ten guineas

P

of the money; for there was a Great Italian Singing Woman, with her Chambermaid, her Valet de Chambre, a Black Boy, and a Monkey, bound for the King's Opera House in the Haymarket, very anxious to reach England, and willing to pay Handsomely—out of English pockets in the long-run—for the accommodation we had to give ; but my capricious Master flies into a Tiff, and vows that he will have no Foreign Squallers on board his Yacht with him. So the poor Signora—who was not at all a Bad-looking woman, although mighty Brown of visage—was fain to wait for the next Packet ; and we went off in very great state, but still having to Pay with needless heaviness for our Whistle. And, of course, all the way there was nothing but whining and grumbling on his Worship's part, that so short a trip should have cost him Twenty-five Guineas. The little Brute was never satisfied ; and when I remembered the Life I had led with him, despite abundant Victuals, good Clothes, and decent Wages, I confess that I felt half-inclined to pitch him over the Taffrail, and make an End of him, for good and all.

The villanous Tub which the Rascals who manned it called a Yacht was not Seaworthy, wouldn't answer her Helm, and floundered about in the Trough of the Sea for a day and a half; and even then we did not make Dover, but were obliged to beat up for Ramsgate. We had been fools enough to pay the Fare beforehand; and these Channel Pirates were unconscionable enough to demand Ten Guineas more, swearing that they would have us up before the Mayor —who, I believe, was in league with 'em—if we did not disburse. Then the Master of the Port came upon us for Dues and Light Tolls ; and a Revenue Pink Boarded us, the Crew getting Half-Drunk at our Expense, under pretence of searching for contraband, and sticking to us till we had given the Midshipman a guinea, and another guinea to the Crew, to drink our Healths.

CHAPTER THE SIXTEENTH.

JOHN DANGEROUS IS IN THE SERVICE OF KING GEORGE.

IT now becomes expedient for me to pass over no less than Fifteen Years of my momentous Career. I am led to do this for divers cogent Reasons, two of which I will forthwith lay before my Reader. For the first, let me urge a Decent Prudence. It is not, Goodness knows, that I have any thing to be ashamed of, which should hinder me from giving a Full, True, and Particular Account of all the Adventures that befell me in these same Fifteen Years, with the same Minute Particularity which I bestowed upon my Unhappy Childhood, my varied Youth, and stormy Adolescence. I did dwell, perhaps, with a fonder circumspection and more scrupulous niceness upon those early days, inasmuch as the things we have first known and suffered are always more vividly presented to our mind when we strive to recall 'em, sitting as old men in the inglenook, than are the events of complete manhood. Yet do I assure those who have been at the pains to scan the chapters that have gone before, that it would be easy for me to set down with the Fidelity of a Ledger-Keeper all the things that happened unto me from my eighteenth year, when I last bade them leave, and the year 1747, when I had come to be three-and-thirty years of age. I remember all: the Ups and Downs; the Crosses and the Runs of Luck; the Fortunes and the Misfortunes; the Good and the Bad Feasts I sat me down to, during an ever-changing and Troublous Period. But, as I have said, I have been moved thus to skip over a vast tract of time through Prudence. There may have been certain items in my life upon which, now that I am respectable and prosperous, I no more care to think of. There may be whole pages, close-written and full of Stirring Matter, which I have chosen to cancel; there may be occurrences treated of which it is best, at this time of Day, to draw a Veil over. Finally, there may be Great Personages still Living who would have just cause to be Offended were I to tell all I know. The dead belong to all the World, and their Bones are oft-times Dug up and made use of by those who in the Flesh knew them not; but Famous Persons live to a very Great Age, and it is sometimes scandalous to recount what adventures one has had with 'em in the days of their hot and rash Youth. Had I permission to publish all I am acquainted with, the very Hair upon your Head might stand up in Amazement at some of the Matters I could relate :—how Mean and Base the Great and Powerful might become ; how utterly Despisable some of the most Superb and Arrogant Creatures of this our Commonwealth might appear. But I am prudent and Hold my Tongue.

Again, and for the Second Reason, I am led to pass over these fifteen years through a feeling that is akin to Mercy and Forbearance towards my Reader. For I well know how desperately given is John Dangerous to a wordy Garrulity—how prone he is to make much of little things, and to elevate to the dignity of Important and Commanding Events that which is perchance only of the very slightest moment. By Prosing and Amplifying, by Moralising and Digressing, by spinning of yarns and wearing of reflections threadbare, I might make a Great Book out of the pettiest and most un-eventful career ; but even in honestly transcribing my actual adventures, one by one,—the things I have done, and the Men and Women I have known,—I should imperceptibly swell a Narrative, which was at first meant to attain no great volume, to most deplorable dimensions. And the world will no longer tolerate Huge Chronicles in Folio, whether they relate to History, to Love or Adventure, to Voyages and Travels, or even to Philosophy, Mechanics, or the Useful Arts. The world wants smart, dandy little volumes, as thin as a Herring, and just as Salt. For these two reasons, then, do I nerve myself to a sudden leap, and entreat you now to think no longer of John Dangerous as a raw youth of eighteen sum-mers, but as a sturdy, well-set man of thirty-three.

Yet, lest mine Enemies and other vile Rascal Fellows that go about the town taking away the characters of honest people for mere Envy and Spitefulness' sake, lest these petty curmudgeons should, in their own sly saucy manner, Mop and Mow, Grin and Whisper, that If I am silent as to Fifteen Years of my Sayings and Doings, I have good cause for hold-ing my peace,—lest these scurril Slanderers should insinuate that during this time I lay in divers Gaols for offences which I dare not avow, that I was concerned in Desperate and Unlawful Enterprises which brought upon me many Indictments in the King's Courts, or that I was ever Pilloried, or held to Bail for contemptible misdemeanours,—I do here declare and affirm that for the whole of the time I so pass over I earned my bread in a perfectly Honest, Legal, and Honourable Manner, and that I never once went out of the limits of the United Kingdom. I have heard, indeed, a Ridiculous Tale setting forth that, finding myself Destitute in London after the Chaplain, Mr. Pinchin, and I had parted company for good and all, I enlisted—being a tall, strapping Fellow—in the Foot Guards. The preposterous Fable goes on to say that quickly mastering my Drill, and being a favourite with my officers, whom I much pleased with my Alacrity and Intelligence, although they were much given to laugh at my assumptions of superior Birth, and nicknamed me "Gentleman Jack,"—I was promoted to the rank of Corporal, and might have aspired to the dignity of a Sergeant's Halbert, but that in a Mad Frolic one night I betook myself to the road as a Footpad, and robbed a Gentleman, coming from the King's Arms, Kensington, towards the Weigh House at Knightsbridge, of fourteen spade guineas, a gold watch, and a bottlescrew. And that being taken by the Hue and Cry, and had before Justice De Veil then sitting at the Sun Tavern in Bow Street, I should have been committed to Newgate, tried, and most likely have swung for the robbery, but for the strong intercession of my Captain, who was a friend of the Gentleman robbed. That I was indeed enlarged, but was not suffered to go scot-free, inasmuch as, being tried by court-martial for absence without leave on the night of the gentleman's misfortune, I was sentenced to receive three hundred lashes at the halberts. Infamous and Absurd calumnies ! Three hundred lashes, forsooth ! John Dangerous has scars enow on his body, but none from the cat-o'-ninetails. His cicatrices (save those which result from his illusage by his Barbarous Tormentors when he was a slave among the Moors) were all gotten in Fair and Honourable Warfare. This precious History of my ever being a Common Soldier is about on a piece with that other Impudent Farrago setting forth that, having spent what Money was bestowed upon me by Mr. Pinchin when I left his service in riotous Debauchery, and wandering about the Eastern end of the town in sore distress, I was pounced upon by a Press Gang, and taken on board the Tower Tender, whence I was shipped to Portsmouth, and served ten years Before the Mast in a Man of War. A foul libel again ! I should never be ashamed of eating the King's bread, God bless him ! and fighting for him, either as a private Fusilier or as a Foremast man in the Fleet ; but it has been my happy fortune to serve his Majesty, both by Sea and Land, in capacities far higher than either of these.

Behold me, then, in the beginning of the year 1747, in the Service of his Sacred Majesty King George the Second. Behold me, further, installed in no common Barrack, mean Guard-house, or paltry Garrison Town, but in one of the most famous of his Majesty's Royal Fortresses :—a place that had been at once and for centuries (ever since the days of Julius Cæsar, as I am told) a Palace, a Citadel, and a Prison. In good sooth, I was one of the King's Warders, and the place where I was stationed was the Ancient and Honourable Tower of London.

Whether I had ever worn the King's uniform before, either in scarlet as a Soldier in his armies, or of blue and tarpaulin as a Sailor in his Fleets, or of brown as a Riding Officer in his customs,—under which guise a man may often have doughty encounters with smugglers that are trying to run their contraband cargoes, or to hide their goods in far-mer's houses,—or of green, as a Keeper in one of the Royal Chases,—I absolutely refuse to say. Here I am, or rather here I was, a Warder and in the Tower.

I was bravely accoutred. A doublet of crimson cloth, with the crown, the Royal Cipher, G. R., and a wreath of laurel embroidered in gold, both on its back and front; a linen ruff, well plaited, round my neck, sleeves puffed with black velvet, trunk-hose of scarlet, rosettes in my slashed shoes, and a flat hat with a border of the red and white roses of York and Lancaster in satin ribbon,—these made up my costume. There were forty of us in the Tower, mounting guard with drawn swords at the portcullis gate and at the entrances to the lodgings of such as were in hold, and other-wise attending upon unfortunate noblemen and gentlemen who were in trouble. On state occasions, when taking pri-soners by water from the Tower to Westminster, and in pre-ceding the Lieutenant to the outward port, we carried Hal-berts or Partisans with tassels of gold and crimson thread.

But although our dress was identical, as you may see from the prints, with that of the Beef-Eaters, we Tower Warders were of a very different kidney to the lazy hangers-on about St. James's. Those fellows were Anybodies, Parasites of Back-Stairs favourites, and spies and lacqueys, transformed serving-men, butlers past drawing corks, grooms and porters, even. They had nothing to do but to loiter about the ante-chambers and staircases of St. James's, to walk by the side of his Majesty's coach when he went to the Houses of Parliament, or to fight with the Marshalmen at Royal Funerals for petty spoils of wax candles or shreds of black hangings. The knaves actually wore wigs, and powdered them, as though they had been so many danglers on the Mall. They passed their time, when not in requisition about the Court, smoking and card-playing in the taverns and mug-houses about Scotland Yard and Spring Gardens. They had the run of a few servant-wenches belonging to great people, but we did not envy them their sweethearts. Some of them, I verily believe, were sunk so low as, when they were not masquerading at court, to become tavern-drawers, or ushers and cryers in the courts of law about Westminster. A very mean people were these Beef-eaters, and they toiled not, neither did they spin, for the collops they ate.

But we brave boys of the Tower earned both our Beef and our Bread, and the abundant Beer and Strong Waters with which we washed our victuals down. We were military men, almost all. Some of us had fought at Blenheim or Ramilies —these were the veterans : the very juniors had made the French Maison du Roy scamper, or else crossed bayonets with the Irish Brigade (a brave body of men, but deplorably criminal in carrying arms against a Gracious and Clement Prince) in some of those well-fought German Fields, in which His Royal Highness the Duke and my Lord George Sackville (since Germaine, and my very good friend and Patron) covered themselves with immortal glory. Nay some of us, One of us at least, had fought and bled, to the amazement of his comrades and the admiration of his commanders,—never mind where. 'Tis not the luck of every soldier to have had his hand wrung by the Great Duke of Cumberland, or to have been presented with ten guineas to drink his health withal by Field-Marshal Wade. We would have thought it vile poltroonery and macaronism to have worn wigs—to say

nothing of powder—unless, indeed, the peruke was a true
Malplaquet club or Dettingen scratch.

Our duties were no trifling ones, let me assure you.   The
Tower, as a place of military strength, was well looked after
by the Regiment of Foot Guards and the Companies of Artillery that did garrison duties on its ramparts and at the
foot of its drawbridges; but to us was confided a charge
much more onerous, and the custody of things much more
precious.   We had other matters to mind besides seeing that
stray dogs did not venture on to the Tower Green, that dust
did not get into the cannons' mouths, or that Grand Rounds
received proper salutes.   Was not the Imperial Crown of
England in our keeping?   Had we not to look after the
Royal diadem, the orb, the sceptre, the Swords of Justice
and of Mercy, and the great parcel-gilt Salt Cellar that is
moulded in the likeness of the White Tower itself?   Did it
not behove us to keep up a constant care and watchfulness,
lest among the curious strangers and country cousins who
trudged to the Jewel House to see all that glittering and
golden finery, and who gave us shillings to exhibit them,
there might be lurking some Rogue as dishonest and as desperate as that Colonel Blood who so nearly succeeded in
getting away with the crown and other valuables in King
Charles the Second's time?   Oh ! I warrant you that we kept
sharp eyes on the curious strangers and the country cousins,
and allowed them not to go too near the grate behind which
were those priceless baubles.

But another charge had we, I trow.   At all times had
this famous fortress of the Tower of London been a place of
hold for the King's prisoners.   Felons, nor cutpurses, nor
wantons suffered we indeed in our precincts, nor gave we the
hospitality of dungeons to ; but of state prisoners, noblemen
and gentlemen in durance for High Treason, or for other
offences against the Royal State and Prerogative, had we
always a plentiful store.   Some of the greatest Barons—
the proudest names in England—have pined their lives away
within the Tower's inexorable walls.   Walls ! why there were
little dungeons and casemates built in the very thickness of
those huge mural stones.   In ancient days I have heard that
foul deeds were common in the fortress—that princes were
done to Death here—notably the two poor Royal infants
that the wicked Richard of Gloucester bid his hell-hounds

smother and bury at the foot of the stairs in that building which has ever since gone by the name of the Bloody Tower. So, too, I am afraid it is a true bill that Torture was in the bad old days indiscriminately used towards both gentle and simple in some gloomy underground places in this said Tower. I have heard of a Sworn Tormentor and his assistants, whose fiendish task it was to torture poor creatures' souls out of their miserable bodies, and of a Chirurgeon who had to watch lest the agonies used upon 'em should be too much for human endurance, and so, putting 'em out of their misery, rob the headsman of his due, the scaffold of its prey, and the vile mobile that congregate at public executions of their raree show. Of " Scavenger's Daughters," Racks, Thumbscrews, iron boots, and wedges, and other horrible engines of pain, I have heard many dismal tales told; but all that had long fallen into disuse before my time. The last persons tortured within the Tower walls were, I believe, Colonel Faux (Guido) and his confederates, for their most abominable Gunpowder Plot, which was to put an end to the Protestant Religion and the illustrious House of Stuart at one fell blow; but happily came to nothing, through the prudence of my Lord Monteagle, and the well-nigh superhuman sagacity of his Majesty King James the First. Guy and his accomplices they tortured horribly; and did not even give 'em the honour of being beheaded on Tower Hill,—they being sent away as common traitors to Old Palace Yard (close to the scene of their desperately meditated, but fortunately abortive crime), and there half-hanged, cut down while yet warm, disembowelled, their Hearts and Inwards taken out and burnt by Gregory (that was hangman then, and that, as Gregory Brandon, had a coat-of-arms given him as a gentleman, through a fraud practised upon Garter King), and their mangled bodies—the heads severed—cut into quarters, well coated with pitch, and stuck upon spikes over London Bridge, east Portcullis, Ludgate, Temple Bar, and other places of public resort, according to the then bloody-minded custom, and the statute in that case made and provided. But after Colonel Guido Faux, Rack, Thumbscrews, boots, and wedges, and Scavenger's daughters fell into a decline, from which, thank God, they have never, in this fair realm of England, recovered. I question even if the Jesuit Garnett and his fellows, albeit most barbarously executed, were tortured in

prison; but it is certain that when Felton killed the Duke
of Bucks at Portsmouth, and was taken red-handed, the
Courtiers, Parasites, and other cruel persons that were about
the King, would fain have had him racked; but the public,
—which by this time had begun to inquire pretty sharply
about Things of State,—cried out that Felton should not be
tormented (their not loving the Duke of Bucks too much
may have been one reason for their wishing some degree of
leniency to be shown to the assassin), and the opinion of the
Judges being taken, those learned Persons, in full court of
King's Bench assembled, decided that Torture was contrary
to the Law of England, and could not legally be used upon
any of the King's subjects howsoever guilty he might have
been.

But I confess that when I first took up service as a Tower
Warder, and gazed upon those horrible implements of Man's
cruelty and hardheartedness collected in the Armoury, I imagined with dismay that, all rusty as they had grown, there
might be occasions for them to be used upon the persons of
unfortunate captives. For I had lived much abroad, and
knew what devilish freaks were often indulged in by arbitrary and unrestrained power. But my comrades soon put
my mind at ease, and pointed out to me that few, very few of
these instruments of Anguish were of English use or origin at
all; but that the great majority of these wicked things were
from among the spoils of the Great Armada, when the proud
Spaniards, designing to invade this free happy country with
their monstrous Flotilla of Caravels and Galleons, provided
numerous tools of Torture for despitefully using the Heretics
(as they called them) who would not obey the unrighteous
mandates of a foreign despot, or submit to the domination
(usurped) of the Bishop of Rome. And so tender indeed of
the bodies of the King's prisoners had the Tower authorities
become, that the underground dungeons were now never used,
commodious apartments being provided for the noblemen and
gentlemen in hold : and a pretty penny they had to pay for
their accommodation; five guineas a day, beside warder and
gentlemen gaoler's fees, being the ordinary charge for a nobleman, and half that sum for a knight and private esquire.
Besides this, the Lieutenant of the Tower had a gratuity of
thirty pounds from every peer that came into his custody, and
twenty pounds for every gentleman writing himself *Armiger*,

and in default could seize upon their cloaks : whence arose a merry saying—"Best go to the Tower like a peeled carrot than come forth like one."

There were even no chains used in this state prison ; of fetters and manacles we had indeed a plenitude, all of an antique pattern and covered with rust ; but no irons such as are put upon their prisoners by vulgar gaolers in Newgate and elsewhere. I have heard say that when poor Counsellor Layer, that was afterwards hanged, drawn, and quartered as a Jacobite, and his head stuck atop of Temple Bar hard by his own chambers,—was first brought for safer custody to the Tower, breakings out of Newgate having been common, the Government sent down word that, as a deep-dyed conspirator and desperate rebel, he was to be double-ironed. Upon this Mr. Lieutenant flies into a mighty heat, and taking boat to Whitehall, waits on Mr. Secretary at the Cockpit, and tells him plainly that such an indignity towards his Majesty's prisoners in the Tower was never heard of, that no such base modes of coercion as chains or bilboes had ever been known in use since the reign of King Charles I., and that the King's warders were there to see that the prisoners did not attempt Evasion. To which Mr. Secretary answered, with a grim smile, that notwithstanding all the keenness of the watch and ward, he had often heard of prisoners escaping from durance in the Tower, notably mentioning the case of my Lord Nithesdale, who escaped in his lady's clothes ; and without more ado informed the Lieutenant that Counsellor Layer must be chained as directed, even if the chains had to be forged expressly for him. Upon which Mr. Lieutenant took a very surly leave of the Great Man, cursing him as he comes down the steps for a Thief-catcher and Tyburn purveyor, and hied him to Newgate, where he borrowed a set of double-irons from the Peachum or Lockit, or whatever the fellow's name was that kept that Den of Thieves. And even then, when they had gotten the chains to the Tower, none of the warders knew how to put them on, or to sully their fingers with such hangman's work ; and so they were fain to have a blacksmith with his anvil, and a couple of turnkeys down from Newgate, to rivet the chains upon the poor gentleman's limbs ; he being at the time half dead of a Strangury ; but so cruel was justice in those days.

When I first came to the Tower, we had but few prison-

ers ; for it was before the Great Rebellion of the 'Forty-five ;
and for a few years previous the times had been after a manner
quiet. Now and then some notorious Jacobite, Seminarist, or
seditious person, was taken up ; but he was rarely of sufficient
importance to be confined in our illustrious Prison ; and was
either had to Newgate, or else confined in the lodgings of a
King's Messenger till his examinations were over, and he
was either committed or Enlarged. These Messengers kept,
in those days, a kind of Sponging Houses for High Treason,
where Gentlemen Traitors who were not in very great peril
lived, as it were, at an ordinary, and paid much dearer for
their meat and lodging than though they had been at some
bailiff's lock-up in Cursitor Street, or Tooke's Court, or the
Pied Bull in the Borough. We had, it is true, for a long
time a Romanist Bishop that was suspected of being in correspondence with St. Germain's, and lay for a long time under
detention. He was a merry old soul, and most learned man;
would dine very gaily with Mr. Lieutenant, or his deputy, or
the Fort Major, swig his bottle of claret, and play a game of
tric-trac afterwards ; and it was something laughable to watch
the quiet cunning way in which he would seek to Convert us
Warders who had the guarding of him to the Romanist faith.
They let him out at last upon something they called a *Nolle
prosequi* of the Attorney-General, or some such-like dignitary
of the law—which *nolle prosequi* I take to be a kind of
habeas corpus for gentlefolks. He was as liberal to us when
he departed as his means would allow ; for I believe that save
his cassock, his breviary, a gold cross round his neck, and
episcopal ring, and a portmantel full of linen, the old gentleman had neither goods nor chattels in the wide world : indeed, we heard that the Lieutenant lent him, on leaving, a
score of gold pieces, for friendship-sake, to distribute among
us. But he went away—to foreign parts, I infer—with flying
colours ; for every body loved the old Bishop, all Romanist
and suspected Jacobite as he was.

Then came that dreadful era of rebellion of which I have
spoken, and we Tower Warders found that our holiday time
was over. Whilst the war still raged in Scotland, scarcely a
day passed without some person of consequence being brought
either by water to Traitor's Gate, or by a strong escort of
Horse and Foot to the Tower Postern ; not for active partici-
pation in the Rebellion, but as a measure of safety, and to

prevent worse harm being done. And many persons of consequence, trust me, saved their heads by being laid by the
heels for a little time while the hue and cry was afoot, and
Habeas Corpus suspended. Fast bind, safe find, is a true
proverb ; and you may thank your stars, even if your enemies
have for a time bound you with chains and with links of
iron, if, when the stormy season has gone past, you find your
head still safe on your shoulders. Now it was a great Lord
who was brought to the Tower, and from whom Mr. Lieutenant did not forget to claim his thirty-pound fee on
entrance ; for " here to-day, gone to-morrow," he reasoned,
and so shot his game as soon as he had good parview of the
same. Now it was some Cheshire or Lancashire Squire,
snatched away from his Inn, at the Hercules' Pillars, or the
Catherine Wheel in the Borough, as being vehemently suspected of Jacobitism. These gentlemen mostly took their
captivity in a very cheerful and philosophical manner. They
would call for a round of spiced beef, a tankard of ale, and
a pipe of tobacco, so soon as ever they were fairly bestowed
in their lodgings ; drank to the King—taking care not to let
us know whether his name began with a G or a J, with many
jovial ha-has, and were as happy as the day was long, so it
seemed to us, if they had but a pack of cards and a volume
of the Gentleman's Recreation, or Academy of Field Sports.
What bowls of punch, too, they would imbibe o' nights, and
what mad carouses they would have ! Such roaring Squires
as these would have been much better bestowed in the
Messengers' Houses ; but these were all full, likewise the
common gaols ; nay, the debtors' prisons and vile sponging-
houses were taken up by Government for the temporary
incarceration of suspected persons.

How well do I remember the dreadful amazement and
consternation which broke over this city when the news came
that the Prince—I mean the Pretender—had utterly routed
the King's troops commanded by Sir John Cope at Preston-
pans ; that the Misguided Young Man had entered Edinborough at the head of a furious mob of Highlandmen, whose
preposterous style of dress I never could abide, and who in
those days we Southrons held as being very little better than
painted Savages ; that the ladies of the Scottish capital had
all mounted the white cockades, and were embroidering
scarves for the Pretender and his officers, and that the Castle

of Edinborough alone held out 'gainst this monstrous up-
rising to destroy authority! But how much greater was the
Dismay in London when we learnt that the Rebels, not
satisfied with their conquests in his Majesty's Scottish
Dominions, had been so venturous as to invade England
itself, and had actually advanced so far as the trading town
of Derby! Then did those who had been long, albeit
obscurely, suspected of Jacobitism, come forth from their
lurking holes and corners, and almost openly avow their
preference for the House of Stuart. Then did very many
respectable persons, formerly thought to be excellently well
affected towards King George's person and Government, become waverers, or prove themselves the Turncoats they had
always, in secret, been, and seditiously prophesy that the
days of the Hanoverian dynasty were numbered. Then did
spies and traitors abound, together with numbers of alarming
rumours, that the Chevalier had advanced as far as Barnet
on the Great North Road; that his Majesty was about to
convey himself away to Hanover; that the Duke of Cumberland was dead; that barrels of gunpowder had been discovered in the crypt beneath Guildhall, and in the vaults of
the Chapel Royal; that mutiny was rife among the troops;
that the Bank of England was about to break; with sundry
other distracting reports and noises.

Of course authority did all it could to reassure the public mind, tossed in a most tempestuous manner as it was by
conflicting accounts. Authority bestirred itself to put down
seditious meetings by proclamation, and to interdict residence
in the capital 'to all known Papists; whereby several most
estimable Catholic gentlemen (as many there be of that old
Faith) were forced to leave their Town Houses, and betake
themselves to mean and inconvenient dwellings in the
country. The gates of Temple Bar were now shut, on sudden
alarms, two or three times a week; as though the closing of
these rotten portals could in any way impede the progress of
rebellion, or do any thing more than further to hamper the
already choked-up progress of the streets. The Lord Mayor
was mighty busy calling out the Train-bands, and having
them drilled in Moorfields, for the defence of the City; and
a mighty fine show those citizen soldiers would have made no
doubt to the bare-legged Highlandmen, had they come that
way. The Guards at all the posts at the Court end of the

town were doubled, and we at the Tower put ourselves into a perfect state of defence. Cannon were run out ; matches kept lighted ; whole battalions maintained under arms ; munitions and provisions of war laid in, as though to withstand a regular siege ; drawbridges pulled up and portcullises lowered, with great clanking of chains and gnashing of old iron teeth ; —and rich sport it was to see those old rust-eaten engines once more brought into gear again.

But, as the Wise Man saith that a soft answer turneth away wrath, so do we often find that a merry word spoken in season will do more than all your Flaming Ordinances and Terrific Denunciations of Fire and Sword. And although at this time (beginning of the year 1746) authority very properly exerted itself to procure obedience to the constitution, by instilling Awe into men's minds, and did breathe nothing in its official documents but heading, hanging, and quartering, with threats of bombardments, free quarters, drum-head courts-martial, chains, gags, fines, imprisonment, and sequestration,—yet I question whether so much good was done by these towards the stability of the cause of the Protestant Religion and King George, or so much harm to that of the Pretender, Popery, brass money, and wooden shoes, as by a little series of Pamphlets put forth by the witty Mr. Henry Fielding, a writer of plays and novels then much in vogue ; but a sad loose fish, although he afterwards, as I am told, did good service to the State as one of the justices of peace for Middlesex, and helped to put down many notorious gangs of murderers, highwaymen, and footpads infesting the metropolis. This Mr. Fielding—whom his intimates used to call Harry, and whom I have often seen lounging in the Temple Gardens, or about the gaming-houses in St. James's Street, and whom I have often met, I grieve to say, in the very worst of company under the Piazzas in Covent Garden much overtaken in liquor, and his fine Lace clothes and curled periwig all besmirched and bewrayed after a carouse—took up the Hanoverian cause very hotly,—having perhaps weighty reasons for so doing,—and, making the very best use of his natural gifts and natural weapons, namely, a very strong and caustic humour, with most keen and trenchant satire, did infinite harm to the Pretender's side by laughing at him and his adherents. He published, probably at the charges of authority,—for he was a needy gentleman, always in love, in liquor, or in debt,—a paper called the *True Patriot*, in which the Jacobites were most mercilessly treated. Notably do I recall a sort of sham diary or almanack, purporting to be written by an honest tradesman of the City during the predicted triumph of the Pretender, and in which such occurrences were noted down as London being at the mercy of Highlanders and Friars; Walbrook church and many others being razed to the ground; Father O'Blaze, a Dominican, exulting over it; Queen Anne's statue at Paul's taken away, and a large Crucifix erected in its place; the Bank, South-Sea, India Houses, &c. converted into convents; Father Macdagger, the Royal confessor, preaching at St. James's; three Anabaptists hung at Tyburn, attended by their ordinary, Mr. Machenly (a grotesque name for the ranting fellow who was wont to be known as Orator Henley); Father Poignardini, an Italian Jesuit, made Privy-Seal; four Heretics burnt in Smithfield; the French Ambassador made a Duke, with precedence; Cape Breton given back to the French, with Gibraltar and Port Mahon to the Spaniards; the Pope's nuncio entering London, and the Lord Mayor and Aldermen kissing his feet; an office opened in Drury Lane for the sale of papistical Pardons and Indulgences; with the like prophecies calculated to arouse the bigotry of the lower and middle orders, and to lash them into a religious as well as a political frenzy. For a cry of " No Popery" has ever acted upon a true-born Englishman as a red rag does on a bull. Perhaps the thing that went best down of all Mr. Fielding's drolleries, and tickled the taste of the town most amazingly, was the passage where he made his honest London tradesman enter in his diary to this effect: " My little boy Jacky taken ill of the itch. He had been on the parade with his godfather the day before to see the Life Guards, and had just touched one of their plaids." One of the King's Ministers said long afterwards that this passage touching the itch was worth two regiments of horse to the cause of government. At this distance of time one doesn't see much wit in a scurrilous lampoon, of which the gist was to taunt one's neighbours with being afflicted with a disease of the skin : and, indeed, the lower ranks of English were, in those days, any thing but free from similar ailments, and, in London at least, were in their persons and manners inconceivably filthy. But 'tis astonishing what a mark you can make with a coarse jest, if you only go far enough, and forswear justice and decency.

Strange but true is it to remark that, in the midst of all such tremendous convulsions as wars, battles, sieges, rebellions, and other martial conflagrations, men and women and children do eat and drink, and love and marry, and beget other babes of humanity, and at last Die and turn to dust, precisely as though the world—or rather the concerns of that gross Orb —were all going on in their ordinary jog-trot manner. Although from day to day we people in London knew not whether before the sun set the dreaded pibroch of the Highland Clans might not be heard at Charing Cross, and the barbarian rout of Caterans that formed the Prince,—I mean the Chevalier,—I mean the Pretender's Army, scattered all about the City, plundering our Chattels, and ravaging our fair English homes ; although, for aught men knew, another month, nay another week, might see King George the Second toppled from his Throne, and King James the Third installed, with his Royal Highness Charles Edward Prince of Wales as Regent ; although it was but a toss-up whether the Archbishop of Canterbury should not be ousted from Lambeth by a Popish Prelate, and the whole country reduced to Slavery and Bankruptcy ;—yet to those who lived quiet lives, and kept civil tongues in their heads, all things went on pretty much as usual : and each day had its evil, and sufficient for the day was the evil thereof. That the Highlandmen were at Derby did not prevent the Hostess of the Stone Kitchen—that famous Tavern in the Tower—from bringing in one's reckoning and insisting on payment. That there was consternation at St. James's, with the King meditating flight and the Royal Family in tears and swooning, did not save the little schoolboy a whipping if he knew not his lesson after morning call. It will be so, I suppose, until the end of the world. We must needs eat and drink, and feel heat and cold, and marry or be given in marriage, whatsoever party prevail, and whatsoever King carries crown and sceptre ; and however dreadful the crisis, we must have our Dinners, and fleas will bite us, and corns pinch our Feet. So while all the Public were talking about the Rebellion, all the world went nevertheless to the Playhouses, where they played loyal Pieces and sang " God save great George our King" every night ; as also to Balls, Ridottos, Clubs, Masquerades, Drums, Routs, Concerts, and Pharaoh parties. They read Novels and flirted their fans, and powdered and patched themselves, and distended their

Q

coats with hoops, just as though there were no such persons in the world as the Duke of Cumberland and Charles Edward Stuart. And in like manner we Warders in the Tower, though ready for any martial emergency that might turn up, were by no means unnecessarily afeard or distraught with anxiety; but ate and drank our fill, joked the pretty girls who came to see the shows in the Tower, and trailed our halberts in our usual jovial devil-me-care manner, as true Cavaliers, Warders in the service of his Majesty the King, should do.

By and by came the news of Stirling and Falkirk, after the disastrous retreat of the Highlandmen back into Scotland. And then happened that short but tremendous fight of Drummossie Moor, commonly called the Battle of Culloden, where claymores and Lochaber axes clashed and glinted for the last time against English broadswords and bayonets. After this was what was called the pacification of the Highlands, meaning that the Duke and his dragoons devastated all before them with fire and sword; and then " retributive justice" had its turn, and the work of the Tower Warders began in earnest.

Poor creatures! theirs was a hard fate. At Carlisle, at Manchester, at Tyburn, and at Kennington Common, London, how many unhappy persons suffered death in its most frightful form, to say nothing of the unspeakable ignominy of being dragged on a hurdle to the place of execution, and mangled in the most horrible manner by the Hangman's butcherly knife, merely because they held that King James, and not King George, was the rightful sovereign of these realms! Is there in all History—at least insomuch as it touches our sentiments and feelings—a more lamentable and pathetic narration than the story of Jemmy Dawson? This young man, Mr. James Dawson by name,—for by the endearing aggravative of Jemmy he is only known in Mr. William Shenstone's charming ballad (the gentleman that lived at the Leasowes, and writ The Schoolmistress, among other pleasing pieces, and spent so much money upon Ornamental Gardening),—this Mr. James Dawson, I say, was the son of highly reputable parents, dwelling, by some, 'tis said, in the county of Lancashire, by others, in the county of Middlesex. At all events, his father was a Gentleman of good estate, who strove hard to bring up his son in the ways of piety and virtue. But the youth was wild and froward, and would not listen to the sage Counsels that were continually given him. After the ordinary grammar-school education, during which course he much angered his teachers, —less by his reckless and disobedient conduct than by his perverse flinging away of his opportunities, and manifest ignoring of the parts with which he had been gifted by Heaven,—he was sent to the University of Oxford to complete the curriculum of studies necessary to make him a complete gentleman. And I have heard, indeed, that he was singularly endowed with the properties requisite for the making of that very rare animal,—that he was quick, ready, generous, warm-hearted, skilful, and accomplished,—that he rode, and drove, and shot, and fenced, and swam, and fished in that marvellously finished manner only possible to those who seem to have been destined by a capricious fate to do so well that which they have never learned to do. And at college, who but Jemmy Dawson — who but he? For a wicked prank, or a mad carouse; for a trick to be played on a proctor, or a kiss to be taken by stealth,—who such a Master of Arts as our young Undergraduate? But at his lectures and chapels and repetitions he was (although always with a vast natural capacity) an inveterate Idler; and he did besides so continually violate and outrage the college rules and discipline, that his Superiors, after repeated admonitions, gatings, impositions, and rustications (which are a kind of temporary banishment), were at last fain solemnly to expel him from the University. Upon which his father discarded him from his house, vowing that he would leave his broad acres (which were not entailed) to his Nephew, and bidding him go to the Devil; whither he accordingly proceeded, but by a very leisurely and circuitous route. But the young Rogue had already made a more perilous journey than this, for he had fallen in Love with a young Madam of exceeding Beauty, and of large Fortune in her own right, the daughter of a neighbouring Baronet. And she, to her sorrow, poor soul, became as desperately enamoured of this young Scapegrace, and would have run away with him, I have no doubt, had he asked her, but for a spark of honour which still remained in that reckless heart, and forbade his linking the young girl, all good and pure as she was, to so desperate a life as his. And so he went wandering for a time up and down the country, swaggering with his boon companions, and pawning his Father's credit in whatsoever inns and pothouses he came unto, until, in the beginning of that fatal year '46, he must needs find himself at Manchester without a Shilling in his pocket, or the means of raising one. It was then the time that the town of Manchester had been captured, in the Pretender's interest, by a Scots Sergeant and a Wench ; and the notorious Colonel Towneley was about raising the Manchester Regiment of Lancashire Lads to fight for Prince Charlie. Desperate Jemmy Dawson enlisted under Towneley ; and soon, being a young fellow of good figure and shining talents, was made a Captain. But the ill-fated Manchester Regiment was ere long broken up ; and Jemmy Dawson, with Colonel Towneley himself, and many other of the officers, were captured. They were all tried at 'the Assizes held after the Assizes at St. Margaret's Hill, Southwark ; and James Dawson, being convicted of high treason, was sentenced to the usual horrible punishment for that offence. He was drawn on a hurdle to Kennington Common ; he was hanged, disembowelled, and quartered : but the young Madam of whom I have spoken was true to him unto the last. For many days following the sentence she vainly solicited his pardon ; but finding all useless, she on the fatal morning (having trimmed a shroud for him overnight, in which, poor Soul, his mangled remains were not to rest) followed him in a Mourning Coach to Kennington Common. She saw the Dreadful Tragedy played out to its very last Act ; and then she just turned on her Side in the Coach, and with a soft murmur, breathing Jemmy's Name, she Died. Surely a story so piteous as this needs no comment. And by Heaven it is True !

CHAPTER THE SEVENTEENTH.

REBELLION IS MADE AN END OF, AND AFTER SOME FURTHER SERVICE WITH
HIS MAJESTY I GO INTO BUSINESS ON MY OWN ACCOUNT.

MEMORANDUM.—About a year before the Rebellion, as the
Earl of Kilmarnock was one day walking in his Garden, he
was suddenly alarmed with a fearful Shriek, which, while he
was reflecting on with Astonishment, was soon after repeated.
On this he went into the House, and inquired of his Lady
and all the Servants, but could not discover from whom or
whence the Cry proceeded; but missing his Lady's Woman,
he was informed that she was gone into an Upper Room
to inspect some Linen. Whereupon the Earl and his Lady
went up and opened the Door, which was only latched. But
no sooner did the Gentlewoman within set eyes on his Lordship's face than she fainted away. When, proper aid being
given to her, she was brought to herself, they asked her the
meaning of what they had heard and seen. She replied, that
while she sat sewing some Linen she had taken up to mend,
the Door opened of itself, and a *Bloody Head* entered the
Room, and rolled upon the Floor; that this dreadful Sight
had made her cry out, and then the Bloody Head disappeared;
that in a few Moments she saw the same frightful Apparition
again, on which she repeated her Shrieks; and at the third
time she fainted away, but was just recovered when she saw
his Lordship coming in, which had made the Impression on
her they had been witness of.

This Relation given by the affrighted Gentlewoman was
only laughed at and ridiculed as the Effect of Spleen-Vapours,
or the Frenzy of a deluded Imagination, and was thought no
more of, till one Night, when the Earl of Kilmarnock, sitting
round a Bowl by the Winter Fire with my Lord Galloway,—
and it is at such a Time that men are most prone to fall-to
telling of Ghost Stories,—and their Lordships' conversation
turning on Spectres and Apparitions, the vulgar notions of
which they were deriding, the terrible tale of the Bloody
Head was brought up, and then dismissed as the idle fancy of
a Hoity-toity Tirewoman. But after Kilmarnock had engaged
in the Rebellion, and Lord Galloway was told of it, he instantly recollected this Story, and said, " I will wager a dozen

Magnums of Claret, and my best silver-laced Justaucorps, that my Lord Kilmarnock will lose his Head.

Nobody took his bet, not daring thus to trifle with the lives of the Quality; but that Scots Lord lost his Head, notwithstanding; and I saw it cut off on Tower Hill in the latter summer of the year '46.

This story of the Bloody Head was common Talk among us Warders at the time,—who were full as superstitious as other Folks, you may be sure. Many such Legends are there, too, current of Persons who were to die Violent Deaths at the hands of the Public Executioner, being forewarned many years before of their Impending Fate. And sometimes hath the Monition come nearer to the Catastrophe, as in the case of K. C. the Ist, who, entering Westminster Hall at that Unnatural Assize presided over by Bradshaw, the Gold Head fell off his Walking-Staff, and rolled on the Pavement of the Hall among the Soldiers; nor, when it was restored to him, could any Efforts of his make it remain on. Also it is said of my Lord Derwentwater, that the last time he went a hunting in the north, before he joined the Old Chevalier of St. George, his whippers-in uncarthed a litter of Fox-cubs, every one of which Vermin had been born without Heads. And as well authenticated is it, that when my Lord Balmerino (that suffered on Tower Hill with the Earl of Kilmarnock) was coming back condemned to Death from his Trial before his Peers at Westminster, his Lordship being of a merry, Epicurean temper, and caring no more for Death than a Sailor does for a wet Shirt, stopped the coach at a Fruiterer's at Charing Cross, where he must needs ask Mr. Lieutenant's Attendant to buy him some Honey-Blobbs, which is the Scottish name for ripe Gooseberries.

"And King Geordie maun pay for the bit fruitie; for King James's auld soldier has nae siller of his ain save twa guineas for Jock Headsman," quoth he in his jocular manner, meaning that those about him must pay for the Gooseberries; for indeed this Lord was very poor, and I have heard was, when in town, so much driven as to borrow money from the Man who keeps the Tennis-court in James Street, Haymarket.

Well, it so happened that the Season was a backward one; and the Fruiterer sends his duty out to his Lordship, saying that he has no ripe Gooseberries, but that of green ones he has a store, to which that unfortunate Nobleman is heartily welcome.

"I'll e'en try one," says my Lord; and from a Punnet they brought him he picks a Green Gooseberry; when, wonderful to relate, it swells in his hand to the bigness at least of an Egg-plum, and turns the colour of Blood. "The de'il's in the Honey-Blobb," cries my Lord in a tiff, and flings it out of window, where it made a great red stain on the pavement.

And this the Warder who stood by, and the Messenger who was in the coach itself, told me.

Less need is there to speak of such strange adventures as my Lady Nithisdale's child (that was born soon after her Lord's escape from the Tower, in which, with such a noble valour and self-sacrifice, she aided him) being brought into the World with a broad Axe figured, as though by a Limner, on its Neck; or of the Countess of Cromartie's infant (she likewise Lay-in while the Earl was under sentence) having a thin red line or thread right round its neck. These things are perhaps to be accounted more as Phenomena of nature than as ominous prognostications, and I so dismiss 'em. But it is worth while to note that, for all the good authority we have of Lord Kilmarnock's Waiting-woman being affrighted by the vision of a Bloody Head, the story itself, or at least something germane to it, is as old as the Hills. During my travels in Sweden, I was told of a very strange mischance that had happened to one of their Kings who was named Charles;—but Charles the what, I do confess I know not;—who walking one evening in his garden, saw all at once a Wing of the Palace, that had been shut up and deserted for Twenty years, all blazing with Light from the Windows, as for some great Festival. And his Majesty, half suspecting this might be some Masquerading prank on the part of the Court Ladies, and half afraid that there was mischief in it, drew his Sword, and calling upon a brace of his Gentlemen to follow him, stave-in a door and came into a Great Old Hall, that was the principal apartment in the said Wing. And at the upper End, where the ancient Throne of his ancestors was long since gone to Rags and Tatters, and abandoned to Dust and Cobwebs, he saw, sitting on the chair of Estate, and crowned, a little child that was then but a boy— the Duke of Sudermania. And lo! as he gazed upon him a

Dreadful Ball, that seemed fashioned in the similitude of
his own Head, showed itself under the Throne, rolled down
the steps, and so came on to his very Feet, where it stopped,
splashing his Boots unto the very ancle with Gore. The tale
of the Bloody Boots, as 'tis called, is still quite familiar to
every Nurse in Sweden; but I never heard how it ended,
or whether King Charles had his Head cut off in the Long-
run; but every Swede will swear to the Story; and as for
the Boots, I have heard that they are to be seen, with the
dark-brown stains of the Blood still upon 'em, in a glass
case at the House of one Mr. Herdström, who sells Aqua
Vitæ over the Milliner's in the Bogbindersgade at Stock-
holm.

'Twas in the summer of 1747 that I put off my Warder's
dress for good and all, the Rebellion being by this time quite
Dead and crushed out; but before I laid down my halbert
'twas my duty to assist at the crowning consummation of
that disastrous Tragedy. One of the Prime Traitors in the
Scottish Risings had been, it is well known, the notorious
Simon Fraser, Lord Lovat, of Castle Downie, in Scotland,
then come to be Eighty years old, and as atrocious an old
Villain as ever lived, but so cunning that he cheated the
Gallows for three-quarters of a century, and died like a Gentleman, by the Axe, at last. He had been mixed up in every
plot for the bringing back of King James ever since the Old
Chevalier's Father gave up the Ghost at St. Germain's, yet
had somehow managed to escape scot-free from Attainder and
Confiscation. Even in the '45, when he sent the Clan Fraser
to join the Young Chevalier, he tried his best to make his
poor Son, the Master of Lovat (a very virtuous and gallant
young Gentleman), the scapegoat for his misdeeds, playing
Fast and Loose between France and the Jacobites on one
side, and the Lord Justice Clerk and the King's Government
on the other. But Justice had him on the hip at last, and
the old Fox was caught. They brought him to London by
Easy Stages, as he was, or pretended to be, mighty Infirm;
and while he was resting at an Inn at St. Alban's, Mr. Hogarth the Painter (whom I have seen many a time smoking
a pipe and making Caricatures of the Company at the Tavern
he used—the Bedford Head, Maiden Lane, Covent Garden:
a skilful Draughtsman, this Mr. Hogarth, but very Uppish
and Impudent in his Tone; for I remember that he once

called me Captain Compound, seeing, as the fellow said, that
I was made up of three—Captain Bobadil, Captain Macheath,
and Captain Kyd),—this Mr. H. went down to St. Alban's,
and took a picture of the old Lord, as he sat in his great
chair, counting the strength of the Scottish clans on his
fingers. 'Twas afterwards graved on copper, and had a prodigious sale.

Monday, March 9th, began this Lord's Trial, very Grand
and Stately, which took place in Westminster Hall, fitted
up anew for the occasion, with the Throne, and chairs for
the Prince and the Duke, brave in Velvet and Gold, Scarlet
benches for the Peers, galleries for Ladies and Foreign Ambassadors, boxes for the Lawyers and the Managers of the
House of Commons that preferred the Impeachment, and a
great railed platform, that was half like a Scaffold itself, for
the Prisoner. So we Warders, and a Strong Guard of Horse
Grenadiers and Foot-Soldiers, brought him down from the
Tower to Westminster, Mr. Fowler, the Gentleman Gaoler,
attending with the Axe ; but the Edge thereof turned away
from his Lordship. The Crown Lawyers, Sir William Yonge,
Sir Dudley Rider, and Sir John Strange, that were of Counsel
for the Crown, opened against him in a very bitter manner ;
at which the Old Sinner grinned, and likened them to hounds
fighting for a very tough Morsel which was scarce worth the
Tearing. Then he plagues the Lord Steward for permission
for Counsel to be granted to him to speak on his behalf,
which by law could not be granted, and for a short-hand
writer to take minutes, which, after some delay, was allowed.
One Schield, that was the first Witness called, deposing that
Lord Lovat made one of a company of gentlemen who in 1740
drank healths and sang catches, such as " Confusion to the
White Horse" (meaning the heraldic cognizance of Hanover)
"and all his generation," and

> "When Jemmy comes o'er,
> We shall have blood and blows galore,"

my Lord cries out upon him as a False Villain and Perjured
Rascal. And was thereupon admonished by the Lord Steward
to more decorous behaviour. Item : that he laid all the blame
of the Frasers rising upon his Son, saying with Crocodile
Tears that he was not the first who had an Undutiful Son ;
whereupon the young gentleman cries out in natural Resent-

ment that he would put the Saddle on the right Horse. But
this and many other charges were brought home to him, and
that he had long foregathered with the Pretender, of whom
he spoke in a mock-tragedy style as " the young man Thomas
Kuli Khan." When upon his defence, he told many Lies,
and strove to Butter their Lordships with specious Compliments and strained Eulogies ; but 'twould not serve. The
Lords being retired into their own chamber, and the question
being put whether Simon Lord Lovat was guilty of all the
charges of high treason brought against him, every one, laying
his hand on his left breast, and beginning with the Junior
Baron, answered, " GUILTY, upon my honour." And the
next day, which was the seventh of the Trial, he was
solemnly sentenced to Die as a Traitor ; his Grace the Lord
Steward making a most affecting Speech, in which he reproached the Lord at the Bar with having unnaturally endeavoured to cast the blame of his malpractices on his son ;
" which," said his Grace, " if it be true, is an impiety that
makes one tremble : for, to quote a wise author of antiquity,
the love of our country includes all other social affections,
which," he continued, " shows a perfect knowledge of human
nature ; for we see, when that is gone, even the tenderest of
all affections—the parental—may be extinguished with it."
Upon which Admirable Discourse, my fellow-Warder, Miles
Bandolier, fell a blubbering, and wiping his eyes with his
laced sleeve, whimpers that it is something, after all, to be a
Lord to be cast for Death in such Sweet Terms ; for no Judge
at the Old Bailey would think of wasting Sugared words upon
the rogue he sent to Tyburn. Which is true.

When all was done, and the Lord Steward had, by breaking his Staff, declared the commission void, the Prisoner, with
a grimace twinkling about his wicked old mouth, bespoke his
Majesty's good consideration, and, turning to the Managers
of the Commons, cries out, " I hope, as ye are stout, ye will
be merciful !" Upon which one Mr. Polwhedlyan, that sate
for a Cornish borough, and was a very Fat Man, thinking
himself directly concerned, shook his head with great gravity
of countenance. But the old Villain was but Play-acting
again, and could but see that the Game was up ; for as the
Lords were filing back to the House, he calls after them,
" God bless you all ! I bid you an everlasting farewell; for
in this place we shall never meet again." He said, "God

bless you !" with a kind of fiendish yowl quite horrible to behold; and if ever man's benison sounded like a curse, it was that of bad old Lord Lovat.

A very sad sight at this memorable Trial was the Appearance and Demeanour of J. Murray, of Broughton, Esq., that had been the Chevalier's Secretary,—deepest of all in his Secrets, and most loved and trusted by him. The unhappy man, to save his Life, had betrayed his master and turned King's Evidence, not only against Lord Lovat, but many other unhappy Gentlemen. I never saw such a shrinking, cowering, hang-dog figure as was made by this Person in the Box; and burned with shame within myself to think that this should be a Man of Gentle birth, and that had touched the hand of a King's Son,—Grandson, I mean. Accomplished scoundrel as Lovat was, even a deeper abhorrence was excited by this Judas: when he first stood up, the Lords, after gazing at him for a moment with Contempt, turned their Backs upon him. The Crown Lawyers treated him in the manner that an Old-Bailey Counsellor would cross-examine an approver in a case of Larceny; and as for the Prisoner, he just shut his eyes while Murray was giving evidence; and when he had finished turns to the Gentleman Gaoler and asks, with his eyes still shut, "Is IT gone?" meaning Judas. At which there was some merriment.

'Twas just a month after this trial, on April 9th, that Justice was done upon Simon Fraser. He had eaten and drunk heartily, and cracked many scurril Jokes while under sentence, and seemed not to care Twopence whether he was Reprieved or Not. On the fatal day he waked about three in the morning, and prayed, or pretended to pray, with great Devotion. At all events, we Warders heard him; and he made Noise enough. At five he rose and called for a glass of Wine-and-Water, after drinking which he Read till seven. Then he took some more Wine-and-Water, and at eight desired that his Wig might be sent to the Barber to be combed out genteelly. Also, among some nicknacks that he kept in a casket, he looked out a Purse made somewhat in the Scotch fashion, of sealskin, to hold the money which he desired to give to the Executioner. At half after nine he breakfasted very heartily of Minced Veal, which he hoped would not indigest, he facetiously remarked, ordering Chocolate and Coffee for his Friends, whose Health he drank himself in Wine-and-

Water.   At eleven the Sheriffs sent to demand his Body, when he desired all present, save we who were at the Door, to retire, that he might say a short prayer.   Presently he calls 'em again, saying, " I am ready."   At the bottom of the first Pair of Stairs from his Chamber, General Williamson, the Commandant of the Garrison, invited him into his room to rest himself.   He complied most cheerfully, and in French desired that he might be allowed to take leave of his Lady, and thank her for all the civilities—for she had sent him victuals every day from her own Table, dressed in the French fashion, which he much affected—which she had shown him during his confinement.   But the General told him, likewise in French, that she was too much afflicted by his Lordship's Misfortunes to bear the shock of parting with him, and so begged to be excused.   Which means, that she did not care about being pawed and mauled by this wicked Old Satyr in his last Moments ; though, with the curiosity natural to her Sex, I saw with my own eyes Madam Williamson, in a new Hoop and a grand silk Calash, and with half-a-dozen of her gossips, at a window of the House on Tower Hill hard by the Sheriff's, and overlooking the Scaffold.

Now we Warders closed up about him ; and preceded and followed by Foot-Soldiers, he was conveyed in the Governor's Coach to the Outward Gate, and so delivered over to the Sheriffs, who, giving a Receipt for his Body, conveyed him in another coach (hired for the two former Lords, Kilmarnock and Balmerino) to the said House close to the Scaffold, in which (the House) was a room lined with Black Cloth and hung with Sconces.

A gentleman of a Pious Mien here beginning to read a Prayer for him, he bade me help him up that he might Kneel. One of the Sheriffs then asked him if he would take a Glass of Wine ; but he said that he would prefer Negus.   But there was no warm water, unhappily, at hand, and says his Lordship, with his old Grin, " The warm bluid is nae tappit yet;" so they brought him a glass of burnt brandy-and-bitters, which he drank with great Gusto.

He desired that all his Clothes should be given to his friends, together with his Corpse, remarking that for such end he would give the Executioner Ten instead of Five guineas, which is the customary Compliment.   To each of the dozen

Warders there present he gave a Jacobus ; to Miles Bandolier fifty shillings ; and on myself, who had specially attended on him ever since he was first brought to the Tower, he bestowed Five gold pieces. As I pouched the money, he clapped me on the shoulder, and says in his comical way,

" I warrant, now, that beer and pudding would sit as easy under thy laced jerkin were ' J. R.,' and not ' G. R.,' blazoned on thee, back and breast."

But anon a light cloud passed over his visage, and I heard him mutter to himself in the Scottish dialect, "Beef and pudding ! 'tis cauld kail for Fraser the morn."

Then turning to the Sheriffs, he desired that his Head might be received in a Cloth and put into the Coffin, the which they promised him ; likewise that (if it could be done without censure) the ceremony of holding up the Head at the Four Corners of the Scaffold should be dispensed with. His Lordship seemed now indeed very weak in his Body, albeit in no way disconcerted as to his Mind ; and, as Miles Bandolier and your Humble Servant escorted him up the steps of the Scaffold, he looked around, and gazing upon the immense concourse of people,

" God save us !" says he ; " why should there be such a bustle about taking off ane gray head, that cannot get up Three Steps without Three Bodies to support it !"

From which it will be seen that his Lordship had a Merry Humour until the last.

No sooner was he on the fatal Platform than, seeing me (as he condescended to think) much dejected, he claps me on the shoulder again, saying, " Cheer up thy heart, laddie in scarlet. I am not afraid ; why should you ?"

Then he asks for the Executioner,—that was none other, indeed, than Jack Ketch, the Common Hangman, dressed up in black, with a Mask on, for the days of Gentlemen Headsmen have long since passed away ; though some would have it that this was a Surgeon's Apprentice, that dwelt close to their Hall in the Old Bailey, and turned executioner for a Frolic ; but I am sure it was Ketch, for he came afterwards to the Stone Kitchen, wanting to treat all present to Drink ; but the meanest Grenadier there would have none of the Hangman's liquor, for all that the Blood on his jerkin was that of a Lord ; and the fellow grew so impertinent at last that we Warders were constrained to turn him out of the

Fortress, and forbid him to return under pain of a Drubbing. "I shall see you no more in the Tower," quoth the impudent rascal; "but, by ——, you shall all of you meet me at Tyburn some day, and I'll sell your lace doublets in Rosemary Lane after that your throttles are twisted." But to resume. Lord Lovat gave this murderous wretch with the Axe Ten Guineas in a Purse. Then he felt the edge of the Instrument itself, and said very quietly that he "thought it would do." Soon after, he rose from an Armchair which had been placed for him, and walks round and round his Coffin, which was covered with Black Velvet, studded with Silver Nails, and this Inscription on it (the which I copied off on my Tablets, at the time) :

SIMON DOMINUS FRASER DE LOVAT,
Decollat. April. 9, 1747,
Ætat. suæ 80.

Then he sat down again, and recited some Latin words which I did not understand, but was afterwards told they were from Horace, and signified that it is a sweet and proper thing to Die for one's Country; at the which a Wag in one of the Gazettes of the time must needs turn this decorous Sentiment into Ridicule, and compose an Epigram insulting Misfortune, to this Effect :

" With justice may Lovat this adage apply ;
For the good of their country ALL criminals die."

Then did the unfortunate Nobleman desire all the people to stand off except his two Warders, who again supported him while he prayed ; after which he calls up his Solicitor and Agent in Scotland, Mr. William Fraser, and, presenting his Gold-headed Cane to him, said, "I deliver you this cane in token of my sense of your faithful services, and of my committing to you all the power I have upon earth ;" which is a Scotch fashion, I believe, when they are Executed. And with this he kissed him upon both cheeks ; for this Lord was much given to hugging and slobbering.

He also calls for Mr. James Fraser, likewise a Kinsman (and these Northern Lords seem to have them by Hundreds), and says, "My dear Jamie, I'm gaun ta Haiv'n ; but ye must e'en crawl a wee langer in this evil Warld." And with this, the old Grin.

Then he took off his Hat, Wig, and Upper Clothes, and

delivered them to Mr. W F., charging him to see that the Executioner did not touch them. He ordered his Nightcap to be put on, and, unloosening his Neckcloth and the Collar of his Shirt, he kneeled down at the Block, and pulled the Cloth which was to receive his Head close to him; but he being too near that fatal Billet, the Executioner desired him to remove a little further Back, which, with our assistance, was Immediately done; and his Neck being properly placed, he told the Headsman he would say a short Prayer, and then give the Signal by dropping his Handkerchief. In this posture he remained about Half a Minute. Then, throwing down the Kerchief, the Executioner, at ONE BLOW, severed his Head from his Body. Then was a dreadful Crimson Shower of Gore all around; and many and many a time at the Playhouse have I thought upon that Crimson Cascade on Tower Hill, when, in the tragedy of *Macbeth*, the wicked Queen talks of " the old man having so much blood in him."

The Corpse was put into the Coffin, and so into the Hearse, and was carried back to the Tower. At four o'clock came an Undertaker from Holborn Hill, very fine, with many mourning coaches full of Scots gentlemen, and fetched away the Body, in order to be sent to Scotland, and deposited in his own Tomb at Kirkhill. But leave not being given by Authority as was expected, it was again brought back to the Tower, and buried by the side of Kilmarnock and Balmerino, close to the Communion-rails in the little church of St. Peter-on-the-Green, where so much Royal and Noble Dust doth moulder away.

Memorandum.—The Block on which this Nobleman suffered was but a common Billet of Oak wood, such as Butchers use, and hollowed out for the purpose of accommodating the neck, but it had not been stowed away in the White Tower for a month before it was shown to the Public for Money, and passed as the Block whereon Queen Anne Boleyn was beheaded. So with the Axe, which was declared to be the one used in decapitating K. C. Ist.; but there's not a word of truth in the whole story. The Block was hewn and the Axe was forged after the '45, and specially for the doing of justice on the Rebel Lords.

Note also that Lord Lovat left it in a Codicil to his Will that all the Pipers from Jonie Groat's house to Edinburgh were to play before his Corpse, and have a handsome allowance in Meal and Whisky (on which this sort of People mostly live) for so doing. Likewise that all the good old Women of his county were to sing what they call a *Coronach* over him. And indeed Women, both young and old, are so good when there's any thing pitiful to be done, that I make no doubt that the *Coronach* would have been sung if the old Rebel had gone back to Scotland; and if there were found those to weep for Nero, I see no reason why some tears should not have been shed for Simon Lord Lovat.

But there is no denying, after all, that Simon Fraser was a very complete Scoundrel. His whole life, indeed, had been but one series of Crimes, one calendar of Frauds, one tissue of Lies. For at least seventy out of his eighty years of life he had been cheating, cogging, betraying, and doing the Devil's service upon earth; and who shall say that his end was undeserved? A Scots Lord of his acquaintance was heard to say that he deserved to be hung twenty times in twenty places for twenty heinous Crimes that he had committed; and let this be borne in mind, that this was the same Lord Lovat that, as Captain Fraser, and being then a Young Man, was outlawed for a very atrocious Act of Violence that he committed upon a young Lady of Fashion and Figure, whom he carried away (with the aid of a Band of his brutal Retainers) in the dead of night, married by Force, with the assistance of a hireling Priest of his, cutting the very clothes off her body with his Dirk, and bidding his Pipers strike up to drown her cries. And yet such a Ruffian as he undoubtedly was could maintain an appearance of a facete disposition to the last; and he seems to have taken great pains to quit the Stage, not only with Decency, but with that Dignity which is thought to distinguish the Good Conscience and the Noble Mind. There is only one more thing to be set down, and that is one that I, being the Warder who (with Bandolier) attended him throughout his confinement, can vouch for the truth of. It was falsely said at the time that this Lord sought to defraud the Axe by much drinking of Wine : now I can aver that while in custody he never drank above two pints a day ; and the report may have arisen from the considerable quantities of Brandy and Rum which were used, night and morning, to bathe his poor feet and legs.

Now, Tranquillity being happily restored to these Kingdoms, and the Chevalier safely gotten away to France (whither, however, that luckless young Man was expelled, and in a very ignominious manner, at the Peace of Aix-la-Chapelle), I do confess that I began to weary somewhat of my fine Red Doublet, and of the Rosettes in my shoes; and although my Loyalty to King George and the Protestant Succession was without stain, I felt that it was somewhat beneath the dignity of a Gentleman Cavalier to dangle all day beneath a Portcullis with a Partisan on one's shoulder, or act as Bear Leader to the Joskins and simpering City Madams that came to see the Curiosities. And I felt my old roaming Fit come upon me as fierce as ever, and longed to be off to Foreign Parts again. I could have taken service under the Duke of Cumberland in the wars of Germany, and could have procured, perhaps, a pair of Colours in his Royal Highness's army; but, odd to relate, ever since my Misadventure at Vienna what time I was in little Squire Pinchin's service, I had conceived a great Distaste for those High Dutch countries, and cared not to go a campaigning there. Then there was fighting going on, and to spare, in Italy, where the Austrians were doing their best to reduce Genoa, the French opposing 'em tooth and nail. But I misliked the Germans as well as their country, and saw not the Profit of getting shot under the command of an Austrian Archduke. There were many other Continental countries open to the enterprise of Gentlemen Adventurers from England, but in most of them only Papists would go down; and to turn Romanist, for whatever reward of Place or Dignity, was against my principles.

Pending, however, my coming to some Determination as to my future mode of life, I resolved to throw up my Post of Tower Warder, receiving the gratuity of Twenty Guineas which was granted to those resigning by the bounty of his Majesty the King. Those who state that I left my Employment in any thing like Disgrace are surely the vilest Traducers and Libellers that ever deserved to have their tongues bored through with a Red-hot Iron; but I do not mind myself admitting that my situation had become somewhat unpleasant, and that I was sufficiently anxious to change the scene of my Adventures. There was a certain Waiting-maid belonging to Madam Williamson (that was General Williamson's lady, Military Commandant) who had long cast Sheep's Eyes upon me. I declare that I gave the Lass no encouragement; but what would you have? I was in the prime of life, and she a buxom kind of Wench, about twenty-two years of age. 'Twas following me here, and ogling me there, and leaving love-billets and messages for me at the Guard-Room. I will not deny but that from time to time I may have passed a jest with the girl, nay, given her some few trinkums, and now and then treated her to chocolate or sweet wine at Marylebone Gardens or the Flask at Hampstead. You may be sure that on these occasions I did not wear my Antiquated costume as a Tower Warder, but a blue Culloden frock, gold-corded, and with crown buttons ; a scarlet waistcoat and breeches ; a hat with a military cock ; and a neat hanger by my side. By drawers, masters of the games, and others, I was now always known as Captain.

Had I not been exceedingly wary and circumspect in all my dealings with this Waiting-woman,—poor thing ! her name was Prue,—the affair might have ended badly ; and there might have been Rendezvous on the ramparts, moonlight trysts on the Tower Green, and the like Follies. But I saw that our Flirtation must not be permitted to go any further. The Commandant's wife, indeed, had come to hear of it ; and, sending for me to her Parlour, must needs ask me what my Intentions were towards her Maid. "Madam," I answered, taking off my hat, and making her a very low bow, "I am a soldier ; and I never knew a soldier yet that Intended any thing ; all he does is without any Intention at all." Upon which she bade me to go for an Impudent fellow ; and I doubt not, had I been under her Husband's orders, would have had me set upon the Picket on the Parade for my free speaking ; but we Tower Warders were not amenable to such Slavish Discipline ; and, indeed, General Williamson, who stood by, was pleased to laugh heartily at my answer, and gave me a crown to drink the King's health, bidding me, however, take care what I was about, and see that the poor girl came to no Hurt. And I being at that time somewhat chary of imperilling my Independence, and minded to take neither a Wife nor a Mistress, thought the very best thing I could do was to kiss, shake hands, and Part, lest worse should come of it.

CHAPTER THE EIGHTEENTH.

I SEE MUCH OF THE INSIDE OF THE WORLD, AND THEN GO RIGHT ROUND IT.

1748. I was not yet Forty years of age, Hale and Stout, Comely enough,—so said Mistress Prue and many other damsels,—with a Military Education, an approved reputation for Valour, and very little else besides. A gentleman at large, with a purse well-nigh as slender as an ell-wand, and as woebegone as a dried eel-skin. But I was never one that wanted many Superfluities; and having no Friends in the world, was of a most Contented Disposition.

Some trouble, indeed, must I have with that luckless Mistress Prue, the Waiting-Maid—sure, I did the girl no Harm, beyond whispering a little soft nonsense in her ear now and then. But she must needs have a succession of Hysterical Fits after my departure from the Tower, and write me many scores of Letters couched in the most Lamentable Rigmarole, threatening to throw herself into Rosamond's Pond in St. James's Park (then a favourite Drowning-Place for Disconsolate Lovers), with many other nonsensical Menaces. But I was firm to my Determination to do her no harm, and therefore carefully abstained from answering any of her letters. She did not break her heart; but (being resolved to wed one that wore the King's cloth) she married Miles Bandolier about three months after my Departure, and broke his head, ere the Honeymoon was over, with a Bed-staff. A most frivolous Quean this, and I well rid of her.

Coming out of the Tower, I took lodgings for a season in Great Ryder Street, St. James's, and set up for a Person of Pleasure. There were many Military Officers of my Acquaintance who honoured me with their company over a Bottle, for even as a Tower Warder I had been a kind of a Gentleman, and there was no treating me as one of base Degree. They laughed somewhat at my Brevet rank of Captain, and sometimes twitted me as to what Regiment I was in; but I let them laugh, so long as they did not go too far, when I would most assuredly have shown them, by the

length of my Blade, not only what Regiment I belonged to,
but what Mettle I was of. By favour of some of my martial
Friends, I was introduced to a favourite Coffee-House, the
" Ramilies," in Jermyn Street ('tis Slaughter's, in St. Martin's
Lane, now, that the Soldier-Officers do most use) ; and there
we had many a pleasant Carouse, and, moreover, many a
good game at cards ; at the which, thanks to the tuition of
Mr. Hodge, when I was in Mr. Pinchin's service, I was a
passable adept, being able to hold my own and More, in
almost every Game that is to be found in Hoyle. And
so our card-playing did result, not only to mutual pleasure,
but to my especial Profit ; for I was very lucky. But I
declare that I always played fair ; and if any man doubted
the strict probity of my proceeding, there was then, as
there is now, my Sword to vindicate my Honour.

'Tis ill-living, however, on Gambling. Somehow or another the Money you win at Cards—I would never touch
Dice, which are too chaney, liable to be Sophisticated, and,
besides, sure to lead to Brawling, Stabbing, and cracking of
Crowns—this Money, gotten over Old Nick's back, I say,
never seems to do a Man any Good. 'Tis light come, and
light go ; and the Store of Gold Pieces that glitter so bravely
when you sweep them off the green cloth seems, in a couple
of days afterwards, to have turned to dry leaves, like the
Magician's in the Fairy Tale. Excepting Major Panton, who
built the Street and the Square which bear his name out of
One Night's Profit at the Pharaoh table, can you tell me of
one habitual Gambler who has been able to realise any thing
substantial out of his Winnings ? No, no ; a Hand at Cards
is all very well, and 'tis pleasant to win enough to pay one's
Reckoning, give a Supper to the Loser, and have a Frisk
upon Town afterwards ; but I do abhor your steady, syste-
matic Gamblers, with their restless eyes, quivering lips, hair
bristling under their wigs, and twitching fingers, as they
watch the Game. Of course, when Cards are played, you
must play for Money. As to playing for Love, I would as
soon play for nutshells or cheese-parings. But the whole
business is too feverish and exciting for a Man of warm temperament. 'Tis killing work when your Bed and Raiment,
your Dinner and your Flask, depend on the turn-up of a
card. And so I very speedily abandoned this line of life.

'Twas necessary, nevertheless, for something to be done

to bring Grist to the Mill. About this time it was a very common practice for Great Noblemen—notably those who were in any way addicted to pleasure, and ours was a mighty Gay Nobility thirty or forty years since—to entertain Men of Honour, Daring, and Ability, cunning in the use of their Swords, and exceedingly discreet in their conversations, to attend them upon their private affairs, and render to them Services of a kind that required Secrecy as well as Courage. One or two Duels in Hyde Park and behind Montagu House, in which I had the honour to be concerned as Second,—and in one of which I engaged the Second of my Patron's Adversary, and succeeded, by two dexterous side slices, in Quincing his face as neatly as a housewife would Slice Fruit for a Devonshire Squab Pie,—gained me the notice of some of the Highest Nobility, to whom I was otherwise recommended by the easiness of my Manners, and the amenity of my Language. The young Earl of Modesley did in particular affect me, and I was of Service to his Lordship on many most momentous and delicate Occasions. For upwards of Six Months I was sumptuously entertained in his Lordship's Mansion in Red Lion Square;—a Kind of Hospitality, indeed, which he was most profuse in the dispensation of:—there being at the same time in the House a French Dancing-Master, an Italian Singer, a Newmarket Horse-Jockey, and a Domestic Chaplain, that had been unfrocked for too much fighting of Cocks and drinking of Cider with clowns at his Vicarage; but to whom the Earl of Modesley was always a fast friend. Unfortunate Young Nobleman! He died of a malignant Fever at Avignon, just before attaining his Thirtieth Year! His Intentions towards me were of the most Bounteous Description; and he even, being pleased to say that I was a good-looking Fellow enough, and come to an Age when it behoved me to be settled in Life, proposed that I should enter in the bonds of Wedlock with one Miss Jenny Lightfoot, that had formerly been a Milliner in Liquorpond Street, but who, when his Lordship introduced me to her, lived in most splendid Lodgings under the Piazza, Covent Garden, and gave the handsomest Chocolate Parties to the Young Nobility that ever were seen. So Boundless was his Lordship's generosity that he offered to bestow a portion of Five Hundred Pounds on Miss Lightfoot if she would become Madam Dangerous—said portion to be at my absolute disposal—and to give me besides

a long Lease at a Peppercorn Rent of a Farm of his in Wilt-
shire. The Match, however, came to nothing. I was not
yet disposed to surrender my Liberty; and, indeed, the
Behaviour of Miss Lightfoot while the Treaty of Alliance
between us was being discussed, did not augur very favour-
ably for our felicity in the Matrimonial State. Indeed, she
was pleased to call me Rogue, Gambler, Bully, Led Captain,
and many other uncivil names. She snapped off the silver
hilt of my dress-sword (presented to me after I had fought
the Second in Hyde Park) and obstinately refused to restore
that gewgaw to me, telling me that she had given it to her
Landlady (one Mother Bishopsbib, a monstrous Fat Woman,
that was afterwards carted, and stood in the Pillory, in Spring
Gardens, for evil practices) in part payment for rent owing.
Moreover, she wilfully spoilt my best periwig by overturn-
ing a Chocolate Mill thereupon; and otherwise so miscon-
ducted herself that I bade her a respectful Farewell,—she
leaving the marks of her Nails on my face as a parting Gift,
—and told my Lord Modesley that I would as lief wed a
Roaring Dragon as this Termagant of the Piazza. This Refusal brought about a Rupture between myself and my Lord.
He was imprudent enough to talk about my Ingratitude, to
tell me that the very coat on my back was bought and paid
for with his Money, and to threaten to have me kicked out
of doors by two of his Tall Lacqueys. But I speedily let
him have a piece of my Mind. "My Lord," says I, going
up to him, and thrusting my face full in his, "you will be
pleased to know that I am a Gentleman, whose ancestors
were ennobled centuries before your rascally grandfather got
his peerage for turning against the true King."

He began to murmur something (as many have done
before when my blood was up, and I have mentioned Royalty) about my being "a Jacobite."

"I'll Jacobite your jacket for you, you Jackadandy!" I
retorted. "You have most foully insulted me. I know your
Lordship's ways well. If I sent you a cartel, you and your
whippersnapper Friends would sneer at it, because I am
poor, and fling Led Captain in my teeth. You won't fight
with a poor Gentleman of the Sword. I am too much of a
Man of Honour to waylay you at night, and give you the
private Stab, as you deserve; but so sure as you are your
father's son, if you don't make me this instant a Handsome

Apology, I will cudgel you till there is not a whole bone in your body."

The young Ruffian—he was not such a coward as Squire Pinchin, but rather murderous—makes no more ado but draws upon me. I caught up a quarter-staff that lay handy (for we were always exercising ourselves at athletic amusements), struck the weapon from his grasp, and hit him a sounding thwack across the shins that brought him down upon his marrow-bones.

"Below the Belt!" he cries out, holding up his hands. "Foul! foul!"

"Foul be hanged!" I answered. "I'm not going to fight, but to Beat You;" and I rushed upon him, shortening the Staff, and would have belaboured him Soundly, but that he saw it was no use contending against John Dangerous, and very humbly craved a parley. He Apologised as I had Demanded, and lent me Twenty Guineas, and we parted on the most friendly terms.

This Lord essayed, notwithstanding, to do me much harm in Town, saying that I had used him with black Cruelty, had requited his many favours with gross Treachery, and the like Falsehoods, until I was obliged to send him a Message to this purport: that unless he desisted, I should be obliged to keep my promise as to the Cudgel. Upon which he presently surceased. So much meanness had he, even, as to fudge up a pretended debt of nineteen guineas against me as for money lent, for the which I was arrested by bailiffs, and conveyed—being taken at Jonathan's—to a vile spunging-house in Little Bell Alley, Moorfields; but the keeper of the House stood my friend, and procured a Bail for me in the shape of an Honest Gentleman, who was to be seen every day about Westminster Hall with a straw in his shoe, and for a crown and a dinner at the eating-house would suddenly become worth five hundred a year, or at least swear himself black in the face that such was his estate:—which was all that was required. And when it came to justifying of Bail before the Judges, what so easy as to hire a suit of clothes in Monmouth Street, and send him into court fully equipped as a reputable gentleman? However, there was no occasion for this, for on the very night of my enlargement I won fifty guineas at the tables; and walking very Bold to my Lord's House, send up the nineteen guineas to my Lord with a note, asking to what lawyer I should pay the cost of suit, and whether I should wait upon him at his Levee for a receipt. On the which he, still with the fear of a cudgelling before his eyes, sends me down a Receipt in Full, *and the Money back to boot*, begging me to trouble myself in no way about the lawyer ; which, I promise you, I did not. And so an end of this troublesome acquaintance,—a profitable one enough to me while it lasted. As for Miss Jenny, her Behaviour soon became as light as her name. I have heard that she got into trouble about a Spanish Merchant that was flung down stairs and nigh killed, and that but for the Favour of Justice Cogwell, who had a hankering for her, 'twould have been a Court-Job. Afterwards I learnt that she had been seen beating Hemp in Bridewell in a satin sack laced with silver ; and I warrant that she was fain to cry, " Knock ! oh, good Sir Robert, knock !" many a time before the Blue-coated Beadles on Evil Thursday had done swingeing of her.

There are certain periods in the life even of the most fortunate man when his Luck is at a desperately low ebb,— when every thing seems to go amiss with him,—when nothing that he can turn his hand to prospers,—when friends desert him, and the companions of his sunshiny days chide him for not having made better use of his opportunities,—when, Do what he will, he cannot avert the Black Storm,—when Ruin seems impending, and Catastrophe is on the cards,—when he is Down in a word, and the despiteful are getting ready to gibe at him in his Misfortune, and to administer unto him the last Kick. These times of Trial and Bitter Travail ofttimes strike one who has just attained Middle age,—the Halfway House of Life ; and then, 'tis the merest chance in the world whether he will be enabled to pick himself up again, or be condemned for evermore to poverty and contumely,— to the portion of weeds and outworn faces. I do confess that about this period of my career things went very badly with me, and that I was grievously hard-driven, not alone to make both ends meet, but to discover any thing that could have its ending in a Meal of Victuals. I have heard that some of the greatest Prelates, Statesmen, Painters, Captains, and Merchants—I speak not of Poets, for it is their eternal portion, seemingly, to be born, to live, and to Die Poor—have suffered the like straits at some time or another of their lives. Many times, however, have I put it on record in these pages, that Despair and I were never Bedfellows. As for Suicide, I do condemn it, and abhor it utterly, as the most cowardly, Dishonest, and unworthy Method to which a Man can resort that he may rid himself of his Difficulties. To make a loathsome unhandsome corpse of yourself, and deny yourself Christian Burial, nay, run the risk of crowner's quest, and interment at the meeting of four cross-roads with a Stake driven through your Heart. Oh, 'tis shameful! Hang yourself, forsooth! why should you spend money in threepenny cord, when Jack Ketch, if you deserve it, will hang you for nothing, and the County find the Rope? Take poison! why, you are squeamish at accepting physic from the doctor, which may possibly do you good. Why, then, should you swallow a vile mess which you are *certain* must do you harm? Fall upon your sword as Tully—I mean Brutus—or some of those old Romans, were wont to do when the Game was up! In the first place, I should like to see the man, howsoever expert a fencer, who could so tumble on his own blade and kill himself. 'Tis easier to swallow a sword than to fall upon one, and the first is quite as much a Mountebank's Trick as t'other. Blow your brains out! A mighty fine climax truly! to make a Horrible Mess all over the floor, and frighten the neighbours out of their wits; besides, as a waggish friend of mine has it, rendering yourself stone-deaf for life. If it comes to powder and ball, a Man of courage would much sooner blow out somebody else's Brains instead of his own.

I did not, I am thankful to say, want Bread during this my time of ill luck; and I never parted with my sword; but sure it is that Jack Dangerous was woundily pushed, and had to adopt many extraordinary shifts for a livelihood. Item: I engaged myself to one Mr. Macanasser, an Irishman, that had been a pupil of the famous Mr. Figg, Master of the Noble Art of Self-Defence, at his Theatre of Arms, on the right hand side of the Oxford Road, near Adam and Eve Court. Mr. Figg was, as is well known, the very Atlas of the Sword; and Mr. Macanasser's body was a very Mass of Scars and Cicatrices gotten in hand-to-hand conflicts with the broadsword on the public stage. He had once presumed to rival Mr. Figg, whence arose a cant saying of the time, "A fig for the Irish;" but having been honourably vanquished by him, even to the slicing of his nose in two pieces, the cracking of his crown in sundry places, and the scoring

of his body as though it had been a Loin of Pork for the
Bakehouse, he was taken into his service, and became a principal figure in all the grand gladiatorial encounters, at wages
of forty shillings a week and his meat. As for Mr. Figg
himself, who was as good at backsword as at broadsword, at
quarter-staff as at foil, and at fisticuffs as any one of them,—
to say nothing of his Cornish wrestling,—I saw him once,
and shall never forget him. There was a Majesty blazed in
his countenance and shone in all his actions beyond all I
ever beheld. His right leg bold and firm ; and his Left,
which could hardly ever be disturbed, gave him the surprising advantages he so often proved, and struck his Adversary with Despair and Panic. He had that peculiar way of
stepping in, in a Parry, which belongs to the Grand School
alone : he knew his arm, and its just time of moving ; put a
firm faith in that, and never let his foe escape a parry. He
was just as much, as great a master as any I ever saw, as he
was a greater judge of time and Measure. It was his method,
when he fought in his Amphitheatre, to send round to a
select number of his scholars to borrow a shirt for the en-
suing combat, and seldom failed of half-a-dozen of superfine
Holland from his prime Pupils. Most of the young Nobility
and Gentry made it a part of their education to march under
his warlike banner. Most of his Scholars were at every
battle, and were sure to exult at their great master's victories ; every person supposing he saw the wounds his shirt
received. Then Mr. Figg would take an opportunity to inform his Lenders of the charm their Linen had received, with
an offer to send the garments home ; but he seldom received
any other answer than " Hang you, keep it." A most ingenious and courageous person, and immeasurably beyond
all his competitors, such as Macanasser, Will Holmes, Felix
Maguire, Broughton, Sutton, and the like.

Many good bouts with all kinds of weapons did we have
at Mr. Macanasser's theatre, which was down a Stable-yard
behind Newport Market, not far from Orator Henley's chapel.
The shirt manœuvre we tried over and over again with varying success ; but we found it in the end impossible to preserve order among our Patrons, the greater part of whom
were Butchers ; and I am fain to admit that many of these
unctuous sky-blue jerkins could fight as well as we. Then
Mr. Macanasser was much given to drinking, and in his pota-

tions quarrelsome. 'Twas all very well fighting on a stage for profit, and with the chance of applause, a clean shirt, and perchance a Right Good Supper given to us by our admirers afterwards at some neighbouring Tavern; but I never could see the humour of Swashbuckling for nothing, and without occasion; and as my Employer was somewhat too prompt to call in cold iron when his Head was so Hot, I shook hands with him, and bade him find another assistant. This was the Mr. Macanasser that was afterwards so unfortunate as to be hanged at Tyburn for devalising a gentleman at Roehampton. Great interest was made to save him; his very prosecutor (who knew not at the first his assailant, or that he had been driven to the road by hard times) heading the signatures to a petition for him. But 'twas all in vain. He made a beautiful end of it in a fine white nightcap fringed; and his funeral was attended by some of the most eminent swordsmen in town, who had a gallant set-to afterwards for the benefit of his widow. 'Tis sad to think of the numbers of brave men that I have known, and how many of them are Hanged.

About this time I was much with the Players, but misliked them exceedingly; and although numbers of brilliant offers were made to me, I could not be persuaded to try the sock and buskin. Hard as were the names by which my enemies would sometimes call me, I could never abide that of Rogue and Vagabond, and such, by Act of Parliament, was the player at that time. No, I said; whatever straits I am driven to, I will be a Soldier of Fortune, and Captain Dangerous to the last.

Of my Adventure with Madam Taffetas the Widow, I am not disposed to say much. Indeed, until my being finally settled, and made the Happiest Man upon earth by my union with the departed Saint who was the mother of my Lilias, it must be admitted that my commerce with the Sex was mostly of the unluckiest description. I have been used most shamefully by women; but it behoves me not to complain, seeing how much felicity I was permitted to enjoy in my latter days. This much, however, I will discreetly set down. That meeting Madam Taffetas in a side box at Drury Lane playhouse, She was pleased to accept my Addresses, and to inform me that my conversation was in the highest degree tasteful to her. I entertained her very handsomely—indeed

much beyond my means, for I was very heavily in debt for
necessaries, and I could scarcely walk the streets without
apprehensions of the grim Sergeant with his capias. Madam
Taffetas was an exceedingly comely person, amazingly well
dressed, and, as I was given to understand, in very prosperous
circumstances. She kept an Italian Warehouse by the Sign
of the two Olive Posts, in the broad part of the Strand, almost
opposite to Exeter Change, and sold all sorts of Italian Silks,
Lustrings, Satins, Paduasoys, Velvets, Damasks, Fans, Leghorn Hats, Flowers, Violin Strings, Books of Essences, Venice
Treacle, Balsams, Florence Cordials, Oil, Olives, Anchovies,
Capers, Vermicelli, Bologna Sausages, Parmesan Cheese, Naples Soap, and similar delicate cates from foreign parts. All
her friends put her down as a forty-thousand-pounder. In
Brief, she professed to be satisfied with my gentility and
Ancient Lineage, though worldly goods I had none to offer
her. All congratulated me on my Good Fortune ; and not
wanting to make any unnecessary bustle about the affair,
we took coach one fine Monday morning down to Fleet
Market, and were married by a Fleet parson—none other,
indeed, than my old Friend Chaplain Hodge, who had taken
to this way of life and found it very profitable, marrying his
twenty or thirty couple a week, when Business was brisk, at
fees varying from five guineas to seven-and-sixpence, and from
a dozen of Burgundy to half a pint of Geneva. But 'twas a
rascally business, the venerable man said, and he sorely longed
for the good old days when he, and I, and Squire Pinchin,
made the Grand Tour together. Alas, for that poor little
man : His Reverence told me that he had gone from bad to
worse ; that his Mamma had married a knavish lawyer, who
so bewildered Mr. Pinchin with Mortgages and Deeds of
Gift, and Loans at usurious interest, that he got at last the
whole of his property from him, brought him in many thousands in debt besides, and, after keeping him for three years
locked up and half-starved in the Compter, was only forced
to consent to his enlargement when the unhappy little man—
whose head was never of the strongest, and his wits always
going a wool-gathering—went stark-staring mad, and was, by
the City charity, removed to Bedlam Hospital in Moorfields.
There he raved for a time, imagining himself to be the Pope
of Rome, with a paper-cap for a tiara, an ell-wand for a cro-
sier, a blanket for a rochet, and bestowing his blessings on

the other Maniacs with much force and vehemence; and there, poor demented creature, he died in the year 1740.

Much better would it have been for me, had I gone straight off my Head and had been sent to howl in Bedlam, than that I should have married that same thievish catamaran, Madam Taffetas. Surely never Madman deserved a Dark House and a Whip more than I did for that most foolishly contracted union. I defy Calumny to prove that I ever used any thing approaching false Representations in this matter. I told her plainly that my Hand, Sword, and Deep Devotion were all I had to offer, and that for mere vile pounds, shillings, and pence, and other Mercantile Arrangements, I must look to her. Absolutely I borrowed ten pieces, although I was then at a very Low Ebb, to defray the expenses of the wedding Treat, which was done most handsomely at the Bible and Crown, in Pope's Head Alley, Cornhill. "Now then," I said to myself, as we came home towards the Strand (for we were resolved to have no foolish honeymooning in the Country, but to remain in town and keep an eye to Business),— "now then, Jack Dangerous, thou art at last Married and Settled, and need trouble thyself no more about the cares and anxieties of money-grubbing and bread-getting. Thou art tiled-in handsomely, Jack; thatched and fenced, and girt about with Comfort and Respectability. Thy hat is on, and thy house is covered." Alas, poor fool! alas, triply distilled zany and egregiously doting idiot! No sooner did a Hackney coach set us down at the Leghorn Warehouse in the broad part of the Strand, than we found Margery the maid and Tom the shopboy in a great confusion of tears on the threshold; and immediately afterwards we heard that during our absence to get married, Bailiffs had made their entrance, and seized all the Merchandise for a bill owing by Madam Taffetas to her Factor of Seven Hundred Pounds. The false Quean that I was wedded to was hopelessly bankrupt, and with the greatest impudence in the world she calls upon me to pay the Money; the Bailiffs adding, with a grin, that to their knowledge she owed much more than their Execution stood for, and that no doubt, as soon as it was bruited abroad that I was her Husband, the Sheriff of Middlesex would have something to say to me in the way of a capias against my person. In vain did I Rave and Swear, and endeavour to show that I could in no way be held liable for Debts which I had never contracted.

Such, I was told, was the Law ; and such it remains to this day, to the Great Scandal of justice and the detriment of Gentlemen cavalieros who may be entrapped into marrying vulgar Adventuresses whom they deem Gentlewomen of Property, and who turn out instead to be not worth twopence-halfpenny in the world.   Nor were words wanting to add dire Insult to this astounding Injury ; for Madam Taffetas, now Dangerous, as I groaningly remember, must needs call me Mercenary Rascal, Shuffling Pickthank, Low-minded Fortune-hunter, and the like unkind names.

Madam Dangerous indeed !   But I am thankful to Providence that the title she assumed very soon fell away from her, and that I was once more left free and Independent. For whilst we were in the very midst of Hot Dispute and violent Recrimination comes a great noise at the door as though some one were striving to Batter it down.   And then Margery the Maid and Tom the shop-lad began to howl and yelp again, crying out Murder and thieves, and that they were undone, the Bailiffs smoking their Pipes and drinking their Beer meanwhile, as though they enjoyed the Humours of the Scene hugely, and my wicked wife now pretending to faint, and now making at me with the avowed Design of tearing my eyes out.   Presently comes lurching and staggering into the room a Great Hulking Brute of a Man that was attired like a Sea Captain ; and this Roystering Tarpaulin makes up without more ado to my Precious Partner, gives her two sounding Busses on either side of her cheeks, and salutes her as his wife.

"Your wife !" I cried, starting up ; "why, she's my wife ! I married her this very morning, and to my sorrow, before Parson Hodge, the Couple-Beggar, at the Fleet."

"That may be, Brother," answers the Sea Captain, with drunken gravity ; "but she's my wife, for all that.   You married her this morning, you say.   I married her five years ago at Horsleydown, and in the Parish church.   I've got the 'Stifficate to prove it ; and though I say it that shouldn't, there's not a Finer woman, with a neater ancle and such a Devil of a temper, to be found 'twixt Beachy Head and Cape Horn."

"A fig for both of you !" bellows Madam Taffetas, who had gone into one of her Sham Faints in the arm-chair, but was now conveniently recovered again.   "If I'm married to

both of you—to you, you pitiless Grampus" (this was to the
Sea Captain), "and to you, Ruffian, Bully, and Stabster"
(this was to *me*), "I'm married to somebody else, and my
real Husband is a Gentleman, who, if he were here, would
quoit the pair of you into the street from Exeter Change to
the Fox under the Hill."

She said this in one Scream, and then Fainted, or pretended to Faint again.

"Brother," said the Sea Captain to me, staggering a
little (for he confessed to having much mixed punch under
hatches), but still very grave,—"brother, I think as how it's
clear that we're both of us d—d fools, and d—d lucky fellows
at the same time."

"Amen!" cries one of the Bailiffs, with a guffaw.

"*You* belay," remarked the Captain, turning towards the
vermin of Law with profound disdain. "Brother" (turning
to me), "is the Press out?"

"What do you mean?" I inquired. "You know that
there's no warrant for press-gangs in this part of the Liberties
of Westminster."

"Liberty be Hanged!" quoth the Sea Captain. "If
there was any liberty, there couldn't be a press, for which I
don't care a groat, for I'm a master mariner. This is what I
mean. Is them landlubbers there part of a press-gang? Are
you trapped, brother? Are you in the bilboes? Are you in
any danger of being put under hatches?"

"Why," upspoke one of the Bailiffs, answering for me,
"the truth is that we are Sheriff's Sergeants, and have made
seizure, according to due writ of *fi. fa.* of this worthy lady's
goods. We've nothing at all against the gentleman who says
that he married her this morning; but as you said that you'd
married her five years ago, it's very likely that we, or some
of our mates, shall have something to say to you, in the form
of parchment, between this and noon to-morrow."

"Very well," answers the Strange Seaman. "You speak
like a Man o' War's chaplain, some Lies and some Lingo, but
all of it d—d Larned. Have you got ere a drop of rum,
brother?"

"There's nothing here but some Three-Thread Swipes,"
responds Mr. Bailiff; "and, indeed, we were waiting until
the gentleman treated us to something better."

"Then," continues the Captain, "you shall have some

rum. Younker, go and fetch these gentlemen some liquor;"
and he flings a crown to the shop-lad. "You may drink
your grog and blow your baccy," he went on, "as long as
ever you like, and much good may it do you. And as for
you, Pig-faced Nan,"—in this uncivil manner did he address
the false Madam Taffetas,—"you may go to bed, or to the
Devil, 'zactly as you choose, and settle your Business with
the Bailiffs in the morning 'zactly as you like. And you and
I, brother," he wound up, taking me by the arm in quite a
friendly manner, "will just go and take our grog and blow
our baccy in peace and quietness, and thank the Lord for it."

All this he said with great thickness and indistinctness
of utterance, but with an immovable gravity of countenance.
I never saw a Man who was manifestly so Drunk speak so
sensibly, and behave himself in such a proper manner in
my life. ¡

As he turned on his heel to leave the parlour where all
this took place, I saw one of the Bailiffs rise stealthily as if
to follow us.

"Belay there !" the Captain cried, advancing his mahogany
Paw in a warning manner. "Hold hard, shipmates. I'm a
peaceable man, and aboard they call me Billy the Lamb ; but,
by the Lord Harry, if I catch you sneaking about, or trying
to find out where I and this noble gentleman be a going, I'm
blest if I don't split your skull in two with this here speak-
ing-trumpet." And so saying the Captain produced a very
long tin tube, such as Mariners carry to make their voices
heard at a distance at sea, but which they generally have
aboard, and do not carry with them in their walks.

The Bailiffs were sensible men, and forbore to intermeddle
with us any more. So we marched out of the House, it
being now about nine o'clock at night ; and, upon my word,
from that moment to this, I never set eyes upon Madam
Taffetas, or Dangerous, or Blokes,—for the Sea Captain's
name, he afterwards told me, was Blokes,—or whatever her
real Name was. It is very certain that she used me most
scandalously, and cruelly betrayed the trusting confidence of
one that was not only a Bachelor, but an Orphan.

Captain Blokes was a strange character. We had a grand
Carouse that night, he paying the Shot like a Gentleman :
and over our flowing Bowls, he told me that he had long had
suspicions of his wife's real character ; and was, indeed, in

possession of evidence (though he had kept it secret) to prove
that she had given herself in marriage to another man before
she had wedded him. And then, through the serving-lad, he
had heard that very morning, on his coming into the Pool
from Gravesend and Foreign Parts, that Madam, who thought
him in China at least, and hoped him Dead, was about to
enter into Wedlock once again; so that, determined to have
Sport, he had well Primed himself with Punch, and lurked
about the neighbourhood until Monsieur Tomfool and his
Spouse (by which I mean myself, although no other man
should call me so) had come home from the Fleet. And so
all the Crying, and Lord ha' Mercies, of the Wench and the
Boy, were all subterfuges; and they knew very well, the sly
rogues, that the Sea Captain would soon be to the Fore.

Nothing would suit him after this but that we should
have Supper at the King of Prussia's Head, in the Savoy, and,
as I had given up my Lodgings as not Grand enough for me
on the eve of my Wedding, and the Vessel of which he was
Commander was lying in the Pool, that we should have Beds
—at his charges—at the same Tavern; and, indeed, your Seafaring Men, although rough enough, and smelling woundily
of tar and bilge-water, are the most Hospitable Creatures
breathing; and that makes Me so free with my Money when
there is a Treat afoot; albeit I can, without Vanity, declare
myself Amphibious, for I have seen as much service by Sea
as by Land, and have always approved myself a Gentleman
of Courage, Honour, and Discretion, on both Elements.

The next morning, after a Nip of Aquavitæ, to clear the
Cobwebs out of our throats, we went down to Billingsgate,
where we saw my old humorous acquaintances, Brandy Sall,
the fishwife, and the humorous porter, the Duke of Puddle-
dock; likewise a merry Wag, that did porterage work for the
Fish Factors in the Market, and thereby seemed to have
caught somewhat of the form of the fish beneath which his
shoulders were continually groaning, so that all who could
take that liberty with him called him Cod's Head and
Shoulders. Here we breakfasted on new Oysters and Fried
Flounders, with a lappet of Kippered Salmon, for Goodman
Thirst's sake, and a rare bowl of hot Coffee, which made us
relish a Jug of Punch afterwards in a highly jocund manner.
And then we fell to conversation; and I, who had nothing to
Conceal, and nothing to be Ashamed of, did recount those of

S

my Adventures which I deemed would be most diverting (for
I forbore to tell him those which were tedious and unevent-
ful) to Captain Blokes. And he, not to be behindhand in
frank confidence, told me how many years he had been at sea;
how many merchant vessels he had commanded ; and what
Luck he had had in his divers Trading Adventures. Likewise that he was now under engagement with some very
worthy Merchants of Bristol, to man, equip, and command a
vessel called the *Marquis*, which, in company with two
others, the *Hope* and the *Delight*, were about to undertake a
Cruising Voyage round the World. Finding from my speech
that I was not wholly unaccustomed to the Sea, and being
made acquainted with what I had done in the West Indies
and elsewhere, Captain Blokes was pleased to say, that I was
the very man for him, if I would join him. And at this time,
in verity, it seemed as though nothing could suit me better ;
for my Resources were quite exhausted, and I was brought
very Low. So, after some further parley, and a good Beefsteak
and Onions, and a bottle of Portugee Wine for dinner, we
went to the Scrivener's in Thames Street, by the name of
Pritchett, that was Agent for the Company of Merchant
Adventurers at Bristol ; and an Agreement was drawn up, by
which, for Fifty Shillings a Month pay, all due rations and
allowances, and a certain proportion of the profits to be
divided among the Ship's Company at the termination of our
Adventure, I bound myself to serve Captain Blokes as Secretary and Purser of the ship *Marquis*.

" Which means," says he, when we had taken a Dram
and shaken hands on signing articles, "that you are to Write,
Fight, Drink, and keep Accompts, play put with me in the
Cabin, assist me in preserving the Discipline of the Ship, sing
a good song when you are called upon, help the Doctor to take
care of the sick, and see that the Steward don't steal the Grog
and Tobacco ; and if you'll stick to me, by the Lord Harry,
Billy Blokes will stick to you. I like you because you were
such a d—d fool as to go and marry that old woman."

The next day we took Coach at the Swan, by Paddington
Church, for Bristol, and two days afterwards arrived at that
great and flourishing Mercantile city. Nothing worthy of
note on the road ; the Highwaymen, that were wont to be so
troublesome, being mostly put down, owing to Justice Fielding and De Vit's stringent measures. We were much beset

with gangs of wild Irish coming over from their own country a-harvesting in our fertile fields; and those gentry were like to have bred a riot, quarrelling with the English husbandmen at Stow. Being at Bristol, comfortably housed at the Bible and Crown in Wine Street,—the landlord much given to swearing, but one of the best hands at making of Mum that ever I knew,—Captain Blokes had great work in settling business with the Company of Merchant Adventurers and Alderman Quarterbutt, their President. As it seems we were at war with the French and Spaniards, the *Marquis* (burden about 320 tons) was to carry twenty-six guns and a complement of 108 men, letters of marque being granted to us by private Commission, with secret instruction as to Prizes and Plunder, so that the disposal of both should redound to the advantage of the Mariners, the Profit of our Employers, and the honour of His Majesty's arms. We had nigh double the usual complement of officers usual in private ships, to prevent mutinies, which ofttimes happen in long voyages, and that we might have a large provision for a succession of officers in case of Mortality. In the *Marquis* we had Captain Blokes, commander-in-chief of the whole Armament, a Mariner; a Second Captain who was a Dr. of Physick, and also acted as President of our Committee (having much book-learning) and Commander of the Marines; two Leftenants; a Sailing Master; a Pilot that was well acquainted with the South Seas, having been in those Latitudes twice before; a Surgeon and his Mate, or Loblolly Boy; Self as Secretary and Purser; two young lawyers, designed to act as Midshipmen; Giles Cash, as Reformado,—that was the title of courtesy given to those who were sent to sea in lieu of being hanged; a Gunner and his crew; a Boatswain, cooper, carpenter, sailmaker, smith, and armourer, ship's corporal, Sergeant of Marines, cook; a Negro that could shave and play the fiddle; and the Ship's company as aforesaid, one-third of whom were foreigners of every nation under the Sun, and of those that were His Majesty's subjects many Tinkers, Tailors, Haymakers, Pedlars, &c.—a terribly mixed Gang, requiring much three-strand cord to keep 'em in order.

On the 2d August 1748 we weighed from King's Road, by Bristol, and at ten at night, having very little wind, anchored between the Holms and Minehead. Coming on a fresh gale at S.E. and E.S.E., we ran by Minehead at six in the morning. Next day the wind veered to N.E. and E.N.E.; on the 4th there was but little wind, and smooth water; on the 5th we saw Land; and finding that we had overshot our port, which was Cork, came to an anchor at noon off the two rocks near Kinsale. At eight at night we weighed, having a Kinsale Pilot on board, who was like to have endangered our safety, the night being dark and foggy, and the Pilot not understanding his Business; so that he nearly turned us into the next Bay to the westward of Cork, which provoked Captain Blokes to chastise him publicly on the quarter-deck. Our two consorts got into Cork before us, and we did not anchor in the Cove until the 7th August, at three in the afternoon. We stayed here until the 28th of the month, getting in stores and provisions, and replacing as many of our tailors and haymakers as we could with real Sailors that could work the Ship. Our crew, however, were continually Marrying while we were at Cork, to the great Merriment of Self and Captain Blokes, who had seen enough and to spare of that Game; but they *would* be Spliced, although they expected to sail immediately; among others, there was a Danish man coupled by a Romish Priest to an Irish woman, without understanding a word of each other's language, so that they were forced to use an interpreter; yet I perceived this pair seemed more afflicted at separation than any of the rest. The Fellow continued melancholy for many days after we were at Sea. The rest, understanding each other and the world better, drank their cans of Flip till the very last Minute, concluded with a health to our good voyage and their next Happy Meeting, and then Departed, quite unconcerned.

We took sailing orders on the 1st of September; and then Captain Blokes discovered to the crew whither we were bound,—that is to say, on a four years' voyage,—in order that, if any Disorders should arise among us, we might exchange our Malcontents while in company with one of his Majesty's ships. But no complaint was found on board the *Marquis*, except from one fellow who was expected to have been Tithing man that year in his Parish, and said his wife would be obliged to pay Forty shillings in his absence; but seeing all hands satisfied, he was easily quieted, and drank with the rest to a prosperous voyage. On the 2d September we, having cleaned and tallowed our ships five streaks below the Water-line, the fiddler struck up "Lumps o' Pudding," and to follow that "Cold and Raw," the Ship's company joining chorus with a will, and so fell down to the Spit End by the *Culloden* Man of War, as our two Consorts had done the Night before. When we came to the Spit End, Captain Blokes saluted the *Culloden* with Seven Guns, to which they returned Five in courtesy, and then we again Three for thanks. And so commenced my Journey round the World.

CHAPTER THE NINETEENTH.

MERCATOR HIS PROJECTION, AND WHAT CAME OF IT.

MEANING simply this, that I have often and often, as a little
Lad, gazed upon the Great Map—very yellow, and shiny,
and cracked on its canvas mounting it was—of the World,
upon Mercator's Projection, and devoutly longed for the day
to arrive when it might be my fortune to make a Voyage of
Circumnavigation. Such a Map, I remember, hung in the
Schoolroom at Gnawbit's; and I have often been cruelly
beaten for gazing at it and pondering over it, instead of
endeavouring to commit to memory a quantity of Words,
the meaning of which I could not for the life of me understand.

Now, indeed, I had got my Desire, and was going round
the World in a Ship well found with Men and Stores, occupying myself a responsible position, and one giving me some
Authority, and enjoying the full Confidence of my Commander, who was, both when sober and inebriated (and he
was mostly the latter), one of the most sagacious men I ever
knew. He spoke seldom, and then generally with a Hiccup;
but what he said was always to the Purpose. I doubt not,
if Captain Blokes had been in the Royal Navy, he would by
this time be flying his pendant as Admiral.

'Twould fill a volume to give you a Narrative, however
brief, of our Voyage. One does not go round the World
quite so easily as a Cit taking a Wherry from Lambeth
Walk to Chelsea Reach. No, no, my Masters; there are
Perils to encounter, Obstacles to overcome, Difficulties to
surmount; and I flatter myself that Jack Dangerous was
not found wanting when a Stout Heart, a Strong Hand, and
a Clear Head were needed. I repeat that 'tis impossible for
me to give you an exact Log of so lengthy a Cruise; and you
must needs be content if I set down a few bare Items of the
most notable Things that befell us.

On the 11th September we chased a strange Sail, and
after three hours came up with her. She proved to be a
Swedishman. After firing a couple of Shots at full Random
at her, to show that we meant Mischief if provoked, and one

of which Shots, I believe, passed over her Taffrail, and killed
a Black Servant and the Captain's Monkey, Captain Blokes
boarded her in his Yall; examined the Master, and searched
the Ship for Contraband of War; but not finding any save
a suspicious quantity of salted Reindeer's Tongues, our Committee agreed that she could not be considered a lawful Prize;
and not being willing to hinder time by carrying her into
any Harbour for further Examination, we let her go without
the least Embezzlement. The Master gave us a dozen of his
Reindeer Tongues, and a piece of dry Rufft Beef; and we
presented him with a dozen bottles of Red-streak Cider. But
while Captain Blokes and the Doctor of Physic and Self
were aboard the Swede taking a social Glass with him, our
rascally crew took it into their heads to Mutiny, their Grievance being that the vessel was a Contraband, and ought to
be made a Prize of. The plain truth was, that the Rogues
thirsted for Plunder. The Boatswain was one of the Mutineers. Him we caused to receive Four Dozen from the
hands of his own Mates, and well laid on; about a dozen of
the rest we put in Irons, after having Drubbed 'em soundly,
and fed 'em on Bread-and-Water; but at the end of a few
days they begged Pardon, and, on promising Amendment,
were allowed to return to their Duty.

18th September we came in sight of Pico Teneriffe, bearing S.W by W., distance about eight leagues. This day
we spied a sail under our Lee Bow, between the Islands of
Grand Canaries and Forteventura. She showed us a clean
Pair of Heels; but we gave Chase, and after seven hours
came up with her. She proved a Prize, safe enough: a
Spanish Bark, about 25 tons, with some 45 Passengers, who
rejoiced much when they found we were English, having
fancied that we were Turks or Sallee Rovers. Amongst our
Prisoners were four Friars, and with them the Padre Guardian of Forteventura, a good, honest old fellow, fat, and
given to jollity. Him we made heartily merry, drinking the
Spanish King's Health, for nought else would he Toast. After
we had made all Snug, we stood to the Westward with our
Prize to Teneriffe, to have her ransomed, that is to say, her
Hull; for her Cargo was not worth redeeming, being extremely shabby,—one or two Butts of Wine, a Hogshead of
Brandy, and other small matters, which we determined to
keep for our own use. The Spanish Dons made a mighty

pother about paying, pleading that the Trade of these Islands enjoyed an immunity from Privateering by arrangement between his Catholic Majesty and the King of Great Britain, and were even seconded by some English Merchants of Teneriffe, that were frightened at the thought of the cruel Reprisals the Dons might exercise after we went away, both on their Persons and Properties; for Jack Spaniard is one that, if he cannot have Meal will have Malt. But we soon let 'em know that Possession was Nine Points of the Law, and that we were resolved to stick to our Prize unless we got Ransom, which they presently agreed to. At eight o'clock the next morning we stood into the Port, close to the Town, and spied a Boat coming off, which proved to be the Deputy Governor, a Spanish Don with as many names as an English pickpocket has Aliases, and one Mr. Harbottle, that was English Vice-Consul. They brought us Wine, Figs, Grapes, Hogs, and other Necessaries, as Ransom in Kind for the Bark; and accordingly we restored her, as also the Prisoners, with as much as we could find of what belonged to their Persons; although, Truth to tell, some of our wild Reformadoes had used them somewhat unhandsomely. All the Books, Crucifixes, Reliques, and other superstitious things, we carefully gave back to the Friars; to the Padre a large Cheese, at which he was much delighted; and to another Religious, who had been stripped nearly as bare as a Robin, a pair of Breeches and a Red Nightcap. And so stood off, giving Three Cheers for King George, and one, with better luck next time, for the King of Spain; and I doubt not that they cursed us heartily that same night in their Churches, for Heretics. Now we had an indifferent good stock of Liquor, to be the better able to endure the Cold when we got to the length of Cape Horn, which, we were informed, had always very Cold Weather near it.

On the 25th, according to custom, we Ducked those that had never passed the Tropic before. The manner of doing it was to reeve a Rope in the Mainyard, to hoist 'em about halfway up to the Yard, and let 'em fall at once into the Water; they being comfortably Trussed by having a Stick 'cross through their Legs, and well fastened to the Rope, that they might not be surprised and let go their Hold. This proved of great use to our Fresh-water Sailors, to recover the Colour of their Skins, which had grown very Black and Nasty.

Those that we Ducked in this manner Three Times were about 60; and others that would not undergo it could redeem themselves by a Fine of Half-a-Crown, to be Levied and Spent at a Public Meeting of all the Ships' Companies when we returned to England. The Dutchmen we had on board, and some few English, desired to be Ducked, some six, others eight and ten times, to have the better title for being Treated when they came home.

On the 1st October we made St. Vincent, where our Water began to smell insufferably; so had some Coopers from the *Hope* and *Delight* to make us Casks, and take in a fresh Stock.

On the 3d we sent a boat to St. Antonio, with one of our Gunner's Crew that was a very fair Linguist, to get Truck for our Prize Goods what we wanted; they having plenty of Cattle, Pigs, Goats, Fowls, Melons, Potatoes, Limes, and ordinary Brandies, Tobacco, Indian Corn, &c. Our people were very meanly stocked with Clothes; yet we were forced to watch our men very narrowly, and Punish some of 'em smartly, to prevent their selling what Garments they had, for mere Trifles, to the Negroes.

We got all we wanted by the 8th; but our Linguist gave us leg-bail; and as he was much given to telling of Lies, we did not go to the pains of sending a party of Marines on shore after him. This is the place whither the Blacks come from St. Nicholas to make Oil of Turtle for the anointing of their Nasty Bodies withal. There was much good Green Turtle at this time of the year, which made me think of my old Jamaica days; but our men, in a body, refused to eat it, much preferring Salt Junk.

Item.—Many Flying Fish about here.

Nothing more worthy of note till the 22d October, when Mr. Page, Second Mate, made an attack on his superior officer, the Doctor of Physic, with a Marline-spike; and, but for a very large Periwig he wore, which was accounted odd in one having a Maritime Command, would have finished him. Mr. Page was had to the Forecastle and clapped in the Bilboes, and Captain Blokes was for Hanging him off-hand as an Example to the rest; but I, as Secretary, pointed out to him that there was no Power of Life and Death in our Instructions, and that it would be folly to run the risk of a Præmunire when we made Home again. With much trouble

I succeeded in dissuading him from his Design; so that the
Mate was only lashed to the Main-gears and soundly Drubbed.
Fair, pleasant Weather, and a fresh Gale. One that had
secreted a Peruke, and a pair of scarlet Stockings with silver
Clocks, out of the plunder of the Spanish Bark, did also
receive Rib-roasting enough (this was on a Sunday, after
Prayers) to last him for a Fortnight.

On the 10th of November, after a terrific Tornado and
Thunder and Lightning, that frightened some of our Tailors
and Haymakers half into Fits, we came to an Anchor in
22-fathom water, in a sandy bay off the land of Brazil.
Caught some Tortoises for their Shells, for they have too
strong a taste to be Eatable. A Portugee boat came from a
Cove in the Island of Grande, on our Starboard side, and
said they had been robbed by the French not long since.
Captain Blokes, the Doctor, and Self went ashore to Angre
de Keys, as it is called in Sea-Draughts; but, as the Portugee
call it, Nostra Senora de la Concepcion, a small village about
three leagues distant, to wait on the Governor, and make him
a present of Butter and Cheese. As we neared the shore, the
People, taking us for Mounseers, fired a few Musquetoons at
us, which did us no Hurt; and when they found out who
we were, they very Humbly Begged our Pardon. The
Friars invited us to their Convent, and told us they had been
so often stripped and abused by King Lewis's frog-eating
Subjects, that they were obliged to take measures to Defend
themselves; and, indeed, 'twas these said Padres who had
fired at us. The Governor was gone to Rio Janeiro, a city
about twelve leagues distant, but was expected back next
day. We got our empty Casks ashore, and sent our Carpenter, with a friendly Portugee, to look out Wood for
Trustle-trees, both our Main and Fore being broke; but the
Weather was so Wet and violent Sultry, that we could do
nothing. Here are abundant Graves of Dead Men; and the
Portugees told us that two great French Ships, homeward
bound from the South Seas, that Watered in this same place
about nine months before, had buried nearly half their men
here; but 'twas at the Sickly season, and the French had a
marvellous foul way of Living. The people very Civil; and
we offered 'em handsome Gratuities if they would catch such
of our men as might run away, which they promised to do
most Cheerfully.

Hearing of a Brigantine (this was some days afterwards) at the entrance of the Bay of Grande, we sent our Pinnace manned and armed to know all about her. She turned out to be a Portugee laden with Negroes, poor Creatures! for the Gold-mines. Our boat returned, and brought as presents a Roove of Fine Sugar and a Pot of Sweetmeats from the Master, who spoke a little English, and had formerly sailed with 'em. The Portugee are cautious in saying how far it is to the Gold-mines; but, I believe, the distance by water is not great; and there is certainly abundance of Gold in the country. The French took about 1200*l.* worth out of their boats last autumn at one Haul, which makes the Portugees hate 'em so. Some of 'em brought us a Monstrous Creature which they had killed, having Prickles or Quills like a Hedgehog, and the head and tail of a Monkey. It stank abominably, which the Portugees said was only the Skin, and that the Meat of it was very Delicious, and often used for the table; but our men not being yet on Short Commons, none of 'em had Stomach enough to try the Experiment, so that we were forced to throw it overboard to make a Sweet Ship. Our people could now hardly go ashore without being frightened, as they thought, by Tigers, and holloaing to be taken on board again; but there was nothing more dangerous hereabouts than Apes and Baboons.

Twenty-seventh November was a grand Festival at Angre de Keys, in honour of one of their Saints. We, and most of our officers from the *Hope* and the *Delight*, went ashore and were received by the Governor, Signor Raphael da Silva Lagos, with much civility. He asked if we would see the Convent and Procession; and on our telling him our Religion differed very much from his, answered that we were welcome to see it without partaking in the Ceremony. We waited on him in a Body, being ten of us, with two Trumpets and Hautboys, which he desired might play us to Church, where our Music did the office of an Organ, but separate from the Singing, which was very well chanted by the Padres. Our Trumpets and Hautboys played "Hey, Boys, up go we!" and all manner of paltry noisy tunes; and, after service, the Musicians, who were by this time more than half-drunk, marched at the head of the Company: next to them an old Padre and two Friars, carrying Lamps of Incense. Then the Image of the Saint, as Fine as a Milkmaid's Gar-

land, borne on a Bier, all spangled, on the shoulders of four
men, and bedizened out with Flowers, Wax-candles, &c.
After these, the Padre Guardian of the Convent, and about
forty Priests in their full Habits. Next came the Governor;
Captain Blokes, in a blue Navy 'Coat laced with Gold, a pair
of scarlet-velvet Breeches, and a Military Hat; and the rest
of the English officers in their very best Apparel. I was fit to
die a'laughing, and whispered to our Doctor of Physic, that
had I known I was fated to walk in such a Procession, I
would never have sold my old Tower Warder's slashed
doublet to the Frippery Man in Monmouth Street, but would
have brought it round the World with me to wear at this
Outlandish place. Each of us had moreover, in Compliment
to his Saintship, a long Candle, lighted, in his hand; the
which gave us great Diversion, flaring the tapers about, and
seeking to smoke one another. The Ceremony held about
two hours, after which we were splendidly entertained at the
Convent, and then by the Governor at the Guard-house, his
own habitation being about three leagues off. It is to be
noted, they Kneeled at every Crossway, and turning, walked
round the Convent, and came in at another door, bowing
down and paying their devotion to the Images and the Wax-
candles, with the like superstitious observances. They unani-
mously told us, however, that they expected nothing from
us but our Company; and, beyond the Trumpets and Hautboys, and a jolly Song or two from us, they had no more.
Many Sharks were in the Road, that keep the Negro Slaves
in good order, should they, poor Black Fellows, attempt
Escape to any foreign ship by swimming to her. But the
Portugees are not very hard with their Negroes, save up at
the Gold-mines, where Mercy is quite unknown. *Aqua d'oro*
may be a very good Eye-water; but, sure, there's nothing like
it for hardening of the Heart.

On the 28th of this Month we bade farewell to our kind
friends of Angre de Keys. Just before sailing we sent a Boat
to the town for more Necessaries, and brought off some Gentlemen, whom we treated to the very best we could. They
were very glorious, and in their Cups proposed the Pope's
Health to us; but we were quits with 'em by toasting that of
the Archbishop of Canterbury; and, to keep up the humour,
we also proposed Martin Luther: but this fell flat, as they
had never Heard of him; whereas that of his Grace at Lam-

beth turned out rather against us than for us; for they cried out that they knew him very well, and that he was a Catholic Saint, under the style and title of San Tomaso de Cantorberi.

December 1st, we weighed with a breeze at N.E.; but later came on a gale S.S.W., forcing us to anchor close under the Island of Grande. About 10 next morning we weighed again, and bore away and steered away S.W. Now the product of Brazil is well known to be Red Wood, Sugars, Gold, Tobaccos (of every kind, and very choice), Whale Oil, Snuff, and several sorts of Drugs. The Portugees build their best ships here. The people very Martial; and 'tis but a few years since they would be under no Government, but have now submitted to the House of Braganza, which makes a Pretty Penny out of them. Their Customs are very nasty; their Houses marvellously foul; and they are for ever smoking of Tobacco; but the Portugees are still a very friendly folk, cordial to us English, although they call us Heretics, and, but for their great love for roasting Jews, very tenderhearted. I like them much better than those Proud Paupers the Spaniards. A Beggar on Horseback is bad enough; but Goodness deliver us from a Beggar on an Andalusian Jackass!

Memorandum.—Brazil discovered by the famous Americus Vespucius, that came after Captain Christopher Colomb.

Nothing remarkable happened until December 6th, when we had close cloudy Weather, with Showers; and, after that, some pretty sharp Gales. On the 15th the colour of the water changed; and we sounded, but had no ground. On the 18th one of the *Hope's* men fell out of the Mizentop on the Quarter-deck, and broke his Skull; so that he died, and was buried next day. A brisk fellow, that; from his merry ways used to be called Brimstone Jemmy. After this, cold airy weather, and numbers of Porpoises, black on their backs and fins, with sharp white Noses. They often leaped high up in the water, showing their white bellies. Also, a plenty of Seals. December 23d we saw Land, appearing first in three, and afterwards in several Islands. The Wind being westerly, and blowing fresh, we could not weather it, but were forced to bear away and run along Shore from three to four leagues distant.

This we saw first was Falkland's Land, described in few Draughts, and none lay it down right, though the Latitude agrees pretty well. December 25th saw Land again; but could not get near enough to see whether it was inhabited; in truth we were too much in a hurry to think of making Discoveries; for at four in the Afternoon we sighted a sail under our Leebow, gave chase, and got ground of her apace till Night came on. In the Morning we saw nothing, it being thick hazy Weather; then, as ill luck would have it, it fell Calm, and having nothing else to do we Piped all hands to Punishment, and gave the Cook three dozen for burning Captain Blokes' burgoo. Then Grog served out, and we took an Observation. Lat. 52·40.

We kept on rowing and towing with Sweeps, and our Boats ahead, until about six in the Evening; and the Chase appearing to be a large ship, we sent Boats aboard our Consort, and agreed to engage her. A fine breeze sprang up, and we got in our Sweeps and Boats, making all possible sail; it came on thick again; but we kept her open on the Larboard, and the *Hope* and *Delight* on the Starboard bow, and it being now Short Nights, we thought it impossible to lose one another. But the Master persuaded our Commander to shorten sail, saying that we should lose our Consorts if we kept on. Another Fog, and be hanged to it; but the next morning the Yellow Curtain was lifted up, and we saw the Chase about four miles ahead, which gave us a new Life. We ran at a great Rate, it being smooth water; but it coming on to blow more and more, the Chase outbore our Consorts, and being to windward, she gave off, and came down very melancholy to us, supposing her to be a French Homeward-bound Ship from the South Seas. Thus, this Ship escaped; and left us all, from the Commander to the Cabin-boys (who had a hard time of it that night, you may be sure), in the most doleful Dumps.

Strong Gales to the 1st of January. This being New-Year's Day, every officer was wished a Merry New Year by our Trumpets and Hautboys; and we had a large tub of Punch, hot, upon the Quarter-deck, where every man in the Ship had above a Pint to his share, and drank to our Owners and Friends' healths in Great Britain, to a Happy New Year, a good Voyage, plenty of Plunder (Wo is me for that Homeward-bound Frenchman from the Southern Seas!), and a

Safe Return. And then we bore down on our Consorts and gave them three Huzzas, wishing them the like.

Now, it being very raw cold Weather, we very much dreaded scudding upon Ice; so we fired Guns as Signals for the *Hope* and *Delight* to bring to, and on the 5th of January brought ourselves to, under the same reef'ed Topsails. We feared at one time, from our Consorts having an Ensign in their Maintop Mastshrouds, as a Signal of Distress, that they had sprung their Mainmast; so we made the Large again, our Ship working very well in a mighty great sea. When we were able to get within Hail of our Consorts, we asked them how they did, and how they had come to hoist the Wretched Rag. They answered, Pretty well, but that they had shipped a great deal of Water in lying by, and being forced to put before the wind, the Sea had broke in at the Cabin Windows, filling the Steerage and Waste, and was like to have spoiled several Men; but, Heaven be thanked, all else was indifferent well with 'em; only it was intolerably Cold, and everything Wet. Captain Blokes sent me on board the *Delight* in our Yall, and I found them in a very disorderly Pickle, with all their Clothes a'drying: the Ship and Rigging covered with 'em from the Deck to the Maintop. They got six of their Guns into the Hold, to make the Ship lively.

Aboard the *Marquis* died, on the 8th, John Veale, a Landsman, having lain ill a Fortnight, and had a Swelling in the Legs ever since he left the Island of Grande. At nine at night we buried him; and this was the first we had lost by Sickness since we left England. Until the 15th, cloudy Weather with Squalls of Rain, and fresh Gales at S.W We now accounted ourselves round Cape Horn, and so in the South Seas. The French ships that first came to trade in these seas were wont to come through the Straits of Magellan; but Experience has taught 'em since, that this is the best Passage to go round the Horn, where they have Sea Room enow, without being crushed and crowded as at a Ranelagh Masquerade; and the Straits are in many places very narrow, with strong Tides and no Anchor Ground.

On the 31st of January, at seven in the Morning, we made the Island of Juan Fernandez, bearing W.S.W., and about two in the Afternoon we hoisted our Pinnace out, and essayed to send one of our Lieutenants ashore, though

we could not be less than four leagues off. As soon as it was
Dark our men cried out that they saw a Light ashore; our
Boat was then about a mile from the Shore, and bore away
for the Ship on our firing a Quarter-deck Gun, and several
Muskets, showing Lanterns in our Mizen and Foreshrouds,
that the Pinnace might find us again, whilst we plied to the
lee of the Island. About two in the Morning she came
aboard, all safe. Next day we sent our Yall ashore about
noon with the Master and Six Men, all well Armed; meanwhile we cleared all ready for Action on board the *Marquis.*
Our Boat did not return, so we sent our Pinnace, with the
Crew, likewise Armed: for we were afraid that the Spaniards
might have had a Garrison there, and so seized 'em. However, the Pinnace returned, and brought abundance of Craw-
fish, but found nothing human; so that the alarm about the
Light must have been a mere superstition of the Ship's
Company.

*It was at this same Island of Juan Fernandez, in the year
of our Lord 1708-9, that Captain Woodes Rogers, commanding the "Duke" Frigate, and with whom also Captain Dam-
pier, that famous Circumnavigator, sailed, found a Man
clothed in Goatskins, who looked wilder than they who had
been the first owners of 'em. He had been on the Island four
years and four months, being left there by Captain Stradling
in the "Cinque Ports;" his name was* ALEXANDER SELKIRK, *a
Scottish man, who had been Sailing Master to the "Cinque
Ports;" but quarrelling with the Commander, was by him
accused of Mutiny, and so Abandoned on this Uninhabited
Island. During his stay he saw several Ships pass by, but
only two came to an Anchor. As he went to view 'em he found
they were Spaniards, and so retired, upon which they Shot at
him. Had they been French, he would have submitted; but
chose to risk his dying alone on the Island rather than fall
into the hands of the Spaniards, because he apprehended they
would Murder him, or make a Slave of him in the Mines;
for he feared they would spare no Stranger that might be
capable of Discovering the South Sea. He had with him
when left his Clothes and Bedding, with a Firelock, some
Powder, Bullets, and Tobacco, a Hatchet, a Knife, a Kettle,
a Bible, some practical Pieces, and some Mathematical Instruments and Books. During the first eight months of his
stay he suffered much from Melancholy and Terror; but*

afterwards got on pretty well. He built two Huts with Pimento Wood, which he also burnt for Fuel and Candle; and which, besides, refreshed him with its fragrant smell. He had grown very Pious in his Retreat, and was much given to singing of Psalms, having before led a very naughty life. Being a very good sailor, Captain Woodes Rogers took him away with him as Second Mate. He told 'em that he had been at first much pestered with Cats and Rats, the latter of which gnawed his feet and clothes, so that he was obliged to cherish the Cats with Goat's-flesh, and they grew so familiar with him as to lie about him in hundreds. But I cannot stay to recount half the wonderful Adventures of Mr. Selkirk. I knew him afterwards, a very old man, lodging with one Mrs. Branbody, that kept a Chandler's Shop over against the Jews' Harp Tavern at Stepney. He was wont bitterly to complain that the Manuscript in which he had written down an Account of his Life at Juan Fernandez had been cozened out of him by some crafty Booksellers; and that a Paraphrase, or rather Burlesque, of it, in a most garbled and mutilated form, had been printed as a Children's Story-book, under the name of ROBINSON CRUSOE. *This was done by one Mr. Daniel Foe, a Newswriter, who, in my Youth, stood in the Pillory by Temple Bar, for a sedition in some plaguey Church-matters. But it is fitting to let these Gentry know that they have Ears, lest they become too Saucy.*

CHAPTER THE TWENTIETH.

Now, being got away from Juan Fernandez, did an unconquerable Greed and Longing for Prize and Plunder come
over us; and did we sweep the Horizon hour after hour as
long as it was Light, in hope of satisfaction to our long-de-
ferred Hope. March 2d we sighted Land, and a vast high
ridge of Mountains they call the Cordilleras, and are in the
Country of Chili. Some parts are, I believe, full as high, if
not higher, than the Pico of Teneriffe, and the tops of all of
'em covered with Snow. This day we came to an allowance
of Three Pints of Water a day for each man; judging it best
to be Economical, although we had a good stock of water
aboard (taken in at Juan Fernandez); but Captain Blokes'
reason was, to be able to keep at Sea for some time longer,
and take some Prizes to keep the Deuce out of our pockets,
without being discovered by Watering; for our South-Sea
Pilot told us that the timorous people of these Latitudes once
smelling an Enemy hovering about, will put to sea with nothing of value from one end of the Coast to the other. Much
baffled by several white Rocks that looked like Ships, and
Captain Blokes much incensed at continual Disappointments,
takes to making the Cabin-boy weary of his life; and after
drubbing him with a Rope's end three times doubled, was
for sousing him in the Pickle-tub; but I dissuaded him (remembering the Torments I had myself endured as a Moose;
and even now when I think of 'em I am Afraid, and Trembling takes hold of my Flesh), and so no more was Done to
him, beyond a Threat that he should be Keel-hauled next
time; although the poor lad had in no way misbehaved himself. We got the two Pinnaces into the water, to try 'em
under sail, having fixed each of 'em with a Gun, after the
manner of a Patterero, to be useful as small Privateers,
hoping they'd be serviceable to us in little winds to take
vessels. March 15th, Land again, and we supposed it was
Lobos; and sure enough, on the 17th, we got well unto
anchor off that Island, but found nobody at the place. On
the 19th we determined to fit out our small Bark for a Priva-

teer, and launched her into blue water, under the name of the *Beginning*. To his great pride and delight, Captain Blokes appointed the Doctor of Physic to command her. She was well built for sailing, so she was had round to a small Cove in the Southernmost part of Lobos. A small Spar out of the *Marquis* made a Mainmast for her, and one · of our Mizen Topsails was altered to make her a Mainsail. March 21st, all being ready, and the *Beginning* christened by Captain Blokes' emptying a Bowl of hot Punch over her bow, she was victualled from the general store ; and the Doctor of Physic, who, for all his Degree, claimed to be a good Mariner, took possession of his high and important command. Twenty men from our ship, and ten from our Consorts, were put aboard her, all well Armed. We saw her out of the Harbour, and she looked very pretty, having all Masts, Sails, Rigging, and Materials, like one of those Half Galleys fitted out for his Majesty's Service in England. They gave our Ship's Company three Huzzas, and we returned them the like at parting. We told the Captain-Doctor that if we were forced out of the Road, or gave chase hence, we would leave a Glass Bottle, buried under a remarkable Great Stone agreed upon, with Letters in it, to give an Account of how it was with us at the moment of our Departure, and where to meet again. And he was to do the like. When the *Beginning* was gone we fell to and scrubbed Ship, getting abundance of Barnacles off her much bigger than Mussels. Seals numerous, but not so many as at Juan Fernandez. A large one seized upon a fat Dutchman that belonged to us, and had like to have pulled him into the water, biting him to the bone about the arms and legs. This Hollander was henceforth known as the Lord Chancellor, having been so very near the Great Seal. After barnacling, we gave the *Marquis* a good Keel, and Tallowed her low down. Another Dutchman we had died of the Scurvy. His Messmates said that it was because we had no more Cheese aboard, and that he could not catch Red Herrings by angling for them in Blue Water.

March 28th. The little *Beginning* came in with a Prize, called the *Santa Josepha*, bound from Guayaquil to Truxillo, 50 tons burden, full of Timber, with some Cocoa-nuts and Tobacco. A very paltry Spoil. There were about twelve Spaniards aboard, who told us (after some little Persuasion, in the way of Drubbing) that the Widow of the late Viceroy of Peru would shortly embark at Acapulco, with her Family and Riches, and stop at Payta to Refresh ; and that about eight months ago there was a Galleon with 200,000 pieces of Eight on board, that passed Payta on her way to Acapulco. They continued, however, to Lie and Contradict themselves when questioned ; and so (as they howled most dismally on deck while under Punishment) they were had down to the Cockpit, where the Boatswain and his Mates had their Will of them, and I don't know what became of them afterwards. These Spanish Prisoners give a great deal of Trouble.

April 2d. The Superstitious among us were heartily frightened at the Colour of the Water, which for several miles looked as Red as any Blood. Some fellows among the crew that were of a Preaching Turn, gave out that this un-usual appearance was an Omen, or Warning to us of Judg-ments coming for what had been done to the Spanish Prison-ers (in the which Duresse I declare I had no hand ; 'twas all done by Captain Blokes' orders, and 'tis very likely that the Boatswain, who was a Rough Fellow, very ignorant, exceeded his instructions). It was explained, however, that this San-guinary Hue in the water was a perfectly natural appearance, caused by the Spawn of Fish ; and two or three of the preach-ing fellows being had to the Maingears and well Drubbed, Grog was served out to the rest, and an Alarm, which might have bred a Mutiny, soon subsided.

But Huzza ! on the 5th of April we had things more sub-stantial to think of than Red Seawater ; for we took, after a very slight Resistance, a Ship called the *Ascension*, built Galleon-fashion, very high, with Galleries, Burden between 400 and 500 tons, and two Brothers Commanders, both Dons of families that were Grandees 500 years before Adam was born, and of course with five-and-twenty Christian Names apiece. She had a number of Passengers and some fifty Negroes ; but the former being persons of Condition, far above the Common Sort, and not poor Coasting people, such as were those in the Timber Bark, we used 'em handsomely. They, without any such persuasion as was employed to their forerunners, told us that the Bishop of Chokeaqua, a place far up the Country in the South Parts of Peru, was to have come from Panama in this vessel for Lima, but would stop at

Payta to Recruit. Being near that place, we resolved to Watch narrowly, in order to catch his Lordship.

Now to the Norrard, and on the 10th of April we were off the Hummocks they call the Saddle of Payta; and being very Calm, we held a Court Martial on one of our Midshipmen who had threatened to shoot one of our men when at Lobos, merely for refusing to carry some Crows that he had shot. The Court was held in Captain Blokes' Cabin, and consisted of the Commander, Self, First-Lieutenant, assisted in our deliberations by sundry pipes of Tobacco and a great Jug of Punch. Found Guilty. Sentenced to be Degraded before the Mast, to have his Grog stopped for a Fortnight, and to receive Four Dozen at the Gun (for he being a kind of Officer, we did not wish to Humiliate him on deck). Half of his punishment he endured with more doleful Squalling than ever I heard from a Penitent in my Life, although the Boatswain was very tender with him, and three Tails of the Cat were tied up. He begged pardon, and so Captain Blokes remitted him the rest of his Punishment. This Midshipman was one who sang a very good Song; and so a Cushion being brought to Ease him, we finished the Evening and the Punch jovially enough, he being before the end in high favour with the Commander, and promised his Rating back again.

April 15. The Officers of all three Ships met on board the *Marquis*, and the Committee came to a Resolution to attack Guayaquil at once. The Bark we had called the *Beginning* by this time had come back to us, having done nothing and found nothing, since its first prize, except a great Sea Lubber, some kind of Monster that the Doctor of Physic had caught and wanted to preserve in Rum, to make a Present of to the Royal Society when we came home; but we forbade his wasting good Liquor for so unworthy an end, and the Monster, smelling intolerably, was thrown overboard. 'Twould have caused me no great sorrow to see the Doctor follow his Prodigy, for he was a very uncomfortable Person, and was much given to cheating at Cards.

April 20th. To our Boats off Guayaquil, a Great Company of Men and Officers all armed to the teeth. We rowed till 12 at night, when we saw Lights, which we judged to be a place called Puna. It blew fresh, with a small rolling Sea, the Boat I commanded being deep laden and crammed with men; some of us said they would rather be in a Storm

at Sea than here; but, in regard we were about a charming
Undertaking, we thought no Fatigue too hard. At daybreak
we saw a Bark above us in the River; and, running down
upon her, found it was a large Pinnace, full of the most considerable Inhabitants of Puna, escaping towards Guayaquil.
Here were at least a dozen handsome genteel young Women,
extremely well dressed, and from them our men 'got some
fine Gold Chains and Earrings. Some of these Nicknacks
were concealed about 'em; but the Gentlewomen in these
parts being very thinly dressed in Silk and Fine Linen, they
could hide but little, and our Linguist was bidden to advise
them to be Wise in Time, and surrender their Valuables,
which they did. And so civil were our Sailors to them,
that they offered to dress some Victuals for us when we got
'em aboard; which made us hope that the Fair Sex would
be kind to us when we returned to England, for our discreet
behaviour to these charming Prisoners.

    *   *   *   *   *   *

I am afraid that during the Attack on Guayaquil, which
took place the next day, and continued for the three following ones, when the place Capitulated to our force, and a
Treaty was signed between our Commanders and the Governor and Corregidor of Guayaquil, sundry proceedings took
place that would not very well have squared with the public
ideas of what is due to the Fair Sex just treated of; but I
declare that I had neither Art nor Part in them, and that I
am entirely Free from any Responsibility that Censure might
cast on the Authors of Cruel Disturbances; for early in the
Attack I was hit by a Musket-ball in the chest, and borne
senseless to our Boats. That I did my Duty bravely, my
Commander was good enough to say, and the whole Ship's
Company to admit. I was carried away to the *Marquis*, and
for a long time lay between Hawk and Buzzard; for a smart
Fever came about the third day, like Burgundy wine after
Sherris, and I was for a while quite off my head and Raving
about Old Times;—about Captain Night and the Blacks,
and Maum Buckey and her Negro Washerwomen, and my
Campaign against the Maroons, and some Other Things that
had befallen me during those fifteen years which I have
chosen to leave a Blank in my life, and which I scorn to
deny did—some of them—lie heavy on my Conscience. All
these were mixed up with the old Gentleman at Gnawbit's,

and my Lord Lovat with his head off, and my Grandmother in Hanover Square; so that I doubt whether those who tended me knew what to make of me. There was some difficulty too as to medical attendance, for we had cashiered our Surgeon—that is to say, he had run away at Grande in the Brazils, to marry a brown Portugee woman; and the Doctor of Physic he was all for Herbal Treatment, demanding Succory, Agrimony, Asarabacca, Knights-pound-wort, Cuckoo-point, Hulver-bush, with Alehoof, and other things not to be found in this part of the World. And Captain Blokes said that he knew nothing half so good for a Gunshot Wound as cold Rum-and-Water; and between the two I had like to have died, but all were very kind to me, even to extracting the Ball with a Pair of Snuffers; and a great clumsy thing the said missile was, being, I verily believe, part of a Door-hinge which these clumsy Spanish Brutes had broken off short to cram into their Guns; and yet it might have gone worse with me had it been a smooth round cast Bullet, and drilled a clean Wound right through my Body.

As I was coming round, even to the taking of some Sangaree and Chicken Panada (for we were now very well provided with Live Stock), the Captain said to me : " You ha'n't murdered a man, Brother, have you ?"

I replied, starting up, that my hands were free from the stain of Blood unrighteously spilt.

" No offence, Brother Dangerous," continued the Captain. " In our line of life we ar'n't particular. It wouldn't take very dirty weather to make our Ensign look like a Black Flag. Piracy and Privateering—they both begin with a P. I thought you had something o' that sort on your mind, because you took it so woundily about being hanged."

" I have had a strange life," I answered faintly.

" No doubt about that," says the Captain. " So have I, Brother, and not an over-good one : that's why I asked you. If the old woman hadn't been in the oven herself, she'd never have gone there to look for her daughter. But have you anything on your mind, Brother ? Is there anything that Billy Blokes can do for you ?"

I answered, very gratefully, that there was nothing I could think of.

" 'Cause why," he resumed, " if there is, you have only to sing out. If you think you're like to slip your Cable, and

would like to say something, we've got a Padre on board out
of the last Prize, and he shall come and do the Right Thing
for you. You don't know anything about his lingo; but
what odds is that? Spanish, or Thieves' Latin, or rightdown
Cockney,—it's all one when the word's given to pipe all
hands."

I answered that I was no Papist, but a humble member
of the Church of England as by Law established.

" Of course," concluded the Captain. " So am I. God
bless King George and the Protestant Succession, and con-
found the Pope, the Devil, and the Pretender! But any
Port in a storm, you know; and a Padre's better than no
Prayers at all. I've done all I could for you, Brother. I've
read you most part of the story of Bel and the Dragon, likewise the Articles of War, and a lot of psalms out of Stern-
hold and Hopkins; and now, if you feel skeery about losing
the number of your mess, I'll make your Will for you, to be
all shipshape before the Big Wigs of London. There must
be a matter of Four Hundred Pounds coming to you already
for your share of Plunder; and no one shall say that Billy
Blokes ever robbed a Messmate of even a twopenny tester
of his Rights."

Again I thanked this singular person, who, for all his
Addictedness to Rum-and-Water, of which he drank vast
quantities, was one of the most Sagacious men I have known.
But I told him that I had neither kith nor kin belonging to
me; that I did not even know the name of my Father and
Mother; and that my Grandmother, even, was an Unknown
Lady, and had been dead nigh forty years. Finally, that if
I made any Will, it would only be to the effect that my Property, if any, might be divided among the Ship's Company of
the *Marquis*, with a donative of Fifty Guineas to the *Hope*
and *Delight* people to drink to my Memory.

"Ay, and to a pleasant journey to Fiddler's Green," cries
out the Captain. " But cheer up, Heart; ye're not weighed
for the Long Journey yet." Nor had I; for I presently recovered, and in less than a month after my Mishap was again
whole and fit for Duty. And I have set this down in order
to confute those malignant men who have declared that all
my Wounds were from Stripes between the Shoulders; whereas I can show the marks, 1°, of an English Grenadier's
bayonet; 2°, of a Frenchman's sword; 3°, of a Spanish bul-

let; with many more Scars gotten as honourably, and which it would be only braggadocio to tell the History of.

Item.—The Corregidores, or Head-Men of Guayaquil, are great Thieves. The Mercenary Viceroys not being permitted to Trade themselves, do use the Corregidores as middle-men, and these again employ a third hand; so that ships are constantly employed carrying Quicksilver, and all manner of precious and prohibited goods, to and from Mexico out of by-ports. Thus, too, being their own Judges, they get vast Estates, and stop all complaints in Old Spain by Bribes. But now and then comes out a Viceroy who is a Man of Honesty and Probity, and will have none of these Scoundrelly ways of Making Money (like Mr. Henry Fielding among the Trading Justices, a Bright exception for integrity, though his Life, as I have heard, was otherwise dissolute), and then he falls to and squeezes the Corregidores, in the same manner as Cardinal Richelieu, that was Lewis Thirteenth's Minister, was wont to do with the Financiers. "You must treat 'em like Leeches," said he; "and when they are bloated with blood, put salt upon them, to make them disgorge." And I have heard that this rigid System of Probity, and putting salt on the gorged Corregidores, has ofttimes turned out more profitable to the Viceroys than trading on their own account.

Many of our men falling sick here, and our Ransom being now fully disbursed by the authorities of Guayaquil, we made haste to get away from the place, which was fast becoming pestiferous.

We set sail with more than fifty men Down with the Distemper (of which they were dying like Sheep with the Rot in the town, and all the Churches turned into Hospitals); but we hoped the Sea Air, for which we longed, would set us all healthy again. So plying to windward, bearing for the Gallipagos Islands, and on the 21st of May made the most Norrard of that Group. Jan Serouder, a West Frieslander, and very good Sailor, though much given to smoking in his Hammock, for which he had many times been Drubbed, died of the Distemper. A great want of Medicines aboard, and the Rum running very low. Sent a Boat ashore to see for Water, Fish, and Turtle, which our men (being now less Dainty by Roughing) had, by this time, condescended to eat. Kept on our course; on the 27th the Easternmost Island

bore S.E. by S., distant about four leagues; and nothing
more remarkable happened till the 6th of June, when we
spied a Sail, the *Hope* being then about two miles ahead of
us; and about seven in the Evening she took her in a very
courageous manner. This was a Vessel of about 90 tons,
bound from Panama to Guayaquil, called the *San Tomaso y
San Demas* (for these Spaniards can never have too much of
a good thing in the way of Saints), Juan Navarro Navarret y
Colza, Commander. About forty people on board, and eleven
Negro Slaves, but little in the way of European goods save
some Iron and Cloth. They had a passenger of note on board,
one Don Pantaleone and Something as long as my Arm, who
was going to be Governor of Baldivia, and said he had been
taken not long since in the North Sea by Jamaica Cruisers.
On the 7th June we made the Island of Gorgona; and, on
the 8th, got to an anchor in 30 fathom water. The next day
sent out our Pinnace a'cruising, and took a prize called the
Golden Sun, belonging to a Creek on the Main,—a twopenny-
halfpenny little thing, 35 tons; ten Spaniards and Indians,
and a Negro that was chained down to the deck to amuse the
Ship Company with playing on the Guitar (a kind of Lute).
However, we found a few ounces of Gold-dust aboard her,
worth some sixty pounds sterling. After examining our Prisoners (who gave us much trouble, for we had no Linguist,
and 'twas a Word and a Blow in questioning them : that is,
the Blow came from us to get the Word from 'em ; but not
more than two or three Spaniards were Expended),—after
this tedious work was over we held a Committee, and agreed
to go to Malaga,* an Island which had a Road, and with our
Boats tow up the River in quest of the rich Gold-mines of
Barbacore, also called by the Spaniards San Juan. But heavy
Rains coming on, we were obliged to beat back and come to
Gorgona again, building a Tent ashore for our Armour and
Sick Men. We spent till the 25th in Careening; on the 28th
we got all aboard agen, rigged and stowed all ready for sea;
the Spaniards who were our Prisoners, and who are very
Dilatory Sailors (for they hearken more to their Saints than
to the Boatswain's Pipe), were much amazed at our Despatch ;
telling us that they usually took Six Weeks or a Month to

---

* There is a River in Macedon and a River in Monmouth, and
more Malagas than one.

Careen one of their King's Ships at Lima, where they are well provided with all Necessaries, and account that Quick Expedition. We allowed Liberty of Conscience on board our floating Commonwealth to our Prisoners ; for there being a Priest in each ship, they had the Great Cabin for their Mass, whilst we used the Church-of-England Service over them on the Quarter-deck. So that the Papists here were the Low Church-men. Shortly after the beginning of July we freed our prisoners at fair Ransom in Gold-dust; but the Village where we landed them was so poor in common Necessaries, that we were obliged to give them some corned beef and biscuit for their subsistence until they could get up the Country, where there was a Town. Same day a Negro belonging to the *Delight* was bit by a small brown speckled Snake, and died in a few hours.

We had with us, too, a very good prize taken by the *Hope*, and continued unloading this and transferring the rich contents to our ships, having promised to restore the Hull itself to the Spaniards, on her being handsomely Ransomed; and the Don that was to be Governor of Baldivia was appointed Agent for us, and suffered to go freely on his Parole to and fro to arrange Money-Matters with the Authorities up the Country.

Memorandum.—Amongst our Prisoners (taken on board the Panama ship) there was a Gentlewoman and her Family, the Eldest Daughter, a pretty young woman of Eighteen, newly Married, and had her husband with her. We assigned them the Great Cabin on board the Prize, and none were suffered to intrude amongst them ; yet the Husband (we were told) showed evident Marks of a Violent Jealousy, which is the Spaniard's Epidemic Disease. I hope he had not the least Reason for it, seeing that the Prize-master (our Second Lieutenant) was above Fifty years of Age, and of a very Grave Countenance, appearing to be the most secure Guardian to females that had the least Charm, though all our young Men (that were Officers) had hitherto appeared Modest beyond Example among privateers; yet we thought it improper to expose them to Temptation. And I am sure, when the Lieutenant, being superseded for somewhat Scorching of a Negro with a stick of fire for answering him Saucily, and Captain Blokes bade me take temporary command of the Prize and Prisoners, that I behaved myself so well as to gain Thanks

and Public Acknowledgments for my civility to the Ladies.
We had notice that more than one of these Fair Creatures
had concealed Treasure about 'em; and so in the most Delicate Manner we ordered a Female Negro who spoke English
to overhaul 'em privately, and at the same time to tell 'em
that it would pain us to the Heart to be obliged to use Stripes
or other Unhandsome Means to come to a Discovery.   Many
Gold Chains, Bracelets, Ouches, and suchlike Whim-Whams
the Sable Nymph found cunningly stowed away; upon which
we gave her half a pint of Wine and a large pot of Sweets,
forgiving her at the same time a Whipping at the Capstan
which had been promised her for Romping and Gammocking
among the people in the Forecastle.   For I suppose there
was never a modester man than Captain Blokes.

August 10th. All Money-Matters being arranged, we disposed of our Prisoners. We burnt down the Village for some
Impertinence of the Head Man (who was a Half-caste Indian),
—but no great harm done, since 'twas mostly Mud and Plantain thatch, and could be built up again in a Week,—and got
to Windward very slowly, there being a constant current
flowing to Leeward to the Bay of Panama.   13th we saw the
Island of Gallo; the 18th we spied a Sail bearing W.N.W
of us, when we all three gave chase, and took her in half an
hour. 70 tons. Panama to Lima. Forty people aboard, upon
examining whom they could tell us little News from Europe,
but said that there came Advices from Portobello in Spain,
and by a French ship from France, not long before they came
out of Panama; but that all was kept private; only, they
heard that his Royal Highness the Duke of Cumberland was
Dead, the which Sad Intelligence we were not willing to Believe, but drank his Health at Night, which we thought
could do him no hurt even if he really happened to be Dead.
By this time we had gotten another Surgeon out of the *Delight*, whom we daily exercised at his Instruments in the
Cockpit, and his Mate at making of Bandages and spreading
of Ointment; and Captain Blokes (who was always giving
some fresh proof of Sagacity), just to try 'em, and imitate
business for 'em a little, ordered Red Lead, mixed with Water,
to be thrown on two of our Fellows, and sent 'em down to
the Hold, when the Surgeon, thinking they had really been
wounded, went about to Dress them; but the Mistake being
discovered, it was a very agreeable Diversion.

After this we made sail to the Marias Islands (for I feel I must be brief in this abstract of my Log, and must compress into a few pages the events of many Months), and all November were cruising about Cape St. Lucas in quest of Prizes. Christmas we spent in a very dismal manner; for a Complaint, something akin to Mumps with Scurvy in the gums, and a touch of Lockjaw to boot, broke out among us, and eight men died. Then we engaged and took a very big Spaniard out of Manilla, 250 tons, and a very rich Cargo, mostly in Gold-dust and embroidered Stuffs. January 10th, 1748-9, at anchor at Port Segura; and here, to our dismal dismay, we heard that Peace had been proclaimed between Spain and England, and that all our Privateering for the present was at an end. Then to Acapulco in Mexico, seeing if we could do some honest trading; but at all the Towns along the Coast they looked upon us as little better than Pirates. But we felt a little comforted at the thought that we had already taken some very rich Prizes, and my own part of the Plunder was now over 1500*l.* January 11th, we weighed from Port Segura, and ran towards the Island of Guam. Our Steward missing some pieces of Pork, we immediately searched and found the Thieves. One of them had been guilty before, and forgiven on promise of Amendment; but was punished now, lest Forbearance should encourage the rest to follow this bad practice. Provisions being so short, and our run now so long, might, without great caution, have brought evil consequences upon us. They (the Thieves) were ordered to the Main-gear, and every man of the watch to give 'em a blow with the Cat-o'-nine-tails. On the 14th February, in commemoration of the ancient English custom of choosing Valentines, a list was drawn up of all the Fair Ladies in Bristol in any way related or concerned in our Ships; and all the Officers were sent for to the Cabin, where every one drew, and drank his Valentine's health in a cup of Punch, and to a happy sight of 'em all. This was done to put 'em in mind of Home.

From Guam, a very poor place, and the Natives uncommonly nasty, we shaped our course to Ternate; and about the 2d of May saw land, which we took for some of the Islands lying about the N.E. part of Celebes, but were satisfied soon after that we were in the Straits of Guiana. 18th May passed several Islands, and the South point of Gillolo.

This was the time of the S.E. Monsoon, which made Weather and Wind very uncertain. May 25th we fell in with a parcel of Islands to the Eastward of Bouton, an island where there is a kind of Indian King, very Savage and Warlike, and with a considerable flotilla of Galleys. We traded with him, and made good profit in the way of Barter; for these Savages will give Gold and Goods for the veriest Trumpery that was ever picked up at a Groat the handful at the hucksters' stalls in Barbican. From Bouton on the 11th June, having well watered and provisioned, and taken a Native pilot on board, we sailed for Batavia, and on the 30th cast anchor in the Road there. We waited on his Excellency the Governor-General (for the States of Holland), and begged permission to refit our Ships, which was granted. Many strange Humours now to be seen aboard. Some of the crew hugging each other; others blessing themselves that they were come to such a glorious place for Punch, where they could have Arrack for Eightpence a Gallon; for now the Labour was worth more than the Liquor; whereas, a few weeks since, a Bowl of Punch was worth more to them than half the Voyage. Now we began to Careen, going over to Horn Island, and a Sampan ready to heave down by, and take in our Guns, Carriages, &c. Several of our men fell ill of Fevers, as they said, from drinking the Water of the Island; but as Captain Blokes opined, more from the effects of Arrack Punch at Eightpence a Gallon. All English ships are allowed by the Government here half a leaguer of Arrack a day for ship's use per man; but boats are not suffered to bring the least thing off shore without being first severely searched. As to the town of Batavia, it lies in a bay full of islands, which so break off the Sea, that though the Road is very large, yet it is safe. The Banks of the Canals through the City are paved with stones as far as the Boom, which is shut up every night at nine o'clock, and guarded by Soldiers. All the Streets are very well built and inhabited; fifteen of 'em have Canals just as in Amsterdam and Rotterdam, and from end to end they reckon fifty-six bridges. The vast number of Cocoa-nut trees in and about the City every where afford delightful and profitable Groves. There are Hospitals, Spin-houses, and so forth, as in Holland, where the idle and vicious are set to work, and, when need arises, receive smart Discipline. The Chinese have also a large Sick House, and manage their charity so well that you never see a Chinaman looking despicable in the street. The Dutch Women have greater privileges in India than in Holland, or, indeed, any where else; for on slight occasions they are often divorced from their Husbands, and share the Estate betwixt 'em. A Lawyer told me at Batavia he had known, out of nifty-eight causes. all depending in the Council Chamber, fifty-two of them were Divorces. The Governor's Palace of Brick, very stately and well laid. He lives in as great splendour as a King: he has a Train and Guards—viz. a Troop of Horse and a Company of Foot with Halberds. in liveries of yellow satin adorned with silver laces and fringe—to attend his Coach when he goes abroad. His Lady has also her Guards and Train. The Javanese. or Ancient Natives. are numerous. and said to be barbarous. and proud. of a dark colour, with flat faces. thin short Black hair, large eyebrows and cheeks. The Men are strong-limbed. but the Women small. The Men have many Wives. and are much given to lying and stealing. They are all Pagans, and worship Devils. The Women tawny, sprightly, and Amorous. and very apt to give poison to their Husbands when they can do it cunningly. There are at least 10,000 Chinese. who pay the Dutch a dollar a month for liberty to wear their Hair. which they are not allowed to do at home since the Tartars conquered 'em. There comes hither from China fourteen or sixteen Junks a year, being flat-bottomed vessels. The Merchants come with their goods. and marvellous queer folks they are. I don't think the whole City is as large as Bristol: but 'tis much more populous.

October 12th. We, according to our Owners' orders to keep our Ships full-manned, whether the War continued or not—and, oh, how we curse this plaguey Peace!—shipped here seventeen men that were Dutch. Though we looked upon our hardships as being now pretty well over. several ran from us here that had come out of England with us. being straggling. lazy good-for-nothings. that can't leave their old Trade of deserting. though now they had a good sum due to each of 'em for Wages. Their shares for Plunder of course were forfeited, and equitably divided among those that stuck by us. From this to the 23d we continued taking in wood and water for our Passage to the Cape of Good Hope; and just before we sailed held a Council on board the *Marquis,* by which 'twas agreed, that if any of our Consorts should happen to part company, the one that arrived first was to stay at the Cape twenty days; and then, if they didn't find the other Ships, to make their utmost despatch to the island of Helena; and if not there, to proceed, according to Owners' orders, to Great Britain.

Nothing particular happened till the 27th of December, when the *Marquis* proved very Leaky, and rare work we had at the Pumps, they being most of them choked up from long disuse. December 28th we came in sight of the Lion's Head and Rump, being two Hills over the Cape Town. Saluted the Dutch fortress with Nine Guns, and got but Three for thanks; it being surprising what airs these Pipe-smoking, Herring-curing, Cheese-making, Twenty-breeches Gentry give themselves. 29th, we moored Ship, and sent our Sick ashore. We stayed here till the end of February, when we went into Sardinia Bay to Careen; for a Survey of Carpenters had reported very badly concerning the Leak. 27th Feb. we had a good Rummage for Bale Goods to dispose of ashore, having leave of the Governor, and provided a Store-house, where I and the Supercargo of the *Delight* took it by turns weekly during the sale of 'em. 28th March came in a Portugee frigate, with news that Five stout French Ships had attempted Rio Janeiro, but were repulsed, and had a great number of men killed, with over 400 taken prisoners by the Portuguese.

April 5th we hoisted a Blue Ensign, loosened our Fore Topsail, and fired a Gun as a Signal for our Consorts to unmoor, and so fell down to Robin and Penguin Islands.

Memorandum.—We buried four while at the Cape; eight ran away to be eaten up, as we heartily hoped, by the Hottentots, who have a great gusto for White Man's Flesh; but reject Negroes as too strong and Aromatic; to say little of the major number of our Ships' Companies getting Married to Black Wenches. But there's no Doctors' Commons at Cape Town; and the best Way of Divorce is by shoving off a boat from Shore, and leaving your Wife behind you.—*Item.* The Dutch generally send a Ship every year to Madagascar for Slaves to supply their Plantations; for the said beastly Hottentots have their Liberty and Ease so much, that they cannot be brought to work, even though they should Starve (which they do pretty well all the year round) for the lack of it. Here, too, we spoke with an Englishman and an Irish-

man, that had been several years with the famous Madagascar
Pirates, but were now pardoned, and allowed to settle here.
They told us that these Miserable Wretches, who once made
such a Noise in the World, dwindled away one by one, most
of them very poor and despicable, even to the Natives, among
whom they had Married. They added, that they had no
Embarkations, only mere Canoes and Rowboats in Madagascar; so that these Pirates (so long a terrible Bugbear to
peaceable Merchantmen) are now become so inconsiderable
as to be scarcely worth mentioning; yet I do think that if
care be not always taken after a Peace to clear all out-of-the-
way Islands of these piratical Vermin, and hinder others
from joining them, it may prove a Temptation for loose
scampish Fellows to resort thither, and make every Creek in
the Southern Seas a troublesome nest of Freebooters.

The Cape having been so frequently described, I shall only
add that the Character of the Hottentots, at which I have
hinted, has been found to be too True, and that they scarce
deserve to be reckoned of the Human Kind : they are such a
nasty, ill-looking, and worse-smelling people. Their Apparel
is the Skins of Beasts; their chief Ornament is to be very
Greasy and Black; so that they besmear themselves with an
abominable Oil, mixed with Tallow and Soot; and the
Women twist the Entrails of Beasts or Thongs of Hides
round their legs, which resemble Rolls of Tobacco. Here's
plenty, however, of all kinds of Flesh and Fowl; there's
nothing wanting at the Cape of Good Hope for a good subsistence; nor is there any place more Commodious for a
Retirement to such as would be out of the Noise of the
World, than the adjacent country in the possession of the
Dutch.

Nothing of note happened till May 1st, only that sometimes we had Thunder, Lightning, Rain, and Squalls of
Wind. On the 7th we made the Island of Ascension, S.
Lat. 8·2. On the 14th at noon we found we had just crossed
the Equator, being the eighth time we had done so in our
course round the World. We had a Dutch Squadron with
us, who expected Convoy Rates, and all manner of Civilities
from us, though there was now Peace, and we wanted nothing
from 'em; but 'tis always the way with this Grasping and
Avaricious People. Soon too we observed that the Dutch
ships began to scrape and clean their sides, painting and

polishing and beeswaxing 'em inside and out, bending new
sails, and the very Mariners putting on half a dozen pair of
new breeches apiece. This it is their custom to do as they
draw near home; so that they look as if newly come out of
Holland.

On the morning of the 15th July we made Fair Island
and Foul Island, lying off Shetland; and sighted two or
three Fishing Doggers cruising off the Islands. Having
little wind, we lay by, and the Inhabitants came off with
what Provisions they had; but they are a very poor people,
wild and savage, subsisting chiefly on Fish. When that
provision fails, I have heard they live on Seaweed.

We being, so to speak, in charge, although unwillingly,
of the Dutch Squadron, which had been willy-nilly our
Convoy, were compelled to put into a port of Holland instead
of into a British one, as we had fondly hoped. On the 23d
July the Dutch Commodore made a signal for seeing Land,
and the whole fleet answered him with all their colours.
The Pilot-boat coming off, we took two aboard, and about
noon parted with some of our Dutch Consorts that were
Rotterdam and Middleburg ships. We gave 'em a Huzza
and a half in derision, and our Trumpet and Hautboy were
for striking up the Rogue's March; but this was forbidden
by the Sagacious Captain Blokes. Some English ships now
hove in sight, and saluted the Dutch Commodore; and afterwards we, though with an ill grace, saluted his Worship to
welcome in sight of the land, which by right belongs to the
Rats (though I have little doubt that for all the Vandykes
and Vandams the long-whiskered Gentry will come to their
own again some of these fine days). As soon as they got
over the Bar the Dutchmen fired all their guns for joy at
their safe arrival in their own country, which they very
affectionately call Fatherland; and, indeed, it was not easy
under these circumstances to be angry with the Poor Souls
that had been so long at Sea and wandering about Strange
Lands. At 8 at night we came to an Anchor in 6-fathom
water, about 2 miles off shore.

On the 24th, in the morning, the Dutch Flag-ship weighed,
in order to go up to the unlivering place. In the Afternoon
Captain Blokes sent me ashore, and up to Amsterdam, with
a letter for our Owners' Agents, to ask how we were to act
and proceed from hence. Coming back with instructions

from the Agent (one Mr. Vandepeereboom, who made me half-fuddled with Schiedam drinking to our prosperous return ; but he was a very Civil Gentleman, speaking English to admiration, and had a monstrous pretty Housekeeper, with eyes as bright as her own Pots and Pans), by Consent of our Council we discharged such men as we had shipped at Batavia and the Cape, and sold the half-dozen Negroes we had from time to time picked up for about a Hundred Dollars apiece. But this last had to be managed by private Contract, and somewhat under the Rose ; for their High Mightinesses, the States-General, allow no Slaves to be sold openly in Amsterdam.

On the 10th we went up the Vlieder, which is a better Road than the Texel, and then to Amsterdam again, where Captain Blokes and his chief officers had to make Affidavits before a Notary Publie to the truth of an Abstract of our Voyage, the which I had drawn up from the Log of the *Marquis*, to justify our proceedings to our own Government in answer to what the East India Company had to allege against us ; they being, as we were informed, resolved to trouble us on pretence that we had Encroached upon their Charter. On the 31st of August comes Mr. Vandepeereboom on board to take Account of what Plate, Gold, and Pearl was in the Ship ; and on the 5th September he took his leave of us.

But not of me ; for as I had been much with him ever since we had lain at Amsterdam, we had become great Chums, and he had persuaded me not to return just yet to England, but to remain with him in Holland, and become his partner in Mercantile Adventure, that should not necessitate my going to Sea again. And by this time, to tell truth, I was heartily sick of being Tossed and Tumbled about by the Waves. No man could say that I had not done my Duty during my momentous Voyage round the World. I had worked as hard as any Moose on board the *Marquis*, doing hand-work and head-work as well. I had been Wounded, had had two Fevers and one bout of Scurvy ; but was seldom in such evil case as to shirk either my Duty or my Grog. I prudently redoubted the Chances of returning in haste to my native Country ; for, although being alone in the world, and the marriage with Madam Taffetas not provable in Law, with no other Domestic Troubles to

grieve me, I knew from long Experience what Ducks and
Drakes Seafaring men do make of their money coming home
from a long voyage with their heads empty and their pockets
full, and was determined that what I had painfully gathered
from the uttermost Ends of the Earth should not be riotously
and unprofitably squandered in the Taverns of Wapping and
Rotherhithe.   Mr. Vandepeereboom entering with me into
the State of his Affairs, proved as far as Ledger and Cash-
book could prove any thing, that he was in a most prosperous way of business, in the Dutch East India trade, of
which by this time I knew something; so that, although
Captain Blokes was loth to part with his old Shipmate and
Secretary, he was yet glad to see me better myself. 'And in
truth Mr. Vandepeereboom's Housekeeper was marvellous
pretty.   I drew my Pay and Allowances, which amounted
to but a small matter; but to my great Joy and Gladness I
found that my share of the Plunder from our Prizes and the
Ransom of Guayaquil came to Twenty Hundred Pounds.
The order for this sum was duly transferred to me, and lodged
to my Account in the Bank of Amsterdam, then the most
famous Corporation of Cofferers (since that of Venice began
to decline) in Europe.   I bade farewell to Captain Blokes
and all my Messmates; left Twenty Pounds to be divided
among the Ship's Company (for which they manned Shrouds
and gave me three Huzzas as the Shoreboat put off); and
after a last roaring Carouse on board the *Marquis*, gave up
for Ever my berth in the gallant Craft in which I had sailed
round the World.

CHAPTER THE TWENTY-FIRST.

OF THE SINGULAR MISFORTUNES WHICH BEFELL ME IN HOLLAND.

'Twas no such very bad Title for a Mercantile Firm, "Vandepeereboom and Dangerous." Aha, Rogues! will you call me Pauper, Cardsharper, Led-Captain, Halfpenny-Jack, now? Who but I was Mynheer Jan van Dangerous? (I took my Gentility out of my Trunk, as the Spanish Don did his Sword when the Sun shone and there were Pistoles galore, and added the Van as a prefix to which I was entitled by Lineage.) Who but I was a wealthy and prosperous Merchant of Amsterdam, the richest city in Holland? Soon was I well known and Capped to, as one that could order Wine, and pay for it, at the sign of the Amsterdammer Wappen, the great Inn here.

Although 'tis now nigh thirty years since, I do preserve the pleasantest remembrance of my life in the Low Countries; for, albeit hating the Dutch when I was Poor, I grew to like 'em as a reputable Merchant Adventurer. 'Twas but a small matter prevented me from setting up my Carriage, and was only hindered by the fact that the Police Laws of Amsterdam are very strict against Wheeled Coaches, allowing only a certain and very small number, lest the rumbling of the Wheels should disturb the good thrifty Burghers at their Accounts. For most vehicles they have what they call a Sley, which is the body of a Coach fastened on to a Sledge with ropes, and drawn by one Horse. A Fellow walks by the side on't, and holds on with one hand to prevent its falling over, while with the other he manages the Reins. A most melancholy Machine this, moving at the rate of about Three miles an hour, and makes you think that you are in a Hospital Conveyance, or else going on a Hurdle to be Hanged, Drawn, and Quartered.

This Amsterdam is the famous town built upon Wooden Piles, as is also Petersburg, and in some order Venice ; and, from its Timber supports, gave rise to the sportive saying of Erasmus when he first came hither, that he had reached a City where the Citizens lived, like Crows, upon the tops of

Trees. And again he waggishly compared Amsterdam to a maimed Soldier, as having Wooden Legs. This Erasmus was, I conjecture, a kind of Schoolmaster, and very learned; but conceited, as are most Bookish Persons.

A Dutchman will save any thing; and this rich place has all come out of saving the Mud and starving the Fishes. Here Traffic is wooed as though she were a Woman, and Gold is put to bed with Time, and there is much joy over their Bantling, which is christened Interest. A strange, cleanly, money-grubbing Country of Botanic Gardens and Spitting-pans, universal Industry and Tobacco-pipes, Gingerbread and Sawing-mills, Tulip-roots and the Strong Waters of Schiedam, Cheese, Red Herrings, and the Protestant Religion. Peculiar to these People is the functionary called the Aanspreeker, a kind of human Bird of Evil Omen, who goes about in a long Black Gown and a monstrous Cocked Hat with a Crape depending from it, to inform the Friends and Acquaintances of Genteel Persons of any one being Dead. This Aansprecker pays very handsome Compliments to the Departed, at so many Stuyvers the Ounce of Butter; and this saves the Dutch (who are very frugal towards their Dead) from telling Lies upon their Tombstones. When a Man quits, they wind up his Accounts, strike a Balance, and go on to a fresh Folio in the Ledger, without carrying any thing forward. At Marriage-time also, it is the custom among Persons of Figure for the Bride and Bridegroom to send round Bottles of Wine, generally fine Hock, well spiced and sugared, and adorned with all sorts of Ribbons. They have also a singular mode of airing their Linen and Beds, by means of what they call a Trokenkorb, or Fire-basket, which is of the size and shape of a Magpie's Cage, and within it is a pan filled with burning Turf, and the Linen is spread over the Wicker-frame; or, to air the Bed, the whole Machine is placed between the Sheets. Nay, there are sundry Dowager Fraws who do warm their Legs with this same Trokenkorb, using it as though it were a Footstool; and considering the quantity of Linsey Woolsey they wear, I wonder there are not more Fires. To guard against this last, there are Persons appointed whose office it is to remain all day and all night in the Steeples of the highest Churches; and as soon as they spy a Flame, they hang out a Flag if it's Day, or a Lantern if at Night, towards the quarter where the Fire is, blowing a Trumpet lustily meanwhile.

Eating and Drinking here very good, save the Water, which is so Brackish that it is not drunk even by the Common People. There are Water-Merchants constantly occupied in supplying the City with drinkable Water, which they bring in Boats from Utrecht and Germany in large Stone Bottles, that cost you about Eightpence a-piece English. The Poor, who cannot afford it, drink Rain-water, which gives rise to the merry saying, that a Dutchman's Mouth is for ever open, either to swallow down Smoke or to drink up Rain. And indeed they are a wide-gaping Generation.

Being as yet a Bachelor, I agreed for my Lodging and Victuals with Mr. Vandepeereboom, who had a fair House, very stately, on one of the Canals behind the Heeren Gragt, or Lord's Street. 'Twould have had quite a princely appearance, but for a row of Elms in front, which, with their fan, almost concealed the Mansion. The noble look of the House, too, was somewhat spoilt by its being next door to a shop where they sold Drugs; which, like all others of this trade in Holland, had for a sign a huge Carved Head, with the mouth wide open, in front of the window: sometimes it rudely resembles a Mercury's Head, and at other times has a Fool's Cap upon it. This clumsy sign is called *de Gaaper*,— the Gaper,—and I know not the origin of it. Some of the Shop-boards they call *Uithang Borden*, and have ridiculous Verses written upon them; and 'tis singular to mark how much of the Jackpudding these Dutchmen, who are keener than Jews in their Cash-matters, have in them.

Mr. Vandepeereboom was high in the College of Magistrates, and I was ofttimes privileged to witness with him the administration of Justice and the infliction of its Dread Awards,—all here very Decent and Solemn. The Awful Sentence of Death is delivered in a room on the basement-floor of the Stadt House: the entrance through a massy folding-door covered with brass Emblems, such as Jove's Beams of Lightning, and Flaming Swords; above, between the Rails, are the old and new City Arms; and at the bottom are Death's Heads and Bones. The inside of the Hall, mighty handsome, in white Marble, and proper History pieces of the Judgment of Solomon, and Zeleucus the Locrian King tearing out one of his Eyes to save one of his Son's, and

Junius Brutus putting his children to Death. On the fore part of the Judgment-seat a fine Marble Statue of Silence, gallantly, but quite falsely, represented by the figure of a Woman on the ground, her finger to her lips, and two Children by her, Weeping over a Death's Head. When the dire Doom of Death is about to be pronounced, the Criminal is brought into this Hall, guarded; and nothing is omitted in point of solemnity to impress on his mind (poor wretch!) and on those about him the awful consequences of violating the Laws of the Country : which is a much better mode, I think, of striking Terror into 'em than the French way, where the Magistrates settle the Sentence among themselves in private, and the *Greffier* comes all of a sudden into the unhappy Person's Cell to tell him that he is to be presently Executed; or even our Old Bailey fashion (though the Black Cap is frightful), where the Culprit is more or less sent to Hang like a Dog,—one down, another come up ; and Jack Ketch Drunk all the while with burnt Brandy. 'Twas a thorough knowledge of Human Nature, too, that thought of placing this Dutch Hall of Justice on the ground-floor, and its Brazen Door opening into a common Thoroughfare through the Stadt House. I never passed by this door without seeing numbers of the Lower Orders of people gazing wistfully through the Rails upon the Emblematic objects within, apparently in Melancholy Meditation, and reflecting upon the Ignominious Effects of deviating from the Paths of Virtue.

Out of the Burgomaster's Parlour in the same building is a passage to the Execution Chamber, or Hall of the Last Prayers, where the Condemned take leave of their Priest, and pass through a Window, the lower part of Wood, so that it opens level with the floor of the Scaffold, which is constructed on the outside, opposite the Waag, or Weigh House.

As associate of one of the Magistrates, I often visited the Dungeons beneath the Stadt House, which are hermetically Sealed unto all Strangers. As places of Confinement, nothing can be more secure ; as places of Punishment, nothing more Horrible. Here, by the faint light of a Rush Candle you gaze only on Emaciated Figures, while out of the Dark Shadows issue faint but dismal Groans. Some are here condemned to linger for Life; yet have I known convicted Creatures in this Rat's hole as merry as French Dancing-Masters, whistling, trolling, and gambolling in the Dark ;

while in the next cell were a number of Women, who, like
the general of their sex when in Durance, did nothing but
Yell and tear their Clothes to Pieces. But 'tis true that all
confined in these dreadful places had committed crimes of a
very Malignant nature, and which heartily warranted their
being thus cut off from Light and Air, and immured in
Regions fit only to be Receptacles for the Dead. Under the
Hall of Justice is likewise the Torture Chamber, where
Miserable Creatures, at the bidding of their Barbarous Judges,
undergo a variety of Torments ; one of which is to fasten the
Hands behind the Neck with a cord through pulleys secured
to the vaulted Ceiling, so as to be jerked up and down..
Weights of Fifty Pounds each are then suspended to the
Feet, until anguish overpowers the senses, and a Confession
of Guilt is heard to quiver on the lips. Public Punishments
are inflicted only Four Times a Year, when a vast Scaffold is
erected in the space between the Stadt House and Waag
House, as before mentioned. Those that are only to be
Whipped endure that compliment with Merciless Severity,
and are not permitted to Retire till those who are to Die have
suffered, which is either by Decapitation or by the Rope.
And this acts as a Warning as to what will happen to 'em
next time. On this occasion the Chief Magistrates attend in
their Robes. But though Strict, they are mighty Just in
administering their Laws, and will not permit the least devia-
tion or aggravation of the Sentence meted out. I did hear
of one jocular Rogue, that was condemned, for the murder of
half-a-dozen women and children, to have his Head severed
from the Trunk at one stroke of the Sword. This Mynheer
Merry-Andrew, previous to quitting the Prayer-Chamber, lays
a Wager with a Friend that the Executioner should not be
able to perform his office according to the exact terms of the
Sentence. So, the moment he knelt to receive the Fatal
Stroke, he rolled his Head in every direction so violently and
rapidly, that the Headsman could not hit him with any
chance of severing his Neck at once ; and after many fruit-
less aims, was obliged to renounce the Task. The Officers
who were to see the Sentence executed were now in a Great
Dilemma. In vain did they try by argument to persuade the
Fellow to remain still, and have his Head quietly taken off.
At last he was remanded back to Prison, and after an hour's
deliberation the Presiding Magistrate, upon his own Responsi-

bility, ordered the Gallows to be brought out, and the Fellow to be straightway Hanged thereupon ; which was done, to the contentment of the Populace, who were howling with Rage at the fear of being deprived of their Sport. But the straight-laced Dutch Judges and Lawyers all took alarm, and declared that the Fellow had been murdered ; and nothing but the high rank and character of the Magistrate preserved him from grievous consequences.

They observe, however, degrees in their Punishments, and are, even in extreme cases, averse from Bloodshed, and willing to try all ways with a criminal before Hanging or Beheading him. Thus have they their famous Rasphuys for the Con-finement and Correction of those whose Crimes are not capital. Over the Gate are some insignificant painted wooden figures, representing Rogues sawing Log-wood, and Justice holding a Rod over them ; and the like of these, with figures of scourg-ing and branding, they stick up in their Public Walks and Gardens, to show what is Done to those who pluck the Flowers or carve Names upon the Trunks of the Trees, and it has a most wholesome effect in frightening Evil-doers. So in the Yard of the Rasphuys is a Whipping-post in Terrorem, with another little figure of Justice flagrant with Execution. Here the Rogues saw Campeachy-wood, which seems to be most toilsome work ; and yet by practice they can saw Two Hundred Pounds' weight every week with ease, and also make many little Articles in Straw, Wood, Bone, and Copper, to sell to Visitors. They are all clad in White Woollen, which, when they are stained with the Red Sawdust, gives them a Hobgoblin kind of appearance. Here too, in a corner of the Yard, they show the Cell in which if the person who was confined in it did not incessantly Pump out the Water let into it, he must inevitably be Drowned; but this Engine, the Gaolers said, had not been used for many Years, and was only kept up as an object of Terror.

In the east quarter of Amsterdam, Justice is administered in its mildest form ; there being the Workhouse close to the Muider Gragt, a place which, I believe, has not its parallel in the whole World. 'Tis partly Correctional and partly Charitable ; and when I saw it, there were Seven Hundred and Fifty Persons within the Walls, the yearly expense being about One Hundred Thousand Florins. In the rooms belong-ing to the Governors and Directresses some exquisite Paint-

ings by Van Dyck, Rembrandt, and Jordaens; and, indeed,
you can go scarcely any where in Holland, from a Pig-stye to
a Palace, without finding Paintings. Here, in a vast room
very cleanly kept, are an immense number of Women occupied in Sewing and Spinning. Among them I saw once a
fine hearty-looking Irishwoman, who had been Confined here
two whole Years, for being a little more fond of true Schiedam
Gin than her lawful Spouse. In another vast Apartment,
secured by many Iron Railings and Grated Windows, are the
Female Convicts in the highest state of Discipline, and very
industriously and silently engaged in making Lace, under the
Superintendence of a Governess. From the Walls of the
Room are suspended Instruments of Punishment, such as
Scourges, Gags, and Manacles, the which are not spared upon
the slightest appearance of Insubordination. Then there are
Wards for the Men; Schoolrooms for a vast number of
Children; and Dormitories, all in the highest state of Neat-
ness. In another part of the Building, which only the Magistrates are permitted to visit, are usually detained ten or a
dozen Young Ladies—some of very high Families—sent here
by their Parents or Friends for undutiful Deportment, or some
other Domestic Offence. They are compelled to wear a particular Dress as a mark of Degradation; are kept apart;
forced to work a certain number of hours a day; and are occasionally Whipped. Here, too, upon complaints of Extravagance, Tipsiness, &c., duly proved, can Husbands send
their Wives, to be confined and receive the Discipline of the
House; *and hither, too, can Wives send their Husbands for
the same Cause, for Two, Three, and Four Years together, till
they show signs of amended Behaviour.* The Food is abundant
and good; but the Work is hard, and the Stripes are many.
Might not such a course be tried with advantage in England,
to abate and cure the frivolities and extravagances of Fashionable People?

So then, as an Honourable Merchant in a city and
country where Commerce is reckoned among the noblest
of Pursuits, I might, but for my Perverse Fate, have grown
Rich, and taken unto myself a Dutch Wife, and had a Brood
of little Broad-beamed Children, that should smoke their
Tobacco and quaff their Schiedam, even from their Cradle
upwards. Indeed, Madam Vanderkipperhaerin of Gouda
(the place where the Cows feed in the Meadows clad in

Blue-striped Jackets and Petticoats) was pleased to look
upon me with Eyes of Favour, and often said it was a Sin
and Shame that such a Proper Man as I (as she was good
enough to say) was not Married and Settled. And, indeed,
why not ? I ofttimes asked myself. I had Florins, Guilders,
and Stuyvers in abundance ; my Partner was a Magistrate,
and well reputed worthy ; why should I not give Hostages
to Fortune, and have done for good and all with the Life of
a Roving Bachelor ? By this time (although by no means
forgetting my own dear native Tongue) I spoke French with
Ease and Fluency, if not with Grammatical correctness ; and
had likewise an indifferently copious acquaintance with the
Hollands Dialect. Why should not I be a Magistrate, a
Burgomaster ? Madam Vanderkipperhaerin was Rich, and
had a beautiful Summer Villa all glistening with Bee's-waxed
Campeachy-wood and Polished Brass on the River Amstel,
some three miles from the City. She had a whole Cabinet
full of Ostades and Jan Steens in ebony frames, and a Side-
board of Antique Plate that might have made Cranbourn
Alley jealous. Why did not I avail myself of the many
Propitious Moments that offered, and demand the Hand of
that most respectable Dutch Dame ?

The Melancholy Truth is, that she chose to be jealous
of Betje, Mr. Vandepeereboom's comely Housekeeper, upon
whom I declare that I had never cast any thing but in-
nocently Paternal Glances, and utterly deny that I ever
foregathered with that young Fraw. She was for moving
Mr. Vandepeereboom to have Betje sent to the Workhouse,
there to be set to Spinning, and to receive the usual unhandsome Treatment ; and when he refused,—having, in truth,
no fault to find with the Poor Girl,—Madam, in a Huff,
withdrew her Countenance and Favour from me, and, with
sundry of her spiteful gossips, revived the old Story of my
having several Wives alive in different parts of Europe and
the New World. Surely there was never yet a man so exposed to calumny as poor John Dangerous !

Then, to make matters worse, there came that sad Affair
of the Beguine. Flesh and blood ! a mortal man (I suppose)
is not to be reckoned among the vilest of Humanity because
he falls in Love. How could I help Wilhelmina van Praag
being a Beguine ? Moreover, a Beguine is not a Nun. The
Beguines belong to a modified kind of Monastic Order. They

reside in a large House with a wall and ditch around it, and that has a Church and Hospital inside, and is for all the world like a little Town. But the Sisterhood is perfectly secular; they mingle with the inhabitants of the city, quit the Convent when they choose, and even marry when they are so minded; but they are obliged, so long as they belong to the Order, to attend Prayers a certain number of times a day, and to be within the Convent-walls at a stated hour every evening. To be admitted to this Order, they must be either unmarried or widows without children; and the only certificate required of them is that of Good Behaviour, and that they have a Competence to live upon. You may ask, if this almost entire Liberty be granted them, what there was to hinder Mynheer Jan van Dangerous and the Fair Beguine Wilhelmina van Praag from coming together as Man and Wife? Wilhelmina was the comeliest Creature (save one) that I have ever seen; and, but that she was a little Stout, would have passed as the living model for the St. Catherine which Signor Raphael the Painter did so well in Oils. I don't think I loved her; but she took my Fancy immensely, and meeting her in the houses of divers Honourable Families in Amsterdam, 'tis not to be concealed that I courted her with much assiduity. This, by some mischief-making Persons, was held to be highly compromising to the Fair Beguine. For all that I had become a Grave Merchant, there was yet somewhat of the Gentleman of the Sword and Adventurer on the High Seas about me; and a great hulking Cousin of the young Fraw, that was a Lieutenant in their High Mightinesses Land Forces,—the Amphibious Grenadiers I call 'em, and more used to Salt-water than Saltpetre, —must needs challenge me to the Duello. The laws against private warfare being very strict in Holland, we were obliged to make a journey into Austrian Flanders, to Arrange our Difficulty; and, meeting on the borders of the Duchy of Luxembourg, I— Well, is Jack Dangerous to be blamed for that he was, in the prime of Life, an approved Master of Fence?

The Lieutenant being dead of his Wounds (received in perfectly fair fight), the whole City of Amsterdam must needs cry out that I had murdered the Man; and the Families who had once been eager to receive me turned their backs upon me. Then the Fair Beguine must go into a craze ; and, upon my word, when I heard how Mad she was,. and how they had been obliged to shut her up in the Hospital, I could not help thinking of the History of my Grandmother, and did mistrust meeting the young Fraw van Praag again (for she was very Sweet, I believe, with the Spark that forced me to fight with him), for fear that she should Pistol me.   But she did not ; and Recovered, to marry a very Wealthy Shipmaster named Druyckx.

While this Ugly Business was the talk of all tongues. (but Mr. Vandepeereboom clapped me on the Shoulder, and bade me take my Diversion while he minded Business, for that all would Blow Over soon), I took an Excursion ('twas in the third year of my Residence here) into North Holland, to visit the famous village of Brock.   Here the streets are divided by little Rivulets, for all the world like Liliputian Canals ; the Houses and Summer-houses all of Wood, painted Green and White, very handsome, albeit whimsical in their shape, and scrupulously neat.   The Inhabitants have a peculiar association among themselves, and scarcely ever admit a Stranger within their Doors.   During my stay I only saw the Faces of two of 'em, and then only by a stealthy Peep. They are said to be very rich, and in some of their Kitchens to have Pots and Pans of solid Gold.   The Shutters of the Windows always kept closed, and the Householders go to and fro by a Back Door, the Principal Entrance being opened only at Marriages and Deaths.   The Street Pavement all set out with Pebbles and Cockleshells, and no Dogs or Cats were seen to trespass upon it ; and formerly there was a law to oblige all Passengers to take off their Shoes.   Here it was that a Man was once Convened and Reprimanded for Sneezing in the Streets ; and latterly, a Parson, I heard, upon being appointed to fill the Church on the Demise of an old Predecessor, gave great offence to his Flock by not taking off his Shoes when he ascended the Pulpit.   The Gardens of this strange Village produce Deer, Dogs, Peacocks, Chairs, and Ladders, all cut out in Box.   I never saw such a Museum of vegetable Statuary in my Life before.   On the whole, Brock resembles a trim, sprightly Ball-room, all garnished, lighted up, and the floor well chalked, but not a Soul to Scrape Fiddle or Foot Minuet.   Farther from here is Saardam, which, at a distance, looks like a City of Windmills.

Item.—I forgot to say, that at Brock they tie up the Cows' Tails with Blue Ribbons.

The Houses of Saardam are principally built of Wood, and every one has a Fantastic kind of Baby Garden. Here is the Wooden Hut where Peter the Great lived, when he wrought as a Shipwright in the Navy-yard. It stands in a Garden, and is in Decent Preservation. The women in North Holland are said to be handsomer than in any other part of the country; but I was out of taste with Beauty when I came hither, and could see naught but ugly Faces.

So, coming back to Amsterdam, I found that Mr. Vandepeereboom's Prediction was fulfilled with a Vengeance, and with Compound Interest. The Business of the Beguine had Blown Over; but another affair had Blown On, and this very speedily ended in a Blow Up. I am sorry to say that this Fairspoken and seemingly Reputable Mr. Vandepeereboom turned out to be a very Great Rogue. Our Firm was in the Batavian trade, dealing in fine Spices, Nutmegs, Cloves, Mace, Cinnamon, and so forth; also in Rice, Cotton and Pepper; and especially in the Java Coffee, which is held to be second only to that of Arabia. In this branch of Trade the Dutch have no competition, and they are able to keep the price of their Spices as high as they choose, by ordering what remains unsold at the price they have fixed upon it to be Burnt. How it came to pass that the Spice Ships consigned to us were all wrecked on the High Seas and never insured; that the Batavian Merchants, to whom we advanced money on their Consignments, all failed dismally; that every Speculation we entered into went against us, and that we always burnt our Surplus Goods just as prices were about to rise,—I know not; but certain it is, that I had not been three weeks back in Amsterdam before the House of Vandepeereboom and Dangerous went Bankrupt. Now 'tis an ugly thing to be Bankrupt in Holland. The people are so thrifty and persevering, and so jealous of keeping their Engagements, that the very rarity of Insolvency makes it Scandalous. A Trading Debtor being a character very seldom to be met with, he is held in more Odium in Holland than in any other part of Europe. Yet are their Laws of Arrest milder than with us in England, where for a matter of Forty Shillings an Honest Man becomes the prey of a Catchpole, and for years after he has paid the Debt itself, with exorbitant Costs to some Knavish Limb of the Law, may still continue to Rot in Gaol for the Keeper's Fees or Garnish. Here, if the Debtor be a Citizen or Registered Burgher (as I was), he is not subject to have his Person seized at the suit of his Creditors, until three regular Summonses have been duly served upon him to appear in the Court, which Processes are completed in about a month; after which, if he does not obey it, he may be laid hold of, but only when he has quitted his House; for in Holland a Man's Dwelling is held even more sacred than in England, and no Writ or Execution whatever is capable of being served upon him so long as he keeps close, or even if he stands on the threshold of his Home. In this Sanctuary he may set at Defiance every Claimant; but if he have the Hardihood to appear Abroad, the Sergeants collar him forthwith; but even in this case he goes not to a common Gaol or Prison for Felons, but to a House of Restriction, where he is properly entreated, and maintained with Liberal Humanity; the Expense of which, as well as the Proceedings, must be defrayed by the Creditors. This regards only the private Gentleman Debtor. But woe betide the Fraudulent Trader! The Bankrupt Laws of Holland differ from ours in this respect, that all the Creditors must sign the Debtor's Certificate, or Agreement of Liberation. If any decline, the Ground of their Refusal is submitted to Arbitrators, who decide as to the merits of the case ; and if the Broken Merchant be found to be a Cheat, no Mercy is shown him. The Rasphuys, the Pillory, nay even the Dungeons beneath the Stadt House, may be his Doom.

This, Mr. Vandepeereboom (being a born Dutchman) knew very well; and he waited neither for Deliberations as to his Certificate, nor for Arbitrators' award. He e'en showed his Creditors a clean Pair of Heels, and took Shipping for Harwich in England. I believe he afterwards prospered exceedingly in London as a Crimp, or Purveyor of Men for the Sea-Service, and submitted to the East India Company many notable plans for injuring the Commerce of the Hollanders. I have likewise reason to think that he did me a great deal of harm amongst my late Owners at Bristol and elsewhere, saying that I had been the Ruin of him with Wasteful Extravagance and Deboshed Ways, and that but for his Intercession I should have been Broken on the Wheel for unhandsome Behaviour to the Fair Beguine. Ere he flitted, he left me a

Letter, in which he had the impudence to tell me that he had long since drawn out my Account from the Bank of Amsterdam, thinking himself much better able to take care of the Money than I was. Furthermore he contemptuously advised me to try some other line than Commerce, for which I was, through my Former Career—or Vagabond Habits, as he had the face to call it—in no wise fitted. Finally, he ironically wished me a Good Deliverance from the hands of the Assessors of the Commercial Tribunal, and with a Devilish Sneer recommended his Housekeeper Betje to my care. O Mr. Vandepeereboom, Mr. Vandepeereboom! if ever we meet again, old as I am, there shall be Weeping in Holland for you—if, indeed, there be any body left to shed tears for such a Worthless Rascal.

This most Dishonest Person, however, did me unwittingly a trifle of good, and at all events saved me from Gyves and Stripes. That Passage of his in the Letter about my Funds in the Bank of Amsterdam was my Deliverance. 'Twas widely known that I was but a simple Seafaring Man, unused to Mercantile Affairs, and that I had really brought with me the considerable sum of Twenty Hundred Pounds. I was arrested, it is true, and lay for many Months in the House of Restriction; but interest was made for me, and the Creditors of the Broken House agreed to sign a Certificate of Liberation. I believe that but for that mournful business of the Beguine, and for that confounded Officer that I sworded, some of the Wealthy Merchants would have subscribed to an Association for setting me up again; but that Rencounter was remembered to my hurt, and says Mynheer van Bommel, when he brought me my Certificate, "Harkye, Friend Englander; you are Free this time. Take my advice, and get you out of Holland as quick as ever you can; for their High Mightinesses, to say nothing of the Worshipful Burgomasters of this City, have a misliking for Men that are too quick with the Sword, and too slow with the Pen; and if you don't speedily mend your way of Life, and bid farewell to this Country, you will find yourself sawing of Campeachy-wood at the Rasphuys, with Dirk Juill, the Beadle, standing over you with a Thong." Upon which I thanked him heartily; and he had the Generosity to lend me Fifty Florins to furnish my present needs.

I was no longer a Young Man. I was now long past my

x

fortieth year, again almost a Pauper, Friendless and Unknown
in the World ; yet did I feel Undaunted, and confident that
Better Days were in store for me.   Pouching my Fifty Florins, I first followed the Burgomaster's advice by getting out
of Holland as quick as ever I could, and betook myself by
Treyckshuyt and Stage Wagon to the city of Bruxelles in
Brabant.   Here I abode for some months in the house of a
clean Widow-woman that was a Walloon, who, finding that
I was English, and besides a very tolerable French Scholar,
procured me several Pupils among the Tradesfolk in the
neighbourhood of the Petit Sablon (hard by the Archduchess
Governante's Palace), where I dwelt on a Sixth Floor.   By
degrees I did so increase my number of Pupils, that I was
able to open a School of some thirty Lads and Lasses.   To
both indifferently I taught the Languages, with Writing and
Accompts ; while for the instruction of the latter in Needlework and other Feminine Accomplishments I engaged my
Landlady's Daughter, a comely Maiden, albeit Red-haired,
and very much pitted with the Small-pox.   Figure to yourself Captain Jack Dangerous turned Dominie !   I am venture-
some enough to believe that I was a very passable Pedagogue ; and of this I am certain, that I was entirely beloved
by my Scholars.   The sufferings I had undergone while a
Captive in the hands of that Barbarous Wretch, Gnawbit,
had never been effaced from my Memory, and had made me
infinitely tender towards little Children.   Indeed I could
scarcely bear to use the Ferula to them, or nip 'em with a
Fescue, much less to untruss and Scourge 'em, as 'tis the
brutal fashion of Pedants to do ; nor do I think, though I
disobeyed Solomon's maxim and Spared the Rod, that I did
much towards Spoiling any Child that was under my care.   I
made Learning easy and pleasant to my Youngsters, by telling them all sorts of moving and marvellous Stories, drawn
from what Books of History I had handy (and these I admit
I Coloured a little, to suit the Imaginations of the Young),
and others concerning my own remarkable Adventures, in
which, however extraordinary they seemed, I always took
care to adhere strictly to the Truth, only suppressing that
which it was not proper for Youth and Innocence to be made
acquainted with.

    But Schoolkeeping is a tiresome trade.   One cannot be
at it day and night too ; and a Man must have some place to

Divert himself in, when the toils of the day are over. I found out a Coffee-House in the Rue de Merinos, or Spaan Scheep Straet, as the Flemings call it, in strange likelihood to our tongue, and there, over my Tobacco, made some strange Acquaintance. There was one De Suaso, an Empiric, that had writ against the English College of Physicians, and was like to have made a Fortune by his famous Nostrum for the Gout, *the Sudorific Expulsive Mixture;* but that Scheme had fallen through, it having been discovered that the Mixture was naught but Quicksilver and Hogslard, which made the Patients perspire indeed, but turned 'em all, to the very Silver in their Pockets, as black as Small-Coal Men. Now he had become a kind of Pedlar, selling Handkerchiefs made at Amsterdam, in imitation of those of Naples, with Women's Gloves, Fans, Essences, and Pomatums—and in fact all the Whim-Whams that are known in the Italian trade as *Galanterie le più curiose di Venezia e di Milano.* But his prime trade was in Selling of Snuff, for the choicer sorts of which there was at that time a perfect Rage among the Quality, both of the Continent and of England. This De Suaso used to Laugh, and say that the best venture he had ever made was from a Parcel of Snuff so bad and rotten, that he was about to send it back to the Hamburg Merchant who had sold it him, when one day, plying at the chief Coffee-House, as was his wont, my Lord Hautgoustham, an English Nobleman, desired him to fill his box with the choicest Snuff he had. Thinking my Lord really a Judge, he gives him some undeniable *Bouquet Dauphine;* but the Peer would have none of it. Then he tries him with one Mixture after another, but always unsuccessfully; until at last he bethinks him of the Musty Parcel he has at home, and accordingly having fetched some of that, returns to the Coffee-House, and says that he has indeed a Snuff of extraordinary Smell and Taste, but that 'tis extravagantly dear. Lord Hautgoustham tries it, and calls out in an ecstasy that 'tis the most beautiful Snuff he ever put to his Nose. He bought a Pound of it, for which De Suaso charged him at the moderate rate of Four Guineas; and desires to know his Lodging, that he may send his Friends to buy some of this Incomparable Mixture. The Artful Rogue then affects the Coy, says that his Stock of the Snuff is very low, and by degrees raises his price to Eleven Pistoles a Pound, until the English in Brussels have been

half-poisoned with his filthy Remnant; when there comes
upon the scene a certain Mr. Dubiggin, a rich old English
Merchant of the Caraccas, who knew all kinds of Snuff as
well as a Yorkshire Tyke knows Horses; and he, telling the
Nobleman and his Friends how they have been duped, my
Lord Hautgoustham, who was of a hot Temper, makes no
more ado, but kicks this unhappy De Snaso half way down
the Montagne de la Cour.

Here, too, I made an Acquaintance who was afterwards
the means of working me much Mischief. This was one
Ferdinando Carolyi, that said he was a Styrian, but spoke
most Tongues, and was a thoroughly accomplished Rascal.
He had been a painter of Flower-pieces, and from what I
could learn had also made the Mill to go in the way of coin-
ing False Money; but at the time I knew him was all for
the occult Science called the Cabala. He showed me a whole
chestful of Writings at his Lodgings—which were very mean
—and declared that he had invented a perfect and particular
System, which he called the Astronomical Terrestrial Cabala.
He had run through the whole Pentateuch, and had reduced
to the Signs of the Zodiac the words of such Scripture Verses
as answered to the same; one to Aries, the second to Taurus,
the third to Gemini, and the like. In short, there appeared
a kind of Harmony in 'em, particularly when the Terrestrial
Cabala (which was of the Dryest) was moistened with a flask
or two of good old Rhenish. The whole of this contrivance
was to tend towards the Discovery of the Philosopher's Stone.
He pretended by these Astronomical Figures to have pene-
trated into the most essential Arcana of Nature, and all the
necessary operations for attaining the *Elixir Philosophorum*,
or some such word. But this Carolyi had such a winning
way with him, that he would well-nigh have talked a Don-
key's Hind-leg off. He began to tell me about Peter of Lom-
bardy and the great adept Zacharias, and of the blessed Terra
Foliata, or Land of Leaves, where Gold is sown to be radically
Dissolved in order to its Putrefaction and Regermination in
a Fixation which has Power over its Brethren the Imperfect
Metals, and makes them like unto itself; and this process
(which I believe to have been only a story about a Cock and
a Bull) he called Re-incrudation. In fact my Gentleman
almost talked me out of my Senses; and as I thought him a
monstrous clever Man, I lent him (although my Purse was

as lean as might be) half-a-score Austrian Ducats, to carry out his experiments in the Universal Menstruum. Alas! I never saw my Ducats nor my Alchemist again. A week after I had lent him the money, he fled on a suspicion of Base Coin; and I had hard work to persuade the Officers of Justice that I had not a hand in his Malpractices. As it was, nearly all my Scholars fell away from my School; and the Impudent Flemings sneered at me as *Mozzoo Kabala,*—in their barbarous Lingo,—and I was pointed out in the streets as a Wizard, a Fortune-teller, a Cunning Man, and what not. So that I was fain, after about ten years' sojourn at Bruxelles, to call in my Dues, gather my few Effects together, and bid farewell to Flanders. It was time; for the Priests were up in arms against me as a Heretic Outlaw, dealing in Magic. The Black Gentry are hereabouts very Bigoted; and although they have no Inquisition, would, I doubt not, have led me a sorry Life, but for my Discretion in timely Flitting.

CHAPTER THE TWENTY-SECOND.

THE Manner of its Coming About was this. I arrived in
Paris very Poor and Miserable, and was for some days (when
that which I brought with me was spent) almost destitute of
Bread. At last, hearing that some Odd Hands were wanted
at the Opera-House to caper about in a new Ballet upon the
Story of Orpheus, the Master of the Tavern where I Lodged,
who had been a Property-Master at the Theatres, and entertained many of the Playing Gentry, made interest for me, as
much to keep me from Starving as to put me in the way of
earning enough money to pay my Score to him. For I have
found that there never was in this world a man so Poor but
he could manage to run into Debt. In virtue of his Influence, I, who had never so much as stood up in a polite
Minuet in my life, and knew no more of Dancing than sufficed to foot it on a Shuffle-board at a Tavern to the tune of
Green Sleeves, was engaged at the wages of one Livre ten
Sols a night to be a Mime in this same Ballet. But 'twas
little proficiency in Dancing they wanted from me. One
need not have been bound 'prentice to a Hackney Caper-
Merchant to play one of the Furies that hold back Eurydice,
and vomit Flames through a Great Mask. They gave me a
monstrous Dress, akin to the *San Benitos* which are worn by
the poor wretches who are burnt by the Inquisition; and my
flame-burning was done by an Ingenious Mechanical Contrivance, that had a most delectable effect, albeit the Fumes
of the Sulphur half-choked me. And they did not ask for
any Characters for their Furies. I had tumbled and vomited
Flames for at least thirty nights, when one evening, standing at the Side-Scenes waiting for my turn to come on, it
chanced that the light gauzy Coats of a pretty little Dancing-
girl, that was playing a Dryad in the Wood where Orpheus
charms the Beast, caught Fire. I think 'twas the Candle
fell out of the Moon-box, and so on to her Drapery; but, at
all events, she was Alight, and ran about the Scene, scream-
ing piteously. The poor little cowardly wretches her Com-

panions all ran away in sheer terror; and as for the two Musqueteers of the Guard who stood sentry at each side of the Proscenium, one dastard Losel fell on his Marrow-bones and began bawling for his Saints, whilst the other, a more active Craven, drops his musket and bayonet with a clang, and clambers into the Orchestra, hitting out right and left among the Fiddlers, and very nearly tumbling into the Big Drum. All this took much less time to pass than I have taken to relate it; but as quick as thought I rushed on to the Stage, seized hold of the little Dancing-girl, tripped her up, and rolled her over and over on the Boards, I encompassing her, till the flames were Extinguished. Luckily there was no Harm done. She was Bruised all over, and one of her pretty little Elbows was scratched; but that was all. One of the Gentlemen of the King's Chamber came round from his Box; and the Sardinian Ambassador sends round at once a Purse of Fifty Pistoles, and an offer for her to become his Madam; "For I should like one," his Excellency said, "that had been half-roasted. All these Frenchwomen look as though they had been boiled." When the Little Girl was brought to her Dressing-room, and had somewhat recovered from her Fright, she began to thank me, her Preserver, as she called me, with great Fervour and Vehemence; yet did I fancy that, although her words were excellently well chosen, she spoke with somewhat of an English Accent. And indeed she proved to be English. She was the Daughter of one Mr. Lovell, an English Gentleman of very fair extraction, who had been unfortunately mixed up in the Troubles of the Forty-five; and having been rather a dangerous Plotter, and so excepted from the Act of Oblivion, had been fain to reside in Paris ever since, picking up a Crust as he could by translating, teaching of the Thrombo and Harpsichord, and suchlike sorry Shifts. But he was very well connected, and had powerful friends among the French Quality. He was now a very old man, but of a most Genteel Presence and Majestic Carriage. The Little Girl's name—she was now about Eighteen years old—was Lilias, and she was the only one. As she had a marvellous turn for Dancing, old Mr. Lovell had (in the stress of his Affairs) allowed her to be hired at the Opera House, where she received no less than a Hundred Ecus a month; but he knew too well what mettle Gentlemen of the King's Chamber and Musqueteers of the

Guard were made of ; and every night after the Performance
he came down to the Theatre to fetch her—his Hat fiercely
cocked, and his long Sword under his arm. So that none
dared follow or molest her. And I question even, if he had
heard of the Ambassador's offer, whether the old Gentleman
would not have demanded Satisfaction from his Excellency
for that slight.

When I discovered that this dear little Creature, who was
as fair as her name and as good as gold, was my Country-
woman, I made bold to tell her that I was English too ;
whereupon she Laughed, and in her sweet manner expressed
her wonder that I had come to be playing a Fury at the
French Opera House. I chose to keep my Belongings private for the nonce ; so the old Gentleman, treating me as
an honest fellow of Low Degree, presented me with ten
Livres, which I accepted, nothing loth, and the Theatre
People even made a purse for me amounting to Fifty more.
So that I got as rich as a Jew, and was much in favour with
my Landlord. But, better than all, the Little Girl, as I was
her Preserver, insisted that I should be her Protector too ;
and old Mr. Lovell being laid up very bad with the rheumatism, I was often privileged to attend her home after the
Theatre, walking respectfully a couple of paces behind her,
and grasping a stout Cudgel. Father and Daughter lived
in the Impasse Mauvaise Langue, Rue des Moineaux, behind
Saint Roque's Church ; and often when I had got my precious
charge home, she would press me to stop to supper, the
which I took very humbly at a side table, and listened to the
stories of old Mr. Lovell (who was very garrulous) about the
Forty-five. " Bless his old heart," thought I ; " I could tell
him something about the Forty-five that would astonish him."

'Twas one night after leaving the Impasse Mauvaise
Langue that, feeling both cold and dry, I turned into a
Tavern that was open late. for a measure of Hot Spiced
Wine as a Night-cap. There was no one there, beyond the
People of the House, save a man in a Drugget Coat, a green
velveteen Waistcoat, red plush Nethers, and a flapped Hat,
all very Worn and Greasy. He was about my own age, and
wore his own Hair ; but the most remarkable thing about
him was his Face. I never saw such a Red Face. 'Twas a
hundred times more fiery than that of Bardolph in the Play.
'Twas more glowing than a Salamander's ; 'twas redder than

Sir Robert Walpole's (the great Whig Minister, who, in my youth, was called by the Commons "Brandy-faced Bob"). This man's Face was terribly puffed and swollen, and the Veins all injected with purplish Blood. The tips of his Ears were like two pendant Carbuncles. His little bloodshot Eyes seemed starting from their Sockets; while the Cheeks beneath puffed out like Pillows for his Orbits to rest upon. Not less worthy of remark was it that this Red-faced Man's Lips were of a tawny White. He was for ever scrabbling with his hands among his tufted Locks, and pressing them to his Temples, as though his Head pained him—which there was reason to believe it did.

This strange Person was, when I entered the Wine-shop, in hot Dispute with the Master about some trifling Liquor Score. He would not Pay, he said; no, not he. He had been basely Robbed and Swindled. He had plenty of Money, but he would not disburse a Red Liard. He showed, indeed, a Leathern Purse with two or three Gold Pieces in it, and smaller Money; but declared that he would Die sooner than disburse. And as he said this, he drew out of his pocket a long Clasp-Knife, two-bladed; and opening it, brandished it about, and said they had better let him go, or Worse would come of it.

The Master of the Tavern and his Wife, decent bodies both, were wofully frightened at the behaviour of this Desperado; but I was not to be frightened by such Racketing. I bade him put up his Toothpick, giving him at the same time a Back-Hander, which drove him into a Corner, where he crouched, snarling like a Wild-beast, but offering to do me no hurt. Then I asked what the To-do was about; and was told that he stood indebted but for Eight Sols, for Half a Litre of Wine, and that they could not account for his Fury. The Man was evidently not in Liquor, which was strange.

These good people were so flustered at the Man's uncommon Demeanour, that, seeing I was Strong and Valiant, they begged me to take him away. This I did, first discharging his Reckoning; for as he had Money about him, I doubted not but that he would recoup me. I got him into the Street (which was close to the Market of the Innocents, and I lived in the Street of the Ancient Comedy, t'other side of the River), and asked him where he was going.

"To get a Billet of Confession," he made answer.

" Stuff and nonsense !" I answered in the French Tongue.. " They sell them not at this Hour of Night. Where do you live ?"

" In the Parvis of Notre Dame," says he, staring like a Stuck Pig. " O Arnault! O Jansenius! O Monsieur de Paris! all this is your fault !"

And he lugs out of his Pocket a ragged Sheet of Paper, which he said was the last Mandement or Charge of the Archbishop of Paris, and was for reading it to me by the Moonlight; but I stopped him short. I had heard in a vague manner that the Public Mind was just then much agitated by some Dispute between the Clergy and the Parliament concerning Billets or Certificates of Confession; but they concerned neither me nor the Opera House. Besides, an Hour after Midnight is not the time for reading Archbishops' Charges in the Public Streets.

" 'Tis my belief, Brother," I said, as soothingly as I could, " that you'd better go Home, and tie a Wet Clout round your Head; or, better still, hie to a Chirurgeon and be let Blood. Have you e'er a Home ?"

He began to tell me that his Name was ROBERT FRANÇOIS DAMIENS; that he had come from Picardy; that he had been a Stableman, a Locksmith, a Camp-follower, and a Servant at the College of Louis-le-Grand; that he had a Wife who was a Cook in a Noble Family, and a Daughter who coloured Prints for a Seller of Engravings. In short, he told me all save what I desired to know. And in the midst of his rambling recital he stops, and claps his Hand to his Forehead again.

" What ails you ?" I asked.

" *C'est le Sang, c'est le Sang, qui me monte à la Tête !*" cries he. " *La Faute est à Monseigneur et à son Mandement. Je périrai; mais les Grands de la Terre périront avec moi.*"*

And with this Bedlamite Speech he broke away from me,. —for I had kept a slight hold of him,—and set off Running as hard as his legs could carry him.

---

* " 'Tis the Blood, the Blood mounting to my Head! 'Tis the Archbishop's fault, and that of his Charge. I shall perish; but the Mighty Ones of the Earth shall perish with me."

I have, contrary to my practice, given these Words as they were spoken, in the French Tongue: for they sunk into my Mind, so as never to be forgotten.—J. D.

I concluded that this Red-faced Man must be some Mad Fellow just escaped out of Charenton; and, having other Fish to fry, let him follow his own devices. Whereupon I kindled a Pipe of Tobacco, and went home to Bed.

Two days after this (March 1757), the whole Troop of the Opera House were commanded to Versailles, there to perform the Ballet of Orpheus before Mesdames the King's Daughters. I had by this time received slight Promotion, and played the Dog Cerberus,—at which my dear little Angel of a Lilias made much mirth. His Majesty was to have waited at Versailles for the playing of the Piece; but after Dinner he changes his mind, and determines on returning to his other Palace of Trianon.

'Twas about Five o'clock in the Afternoon, and there was a great Crowd in the Court of Marble to see the Most Christian King take Coach for Trianon. The Great Court was full of Gardes Françaises, Musqueteers Red and Gray carrying Torches, with Coaches, Led Horses, Prickers, Grooms, Pages, Valets, Waiting Women, and all the Hurly-Burly of a great Court. Some few of the Commonalty also managed to squeeze themselves in—amongst others, your humble Servant, John Dangerous, who was now reckoned no better than a Rascal Buffoon.

'Twas bitterly cold and freezing hard, and the Courtiers had their hands squeezed into great fur Muffs. I saw the King come down the Marble Staircase; a fair portly Gentleman, with a Greatcoat, lined with fur, over his ordinary vestments—then a novelty among the French, and called a *Redingote*, from our English Riding-coat.

"Is that the King?" I heard a Voice, which I seemed to remember, ask behind me, as the Monarch passed between a double line of Spectators to his Coach.

"Yes, Dog," answered he who had been addressed, and who was an Officer in the Gray Musqueteers. "Pig, why dost thou not take off thy Hat?"

I was all at once pushed violently on one side. A Man with a Drugget Coat and Flapped Hat, and whom I at once recognised by the light of the glaring torches as the Red-faced Brawler of the Wine-shop, darted through the line of Guards, an open Knife in his hand, and rushing up to him, stabbed King Lewis the Fifteenth in the side.

I could hear his Majesty cry out, "*Oh! je suis blessé!*"—

" I am wounded !"—but all the rest was turbulence and confusion ; in the midst of which, not caring that the Red-faced Man should claim me as an Acquaintance, I slipped away. I need scarcely say that there was no Ballet at Versailles that night.

A great deal of Blood came from the King's Wound ; for he was a Plethoric Sovereign, much given to High Living ; but he was, on the whole, more Frightened than Hurt. Although when the Assassin was first laid hold of, His Majesty cried out in an Easy Manner that no Harm was to be done to him, he never afterwards troubled his Royal Self in the slightest Manner to put a stop to the Hellish Torments inflicted on a Poor Wretch, who had, at the most, but scratched his Flesh, and for whom the most fitting Punishment would have been a Cell in a Madhouse.

As for this most miserable Red-faced Man, Robert François Damiens, this is what was done to him. At first handling, he was very nearly murdered by the Young Gentlemen Officers of the Body Guard, who, having tied him to a Bench, pricked him with their Sword Points, beat him with their Belts, and pummeled him about the Mouth with the Butt-ends of Pistols. Then he was had to the Civil Prison ; and a certain President, named Machault, came to interrogate him ; who being most zealous to discover whether the Parricide (as he was called) had any Accomplices, heated a Pair of Pincers in the Fire, and when they were red-hot, clawed and dragged away at the Unhappy Man's Legs, till the whole Dungeon did reek with the horrible Odour of Burnt Flesh. Just imagine one of our English Judges of the Land undertaking such a Hangman's Office ! The poor Wretch made no other complaint than to murmur that the King had directed that he was not to be ill-treated ; and when they further questioned him, could only stammer out some Incoherent Balderdash about the Archbishop, the Parliament, and the Billets of Confession.

After many Days, he was removed from Versailles to Paris ; but his Legs were so bad with the Burning, that they were obliged to carry him away on a Mattress. So to Paris ; the Journey taking Six Hours, through his great attendance of Guards and the thickness of the Crowd. He was had to the Prison of the Conciergerie, and put into a Circular Dungeon in the Tower called of Montgomery—the very same one

where Ravaillac, that killed Henry the Fourth, had formerly
lain. There they put him into a kind of Sack of Shamoy
Leather, leaving only his Head free ; and he was tied down
to his bed—which was a common Hospital Pallet—by an
immense number of Leathern Straps, secured by Iron Rings
to the Floor of his Dungeon. But what Dr. Goldsmith, the
Poetry-writer, means by "Damiens' Bed of Steel," I'm sure I
don't know. At the head and foot of his Bed an Exempt
kept watch Night and Day, and every three-quarters of an
hour the Guard was relieved; so that the Miserable Creature
had little chance of Sleeping. He would have sunk under all
this Cruelty, but that they kept him up with Rich Meats and
Generous Wines, which they had all but to force down his
Throat.

But while all this was being done to Damiens, other steps
were being taken by Justice, the which narrowly concerned
me. As he would denounce no Accomplices real or imaginary,
the Police did their best to find out his Confederates for themselves, and by diligent Inquiry made themselves acquainted
with all Damiens' movements for days before he committed
his Crime. They found out the Wine-shop where he had
refused to pay his Reckoning and made a Disturbance ; and
learning from the people of the House what manner of Man
had paid for him and taken him away, they were soon on *my*
track. One night, just before the Ballet began, I was taken
by two Exempts ; and, in the very play-acting dress as Cerberus that I wore, was forced into a Sedan, and taken, surrounded by Guards, to the Prison of the Châtelet. I thought
of appealing to our Ambassador in Paris, and proving that I
was a faithful Subject of King George ; but, as it happened,
I owed my safety to one who disowned that Monarch, and
kept all his Allegiance for King James. For old Mr. Lovell,
hearing of my Arrest, and importuned by poor Pretty Miss
Lilias, who was kind enough to shed many Tears on the occasion, hurried off to his Eminence the Cardinal de ———,
who was all but supreme at Court, and with whom he had
great Influence. The Cardinal listens to him very graciously,
and by and by comes down the President Pasquier to interrogate me ; to whom I told a plain Tale, setting forth how I had
been unfortunate in Business in Holland and Flanders, and
was earning an honest Livelihood by playing a Dog in a
Pantomime. The people in the Wine-shop could not but

bear me out in stating that I had come across the Red-faced
Man by pure Accident, and was no Friend of his. It was
moreover established by the Police, that I had not been seen
in Damiens' company after the Night I first met him, and that
I had a legitimate call to be at Versailles on the day of the
Assassination ; so that, after about a fortnight's detention, I
was set at Liberty, to my own great joy and that of my good
and kind Mistress Lilias, who had now repaid ten-thousand-
fold whatever paltry Service I had been fortunate enough to
render her. Nay, this seeming Misadventure was of present
service to me; for his Eminence was pleased to say that he
should be glad to hear something more concerning me, for
that I seemed a Bold Fellow ; and at an Interview with him,
which lasted more than an Hour, I told him my whole Life
and Adventures, which caused him to elevate his Eyebrows
not a little.

"*Cospetto !* Signor Dangerous," says he (for though he
spoke French like a Native, he was by Birth an Italian, and
sometimes swore in that Language), "if all be true that you
say,—and you do not look like a Man who tells Lies,—you
have led a strange Life. When a Boy, you were nearly
Hanged ; and now at the *mezzo cammin* of Life you have
been on the point of having your Limbs broken on a St.
Andrew's Cross. However, we must see what we can do for
you. Strength, Valour, Experience, and Discretion do not
often go together; but I give you credit for possessing a fair
show of all Four. I suppose, now, that you are tired of
squatting at the Wicket of the Infernal Regions at the Opera-
House ?"

I bowed in acknowledgment of his Eminence's compliments, and said that I should be glad of any Employment.

"Well, well," continued his Eminence, "we will see. At
present, as you say you are a fair Scholar, my Secretary will
find you some work in copying Letters. And here, Signor
Dangerous, take these ten Louis, and furnish yourself with
some more Clerkly Attire than your present trim. It would
never do for a Prince of the Church to have a Flavour of the
Opera Side-Scenes about his house."

Unless Rumour lied, there hung sometimes about his
Eminence's sumptuous hotel a Flavour, not alone of the Opera
Side-Scenes, but of the Ballet-Dancers' Tiring-room. How-
ever, let that pass. I took the ten Louis with many Thanks;

and six hours afterwards was strutting about in a suit of Black, full trimmed, with a little short Cloak, for all the world like a Notary's Clerk.

I had been in the Employ of his Eminence—who showed me daily more and more favour—about a month when all Paris was agog with the News that the Monster Parricide and Hell-Hound (as they called him from the Pulpit), Robert François Damiens, was to suffer the last Penalty of his Crime. I know not what strange horrible fascination I yielded to, but I could not resist the desire to see the End of the Red-faced Man. I went. The Tragedy took place on the Place de Grêve; but ere he came on to his last Scene, Damiens had gone through other Woes well-nigh unutterable. I speak not of his performing the *amende honorable*, bare-footed, in his Shirt, a Halter round his Neck, and a lighted Taper of six pounds' weight in his Hand, at the Church-door, confessing his Crime, and asking Pardon of God, the King, and all Christian Men. Ah! no; he had suffered more than this. Part of his Sentence was that, prior to Execution, he was to undergo the Question Ordinary and Extraordinary; and so at the Conciergerie, in the presence of Presidents, Counsellors of the Parliament, Great Noble-men of the Court, and other Dignitaries, the poor Thing was put into the *Brodequins*, or Boots, and wedge after wedge driven in between his Legs—already raw and inflamed with the Devilries of the President Machault—and the Iron In-casement. He rent the air with his Screams, until the Surgeons declared that he could hold out no longer. But he confessed nothing; for what had he to confess?

Then came the last awful Day, when all this Agony was to end. I saw it all. The Grêve was densely packed; and although the space is not a third so large as Tower Hill, there seemed to be Thousands more persons present than at the beheading of my Lord Lovat. A sorrier Sight was it to see the windows of the Hôtel de Ville thronged with Great Ladies of the Court, many of them Young and Beautiful, and all bravely Dressed, who laughed and chattered and ate Sweetmeats while the Terrible Show was going on. The Sentence ran, that the Assassin's Hand, holding the Knife which he had used, should be Burnt in a Slow-fire of Sul-phur. Then that his Flesh should be torn on the Breast, Arms, Stomach, Thighs, and Calves of the Legs with Pincers; and then that into the gaping Wounds there should be poured Melted Lead, Rosin, Pitch, Wax, and Boiling Oil. And finally, that by the Four Extremities he should be attached to Four Horses, and rent Asunder; his Body then to be Burnt, and his Ashes scattered to the Winds. There was nothing said about the Lord having mercy upon his Soul; but careful injunction was made that he was to be condemned in the Costs of the Prosecution.

All this was done, although I sicken to record it, but in the most Blundering Butcherly manner. The Chief Executioner of the Parliament was Sick, and so the task was deputed to his Nephew, Gabriel Sanson, who being, notwithstanding his Sanguinary Office (which is hereditary), a Humane kind of Young Man, was all in a Shiver at what he had to perform, and quite lost his Head. Both his Valets, or Under-Hangmen, were Drunk. They had forgotten the Pitch, Oil, Rosin, and other things; and at the last moment they had to be sent for to the neighbouring Grocers'. But these Shopkeepers declared, out of humanity, that they had them not; whereupon Guards and Exempts were sent, who searched their Stores, and seized what was wanted in the King's Name. Then the Fiendish Show began. I can hear the miserable man's Shrieks as I sit writing this now.—But no more.

So strong is our Human Frame, that the great strong Brewer's Horses, although Dragged and Whipped this way and t'other, could not pull his limbs Asunder. So the Surgeons were obliged to sever the great Sinews with Knives, and then the Horses managed it somehow.

Note.—When the Horses were Lashed, to make 'em pull Lustily, the Fine Ladies at the windows fluttered their Fans, and, in their sweet little Court Lingo, cried out compassionately, " *Oh, les pauv' Zevaux !*"—" Oh, the poor Dobbins !" They didn't say any thing about a poor Damiens.

Note also, that when they took his Head, to cram it into the Brazier, and burn it with the rest of his Members, they found that his Hair, which when he was arrested was of a Dark Brown, had turned quite White.

This Story is Naked Truth, and it was done in the Christian country of France, and in the Year of our Lord Seventeen Hundred and Fifty-Seven. It all fell out because a poor, ignorant, half-crazy Serving-Man chose to muddle his

Head about the Archbishop of Paris and his Billets of Confession, and because he would not go to a Chirurgeon and be let Blood when Jack Dangerous bade him.

A week after this his Eminence was pleased to send for me into his Cabinet, and told me that he had heard great Accounts from his Secretary of my Parts, Application, and Capacity, and that he designed to restore me to the position of a Gentleman. He asked me if I had a mind for a particular Employment and a Secret Mission ; and on my signifying my willingness to embark in such an Undertaking, bade me hold myself in readiness to travel forthwith into Italy.

CHAPTER THE TWENTY-THIRD.

OF MY SECRET EMPLOYMENT IN THE SERVICE OF THE CARDINAL
DE ——.

PARIS was now clearly no place for me; so bidding adieu to
my kind Protectress, I made what haste I could to quit the
city where I had witnessed, and in some sense been impli-
cated in, so Frightful a Tragedy. There had always been
mingled with my Adventurous Temperament a turn for sober
Reflection; and I did not fail to Reflect with much seriousness upon the appalling perils from which I had just, by the
Mercy of Providence, escaped. Setting altogether on one
side the Pretty Sight I should have presented had I been
subject to the Hellish Tortures which this poor crazy Wretch
Damiens underwent, I justly conceived an extreme Horror
for this fiendish yet frivolous People, who could mingle the
twirling of Fans and the sucking of Sugar-plums with the
most excruciating Torments ever inflicted upon a Human
Being. At least, so I reasoned to myself, if we English
hang and disembowel a Traitor, at least we strangle him
first; and though the sentence is Bloodthirsty, the mob
would rend 'Squire Ketch in pieces were it known that a
Spark of Life remained in the Body of the Patient when the
Hangman's Knife touched his Breast; but these Frenchmen
have neither Humanity nor Decency, and positively pet and
pamper up their Victim in order that he may be the better
able to endure the full effects of their infernal Spite.

Not without considerable Misgivings did I undertake
my new Employment, the more so as I was both forbidden
and ashamed to impart any inkling of its nature to my dear
Mistress. Say what you will, no man that has a spark of
Honesty remaining in him can have much relish for the
calling of a Spy. I tried hard to persuade myself that this
was a kind of Diplomatic Employment; that I was intrusted
with Secrets of State; and that by faithfully carrying out
my Instructions, I was serving the cause of Civilisation, and
in my humble way helping to maintain the Peace of Europe.
For in all ages there have been, and in all to come there
must be, sober and discreet Persons to act as Emissaries, to

inquire into the conditions of the People, and bring back Tidings of the Nakedness or Fertility of the Land. It would never have been known that there was Corn in Egypt, but for the sagacious Investigations of Messengers sent to quest about in the interest· of a Famished Community. Nevertheless I admit that, although I spread much such Balsam upon my galled and chafed Conscience, I could not avoid a dismal Distrust that all these Arguments were vain and sophistical. The words, "Spy, Spy, Spy," haunted me both by day and by night. I saw, in imagination, the Finger of Derision pointed at me, and heard, in spirit, the wagging of the Tongues of Evil-minded Men. The worst of it was, that the occult nature of my Mission prevented me from loudly proclaiming my Honesty in order to vindicate it against all comers, and glued my Sword to its Scabbard, whence it would otherwise furiously have leapt to avenge the merest Slight put upon me.

His Eminence the Cardinal de —— was pleased to equip me for my Journey in the most munificent Manner. First he directed me to procure a plentiful stock of Clothes both for travelling and for gala Occasions, not forgetting a couple of good serviceable Rapiers, as well as a Walking-sword, a Dress-foil, and a Hanger, with a pair of Holster Pistols, and two smaller ones of Steel in case of Emergencies. Also, by his advice, within the lining of my Coat, by the nape of my Neck, just where the bag of my Wig hung, I secreted a neat little Poniard or Dagger. In a small Emerald Ring, of which he made me a Present, was compactly stowed a quantity of very subtle and potent Poison, sufficient to kill Two Men. "One never knows what may happen, dear Captain," says his Eminence to me, with his unctuous Smile. "Your Profession is is one of sudden Risks, leading sometimes to prospects of painful Inconvenience. If you are brought to such a pass that all your Ingenuity will not enable you to extricate yourself from it, and if you have any rational Objection, say, to being Burnt Alive, or Broken on the Wheel, 'tis always as well to have the means at hand of executing oneself with genteel Tranquillity. Such means you will always carry with you on your Little Finger; and I can see, by the circumference of the Ring, that 'tis only by Sawing off that it can be got from off your Digit. Poison yourself, then, *mio caro*, if you see no other way of getting out of the Scrape; but pray remember this : That he who has poison about him, and only enough for one, is an Ass. *Always carry enough for Two.* The immersion of that little finger in a Glass of Wine, and the pressure of a little Spring, would make Hercules so much cold chicken in a Moment. There are times, dear Captain, when you may have to save Half your Potion to kill yourself, but when you may safely lay out the other Half with the view of killing somebody else." A mighty pleasant Way had his Eminence with him; and his conversation was a kind of Borgia Brocade shot with Machiavelism.

My Despatches and other Secret Documents I was to carry neatly folded and moulded within a Ball of Wax not much larger than a Pill. This again was put into a Comfit-box of Gold, and suspended by a minute but strong Chain of Steel round my Neck.

"In difficult Circumstances," says his Eminence, "you will open that Comfit-box and swallow that little Ball of Wax. I have often thought," he pursued, "that Spies, to be perfect in their Vocation, should first of all be apprenticed to Mountebanks. At the Fair of St. Germain, I have gazed with admiration on the grotesquely bedizened fellows who swallow Swords, Redhot Pokers, and Yards of Ribbon without number, and thought of what invaluable service their Powers of Gullet would be in the rapid and effectual concealment of Documents the which it is expedient to conceal from the eyes of the Vulgar."

Again, in the folds of a silken Belt, in the which I was to keep my Letters of Credit and a large unset Diamond, in case I should be pressed for Money in places where there were no Bankers,—for Diamonds are convertible into Cash from one end of the World to the other, except among the Cannibals,—in this Belt was a little Scrap of Parchment secured between two squares of Glass, and bearing an Inscription in minute characters, which I was unable to decipher. I have the Scrap of Parchment by me yet, and have shown it to Dr. Dubiety, who is a very learned man; but even he is puzzled with it; and beyond opining that the characters are either Arabic or Sanscrit, cannot give me any information regarding their Purport.

"This Parchment," observed the Cardinal, when he delivered it to me, "will be of no service to you with Civil or Military Governors, and it will be wise for you not to show it to carnal-minded Men; but if ever you get into difficulties with Holy Mother Church—I speak not of Heretic Communions—you may produce it at once, and it will be sure to deliver you from those Fiery Furnaces and the Jaws of those Devouring Dragons of whom the said Holy Mother Church is sometimes forced (through the perversity of Mankind) to make use."

Finally, this same Belt contained a curious Contrivance, by means of a piece of Vellum perforated in divers places, for deciphering the Letters I might receive from his Eminence or his agents. On placing the Vellum over the Letter sent, the words ·intended to meet the eyes of the recipient, and none other, would appear through the incisions made; while, the Vellum removed, the body of the Epistle would read like the veriest Balderdash. This the French call a *chiffre à grille*, and 'tis much used in their secret Diplomatic Affairs. The best of it is, that when the two Parties who wish to correspond have once settled where the incisions are to be, and have each gotten their *grille*, or Peephole Vellum, no human being can, under ten thousand combinations of letters, and years of toilsome labour, decipher what is meant to be expressed, or weed out the few Words of Meaning from the mass of surrounding Rubbish.

I bade his Eminence farewell, having the honour to be admitted to his *petit lever*, the felicity to kiss his hand and receive his Benediction, and the distinction of being conducted down the Back Stairs by his Maître d'Hôtel, and let out by a Side Door in the Garden-wall of his Mansion. A close Chariot took me one morning in the Spring of '58 to the Barrière de Lyon, and there I found a Chaise and Post-horses, and was soon on my road to the South, with three hundred Louis in Gold in my Valise, and a Letter of Credit for any sum under five hundred, at a time I liked to draw, in my Waist-belt. I was Richer in Purse and more bravely Dressed than ever I had been in my life, and travelled under the name of the Chevalier Escarbotin; but I was a Spy, and, in mine own eyes I was the Meanest of the Mean.

A happy Mercurial Temper and cheerful Flow of Spirits soon, however, revived within me; and, ere Ten Leagues of my Journey were over, the Chevalier Escarbotin became once more to himself Jack Dangerous. " I will work the Mine of my Manhood," I cried out in the Chaise, "to the last Vein of the Ore." *Vive la Joie!* Yet in my innermost heart did I wish myself once more with Captain Blokes as the daring Supercargo of the dear old *Marquis*, or else a Peaceful Merchant at Amsterdam, giving good advice to the Rogues and Sluts in the Rasphuys. O Mr. Vandepcereboom, Mr. Vandepeereboom!

Six days after my departure from Paris, I embarked from Marseille on board a Tartane bound for Genoa. We had fine sailing for about three days, till by contrary winds we were driven into San Remo, a pretty Seaport belonging to the Genoese. This abounds so much with Oranges, Lemons, and other Delicious Fruit, that it is called the Paradise of Italy. So on to Genoa, where the Beggars live in Palaces cheek by jowl with the Nobles, who are well-nigh as beggarly as they; and the Houses are as lofty as any in Europe, and the Streets between them as dark and narrow as Adam and Eve Court in the Strand. The Suburb called San Pietro d' Arena very pretty and full of commodious Villas. There are thirty Parish Churches, and at San Lorenzo they show a large Dish made out of One Emerald, which they say was given to King Solomon by the Queen of Sheba. The Genoese are a cunning and industrious People, with a great gusto for the Arts, but terrible Thieves. The Government a Republic, headed by a Doge, that is chosen every two years from among the Nobility, and must be a Genoese, at least Fifty years of age, and no Byblow. He cannot so much as lie One Night out of the City, without leave had from the Senate. When he is elected, they place a Crown of Gold on his Head, and a Sceptre in his Hand. His Robes are of Crimson Velvet, and he has the title of Serenity.

Here I did business with several Persons of Consideration: the Senators B—c—i and Della G——, the rich Banker L——, and Monsignore the Archprelate X——. So by Cortona, where there is a strong Castle on a Hill, to Pavia, an old decaying City on the River Tessin, which is so rapid that Bishop Burnet says he ran down the Stream thirty miles in three hours by the help of one Rower only. This may be, or t'other way; but I own to placing little faith in the veracity of these Cat-in-Pan Revolution Bishops. Here (at Pavy) is a Brass Statue of Marcus Antoninus on Horseback; though the Pavians will have it to be Charles the Fifth, and others declare it to be Constantine the Great.

After two days here, waiting for Despatches from his Eminence, which came at last in the False Bottom of a Jar of Narbonne Honey, and I answering by a Billet discreetly buried in the recesses of a large Bologna Sausage, I posted to Milan, through a fertile and delicious country, which some call the Garden of Italy. A broad, clean place, with spacious Streets; but the Wine and Maccaroni not half so good as at Genoa. The Cathedral full of Relics, some of which run up as high as Abraham. In the Ambrosian Library are a power of Books, and, what is more curious, the Dried *Heads* of several Learned Men—amongst others, that of our Bishop Fisher, whom King Harry the Eighth put to Death for not acknowledging his Supremacy. About two miles from hence is a Curiosity, in the shape of a Building, where, if you fire off a Pistol, the Sound returns about Fifty times. 'Tis done, they told me by two Parallel Walls of a considerable length, which reverberate the Sound to each other till the undulation is quite spent. The which, being so informed, I was as wise concerning the Echo as I had been before.

It was my Design to have proceeded from Milan either to Venice or to the famous Capital City of Rome; but Instructions from his Eminence forced me to retrace my steps, and at Genoa I embarked for Naples. This is a very handsome place, but villanously Dirty, and governed in a most Despotic Manner. Nearly all the Corn Country round about belongs to the Jesuits, who make a pretty Penny by it. The Taxes very high, and laid on Wine, Meat, Oil, and other Necessaries of Life; indeed on every thing eatable except Fruit and Fowls, which you may buy for a Song. All Foreigners who have here purchased Estates are loaded with Extraordinary Taxes and Impositions. The City is remarkable for its Silk Stockings, Waistcoats, Breeches, and Caps; Soap, Perfume, and Snuff-boxes. They cool their Wine with Snow, which they get out of pits dug in the Mountain-sides. Near here, too, is a Burning Mountain they call Vesuvio. It may be mighty curious, but 'tis as great a Nuisance and Perpetual Alarm to the peaceable Inhabitants of Naples as a Powder Magazine. Very often this Vesuvio gives itself up to hideous Bellowing, causing the Windows, nay the very Houses, in Naples to Shake, and then it vomits forth vast Quantities of melted Stuff, which streams down the Mountain-sides like a pot boiling over. Sometimes it darkens the Sun with

Smoke, causing a kind of Eclipse; then a Pillar of Black
Smoke will start up to a prodigious Height in the air, and
the next morning you will find the Court and Terrace of
your House, be it ten miles away, all strewn with Fine Ashes
from Vesuvio.

CHAPTER THE TWENTY-FOURTH.

I FALL INTO THE HANDS OF RECREANT PAYNIMS, AND AM REDUCED TO A
STATE OF MISERABLE SLAVERY.

I THINK I should have been much better off, if, stopping at
Naples, I had fallen into the blazing Crater of Vesuvio,
and have cast up again into the air in the shape of Red-
hot Ashes. I think it would have been better for me to
be Bitten by the Tarantula Spider (which is about the size
of a small Nutmeg, and when it bites a person throws him
into all kinds of Tumblings, Anger, Fear, Weeping, Crazy
Talk, and Wild Actions, accompanied by a kind of Bedlam
Gambado), than to have gone upon the pretty Dance I was
destined to Lead. However, there was no disobeying the
commands of his Eminence, who, in his Smooth Italian
way, told me at Paris that those of his Servants who did
not attend to his Behests, were much subject to dying
Suddenly after Supper; and so, Willy-nilly, I sped upon
my Dark Errand.

Business now took me to Venice. This is a very grand
City, both for the Magnificence of its Nobles and the Extent
of its Commerce. The Doge is only a Sumptuous kind of
Puppet, the Real Government being invested in the Seignory,
or Council of Ten, that carry matters with a very High Hand,
but, on the whole, give Satisfaction both to the Quality and
the Common. Here are numbers of Priests of a very Free
Life and Conversation, and swarms of Monks that are notorious Evil-doers; for during the Carnival (a very famous
one here) they wear Masks, sing upon Stages, and fall into
many other Practices unbecoming their Profession. The
Venetian Nuns are the merriest in all Europe, and have a
not much better Repute than the Monks, many of them
being the Daughters of the Nobility, who dispose of 'em in
this manner to save the Charges of keeping 'em at home.
They wear no Veils; have their Necks uncovered; and receive the Addresses of Suitors at the Grates of their Parlours. The Patriarch did indeed at one time essay to Reform
the abuses that had crept into the Nunneries; but the Ladies
San Giacomo, with whom he began, told him plainly that

they were Noble Venetians, and scorned his Regulations. Thereupon he attempted to shut up their House, which so provoked 'em that they were going to set Fire to it; but the Senate interposing, commanded the Patriarch to desist, and these Merry Maidens had full liberty to resume their Madcap Pranks.

Here they make excellent fine Drinking-glasses and Mirrors; likewise Gold and Silver Stuffs, Turpentine, Cream of Tartar, and other articles. The Streets mostly with Water running thro' 'em, like unto Rotterdam, all going to and fro done in Boats called Gondoles,—a dismal, Hearse-looking kind of Wherry, with a prow like the head of a Bass-Viol, and rowed, or rather shoved along with a Pole by a Mad, Ragged Fellow, that bawls out verses from Tasso, one of their Poets, as he plies his Oar. The great Sight at Venice, after the Grand Canal and St. Mark's Place, is the Carnival, which begins on Twelfth Day, and holds all Lent. The Diversion of the Venetians is now all for Masquerading. Under a Disguise, they break through their Natural Gravity, and fall heartily into all the Follies and Extravagances of these occasions. With Operas, Plays, and Gaming-Houses, they seem to forget all Habits, Customs, and Laws; lay aside all cares of Business, and Swamp all Distinctions of Rank. This practice of Masking gives rise to a variety of Love Adventures, of which the less said the better; for the Venetian Bona Robas, or Corteggiane, as they call 'em now, are a most Artful Generation. The pursuit of Amours is often accompanied by Broils and Bloodshed; and Fiery Temper is not confined to the Men, but often breaks out in the Weaker Sex; an instance of which I saw one day in St. Mark's Place, where two Fine Women, Masked, that were Rivals for the favour of the same Gallant, happening to meet, and by some means knowing one another, they fell out, went to Cuffs, tore off each other's Mask, and at last drew Knives out of their pockets, with which they Fought so seriously, that one of them was left for Dead upon the Spot.

Another Frolic of the Carnival is Gaming, which is commonly in Noblemen's Houses, where there are Tables for that purpose in ten or twelve Rooms on a floor, and seldom without abundance of Company, who are all Masked, and observe a profound Silence. Here one meets Ladies of Pleasure

cheek by jowl with Ladies of Quality, who, under the protection of a convenient piece of Black Satin or Velvet, are
allowed to enjoy the entertainments of the Season; but are
generally attended either by the Husband or his Spies, who
keep a watchful eye on their Behaviour. Besides these
Gaming-Rooms, there are others, where Sweetmeats, Wine,
Lemonade, and other Refreshments may be purchased, the
Haughty Nobility of Venice not disdaining to turn Tavern-
keepers at this season of the year. Here it is usual for
Gentlemen to address the Ladies and employ their wit and
raillery; but they must take care to keep within the bounds
of Politeness, or they may draw upon themselves the Resentment of the Husbands, who seldom put up with an
Affront of this kind, though perhaps only imaginary, without exacting a severe Satisfaction. For the Common People
there are Jugglers, Rope-dancers, Fortune-tellers, and other
Buffoons, who have stages in the Square of St. Mark, where,
at all times during the Carnival, 'tis almost impossible to
pass along, owing to the Crowd of Masqueraders. Bull Baitings, Races of Gondoles, and other Amusements, too tedious
to enumerate, also take place. But among the several Shows
which attract the eyes of the Populace, I cannot forbear describing one which is remarkable for its oddity, and perhaps
peculiar to the Venetians. A number of Men, by the help
of Poles laid across each other's Shoulders, build themselves
up almost as children do Cards—four or five Rows of 'em
standing one above the other, and lessening as they advance
in height, till at last a little Boy forms the Top, or Point, of
the Structure. After they have stood in this manner, to be
gazed at, some time, the Boy leaps down into the arms of
people appointed to catch him at the Bottom; the rest follow
his example, and so the whole Pile falls to Pieces.

The Nobility of Venice are remarkable for their Persons
as well as for their Polite Behaviour, and have a great deal
of Gravity and Wisdom in their Countenances. They wear
a light Cap with a kind of black Fringe, and a long black
Gown of Paduan Cloth, as their Laws require; though the
English have found means to introduce their Manufactures
among 'em. Underneath these Gowns they have suits of
Silk; and are extremely neat as to their Shoes and Stockings. Their Perukes are long, full-bottomed, and very well
Powdered; and they usually carry their Caps in their Hands.

The Women very well shaped, though they endeavour to
improve their Complexions with Washes and Paint. Those
of Quality wear such high-heeled Shoes, that they can scarce
walk without having two people to support them. In matters of Religion (though their worship is as pompous as Gold
and Jewels can make it) the Venetians are very Easy and
Unconcerned; and neither Pope nor Inquisition is thought
much of in the Dominions of the Seignory. For Music in
their Churches they have a perfect Passion. The City is
well furnished with Necessaries; but the want of Cellarage
makes all the Wine sour. The Inhabitants are of a Fresh
Complexion, and not much troubled with Coughs; which is
strange, they having so much Water about 'em. They begin
their day at Sunset, and count one o'clock an hour after, and
so on to twenty-four; which is likewise a Custom, I believe,
among the Chinese.

They bury their Dead within the Four-and-Twenty Hours,
and sometimes sooner. The Funerals of Persons of Quality
are performed with great Pomp and Solemnity; and the
deceased are carried to the Place of Interment with their
Faces bare. Whilst I was in Venice, their Patriarch (who
is a kind of Independent Pontiff in his own way; for, as I
have said, they reckon but little of his Holiness here) died,
and was buried with this Ceremony. He was carried in one
of his own Coaches, by night, to St. Mark's Church, which
was all hung with Black for the occasion; and next day the
Corpse was laid on a Bed in the very middle of the Church,
dressed in the Sacerdotal Habit, with the Head towards the
Choir, and his Tiara, or Mitre, lying at the feet. At each
corner of the bed stood a *valet de chambre*, holding a Banner
of Black Taffety, with the Arms of the Deceased. A hundred large Wax Tapers were placed in Candlesticks round
the Bed, and High Mass was sung; the Sopranos very beautiful. After Mass was over, all retired; but the Body lay
exposed till evening, when it was stripped of its Vestments
(for though a very Gorgeous people, they are Economical in
their ways), and put into a Leaden Coffin, enclosed in another
of Cypress, and was then let down into the Grave. 'Tis not
usual with the Relations to attend the Funeral, which they
look upon as a Barbarous Custom. But they wear Mourning
longer and more regularly than in many other countries. A

woman in a Mourning Habit appears Black from Head to Foot, not the least bit of Linen being to be seen.

The nature of my Employment now brought me into intimate Commerce with Monsieur B——, a French Merchant of Lyons, who treated me with extraordinary Civility, and made great Offers of being of Assistance to me in my Voyage to Constantinople, whither I was now Bound. This Gentleman, by means of the French Ambassador at the Porte, had gotten a Firman, or Passport, to enable him to Travel to that City, and, with a proper number of Attendants, through any part of the Turkish Dominions. As 'tis inconvenient and dangerous Voyaging through the Territories of the Great Turk without such a Protection, nothing could be more Agreeable than the offer he made me of his Company, the more so as his Eminence had enjoined me to keep a Strict Watch upon every thing that M. B—— said or did. He had designed to reach Constantinople by Land through Bosnia, Servia, Bulgaria, and Roumania ; yet, in compliance with my Inclination (I wish my Inclination had been at the Deuce), which was all for a Sea Passage, he consented to embark on board a Vessel bound to Candia and other Islands of the Archipelago, from which we were to procure a Passage to the Capital of the Ottoman Empire. What made this Gentleman's Society more acceptable, was his thorough Knowledge of the Trade of the Levant, and the Genius and Temper of the People. Thus, he informed me of the Method of Dealing with Jews, Armenians, and Greeks ; of the Eastern manner of travelling in Caravans, and the necessary precautions against such Accidents as are mostly fatal to Strangers ; and instructed me in the Art of concealing Things of Value,—although I think I too could have given him a Lesson in that Device,—and avoiding those Snares which Governors, Military Officers, and Petty Princes make use of in order to plunder Travellers and Merchants. Under these favourable Auspices, we embarked in the Autumn of '37, on board a Trading Vessel called the *San Marco*, bound for Candia, but first for Malta, so famous for its Order of Knights. A fine Gale at North-West carried us pleasantly down the Gulf of Venice, or Adriatic Sea ; and on the fifth day we came in sight of Otranto, a Town destroyed by the Turks nigh Three Hundred years ago, since which time it has hardly regained its Ancient Lustre, but at present well Fortified, and

defended by a High Castle, which I have heard the Honourable Mr. Walpole, a Fine, Lardy-Dardy, Maccaroni Gentleman, that lives at a place called Strawberry Hill, by Twitnam,
in England, has written a silly Romantic Tale about. So we
got clear of the Gulf of Venice, and in three days more, after
making Cape Passaro, in Sicily, entered the Haven of Malta.

This is an Island that lies between Sicily and the Coast
of Africa, and is of an Egg-shaped figure, about twenty miles
long and twelve broad. The City of Malta is divided into
three parts, which are properly so many Rocks jutting out
into the Sea, with large Harbours between them. That called
Valetta, in honour of the Grand Master who so gallantly
defended the place against the Turks, is extremely well Fortified, and also defended by a Castle, held to be impregnable.
The City contains about Two Thousand Houses, well built
with white Stone, and Flat-roofed, surrounded by Rails and
Balusters. On t'other side of the Harbour is another City,
formerly called Il Borgo, or the Borough, but now named
Città Vittoriosa, alluding to the terrible Mauling the Turks
got here in 1566. St. John's Church very handsome, and on
one side of it a fine Piazza, with a Fountain in the corner.
Here are all the Tombs of the Grand Masters, and a great
many Flags taken from the Turks. The Right Hand of St.
John Baptist, wanting but Two Fingers, shown here for
Money, with many other Relics and Ornaments. The Grand
Master lives in a magnificent Palace ; and close by is an
Arsenal, with Arms for Thirty Thousand Men.

The Treasury is a very stately Edifice ; but what gives the
highest Idea of the Charity of this illustrious Order is their
noble Hospital, where all the Sick are received and provided
for with the utmost Care. The Rooms are large and commodious, and in each of them there are but two Patients.
Their Diet is brought to them in rich Silver Plate by the
Knights themselves, who are obliged to this Attendance by
their Constitutions ; and such an exact Decorum is observed,
and every thing performed with such Magnificence, that it
raises the astonishment of Strangers.

But if there be Charity and Benevolence for the Christian
Sick, there is little Mercy shown towards Infidels and Miscreants. The Prison for the Slaves is an enormous Building,
with a Colonnade running round it, and capable of lodging
three or four thousand of those Unhappy People. There are

seldom less than Two Thousand in the House, except when the Galleys of the Order are at Sea upon some Expedition. Then the Poor Wretches are Chained, Night and Day, to the Oar ; but when on Shore they have only a small Lock on their Ankles, like the slaves at Leghorn, and are permitted to go to any part of the Island, from which they have seldom an opportunity of making their Escape.

The Knights of the Order of St. John of Jerusalem, commonly called Knights of Malta, after removing from Jerusalem to Magrath, from thence to Acre, and thence to Rhodes, were expelled from that Island by the Sultan Solyman, having an Army of Three Hundred Thousand Men. The Knights retired, first to Candia, and then to Sicily; but at last the Emperor Charles the Fifth gave 'em the Island of Malta, which they hold to this day. They formerly consisted of Eight Languages or Tongues, according to their Different Nations, viz. those of Provence, Auvergne, France, Italy, Arragon, Germany, Castile, and England; but this last one has been extinct since our Harry the Eighth's time, and what English Knights there be who are Papists are forced to find their Tongue where they can. Each of the Languages has its Chiefs, who are also called Pillars and Grand Crosses, being distinguished by a large White Cross 'broidered on their Breasts. The Seven Languages have their respective Colleges and Halls in Malta, the Head of each House being called the Grand Prior of his Nation ; and to each belongs a certain number of his Commanderies. The Knights, at their entrance into the Order, must prove their Legitimacy, as well as Nobility, by four Descents, and are termed Chevaliers by Right. Those who are raised to the rank of Nobles, for some Valiant Exploit, are called Chevaliers by Favour. None are admitted by the Statutes of the Order under the age of Sixteen; but some are received from their very Infancy on paying a large Sum of Money, or by Dispensation from the Pope. All the Knights oblige themselves to Celibacy, which does not hinder their leading very Disorderly Lives ; and indeed Malta is full of Loose Cattle of all kinds. When they are Professed, a Carpet is spread on the Ground, on which is set a Piece of Bread, a Cup of Water, and a Naked Blade ; and they are told, " This is what Religion gives you. You must procure yourself the rest with your Sword." The which they do, to a pretty considerable Tune, by spoiling of the Turks.

After they make their Vows, they wear a White Cross or Star, with Eight Points, over their Cloaks or Coats, on the Left Side, which is the proper Badge of their Order, the Golden Maltese Cross being only an Ornament. The ordinary Habit of the Grand Master is a kind of Cassock, open before, and tied about him with a Girdle, at which hangs a Purse, alluding to the Charitable ends of their Order ;—but 'tis not to be denied that they have grown very Proud, and Live, many of 'em, in as Shameful Luxury as the Prince Bishops of Germany. Over his Cassock the Grand Master wears a Velvet Gown or Cloak when he goes to Church on Solemn Festivals. He is addressed under the Title of Eminence by all the Knights; but his Subjects of Malta, and the neighbouring Islands, style him Your Highness. As Sovereign, he coins Money, pardons Criminals, and bestows the places of Grand Priors, Bailiffs, &c. ; but in most cases of importance is obliged to seek the advice of his Council, so that he is not wholly Absolute. The Ecclesiastics proper of the Order—for the rest are but Military Monks, that do a great deal more Fighting than Praying, and savour much more of the Camp than of the Convent — are Chaplains, Monastic Clerks, and Deacons. They likewise wear a White Cross, partake of the Privileges of the Institution, and are great Rascals.

'Tis well known that the Knights of Malta are destined to the Profession of Arms for the Defence of the Christian Faith, and the Protection of Pilgrims of all Nations. It is to be observed, that there are also Female Hospitallers of the Order of St. John, sometimes called Chevalières, or She-Knights, of equal Antiquity with the Knights, whose business it is to take care of the Women Pilgrims in a Hospital apart from that of the Men. As the Order look upon the Turks as the Great Enemies of Christianity, they think themselves obliged to be in a state of perpetual Hostility with that people, and, for Centuries, have never so much as signed the preliminaries of a Peace with 'em. They have performed innumerable and astonishing exploits against their much-hated Enemies, the Insolence of whose Rovers they continue to Restrain and Chastise, except when the Rovers, as sometimes happens, get the better of 'em. They have Seven Galleys belonging to the Order, each of which carries Five Hundred Men, and as many Wretches in Fetters tugging away at the

Oar, for Dear Life. Every one of these Galleys mounts Sixteen Pieces of Heavy Artillery; and besides these they fit out a great many Private Ships, by license from the Grand Master, to cruise up and down among the Turks, doing great Havoc, and thereby growing very Rich. Thus it will be plain to the Reader, that a Knight of Malta is a kind of Medley of Seaman, Swashbuckler, and Saint—Admiral Benbow, Field-Marshal Wade, and Friar Tuck all rolled up into one.

I did become acquainted with one of these Holy Roystering Cavalieros, by the name of Don Ercolo Amadeo Sparafucile di San Lorenzo, that was a perfect Model of all these Characteristics. He Confessed with almost as great regularity as he Sinned. The Chaplains must have held him as one of the heartiest of Penitents; for he never came back from a Cruise without a whole Sackful of Misdeeds, and straightway hied him to St. John's Church, to fling his Sinful Ballast overboard and lighten Ship. How he swore! I never heard a man take the entrails of Alexander the Great in vain before; but this was an ordinary expletive with Don Ercolo. He belonged to the Italian Language, though I suspected he had a dash of the Spanish in him; and many a Gay Bout over the choicest of Wines have I had with him at his Inn, as their College-halls are sometimes called. He could drink like a Fish, and fight like a Paladin. He was a good Practical Sailor and Master of Navigation; Rode with ease and dexterity; and was a Proficient in that most difficult trick of the *Manège*, that of riding a horse *en Biais*, as the French term it, and of which our Newcastle has learnedly treated; was an admirable Performer on the Guitar and Viol di Gamba; Sung very sweetly; Fenced exquisitely; must have been in his Youth (he was now about Sixty, and his Hair was grizzled gray) as Beautiful as a Woman, as Graceful as my Sweet Protectress Lilias, as Brave as the Cid, and as Cruel as Pedro of Spain. As it is so long ago, and the Principal Parties in the Affair are all Dead, I don't mind disclosing that my Instructions from his Eminence the Cardinal were to Buy the Cavaliere di San Lorenzo at any Price. I told him so plainly over a Flask of Right Alicant, at a little Feast I had made for him in return for his many Hospitalities, and gave him to understand that he had but to say the word, and Scroppa, the great Goldsmith of Strada Reale, would be glad to cash his

z

Draft for any Sum under Fifty Thousand Ducats. For his Eminence wanted the Cavaliere to be a Friend of France, and France at that time thought that she very much wanted the Island of Malta.

Don Ercolo was not in the least angry; only, he Laughed in my Face.

"Chevalier Escarbotin," he said gaily, "you have mistaken your man. Tell his Eminence the Cardinal de —— that he may go and hang himself. I am not to be bought. I am Rich to Two Hundred and Fifty Thousand ounces of Gold, all got out of spoiling the Infidels. When I die, I shall leave half to the Order, and half to the families of certain Poor Women Creatures whom I have wronged, and who are Dead."

I said, to appease him, that I was but Joking.

"Ta, ta, ta!" retorts he. "I know your Trade well enough. I have been too much among men not to be able to scent out a Spy. But you are a very Jovial Fellow, Escarbotin; and I don't care what you are, so long as you are not a Turk, which, by the way, I don't think you would mind turning."

"O, Signore Cavaliere!"—I began to expostulate.

"What does it matter?" quoth Don Ercolo. "Does it matter any thing at all? Perhaps some of these days, when I am tired of the Eight Points, I shall take the Turban myself."

"A Renegado!" I cried.

"Many a brave Gentleman has turned Renegado ere this," answered he. "Next to the pleasure of Fighting the Turks, I should esteem the condition of being a Turk myself, and fighting against the Order of Malta. But I forgot. You are a Lutheran; although how you came to be a Protestant, with that name of Escarbotin, I can't make out."

I murmured something about belonging to the Reformed Church at Geneva; although I forgot that they were mostly Calvinists there, not Lutherans. But of this Don Ercolo took little notice, and went on.

"When you write to the Cardinal, tell him that Ercolo Amadeo Sparafucile di San Lorenzo is not to be purchased. The sly old Fox! He knows I have great influence with my Uncle the Grand Master. Tell him that I am very much obliged to him for his Offer, and thank him for old Acquaintance' sake. Nay; I believe I am some kind of Kinsman of his Eminence, on the Mother's side. But assure him that I am not in the least Agony with him. If I were Poor, I should probably accept his Offer; but none of the Poor Knights of our Order are worth Buying. It matters little to me whether France, or Spain, or even Heretic England gets hold of this scorching Rock, with its Swarms of Hussies and Rascals; only I prefer amusing myself, and fighting the Turks, to meddling in Politics, and running the risk of a life-long dungeon in the Castle of St. Elmo."

There was a long Silence after this, and he seemed plunged in profound Meditation. Suddenly he fills a Cup with Wine, drains it, and, in his old careless manner, says to me,

" Tell him this—be sure to tell him, lest he should be at the trouble of sending Emissaries to Poison me—I have the best Antidote of any in the Levant, and shall take three drops of it after every Bite and Sup for Six Months to come. Not that I dread you. All Spy as you are, you still look like an Honest Fellow. *You* would not poison an old Friend, would you, Little JACK DANGEROUS ?"

I started to my feet, and stared at the grizzled, handsome Knight in blank amazement. We had been conversing in the French tongue; but the latter part of his Speech he had uttered in mine own English, and with a faultless accent. Moreover, where before had I heard that Voice, had I seen that Face ? My Memory rolled back over the hills and valleys of years; but the Mountains were too high, and the Recesses behind them inaccessible without Mental Climbing, for which I was not prepared.

" Little Jack Dangerous," continued the grizzled Knight, " where have you been these Seven-and-thirty Years ? When I knew you first, you were but a poor little Runaway School-boy, and I was a Tearing Fellow in the Flush and Pride of my hot Youth."

" A Runaway Schoolboy !" I stammered.

" Ay ! had you not fled from the Tyranny of one Gnawbit ?"

" I remember Gnawbit well," I answered, with a shudder.

" Do you remember Charlwood Chase, and the Blacks that were wont to kill Venison there ?"

" I do."

" And Mother Drum, and Cicely, and Jowler, and the

Night Attack, and how near you were being hanged? Do
you remember Captain NIGHT?"

A Light broke in upon me. I recognised my earliest
Protector. I seized his Hand. I was fairly blubbering, and
would have rushed into his Arms; but there was something
Cold and Haughty in his Manner that repulsed me.

"'Tis well," he said. "I am a Knight of the most
Illustrious Order of St. John of Jerusalem, and an Italian
Cavalier of Degree. You—"

"I am a Spy," I cried out, half-sobbing. "What was I
to do? My Malignant Fate hath ever been against me. I
am despicable in your Eyes, but not so despicable as I am in
mine own."

"There, there," he cries out, very placably. "There's no
great harm done, and there's much of a muchness between
us. When you first came across me, was I not stealing the
King's Deer in Charlwood Chase, besides being in Trouble—
I don't mind owning to you now—on account of King
James? 'Twixt you, Jack Dangerous, Flibustier, Saltabadil,
and Spy, and Captain Night, now called Don Ercolo et cetera
et cetera di San Lorenzo, and a Knight of Malta, there is not
much, perhaps, to choose. The World hath its strange Ups
and Downs, and we must e'en make the best of them. Sit
you down, Jack Dangerous, and we will have t'other Flask."

We had t'other Flask, and very good Wine it was; and
for the rest of the time I remained in Malta, Don Ercolo
continued to be my Fast Friend, even as he had been in my
Youth. And yet 'twas mainly through his Instrumentality
that I quitted the Island; for he sent his Page to me with a
Letter, written in our own dear English Tongue, in the which
he instantly desired me, as I valued my Life and the Interests
of my Employers, to put the Broad Seas between myself and
the Grand Master; for that an Inkling of my Errand had got
Wind, and that the Party unfavourable to France being then
uppermost, I ran immediate risk of being cast into a Dungeon,
if not Hanged. For this Reason, said Don Ercolo, he must
forbear any further Commerce with me (not wishing to draw
Suspicion on himself, for the Knights are very jealous in Political Affairs); but he assured me of his continued Friendship, and desired if I stood in Need of any Funds for my
Journey to inform the Page, that he might furnish me secretly with what Gold I needed. But I wanted nothing in

this way, having ample Credits; so making up my Valises with all convenient Speed, the Chevalier Escarbotin bade adieu to Malta.

I took a Passage in a Speronare that was bound to Candia, where I hoped to find some Trading Vessel of heavier Burden to take me to Constantinople. The Mediterranean Sea here very beautiful, and delightful to see the Dolphins, Tunnies, and other Fish, that frequently leapt out of the Water, and followed our Ship in great Numbers. Also a Waterspout, which is a Phenomenon very well known to Seamen in the Levant Trade, and reckoned very dangerous. It looked mighty Fierce and Terrific; and our Sailors, to conjure it away, had recourse to the Superstitious Devices of cutting the air with a Black-Handled Knife, and reading the First Chapter of St. John's Gospel, accounted of great Efficacy in dispersing these Spouts.

Woe is me! After Six Days' most pleasant Sailing, and after doubling Cape Spada, and in very sight of Canea (which is the Port of Candia), a strange Sail hove in Sight, gave Chase, came up to us an hour before sundown, and without as much as, By your leave, or With your leave, opened Fire upon us. A Couple of Swingers from her Double-shotted Guns were a Bellyful for our poor little Speronare, in which there were but Ten Men and a Boy, Passengers included; and we were fain to submit. O, the intolerable Shame and Disgrace! that Jack Dangerous, who had been All Round the World with that Renowned Commander, Captain Blokes, and had Chased, Taken, and Plundered many a good tall Ship belonging to the Spaniards,—ay, and had landed on their Main, Spoiled their Cities and Settlements, Toasted their fine Ladies, and held their Chief Governors to Ransom,—should be laid in the Bilboes by a Rascally African Pirate Vessel mounting Nine Guns, and belonging to the most Heathenish, Knavish, and Bloodthirsty Town of Algiers. My Gall works now to think of it; but Force was against us, and the Disaster was not to be helped. I was in such a Mad Rage as to be near Braining the Captain of the Speronare with a Marline-Spike, and would have assuredly blown out the Brains of the first Moor that boarded us, had not the Italian Captain and his Mate seized each one of my arms, and by Main Force wrested my Weapons from me. And in this (though hotly enraged with 'em at first, and calling them all kinds of Abusive Epi-

thets) I think they acted less like Traitors than like Persons
of Sense and Discretion; for what were we Ten (and the Boy)
against full Fifty powerful Devils, all armed to the Teeth, and
who would assuredly have cut all our Throats had we shown
the least Resistance.

So they had their Will of us, and we were all made Prisoners, preparatory to undergoing the worse Fate of Slaves.
Vain now, indeed, were all his Eminence's Secret Precautions
about the Concealment of Missives; for these Rascal Moors
made no more ado, but stripped us of every Rag of Clothing,
ripping up the Seams thereof, and examining our very Hair,
in quest of Gold and Jewels. The Boatswain, however, that
was appointed to search me, after taking from me all my Stock
of Money, which was Considerable, returned to me the famous
Bit of Parchment between the Glasses, which was to bear me
Harmless against the Claws of Holy Mother Church if she
happened to turn Tiger-Cat; for these Mahometans have a
profound respect for Charms and Amulets, and very like he
took this for one, which could be no good to him, an Infidel,
but might serve a Frank at a pinch. There was another
Article, too, which he restored to me, after Examination, and
of which I have hitherto made no mention. What was this
but a little Portrait of my Beloved Protectress, which I carried with me next my Heart? Not that I had ever ventured
to be so bold as to Ask her for such a pledge, or that she had
favoured me enough to give it me; but while I was in Paris
there had been limned by the great French Painter, Monsieur
Boucher, a Picture of one of the Opera Ballets, not Orpheus's
Story, but something out of Homer's Poetry,—*Ulysse chez
Alcinous*, I think 'twas called,—and this Picture contained
very Life-like Effigies of all the Dancers that stood in the
front rank, of whom my sweet Mistress Lilias was one. From
this an Engraving in the Line Manner was made, which was
put forth by the Printsellers just before I left Paris; and I
declare I gave a Louis d'Or, Ten Livres, Twelve Sols for a
Copy, and cutting out the Pictured Head of my Protectress
with a sharp Penknife, had it pasted down and framed in a
Golden Locket. When the Boatswain saw this, he Grinned,
till the Turban round his tawny Head might have been taken
for a Horse-collar. He wrenched the Portrait out of its Frame,
and put the Gold among the heap of Plunder that was gathered, for after division, on the Deck, and was then about to

throw the dear Bit of Paper into the Sea,—for these Moors think it Sinful to portray the Human Countenance in any way,—but I besought him so Earnestly, both by Signs and supplicatory Gestures, and even, I believe, Tears, to restore it to me, that he desisted ; and putting his Finger to his Lips, as a Hint that I was not to reveal his Clemency to his Commander, gave me back my precious Portrait. He would have, however, the fine Chain I wore round my Neck; so I was fain to make an Opening between the two Sheets of Glass that covered my Amulet, and push in the Portrait, face downwards ; and the two together I hung to a bit of slender Lanyard. But all my brave Clothes were taken from me, and in an Hour after my Capture I was Bare-footed, and with no other Apparel than a Ragged Shirt and a Pair of Drawers of Canvas. To this Accoutrement was speedily added about Twenty-one Pounds of Fetters on the Wrists and Ankles ; and then I, and the Captain, and the Mate, and the Men, and the Boy, were put into a Boat and taken on board the Algerine, where we were flung into the Hold, and had nothing better to eat for many days than Mouldy Biscuit and Bilge-Water. The Cargo of the Speronare was mostly Crockery-ware and Household Stuff, for the use of the Candiotes ; and the Moors would not be at the trouble of Removing, so they Scuttled her, and bore away to the Norrard.

Item.—I swallowed my Despatches ; but the Moors got hold of my Letters of Credit and my Cipher.

CHAPTER THE TWENTY-FIFTH.

AFTER MANY SURPRISING VICISSITUDES, J. DANGEROUS BECOMES BESTUSCHID BASHAW.

So we were all taken into Algiers. 'Tis called "The War-like" by that proud People the Turks ; but with much more Reason, I think, should it be named "The Thievish." Out upon the Robbers' Den ! This most abominable Place, which has, during so many Ages, braved the Resentment of the most powerful Princes of Christendom, is said to contain above 100,000 Mahometans,—among them not above Thirty Rene-gadoes,—15,000 Jews, and 4,000 Christian Slaves. 'Tis full of Mosques and other Heathenish places of Worship, and is strongly Fortified, both towards the Sea and the Land. The Ship that took us was a Brigantine ; and they have nigh a Hundred of 'em (besides Row-boats), mounting from Ten to Fifty Guns, with which they ravage the Trade of Europe. There is little within the City that is Curious, save the Dogs, which are very abundant, and very Fierce and Nasty. The street Bab-Azoun is full of shops, and Jews dealing in Gems and Goldsmiths' Work. The Hills and Valleys round the City are every where beautified with Gardens and Country Seats, whither the Wealthy Turks retire during the Heats of Summer. Some of the Wild Bedoween Tribes up the coun-try go Bare-headed, binding their Temples only with a Fillet to prevent their hair growing troublesome. But the Moors and Turks in Algiers wear on the crowns of their Heads a small Cap of Scarlet Woollen Cloth, that is made at Fez. The Turban is folded round the bottom of these Caps, and by the fashion of the folds you can tell the Soldiers from the Citizens. The Arabs wear a loose Garment called a Hyke, which serves them as a complete Dress by Day, and a Bed and Coverlet by Night. 'Tis observable that when the Moorish women appear in Public, they constantly fold them-selves so close up in their Hykes that very little of their Faces can be seen ; but in the Summer Months, when they retire to their Country Seats, they walk about with less Caution and Reserve, and, at the approach of a Stranger, only let fall their Veils.

What became of the Master and Crew of the Speronare

I know not. They were but Weakly Creatures ; and I conjecture were sold off into private Hands and sent up the
country. Now, although I was past the Middle Age, and
indeed drifting into years, I was still of Unbowed Stature
and great Strength, and a Personable Fellow, hardened in
the furnace of Danger and Adventure. This led to my
being reserved from the public Slave-Market for the Dey
of Algiers' own use. Woe is me, again ! The Distinction
profited me little, for it merely amounted to my being made
Stroke-oar of the third row of the Dey's State-barge, or Galleasse. Imagine me now, in a Tunic and Drawers of Scarlet
Serge, and a White Turban round my Head to keep me from
Sun-stroke, chained by the Ankles to a bench, and with an
Iron Collar round my Neck, from which another Chain
passed to a Bar running fore and aft the whole length of the
Galleasse. Between the benches of Rowers runs a narrow
Planking ; and up and down this continually patrols a great
Tawny Ruffian of a Moorish Boatswain, armed with a Whip
of Rhinoceros Hide, which, with a Will, he lays on to the
Shoulders of those who do not tug hard enough at the Oar.
Miserable and fallen as was my state, I did yet manage to
evade the crowning Degradation of Stripes ; for, being a
Man used to the Sea, and full of Courageous Activity, I got
through my toil so as to make it impossible for my Superiors
to find fault with me ; and besides, in a few words of Lingua
Franca that I picked up, I gave the Boatswain to understand
that if ever he hit me with his Rhinoceros Thong, I should
take the earliest opportunity of Strangling him. As for our
Food, 'twas mainly Beans, and in the morning a Mess of
boiled Maize they call Couscoussou, with some villanous
Rank Butter, melted, poured over it. And sometimes the
Carcass of a Sheep that had died of Disease was given to us.
But whatever we had was eaten on our benches, and the
Cook of the Galleasse passed up and down the planking to
serve out the Rations. We Ate on our benches, we Slept on
our benches, and some of us Died on our benches. There
were Ninety-two Christian Slaves on board the Dey's Galleasse, and Twelve on my Bench. Being Stroke-oar, I was
spared the continual contemplation of a Man's back in front
of me, which other Slaves have told me makes you so mad that
you want to Bite him ; but 'twas scarcely less Vexatious to
have behind, as I had, a Chattering Fellow of a Frenchman,

for ever jabbering forth his complaints, and not bearing them with the surly Dignity of a Briton. I could almost *hear* this fellow grimace; and he was never tired of bemoaning his bygone happy state as a Hairdresser's Journeyman in the Rue St. Honoré at Paris. "Why did a Vain Ambition prompt me to journey from Marseilles to Constantinople?" cried he about Fifty times a day. "Why did I rely on the protection of my Wife's Cousin, who gave me recommendations to his brother, Cook-in-Chief to the Ambassador of France at the court of the Antique Byzantium (*l'antique Byzance*)? Where is my Wife? Where is my Wife's Cousin? They are drinking the wine of Ramonneau; they are dancing at the Barriers. O, my Cocotte! where is my Cocotte?"

"Hang your Cocotte!" I used to cry out in a rage. "'Tis bad enough to be mewed up here like a Bear in a pit, without being worried by a confounded Barber's Clerk!"

I had been Tugging at the Oar full Six Months, when a change came over my lamentable Lot. The Dey of Algiers was at this time one Mahomet Bassa, a very Bold, Fierce, Fighting Man, but of the meanest Extraction, and one, indeed, that had been no more than a common Soldier, from which he had sprung to be, by turns, Oda-Bashee or Lieutenant, Bullock-Bashee or Captain, Tiah-Bashee or Colonel, and Aga or General. For among these strange people every valiant and aspiring Soldier,—I wish 'twas so in England,—though taken yesterday from the Plough, may be considered as Heir-Apparent to the Throne. Nor are they ashamed of the obscurity of their birth. This Mahomet Bassa, in a dispute he once had with the Spanish Consul, said: "My mother sold Sheep's Trotters, and my father Neat's Tongues; but they would have been ashamed to expose for sale on their stalls a Tongue so worthless as thine." Mahomet Bassa was, like most of the Turks, a man of Pleasure, and his Harem was furnished with an extraordinary number of choice Beauties.

His Highness (as he is called), happening to single me out from the rest of the Slaves on board the Galleasse, and being that told I was English—for equally in hopes of Bettering my Condition, and for the purpose of keeping Secret my Employment with his Eminence, I had avowed myself to be of that Nation—ordered me to be released from my Chains, and brought before him at the Divan. Through his Interpreter, a cunning Rogue from Corfu, who spoke most Languages indifferently well, he asked me who I was, and how I came to be aboard the Speronare. I answered, conveniently mixing fact with fiction, that I had been a Captain by Sea and Land in the Service of the King of England; that I had earned a good deal of Prize-Money; had retired from Active Duties, being now nigh upon Fifty years of Age, and was taking my pleasure by voyaging in a part of Europe with which I had hitherto been little acquainted. This Answer seemed to satisfy him pretty well; although he was very curious to know whether I had any Kindred in the Island of Malta, or any foregathering among the Knights. Fortunately for me the Interpreter, to whom I had given a hint of ultimate Reward, deposed that I could not speak twenty words of Maltese (which is a kind of Bastard Italian); and he told me that if it had been discovered that I was in any way Connected with the Order, I should surely have been Impaled; the Dey being then in a towering Rage with the Knights, one of whose Commanders had just captured one of his finest Brigantines, and Dressed Ship, as he humorously put it, by hanging every Man-Jack of the Crew at the Yard-arm, and the Algerine Captain at the Mizen. The Dey then asked me if I had any Friends who I thought would pay my Ransom, the which he placed at the Moderate Computation of Four Thousand Gold Achmedies (about Fifteen Hundred Pounds sterling). I answered, that I thought I could raise about half that Sum, if I were allowed to communicate with one Monsieur Foscue, a Banker at Marseilles, upon whom I had—or rather my Captors had—a Letter of Credit, which they had taken from me. But by Ill-luck this Letter of Credit could not be found. The Captain and Crew of the Rover that took the Speronare were all well bastinadoed about it, but no Letter was forthcoming; and I am more inclined to think that it was thrown, in sheer Ignorance, overboard, than that it was Embezzled. However, as 'twas not to be discovered, the Dey began to look upon me as an Impostor; but I earnestly represented to the Interpreter that, if I had time to write to Monsieur Foscue, all would be right. This I had his Highness's gracious permission to do, and meanwhile was to remain a Slave; but was not sent back to the Galleys. Being a Strong Fellow, and professing to know something about Gardening—Lord help me! I had never touched a Spade ten times in my Life—I was sent to work in his Highness's Gardens at the Castle of Sittcet-ako- Leet. As for my Letter, I penned it in as good French as I could muster, begging Monsieur Foscue to communicate at once with his Eminence, telling him how I had been captured, and that my Letter of Credit had been taken from me, and of the Sorry Plight I was now in. I was given to understand that from Six to Nine Months must pass by be- fore I could expect an Answer; for that Safe Conducts to Christian Packets between Algiers and Marseilles were only granted thrice a year, and the last was but just departed. Whereupon I resigned myself to my Captivity, hoping for Better Days.

The Head Gardener of the Dey was an old Renegado German, named Baupwitz, who tried hard to convert me to the Mussulman Faith. But in addition to my stanch At- tachment to the Protestant Religion, I could see that the State and Condition of the few Renegados in Algiers was very mean and miserable, and that they were despised alike by Turks, Moors, Arabs, Bedoweens, and Jews. And, in- deed, what good had Baupwitz done himself by turning Pay- nim? Thus much I put to him plainly; at which the Old Man was angered, and for some days used me very spitefully; when the Dey, coming to the Castle, took it into his head to have me brought back to Algiers, and enrolled among his Musicians as a Player upon the Cymbals. I declare that although able to troll out a Stave now and then, I could not so much as Whistle "God save the King;" but I managed to clash my two Saucepan-Lids or Cymbals together and to make a Noise, which is all the Turks care for, they having no proper Ear for Music. As one of his Highness's Musi- cians, I was dressed very grandly, with a monstrous Turban all covered with Gold Spangles and Silk Tassels; but I had a Collar of Silver riveted round my Neck, and Silver Shackles round my Ankles, and Silver Manacles round my Wrists; and was still a Slave.

The rest of the Musicians were either Black Negroes or Cophtic Christians, and they used me with Decent Civility; nor did the Master of the Musicians—otherwise a most cruel Moor—go out of his way to flout, much less smite me with his Rattan. If he had dared but to lay one Stripe upon me, I would have sprung upon the Wretch and dashed out his

Brains with my Cymbals, even if I had been put upon the Pale for it half an hour afterwards.

Lodged in the Guard-house at the Dey's Palace, with pretty abundant Rations, and some few Piastres daily to buy Wine (I being a Frank) and Tobacco, and pretty well treated by the Cologlies, or Moorish soldiers, I did not pass such a very bad time of it; and when off Duty, had liberty to go about the City and Suburbs pretty much as I chose. And I was a hundred times better off than the Moslem Slaves are at Malta.

These Algerines are an Uncouth, Savage People; and the Turkish Despotism has quite destroyed that security and Liberty which of old gave birth and encouragement to Learning; hence the knowledge of Medicine, Philosophy, and the Mathematics, which once so flourished among the Arabs, is now almost entirely lost. The Children of the Moors and Turks are sent to School at about Six years old, where they are taught to Read and Write for the value of about a Penny a week of our Money. Instead of Paper or a Plate, each boy has a piece of thin square Board, slightly daubed over with Whiting; on this he makes his Letters, which may be wiped off or renewed at pleasure. Having made some progress in the Koran, he is initiated into the Ceremonies and Mysteries of the Mahometan Religion; and when he has distinguished himself in any of these branches of Learning, he is Richly Dressed, mounted on a Horse finely Caparisoned, and paraded, amidst the Huzzas of his School-fellows, through the Streets; while his Friends and Relations assemble to congratulate his Parents, and load him with Toys and Sweetmeats. And this Observance answers to our Western Rite of Confirmation. But after being three or four years at School, the Boys are put 'Prentice to Trades or enrolled in the Army, where they very speedily forget all they have learnt.

Though such bold Sailors, the Algerines are very despicable as Navigators. Their chief Astronomer, Muley Hamet Ben Daoud, when I was there, who superintended and regulated the Hours of Prayer by the Moon and Stars, had not the skill to make a Sun-dial; and in Navigation they cannot get beyond Pricking of a Chart, and distinguishing the Eight principal Points of the Compass. Even Chemistry, which was once the favourite Science of these people, is at present

only applied to the Distilling of a little Rose-water. The
Physicians chiefly study the Spanish Translation of Dios-
corides (that was a Learned Leech in Olden Times); but the
Figures of the Plants and Animals are more consulted than
the Descriptions : yet are these Knaves naturally Subtle and
Ingenious ; wanting nothing but Application and Patronage
to cultivate and improve their Faculties. They are for the
most part Predestinarians, and pay little regard to Physic,
either leaving the Disorder to contend with Nature, or
making use of Charms and Incantations. They, however,
resort to the Hammam, or Hot Bagnio (a great Sweating-
bath, and a sovereign Remedy for most Distempers), and
have a few Specifics in general use. Thus, in Pleurisy and
the Rheumatics they make several Punctures on the part
affected with a Red-hot Needle; and into simple Gunshot
Wounds they pour Fresh Butter almost boiling hot. The
Prickly Pear roasted in Ashes is applied to Bruises, Swell-
ings, and Inflammations; and a dram or two of the Round
Birthwort is esteemed the best remedy in the world for the
Choler. But few Compound Medicines ; only, for that dreadful scourge the Plague (from which Lord deliver all Men not
being Heathens !), they commonly use a Mixture of Myrrh,
Saffron, Aloes, and Syrup of Myrtle-berries,—which does not
hinder 'em from dying like Sheep with the Rot.

There are no Public Clocks here ; those contrivances,
with Bells, being held an Impious Aping of Providence.
And the only way you have of telling the Time is by the
Fellows up in the Minarets calling 'em to Prayers. Some
of the rich Agas have Watches, bought or stolen out of
Europe ; but they are usually spoilt by the Women of the
Harem playing with 'em. The Dey's principal Wife, Zoraïde
Khanum, is said to have boiled a large Gold Chronometer,
made by Silvain of Paris, with Cream and Sweet Almonds.
Yet does a remnant of their Ancestors' old skill in Arith-
metic and Algebra linger among 'em ; for whereas not one
in Twenty Thousand can do an Equation (and Captain
Blokes taught me, and I have since forgotten How), yet the
Merchants are frequently very dexterous in Reckoning by
Memory, and have also a singular method of Numeration, by
putting their hands into each other's Sleeves, and touching
one another with this or that Finger, or a particular Joint,
each standing for a determined Sum or Number. Thus,

without ere moving their lips,—and your Mussulman has a wholesome horror of squandering Words,—they conclude Bargains of the Greatest Value.

None of the Women think themselves completely Adorned till they have tinged the Lashes and the edges of their Eyelids with the powder of Lead-Ore. This they do by dipping a Bodkin of the thickness of a Quill into the Powder, and dragging it under the Eyelids. This gives their Eyes a Sooty colour, but is thought to add a Wonderful Grace to their Complexions. And was not this that which Jezebel did in the Ancient Time ?* The Old Custom of plighting their Troth by drinking out of each other's Hand is the only Ceremony used by the Algerines at their Marriages. The Bridegroom may put away his Wife whenever he pleases, upon the forfeiture of the Dowry he has settled upon her; but he cannot afterwards take her again until she has been Re-married and Divorced from another Man. After all, the Wives are only held as a better class of Servants, that when their Toil is over become Toys. The greater part of the Moorish Women would be esteemed Beauties even in England, and as Children they have the finest Complexions in the World; but at Thirty they become Wrinkled Old Women. For a Girl is often a Mother at Eleven, and a Grandmother at Twenty-two; and their Lives being generally as long as Europeans, these Matrons often live to see Children of many Generations. They are desperately Superstitious, and hang the Figure of an Open Hand round the Necks of their Children ; and never an Algerine Pirate goes out of Port without such a Hand painted on the Stern, as a counter Charm to an Evil Eye. Truly there are some Christian Folks not much less foolish in their Superstitions; and Rich and Poor among the Neapolitans carry a forked bit of Coral about with them, to conjure away this same Evil Eye, which they call *Gettatura.*

They have a kind of Monks called Marabutts, who are supposed to lead an Austere Life, and pass their lives in counting a Chaplet of Ninety-nine Beads ; but who are, in truth, Impudent Beggars, Thieves, and Profligates. And this is pretty well the Character of the whole body of Algerines, from the Dey in his Palace to his Father who sells Sheep's Trotters. There are a few Grave People, in no

---

* 2 Kings ix. 30.

constant Employ (that is to say, they have made their Fortunes by Murder and Piracy, and are now Retired), who
spend the day, either in conversing with one another at the
Barbers' Shops, or at the Bazaars and Coffee-houses. But the
greater part of the Moorish and Turkish Youth are the wild-
est of Gallants and Roysterers, and waste their time in the
most unseemly Fandangoes.

Item.—These Marabutts are no better than the Mounte-
banks I have seen at the Carnival of Venice or at Southwark
Fair. One Seedy Mustapha tells me that a neighbouring
Marabutt had a solid Iron Bar, which, upon command,
would give the same Report and do as much Mischief as a
Piece of Cannon. At Seteef, too, there was one famous for
Vomiting Fire ; but the Renegado Baupwitz, who had seen
him, assured me 'twas all a Trick ; that his Mouth did certainly seem to be all in a Blaze, while he counterfeited
Violent Agony ; but that on close inspection it appeared
that the Flames and Smoke with which he was surrounded
arose from Tow and Sulphur, which he had contrived to
kindle under his Hyke. The most commendable thing I
can find in the Algerine Character is the great respect they
pay to their Dead. They don't cram 'em into stifling little
Graveyards in the midst of crowded towns, as we do, to our
injury and shame ; but have large Burial-grounds, at a good
distance from their towns and villages. Each Family has
a particular Part, walled in like a garden, where the Bones
of their Ancestors have remained undisturbed for many
Generations. The Graves are all distinct and separate, and
the space between is planted with Beautiful Flowers, bordered round with Stone, or paved over with Tiles. The
Graves of the Great People are likewise distinguished by
Square Rooms with Cupolas built over them, which, being
kept constantly clean, whitewashed, and beautified, nevertheless continue like the Hypocrites, and are but Sepulchres
full within of nothing but Dead Men's Bones.

It happened one fine Autumnal Afternoon, that, my
Services as Cymbal-Player not being required until the
Dey's Supper after Evening Prayers, I was wandering for
mere Amusement in some of the least-frequented Streets of
the City ; which are here, for the sake of Shade, mere
narrow Lanes, without any Pavement but Dust, and without a Door or Window from twenty yards to twenty yards.

In fact they are but Passages between almost dead Walls; the Houses themselves generally standing in the midst of the Gardens. Now I quitted the Street of Baba-zoun by the Street of the Shroffs, or Money-changers, designing to reach the Gate of the River; but the Streets are all so much alike that I lost my Way, and went blundering on from one Lane into another, till I almost despaired of finding my Road back again. I should be too late for the Dey's Supper, thought I; and although Jack Dangerous was never given to Trembling, I began to feel very uncomfortable concerning the Notice that Mahomet Bassa, who was never known to have Pity on any Human Being, Man, Woman, or Child, might take of my Absence. For these accursed Algerines are most cruel in their Punishments. Trials are very swift, and Sentence is always executed within half an hour afterwards. Small Offences are punished with the Bastinado, or the Rhinoceros Whip. For Clipping or Debasing the Public Coin the old Egyptian punishment of cutting off the Hands is inflicted; although the Dey, in one of his Furies, has been known to have the Base Money melted, and poured down the Coiner's Throat. If a Jew or a Christian is guilty of Murder, he is Burnt Alive without the gates of the City; but for the same Crime the Moors and Arabs are either Impaled, hung up by the Neck over the Battlements of the City, or thrown upon Hooks fixed upon the Walls below, where they sometimes hang in Dreadful Torments for Thirty and Forty hours together before they Expire. The Turks, however, out of respect for their Characters, are sent to the Aga's house, where they are either Bastinadoed or Strangled; and when the Women offend, they are not exposed to the populace, but are sent to a private House of Correction; or, if the Crime be Capital, they are sewn up in a Sack, carried out to Sea, and Drowned. And for especial Criminals is reserved the Extraordinary Barbarous punishment of Sawing Asunder; for which purpose they prepare two Boards, of the same length and breadth as the Unfortunate Person, and, having tied him betwixt them, begin sawing at the Head, and so proceed till he is divided into Halves. 'Tis said that Kardinash, a person who was not long since Ambassador at the Court of England, suffered in this wise merely for maintaining, in the face of the Dey, that the King of Great Britain had only One Wife.

All these Grim Probabilities did I revolve in my mind, as the Sun went on sinking, and I could meet nothing but a few Rapscallion Boys that, when I strove to stammer out a few words of Arabic to ask my Way, laughed and jeered in their Impudent manner, and flung handfuls of Dust at me. Just as I was losing all Patience, and determined to Knock at the first door I came to, and make my state known at all hazards, there came upon me at the corner of a street the Figure of a Woman, Muffled up, as 'tis their fashion, in her Hyke and Burnouse, so that I could only see her Eyes, which were smeared over with the usual Black Stuff, but which seemed to have somewhat of a Yellowish Cast. I started, as if she were a Ghost just risen from the ground; but indeed she had only just stepped out from a little Garden-door, that now stood Ajar. From the folds of her White Burnouse now came out a plump Hand, very Glossy, but very Black. She first laid her Finger on that part of her Hyke where her Mouth might be, to command me to Silence; then touched me on the Arm; then pointed to a Latticed Window high up in the wall, to give me to understand that some one had been Watching me from there; and then beckoned me to Follow her. I was wofully perplexed, and, thought I, "The Dey will have no Cymbals to his Supper to-night, that's certain." Still, it is never to be said that J. D. ever shirked an adventure that promised aught of Love or Peril; and had it been into the jaws of a Lion, I must have followed the Negro Emissary. After all, I reasoned, I was a proper-looking Fellow, although no longer in my First Youth, and my hair beginning to Grizzle somewhat; but Love levels ranks, as my Lord Grizzle has it in Tom Thumb; and I was, perhaps, not the first Frank Slave who was favoured by a beauteous Moorish Lady. A Moorish Beauty! Why, this might be, after all, a Princess, a Sultana, a Turkish Khanum! It turned out, however, far differently from what I had expected. Following the Slave, we quitted the street and passed through a Porch, or Gateway, which the Negress carefully locked after her. We now entered upon a Court, with Benches on either side, and paved very handsomely with Marble, covered in the middle with a rich Turkey Mat, and sheltered from the heat of the weather by a kind of Veil, expanded by Ropes from

one side of the Parapet-wall, or Lattice of the Flat Roof, to
the other. So into a little Cloister running round this Court,
and up a little winding stone Staircase into another Cloister
or Upper Gallery. Then at a Door all covered with rich Fili-
gree-work in Gold and Colours did the Negress knock ; and
by and by a soft silvery Voice, of which the sound, somehow,
made me start and tremble much more than that of the Old
Knight of Malta had done, said a few words in Arabic, and
we went in.

I found myself in a large square Apartment, with curious
latticed Windows, through which the Evening Sunlight came,
in the prettiest of patterns, and fell, like so many spangles
disposed by an artful Embroiderer, upon the rich Carpet. A
great Divan, or Stuffed Bench of Crimson Damask, ran all
round the room, with many soft pillows and shawls upon it ;
and on this Divan, upon the side opposite the door, sat an
Eastern Lady, amazingly Dressed. She had laid aside her
Hyke, which was of white silk gorgeously striped with gold
and Crimson Bars, and all dotted with Bullion Tassels, and
sat in a tight-fitting jacket of Red Velvet, open in front,
where you could see the Bosom of her Snowy Smock all
blazing with Emeralds and Rubies. I had never seen so
many of the latter kind of Jewels since the days of my Grandmother, in her Cabinet of Relics. Round her Waist was
swathed a great Cashmerian Shawl, very rich and noble, and
with a heavy Fringe ; and from among the folds peeped out
a little Poniard with a jewelled Hilt, and a knife with a Gold
and Mother-of-pearl Haft to cut her Victuals. She wore
loose Trousers or Drawers of a very fine spun Silk, covered
with a raised pattern in gold thread, that, as is the custom of
the Moorish Women, were fastened at the Knee, and then
fell in quite a torrent of Drapery down to her Ankles, nearly
covering her pretty Feet. A sweet Fashion, and very Modest.
As to the Feet themselves,—the smallest, sure, that mortal
woman ever had,—I could, rapid as was my survey, see that
she wore no Hose ; but her tiny Toes were thrust into Slippers
or Papowshes of blue velvet, all heightened and enriched
with Gold Orris and Seed Pearls. On her head was a dainty
little cap, of the Fez Pattern, but of velvet instead of cloth,
jewelled ; and from it hung a monstrous Tassel of Gold, which
reached half-way down the Back. As for her Hair, it hung
very nearly down to the ground, being all collected into one

Lock, and bound and plaited with Ribbons; and being thus
adorned, were tied close together above the Lock, the several
corners of a Kerchief, made of thin flexible plates of Gold,
cut through, and engraved in imitation of Lace. In one hand
she held a great Fan, of Peacocks' Feathers, with a Mirror in
the midst, and a handle of Gold, Emeralds, and Agate, that
would have driven a Duke's-Place Jew crazy to look at; and
in the other,—well, you know that Oriental Fashions are
different from ours, and that the Paynim nations have the
strangest of Manners and Customs,—I declare that, in the
other Hand—the dexter one—the Lady held the Tube of a
Tobacco-pipe, the which she was smoking with great Deliberation and apparent Relish. But 'twas a very different Pipe
to what we are in the habit of seeing in England—having a
Bowl of fine Red Clay encrusted with Gems, a long straight
tube of Cherry-wood, and a Mouth-piece of Amber studded
with Precious Stones. This Pipe they call a Chibook, and
they smoke it much as we do our common Clay things; but
there's another, which they call a Nargilly, like the Hubble-
bubble smoked by the proud Planters in the Dutch East
Indies. With the Nargilly, the Smoke passes first through
Rose-water, to purify it; and after passing through many
snake-like coils of silk and wire tubing, the Smoker gulps it
down bodily; so that it goes into his Lungs, and must make
them as sooty as a foul Chimney. Many of the Turks are so
handy at this nasty trick, that they can make the Smoke they
have swallowed come out at their ears, eyes, and nostrils; but
I envy them not such Mountebankery, and when I smoke my
Pipe, am content to Blow a Cloud in a moderate and Christian manner.

I have kept you so long describing this Eastern Lady's
Dress, that you must be growing impatient to know whether
her Face matched in handsomeness with her Apparel; but
there was the Deuce of it; for while I stood before her,
staring and wondering over her splendid Habiliments, I
could catch ne'er a glimpse of her Countenance, which was
entirely concealed from view by the Veil they call a *Formah*,
which is made of a very fine gauzy stuff, but painted in body-
colour in a pattern so as to make it Opaque, and so artfully
disposed as to hide the Face without shading any of the
splendour of the Dress. And though I could not make out
so much as the tip of the Lady's Nose, I had a queer sensa-

tion that she was looking at *me*, nay, even that her eyes were twinkling in a merry manner under her Veil. And so I remained Dumbfoundered, quite uncertain as to the kind of Adventure that had befallen me. Had some Moorish or Turkish Dame designed only to Divert herself at the expense of a poor Christian Slave? or was the Veiled Lady only some artful Adventuress of the Jewish, Armenian, or Cophtic Nation, of whom there were many here, affecting great magnificence in their Habits and Living?

Full Ten Minutes had the Lady so gazed upon me, I staring stupidly at her, and the Negress continuing to enjoin me to silence by putting her finger to her Lips. Then clapping her little hands together (I mean that the Lady did, for the Black Woman's were sad Paws), in tumbles from a little door at the side of the Divan a Negro Urchin about eight years of age, very richly clad, who at her command brings Pipes and Coffee; and, signs being made to me, I sat down on a couple of Pillows on the Ground, smoked a Chibook, emptied a Cup, not much bigger than an eggshell, of Coffee,—very Bitter and Nauseous here, for they give you the Dregs as well as the Liquor,—all the while staring at the Lady as though my Eyeballs would have started out of my Head. And by this time the Sun had quite gone down, and as there is but little Twilight in these parts, the Shade of Evening fell like a great black Pall over the Room; so the little Black Urchin came tumbling in again with a couple of Lamps, which he set down before the Divan. These cast a very soft and rosy Light, passing through folds of Pink Silk; and as soon as my eyes grew accustomed to 'em, I could see that the Lady had raised her Veil, that she was looking upon me with a pair of Dark, Roguish, Twinkling Orbs, and that I was sitting in the presence of my kind Protectress, Lilias.

"What think you of this for an Opera Habit, goodman Cerberus?" cried she. "Is this not much better than the Ballet of Orpheus? And, goodness! what strange Accoutrement have you, too, got into?"

When my first ecstasies of Joy and Amazement were over, I explained to my Dear Patroness the reasons (none of my own choosing) for appearing in such a Garb as I then wore; telling her how I had been Galley - Slave, and was now Cymbal-Player, to the Unbelieving Dey of Algiers; and with great Humility did I ask after her Honoured Parent, and seek

to know by what uncommon Accident she, the erst Ballet
Dancer in the King's Opera-House at Paris, had come to be
the tenant of this Outlandish House, and arrayed in this
Heathen Habit. She answered me with that Candour and
Simplicity which I ever found characteristic of her. Old Mr.
Lovell was still alive, and in Paris; and this is how his
Daughter had become separated from her. A very brilliant
Engagement, as First Dancer, indeed, had been offered to her
at the King's Theatre at Palermo; and, after long unsuccess-
ful importunities addressed to the Gentlemen of the French
King's Chamber to cancel her Engagement, these instances,
owing to the untiring influence of Cardinal de ——, had
succeeded, and she was allowed to depart. Full willingly
would she have taken her Papa with her as a Travelling
Companion; but the Old Gentleman was now very Infirm,
and averse from Moving; and so Lilias was placed under the
Guardianship of an old Spanish Lady, the Señora Satisfacion
de Mismar, who was the Palermo Manager's Aunt, made his
engagements for him abroad, and played the Duenna or
Singing Old Woman in his Comedies and Operas at home.
Nothing could be properer than this arrangement, Donna
Satisfacion being a personage of exceeding Discretion and
Propriety of Behaviour; so the two, with half a dozen more
little Dancing-girls that had been hired to fill inferior places,
started for Bordeaux, whence they designed to take shipping
for Palermo. But by ill luck there was no Packet or Merchant Vessel bound for Sicily to be taken up for a long time;
and so they were fain to travel to Toulon, avoiding Marseilles,
where the Plague then was very bad, and thence by way of
Nizza to Genoa, where they found a Brig bound for Messina,
which they thought would serve their turn. And, in truth,
the poor souls found it but too well served; for the Brig
was captured off Bastia in Corsica by one of these diabolical
Barbary Rovers, all on board made Slaves, and carried, not
into Algiers, but into Sallee. There, after much suffering,
poor Donna Satisfacion de Mismar died of a Distemper of
the country, and poor Lilias was left without any other
Protector than her own Virtue and a kind Providence.

'Twas a terrible condition to be left in : Young, Fair,
Friendless, and a Slave among these Moorish Barbarians.
By Heaven's Mercy, however, the dear Girl came to no
Harm. 'Tis the custom, before the Christian Women-cap-

tives are exposed for sale in the public Slave-Market, where they are Handled and put through their paces as though they were so many Cattle, for a Private Inspection of 'em to be made by the rich Persons of the place, who come and take Pipes and Coffee with the Merchant, glance over his Stock in a respectful Manner, and often strike a Bargain there and then. The Girls for sale are apparelled in a sumptuous manner, bathed, perfumed, and trinketed out for their Private View ; and their Captors seek to render 'em docile by giving 'em plenty of Sweetmeats. As if the intolerable pangs of Slavery were to be allayed by Lollipops ! It chanced that among the visitors to the Merchant's House was one Hamet Abdoollah, a very Learned Man, a Physician by Trade, and equally trusted by the Bey of Tunis, the Dey of Algiers, and him who reigned at Tripoli ; but who would not devote himself to the service of any of these Potentates, but, loving an independent life, served all with equal fidelity, sometimes even travelling so far as the Capital of Morocco, where he was in high favour with the Savage who calls himself Emperor of that country, which would be as piratical as the Barbary States, only it has less Seaboard. The father of this Physician had been quite as learned a Man as he, and by the name of Muley Abdoollah had travelled much in Western Europe, where by his Skill and Erudition he had gained so much consideration among the Polite as to be elected a Correspondent Member of the Royal Society of England and the Paris Academy of Sciences. His son was one of the wisest and justest and most merciful of his Species, as you will presently have cause to admit. He was struck at once by the Beauty, Intelligence, and Goodness of Lilias, and his humane heart recoiled at the thought of what her fate might have been among a people given up to Cruelty and Lust. He forthwith bought her of the Merchant at a fair price ; for although that crafty and rapacious Slave-Dealer would have made him pay Through the Nose for his Treasure, knowing the Physician to be a man of great Wealth, he forbore in very shame from his extortion ; for Hamet Abdoollah had but just saved his little son out of a Fever, after he had been given up by all the Ignorant Leeches of Sallee.

So Lilias became the Bond-servant, but only so in name, to this Wise and Good Man. As her dearest wish was now to rejoin her Father, he undertook to send her back to

France, and with that view did remove with his precious
charge to Algiers, only exacting from her a promise that
while she remained under his protection she would wear the
Moorish Habit and pass as his Wife, so as to avoid Insult
when she walked abroad.   But of any thoughts of Love and
Intrigue the Good Man was entirely free.   He was wrapped
up in the study of the Healing Art, and troubled his head
much more about Drugs, Cataplasms, and Electuaries, than
about the Bow and Arrows of Dan Cupid.   Though why the
God of Love should have been christened Daniel, it puzzles
me to comprehend.   This accounts for the manner in which
I had found my dear Protectress caparisoned in every respect
as a Moorish Dame.   She told me that this was by no means
the first time she had seen me, and that my being Cymbal-
Player in the Dey's Musicians was very well known to her,
and that her kind Guardian was on the point of petitioning
the Dey to release me from Servitude, when by accident she
espied me from the Window, and could not resist the temptation of having me called in.

But, in her sweet regard for what was due to Modesty and
Decorum, she would have no Parley with me save in the
presence of the Black slave,—'tis true that she did not understand a word of English,—and directly she had come to an
end of her Narrative, she sent the Tumbling Urchin to inquire whether the Physician had come home, the part of the
House she occupied being quite separate and distinct from
his.   The smutty little Imp comes back bringing word that
Hamet would wait upon her presently; and anon, after discreetly tapping at the door, he came in, a grave, Reverend
Man, in a flowing Robe of Sad-coloured Taffety, and with a
long White Beard and Green Turban; for he had made the
Mecca Pilgrimage, and yet abstained from assuming the title
of Hadji, to which he was entitled.   He spoke very good
French, and even a little English (learned from his Papa);
and when I was made known to him, asked for news of Dr.
Mead and Sir Hans Sloane, although I could tell him but
little of that worthy and deceased Gentleman.

"Happy is the Wooing that is not long a Doing," they
say; and, by this time, you will probably have discovered
that I Loved Lilias Lovell very dearly.   'Twas no Ramping,
Rantipoling, Fiery-Furnace kind of Calf Love on my part,
but a matured and sensible admixture of Gratitude and Sin-

cere Affection. I scorn to conceal that although I knew myself to be by Lineage worthy the hand of a Gentleman's Daughter,* I was aware that, by the Meanness of the condition under which I was first known to the Lovell Family, a Gulf yawned between their Estate and mine; and that, warm and devoted as was my Love for the Pretty Little Creature I had saved from the Flames, I could but deem that she reckoned the Humane Dog Cerberus of the Opera Ballet as of no greater account than a real Doggish Mastiff. But, to my extreme Amazement and Felicity, this was not so. I was beloved by this Amiable Young Person, to whom Ambassadors were proud to go on their knees, and whom Gentlemen of the Chamber would have covered with Diamonds. With a charming frankness, blushing and stammering, yet with Virginal Pride, she confessed that she was enamoured of me, and, if Fortune were propitious, would gladly be my Wife. I could at first scarcely realise the possibility of such great and unmerited Happiness; for well did I know the disparity in Age that existed between us—how Rough and Weather-beaten was I; and she, how Tender, Delicate, and Good! "But does not the Ivy twine round the Oak?" quoth the Physician, as he smote me cheerfully on the Shoulder. And behold, now, gnarled and battered old Jack Dangerous, with this delicious little Parasite creeping toward and Nestling Round him.

---

* I preserve a fragment of what His Eminence was pleased once upon a time to write to me, in his curious Italian way of spelling the French tongue: "*Si cieu che vous m'avez dict sur vostre Naissance è vray, vos esteo digne di monter dedans le carozze du Roy.*"

CHAPTER THE TWENTY-SIXTH AND LAST.

OF MY SERVICE UNDER THE GREAT TURK AS A BASHAW; OF MY ADVEN-
TURES IN RUSSIA AND OTHER COUNTRIES; AND OF MY COMING HOME
AT LAST AND BUYING MY GRANDMOTHER'S HOUSE (WHICH IS NOW MINE)
IN HANOVER SQUARE.

'TWAS the advice of the Good Physician, that, to prevent
Accidents, we should be Married without Delay; for in these
hot countries you are here to-day and gone to-morrow, and
no one can tell what may happen. Difficulties almost insur-
mountable, 'tis true, seemed to stand in the way of our
Union; but Hamet Abdoollah was able to act almost a
Magician's part to bring about our Happiness. I was for the
time being bestowed in his House, and the next morning the
Physician hies him to the Dey, who was in a Fury about me,
and was threatening all kinds of Bowstrings and Bastinadoes.
But his Highness happening likewise to be suffering from
Toothache, and as a Man with a Raging Tooth would give all
the Treasures of Potosi to be quit of his Agony, the Physician
promised to Relieve him forthwith if he would grant his
Suit. The Dey promised him any thing he could wish for,
and so Hamet Abdoollah cures him with a little Phial full of
nothing but Tar Balsam. 'Tis but just to the Mussulmans to
say, that when they have once given their Word of Honour,
they keep it with Extreme Rigour; so that when the Physician begged pardon for me, and License to purchase me out
of the Dey's service and take me into his own, the Suit was
very cheerfully granted. Joyfully Hamet Abdoollah repairs
to us again, with a Firman under the Dey's own Signet
granting me my Liberty; and that very forenoon my silver
Collar, Anklets, and Manacles were stricken off,—the Physician returning them to the Dey's Treasury,—and I was no
longer a Slave.

Although there is no Man alive who mislikes Popery and
its Superstitious Practices more than does J. D., there is one
order of Nuns and one of Monks for whose members I entertain a profound Love and Reverence. Of She-Religious, I
mean those Blessed Sisters of Charity who go about the
World doing good, braving Sickness, succouring Misery, as-
suaging Hunger, drying up Tears, and smiling in the Face of

Death. God bless those Holy Women, say I, wheresoever they are to be found! and in our own Protestant country of England, why should we not have similar Sisterhoods of Women of Mercy, or Deaconesses, bound by no rigid vows, and suffering no ridiculous Penances of Stripes and Macerations, but obeying only the call of Religious Charity, and going Quietly and Trustfully about their Master's Business? Of He-Monks, I mean the Fathers of the Work of Redemption, or Redemptorists, whose sole business it is to travel about Begging and Praying of the Rich for money to Ransom poor Christian bodies out of Slavery; which is a better work, I think, than praying for the deliverance of their Souls out of Purgatory. These Redemptorist Fathers have a permanent Station and Correspondence at all the Piratical Ports of the Barbary Coast; and at stated times, when they have gathered enough Money to redeem a certain number of Christians, a body of the Fraternity visit the Station, take away their Sanctified Merchandise, and by their Humble and Devout Carriage, and exemplary Poverty of Life, extort admiration even from the Bloodthirsty Heathens.

Now at Algiers, about this time, there was suffered to dwell an old Religious of this Order, Le Père Lefanu,—who for his Virtues and Piety was esteemed even by the Mussulman Ulemas, and was thought a good deal more of than any of their Marabutts or Santons, which is a name they give to a kind of wandering Idiots, who, the Crazier they are, are thought the more deserving of Superstitious Veneration. Père Lefanu was nearly ninety years of age, and had dwelt among these Barbarians for full sixty years of his Life, passing his time in Meditation, Prayer, and the Visitation of the Sick and Needy, both among the Unbelievers and the Christian Slaves, and at the same time transacting all necessary business with the Dey's Head-men for periodically redeeming those that were in Bondage. Our good Physician had a profound esteem for this Reverend Person, and often visited him; and now it was through his Ministry that Lilias and I were to be made One. I had forgotten to say, that my departed Saint was of the Communion opposite to mine; but in a land of Pagans 'tis as well to forget all differences between Papists and Protestants, and to remember only that we are Christians. Père Lefanu had been ordained a Secular Priest before he had become a Regular Monk, and he told me that if I had any Conscientious Scruples as to the Husband being a Pro-

testant and the Wife of another way of Thinking, I could
have the marriage done over again in whatever way I thought
proper on our return to Europe. But I was in far too great
a Hurry to be Married to look too narrowly which way the
Cat jumped; and a Romish Wedding is surely better than
jumping over a Broomstick, which, unless we had adopted
the uncouth Moresque custom, would have been all the Ceremony of Matrimony we could have had. So Père Lefanu
came privately, to avoid Gossip, to the Physician's House,
and Lilias Lovell and John Dangerous were made One in the
French Language, the contracting parties being English, the
Bridegroom's best man a tawny Mahometan Moor, and the
only Bridesmaid a Black Negress.

Our Honeymoon (we continuing to dwell in the House of
the good Hamet Abdoollah) was one of unmixed Joy and
Gladness; but 'twas too complete to last long, and soon came
a black Storm to lash into fury the calm surface of our Life's
Lake. Seized with a Malignant Distemper, and after but
three days' Sickness, the good Hamet Abdoollah died. His
Pillow was smoothed by our reverent hands, and with his
dying breath he blessed us. I know not if there be any
Saints in the Mussulman Church; but if ever a man deserved
Canonisation from whatsoever Communion he belonged to, I
am sure it was Hamet Abdoollah, the Moorish Physician.

His Skill in Medicine had brought him great Wealth,
of which, although he was always distributing Alms to the
Poor, he left a considerable Portion behind him. In his last
moments he sent for the Cadi and Ulema of his quarter, for
his will to be made, or at least to assure them by word of
mouth of his Testamentary Intentions, which among this
People would have been as religiously carried out as though
he had written them. But, alas! when the Cadi and the
Ulema arrived, he was speechless, and died without word or
sign of his Wishes.

His Relations came forthwith to administer to his Effects,
and (if truth be not unpalatable to English Heirs, that often
do the same thing) to fight and squabble over the administration thereof. A pretty Noise and Riot they made: now
weeping and howling over the Corse; now bursting open
Trunks, wrenching Trinkets from each other, striving to convey away Garments and Furniture, and even tearing down
the hangings of Rich Stuff. Only the Harem, where my one
True Wife was, remained inviolate from these Harpies; but

me they overwhelmed with the most injurious Invectives and accosted by the foulest epithets, calling me Infidel, Pig, Giaour Dog, Frankish Thief, and the like, telling me that I had fattened long enough on the Substance of a True Believer, with the like opprobious speeches. I let them have their way, only giving them to understand that the first Man who should attempt to cross the Threshold of my Harem, it were better for him that he never had been Born.

Soon, however, came a greater Heir at Law than any of these, to take possession of the Dead Man's heritage. The news of Hamet Abdoollah's decease had come to the ears of the Dey; and straightway he sends down a strong guard of Coglolies to Seize all in his Name, specially enjoining the Bullock Bashee in command to put the big Christian Slave (meaning myself) in Fetters, and equally secure, although with lighter Bonds, the fair Frankish Woman, meaning my dear Wife Lilias. All this was no sooner said than done. The Rough Soldiers burst into the House, and, to prevent any misunderstanding about me, a Cloth (for which I was quite unprepared) was thrown over my head from Behind; and while I was yet struggling to free myself from this blinding Incumbrance, the Gyves were passed over my Wrists and Ankles. And then they removed the Cloth, and, laden with heavy Chains, I had to behold in Despair their Invading the Sanctity of my Harem, and tearing therefrom my Lilias. In vain did I Shout, Threaten, Grind my Teeth, Implore, Promise, and strive to Tear my Hair. They only Laughed; and one Brutish Coglolie made as though to strike me with the flat of his Sabre, when I out with my foot, all fettered as it was, and gave the Ruffian a blow on the Jaw, the which, by the momentum given by the Iron, I thought had stove it in. This much infuriated his Savage Companions; and I doubt not but that they would have finished me, but the Bullock Bashee, who had orders to the contrary, constrained them to stay their hand.

What became of my dear Lilias, I was not allowed to know. She was borne away, shrieking and calling on me, with streaming Eyes, for help; and I saw her no more. Myself they dragged downstairs; and when we were come into the street, flung me, fettered as I was, over the back of an Artillery Horse, where I lay, face downwards, and in a kind of stupor, as listless as a Miller's Sack; and so, my Gyves jingling and clattering, I was conveyed away.

The cruel and remorseless Dey of Algiers I saw no more. Some spark of shame there might perchance be in the Ruffian's Breast that forbade him to gaze upon the man he had pardoned and enfranchised, and had now traitorously Kidnapped. I suppose that in the Thieves' philosophy of this Fellow he reasoned that, if promises are to be kept to Live Men, there is no need to keep them unto Dead ones; that he was released from all his obligations by the demise of Hamet Abdoollah ; and that, as the Physician could not cure him of the Toothache again, if he chanced to get it, 'twas idle to continue bestowing Favours where no Benefits could be derived.

Into a wretched Dungeon of the Arsenal was poor J. Dangerous thrust, with naught for victuals but Musty Beans and Stinking Water. When I had been here, groaning and gnashing my teeth, for seven days,—which seemed to me thrice seven years,—a Rascally Fellow that I knew to be a Scribe belonging to the Divan of the Dey comes into my Dungeon to tell me that the Packet-ship has come in from Marseilles, and that in answer to my letter to Monsieur Foscue, that Merchant sends word that he knows nothing at all about me ; to which the Rascally Scribe adds, in the Lingua Franca, that I was no doubt an Impostor who had trumped up a convenient Fable of my being a Gentleman and having Correspondents who would be Answerable for my Ransom in Europe, in order to get better food and treatment until the real truth could be known. Whereupon he tells me that his Highness the Dey had not yet quite made up his mind as to whether he shall have me Impaled or merely Flayed Alive, and so slams the door in my face.

In this Horrible Dungeon did I continue for seven days more, mostly grovelling on the ground, my face downwards, and praying for Deliverance or Death. I had a mind to dash my Brains out against the slimy walls of the Cell, but was only stayed by the thought of my Lilias. 'Twas always night in this abominable Hole, which was lighted only by a hole in the roof, about four inches square, and which gave not into the open air but into a Corridor above. But on the fifteenth night of my Captivity, for I judged it so by the utter darkness, the door of the Dungeon opened, and the Blessed Old Man that was a Redemptorist Father appeared, bearing a Lantern.

" You have that about you, my son," says he, " which

should be a sign that you are a trusted Agent of Holy Mother Church. Can you show it?"

I pointed with one of my fettered hands to my Breast, and made signs for him to search for that he was in quest of. The which he did, and after reverently kissing the Parchment I had between the Glasses, restored it to me.

"You have been most basely entreated," he continued. "Monsieur Foscue sent ample funds for your Ransom, and his Eminence is most anxious for your safety; but the cruel Moorish Prince who governs this unhappy city, after taking the money, feigned that you had made your Escape from the Arsenal, designing to keep you here in Chains and Hunger until you should Perish."

He paused for a moment, for his Great Age made him very feeble, and then continued:

"I can deliver you from this Abode of Misery; but it is not in my power, my son, to give you entire Deliverance. Would that I could! You have but to follow me to the Quayside, where you will find a boat to convey you on board a Turkish Merchant-ship, that to-morrow morning weighs anchor for Constantinople. You will still be a Slave to the Captain, but to your own ingenuity I leave it to obtain complete Freedom."

"And my Wife—my dear, dear Lilias?" I asked.

The Ancient Man shook his head.

"I can do nothing to bring you together again. She cannot follow you to Stamboul; but by Perseverance, and in Time, you may be restored to her."

"Time!" I cried out, in bitter desperation. "Time! O Father! I am growing an old man. She is the stay and prop of my Life; she is the one ray of sunshine cast on a Black and Wicked Career! And she is taken from me by these Butchers! and I am to see her no more? What care I for Hunger and Chains, and a Dungeon-floor for a Pallet? They have been familiar to me from my earliest youth. If I am not to have my Lilias's sweet companionship again, I will remain here, in this Hole, and die like a Dog, as I am."

"Take comfort, my son," said the Redemptorist Monk. "Time and Perseverance may, I repeat, enable you to attain your heart's desire. Meanwhile, console yourself with the assurance that the Fair and Good Woman, who is your Wife, is out of peril from lawless men. By the same Packet-ship that brought the Letters from Monsieur Foscue came a Sum suffi-

cient Doubly to Ransom the Young Woman. The benignant
protection of his Eminence has been extended to her, and she
will in a few days return to France, and to her Father."

"But can I not see her?—cannot I touch her Hand?—
can I not press her Lip?—for one brief moment, and for the
last time?"

"It is impossible," answered the Monk. "She is watched,
both by Day and Night, by zealous agents of the Dey,
and I have no means of access to her. 'Twould be death
both to you and to myself were I to seek to bring about a
meeting between you. Even now the precious moments are
wasting away. In another hour the Guard will be changed,
and your Escape impossible."

"And how is it possible now?" I asked. "And will no
one come to Hurt through my evasion?"

"It *is* possible," he repeated. "You have to walk but
from hence to the Outer Gate and the Quayside. Immediately you have departed, the Body of a poor Christian Slave,
of your age and stature, who died this morning at the
Arsenal, will be conveyed here, and garnished with your
Chains. The Dey will be told that you have died in Prison.
He loves not to look upon the faces of those he has murdered,
and will take the word of the Aga, who is in our pay.
Come! there is not an instant to be lost. Here is the key to
your Fetters. Unlock them, and follow me."

With a heart that was now elated with the prospect of
Deliverance, and now sunk at the thought that I was still to
be separated from my Lilias, I did as the good Redemptorist
bade me, and, casting my accursed Shackles from me in a
heap, limped slowly forth—for the Iron had wofully galled
me. Outside the Dungeon-door stood a couple of Coglolies,
with their Turban-cloths let down over their faces to serve as
Masks, who swiftly unlocked what Doors remained between
us and the Sea Rampart. The Monk pressed my Hand,
gave me his Blessing, bidding me hope for Better Times, and
disappeared. Guided by the Coglolies, and, indeed, half
supported by them, I was put into a Boat waiting at the
Quayside, as the Monk had told me, and ten minutes' hard
pulling brought us alongside a large craft, on board which, I
being so weak, they were fain to hoist me with Ropes. By
this time I had sunk into a kind of Lethargy, and, being
conveyed below and put into a cot in the Master's Cabin, fell
into a slumber, which lasted for very many hours.

The Captain of this ship was an English Renegado, named Sparkenhoe. He had served as Midshipman and Master's Mate in a King's ship; but having been, as he conceived, unjustly Broken for hot words that passed between him and the Captain,—this took place at Gibraltar,—had deserted, and hid himself on board a Merchant Brig bound for Tangier. At last, being fond of a Roving Life (and having the misfortune to kill the Captain of the Merchant Brig in a dispute concerning some Bullocks they were shipping), he had turned Mussulman; and after living some time among the Buccaneers of the Riff, had come to Algiers, and been made Captain of a Merchantman trading to the Dardanelles, and doing a bit of Piracy when opportunity served. 'Twas full five-and-twenty years since he had Run from the King of Great Britain's service; and although his Blue Eyes and enormous Red Whiskers still gave him somewhat of a Saxon appearance, he had very nearly forgotten his Mother Tongue, and only retained English enough to enable him to mingle a few Billingsgate Oaths with his barbarous Levantine Lingo.

This fellow, whom I heartily despised, for he had kept all the Vices of his former Religion, and had acquired none of the Virtues of his new one, was civil enough to me, and informed me that all he could do for me, in return for the Bribe he had received from his Employers, would be to deliver me to a Slave Merchant at Constantinople, who would place me out in Domestic Service where I should not be ill-treated. But he very strongly advised me to turn Turk or Renegado, as he himself was, saying, that in such a case he would land me perfectly free at the Porte, where I should doubtless find some profitable Employment. This I scornfully refused; whereupon he shrugged his Shoulders, and said that I was a Fool, but might possibly think Better of it, in Time.

After three weeks' coasting among the Isles of the Grecian Archipelago, and so into the Sea of Marmora, we steered into the Bosphorus 'twixt the Castles of Europe and Asia; and the same night the Slave-Dealer comes off in a private Caique,—as the Turks call their Canoes,—and the Renegado delivered me up to him. I was taken to his House at Galata, where I was kept very close for two or three weeks, and was then sold to a Merchant of Damascus in Asia, that had come to Constantinople with the Autumn Caravans, to dispose of his cargo of Silk and Attar of Roses—a very fine and subtle Perfume, one drop of which is sufficient to scent an entire House.

'Twas in the autumn of the year 1759 that I so came to Damascus, and for ten years did I remain in that city, —all the time without hearing one word from my dear Wife. Had I been in the Capital, where Foreign Ambassadors reside, I could not, as a Christian, be detained in Slavery; that being guarded against by Treaties between the Crown of Great Britain and the Sublime Porte. But in this remote part of the Empire, these and many other worse enormities were possible; and I remained as one Dead and Buried. To a few English and French Travellers passing through Damascus did I tell my piteous Tale, and entreat their help; but the account that I gave of myself was so rambling and confused, and contained I could but confess it, so many Incredible Particulars, that I could plainly see no one believed my Tale, or accounted me as aught but a half-mad Fellow that had run away for some misdeed from a Ship in port on the Coast of Syria, and was now trying to cadge Sympathy for a Pretended Grievance. At last I gave up complaining. Slowly, but surely, my memory of my former life began to Decay, and even the knowledge of mine own Language faded away, and became weaker and weaker every day. I dressed, I ate, I drank, I slept in the Eastern Fashion, and in all but religion I was a Turk.

Meanwhile I had gained in the favour of my Master. He was about mine own age when he purchased me, and we grew old Together. At first I was employed as a mere Menial, in carrying of Bales and Packages, and tending of Camels; but by degrees I was promoted to be his Warehouseman, Clerk, Cashkeeper, and at last his Partner. In that capacity he sent me to manage a large silk-plantation of his in the Lebanon; and after two years of that work I left him with a fortune of no less than five hundred Purses of Gold (about 20,000*l.* of our Money), to set up on my own account in the City of Broussa. He made no attempt (nor had he at any time done so) to combat my Religious Scruples, but counselled me to behave in all things outwardly as a Turk; and if any thing was said of my being in countenance a Frank (though I was swarthy enough from my Long Journeyings), to account for it by saying that I was an Affghan, born out of India. He died very soon after I

settled at Broussa, and the secret of my being a Christian
died with him. It is true that, for mere Policy's sake, I did
go through the Mummeries of outward Mahometans, and had
my Rosary and my Prayer-carpet like other Merchants of
Broussa; but I scornfully deny that I was initiated, or submitted to, any Heathenish Rites; and I am ready to maintain now, Cut, Thrust, or Backsword, that I was then as
stanch and leal a Protestant as I am now.

Under the name of Gholab Hassan, of Affghanistan, and
a True Believer, I prospered exceedingly, almost entirely forgetting my own country. 'Tis true I always preserved an
affectionate remembrance of my dear Wife Lilias; but she
seemed to me in the guise of some Departed Angel, whom I
had been privileged to behold but for a Short and Transient
Period. Among these Pagans, as is well known, Polygamy
is permitted; but that is neither here nor there; and I was
now an Old, Old Man.

'Tis ten years since, namely, A.D. 1770, that a great Insurrection against the Authority of the Porte, or rather of
the Bashaw of the Province, who had been laying on the
Taxes with somewhat too heavy a hand, broke out in Broussa.
The infuriate Populace burnt the House of the Bashaw about
his ears, plundered the Bazaar, and were proceeding to further extremities, when, a puff of my old Martial Spirit
reviving within me, I collected a trusty band of Porters and
Camel-drivers, rallied the Turkish Troops, who were flying
in all directions, reformed them, scattered the Insurgent
Mobile, and did (I promise you) speedy execution on some
Scores of them. The Insurrection was very speedily sub-
dued, and all Broussa was filled with the praises of my Valour
and Discretion. The Bashaw was a poor Good-natured kind
of Creature, Brave enough, but so Fat that when he mounted
on Horseback they were obliged to put one of the Pillows of
his Divan on the pummel of his saddle to keep his Stomach
steady. An end, however, was put to the discomfort he suffered through Corpulence, by the arrival, three weeks after
the suppression of the Insurrection, of a Tartar Courier, who
brought with him a Bowstring and a Firman from the Grand
Seignor. By means of the Bowstring, the Fat Bashaw was
then and there strangled,—for they do things in a very off-
hand manner in Turkey,—and when the Firman was opened
by his Vizier it was found to contain, not his own nomina-
tion to the Bashawlik, which he fondly expected, but the

appointment of the Merchant Gholab Hassan, that is to say, JOHN DANGEROUS, that is to say, your Humble Servant, to the vacant Post, and commanding my immediate attendance at the Porte to receive investiture with the Three Horse-tails of Office.

I was at once saluted as Gholab Bashaw, and the next day set forth amidst great Acclamations, and in sumptuous state, for Constantinople. Arrived there, I was handsomely lodged in a Palace close to the Old Seraglio, and admitted to no less than three solemn Audiences with the Commander of the Faithful, the Caliph Al Islam, the Padishaw of Roum, the Great Turk himself.

I could not help smiling at myself, now arrayed in all the pomp and glory of an Exalted Functionary, and in the true Turkish fashion. 'Tis a custom (through Ignorance of those parts) with the Limners of Europe to portray all Os-manlis with long Beards; and, for truth, as a Merchant at Broussa, I had a great grizzled one of most Goatish appear-ance; but among the Bashaws and all those engaged in the Military Service of the Grand Seignor, or holding high Em-ployments in the Seraglio, they wear only a fierce and mar-tial pair of Whiskers. The most distinguishing sign of a true Mussulman is, after all, his Sarik or Turban, made in two parts, namely a Bonnet, and the Linen that is wrapped round it. The former a kind of Cap, red or green, without Brims, and quilted with Cotton. About this they roll seve-ral folds of Linen Cloth; and it is a particular art to know how to give a Turban a good air; it being a trade with 'em, as the Selling of Hats is with us. The Emirs, who boast of being descended from the race of Mahomet, wear a turban all green; but that of the common Turks is red, with a white border, so distinguishing them from the Christians. Next I wore great long Breeches of a 'broidered stuff, and a Shirt of fine soft calico, with wide Sleeves, but no Wristbands or Collar; and over this a Cassock or Vest of fine English Cloth, reaching to the ankles, and buttoned with buttons of gold, about the bigness of a peppercorn. This was tied with a broad Sash or Girdle, which went thrice round the waist, with the ends hanging down before, and two handsome Tas-sels. Over all this another Garment, richly laced, and lined with Furs of the Martin or the Badger. In my Girdle a Dagger, about the size of a case-knife, the handle curiously wrought, and adorned with Precious Stones. And as the

Turkish tailors make no pockets to their vestments, Purse, Handkerchief, Tobacco-box, and things of that nature must needs be put into the Bosom, or thrust under the Girdle. Instead of Shoes, a pair of Slippers of yellow leather; which, whenever you enter a Mosque or the presence of a Superior, you must put off on the threshold. This custom makes the soles of a Turk's feet always ready for the application of the Talack, or Bastinado, from which argument neither high nor low are exempt.

Item.—The Women here very richly dressed, but sad Gossips, and a Lazy, Lolloping kind of creatures; which they must needs be, poor souls, seeing that they have no sort of Education, and are kept mostly in seclusion, talking of scandal, sucking of sugar-plums, showing their brave apparel to each other, and thrumming upon the Mandolin. A galloping, dreary, dull place indeed is a Turkish Harem. As to the qualities of the mind, the Turkish Women want neither Wit, Good Sense, nor Tenderness; but the constraint that is put upon 'em, and the jealous eye with which they are guarded, makes 'em go a great way in a little time, and make an ill use of the Liberty which is sometimes granted them. The old women-slaves of the Armenian and Jew Merchants, who are the confidantes of the Turkish women, enter their apartments at all hours, under the pretence of bringing them Jewels, and often favour their Amours with brisk young fellows. The usual hour for intrigue is the hour of morning and evening Prayers, when the Husbands are away at the Mosques. In case of Discovery the Turks are masters of the Lives of their Wives; and if they have been convicted in form, they are sewn up in Sacks, and thrown into the Sea. And even if a Guilty Woman's life is spared, she is condemned to marry her Gallant, who is sentenced to die, or must turn Mahometan, supposing him to be a Christian. The least punishment for a man who has broken the Seventh Commandment is to ride through the streets upon an Ass, with his face towards the Tail, to receive a certain number of Blows upon the Soles of his Feet, and to pay a Fine in proportion to his Estate.

But though a duly-invested Bashaw of Three Tails, I was not fated to remain long in that Capacity. For once, however, my Destiny, in subjecting me to Change, played me a kind instead of a spiteful Turn. Going to visit the French Ambassador, who was then in high favour at the Porte, I.

found there, living under the protection of his Family, a Lady, who was no other than my dear Wife Lilias, and with her a Daughter, called after her own name, who was now twelve years of age. Her History, as she related it to me, was brief, but amazing. Both her Father and the Cardinal died about two years after her return from Captivity; but she found a new guardian in my old friend Captain Night, or Don Ereolo Sparafucile di San Lorenzo, the Knight of Malta, who had retired from that Island to end his days in France. She was enabled to cheer the declining years of that Gallant Gentleman, who had preserved a lively remembrance of his old *Protégé*, Jack Dangerous; and when he died, left her the whole of his large fortune. All these years she had remained in a dreadful state of uncertainty, till, through the kind offices of the French Minister of Police, she was made acquainted with the last Dying avowal of a Pirate Renegado, named Sparkenhoe, who had expired at the Galleys of Marseille, and stated that, in the year 1759, he had conveyed a refugee Christian Slave from Algiers to Constantinople, where he had been sold to a Merchant of Damascus. In the almost desperate hope of discovering some Tidings of me, my Wife and Child had journeyed to the Porte, where they were most kindly received at the French Embassy. They had given up almost every prospect of meeting me again, when I made my sudden appearance in the strange Guise of a Turkish Bashaw.

Under ordinary Circumstances, it might have gone hard with me; for the Turks reckon it as an unpardonable crime for a Christian to assume the Mussulman Garb, and conform outwardly to that religion, without having gone through the Proper Rites. However, as I have said, the French Ambassador was just then in high favour with the Porte. He made interest with the Captain Bashaw, the Kislar Aga, and the Grand Vizier himself. The Services I had rendered to the Great Turk by suppressing the Insurrection at Broussa were taken into consideration; and it was at length agreed, that if I would convey myself away privately, and take my Wife with me, no more should be said about the matter. It was given out at Broussa that I had been appointed to another and more distant Government; and he who had been Vizier to the unlucky Fat Man got his much-coveted Preferment, and I have no doubt, was very happy in it, till the inevitable Tartar came, and he was Bowstrung, like his predecessor.

So Gholab Bashaw resigned the Three Horse-tails that during so brief a period had waved at his Flagstaff, and became once more plain JOHN DANGEROUS. The Sublime Porte, however, confiscated all my Property at Broussa, including my Wives—I mean, my Women Servants.

With my Wife and Child I now returned to Europe, full of Years, and, I hope, notwithstanding some Ups and Downs, full of Honours too. We were in no hurry, however, to return to England; for I had wandered about Foreign Parts so long in Discredit, and Danger, and Distress, that I thought myself well entitled to see the world a little in Freedom and Independence, and with a Handsome competence at my Back. Therefore, as the Chevalier Captain John Dangerous,—I have dropped my Knightly rank of late years, —and furnished with all necessary passports and safe-conducts, we made our way across the Black Sea to Odessa, a mean kind of place, but rising in the way of trade; and after a most affable reception by the Russian Governor of that place, journeyed at our ease through the Tauric Chersonese, now wrested from the Tartar Khans of Simpheropol, and belonging to the Muscovites. Next, in a handsome wheeled carriage-and-four, we made for the great City of Moscow,— the old Capital of the Great Dukes of Russia,—where we abode two whole years, and went among the very best people in the place; although I had an ugly Equivoque with a young Gentleman of Quality that was an officer of Dragoons, and who, I declare, stole a diamond-mounted Snuff-box of mine off my wife's Harpsichord, putting the same (the Snuff-box, I mean) into the pocket of his pantaloons. Him I was compelled to expel from my house, the Toe of my Boot aiding; and meeting him subsequently at a Coffee-House, and he not seeming sufficiently impressed with the turpitude of his Offence, but the rather inclined to regard it as á venial Prank or Whimsey, I did Batoon him within an inch of his life, and until there were more wheals on his Body than bars of silver-braid on his Jacket. This led to a serious misunderstanding between Justice and myself. I was not Imprisoned, but was summoned no less than fifty-seven times before a kind of Judge they call an Assessor, who addressed a number of interrogatories to me, which, at a moderate computation, reached, in the course of five weeks, three thousand seven hundred and nine questions. This might have gone on till Doomsday, but for the kind offices of a Muscovite friend, who hinted to me that if I discreetly slipped a Bank-bill for five hundred roubles into the hand of the Examining Judge, I should hear no more of the affair. This I did, and was soon after honourably acquitted; after which I gave the young Spark whom I had batooned his revenge, by allowing him to doff me out of a few score pieces at the game of Lansquenet. By and by, being tired of Moscow, we removed to the stately northern Capital, Petersburg, where I had a handsome mansion on the Fintanka Canal, and was on more than one occasion admitted to an audience with the Empress of Russia, the mighty Czarina Catherine; a fine, bold, strapping woman, with a great taste for Politics, Diamonds, the Fine Arts, and affairs of Gallantry. The first time I made my obeisance to her Majesty (which was at her summer residence of Peterhoff, on the River Neva), she deigned, smiling affably, to say to me :

"*Ah, ah ! vous êtes le Sabreur anglais qui avez rossé mes gens là-bas, à Moscou. Je voudrais que vous en fissiez autant pour mes faquins de Chevalier-Gardes à Pétersbourg.*"

I was given to understand in very high quarters that I had only to ask, to receive a lucrative and honourable Appointment in the service of the Czarina,—either as a General by Land, or as an Admiral at Sea ; but I was sick of fighting, and of working too ; so at last, in disgust, I gave up my House, and taking shipping with my family at Cronstadt, retired to Hamburg, whence, after a brief sojourn, I travelled to France.

My sainted Wife, with whom, after our reunion, I lived most happily, died in Paris, in the year 1773 ; and then, feeling my Days drawing to a close, and desiring to lay my Bones in my own Country, I returned to England, after an absence of more than Thirty Years. Finding that the old Mansion that had belonged to my Grandmother was for sale by Public Auction, I purchased the Freehold, repaired and beautified it, and came to reside in it, occupying my long and happy leisure by the composition of these Memoirs. And if any one of my Readers experiences one-hundredth part the pleasure in Reading these Pages (and that I dare scarcely hope) that I have experienced in Writing them, John Dangerous will, indeed, be amply repaid.

THE END.

www.ingramcontent.com/pod-product-compliance
Lightning Source LLC
Chambersburg PA
CBHW021544110726
47902CB00004B/1016